ESCAPE TO THE SWISS CHALET

Also by Carrie Walker

Escape to the Tuscan Vineyard

ESCAPE TO THE SWISS CHALET

Carrie Walker

An Aria Book

First published in the UK in 2023 by Head of Zeus,
part of Bloomsbury Publishing Plc

9 7 5 3 1 2 4 6 8

A catalogue record for this book is available from the British Library.

ISBN (PB): 9781804547311
ISBN (E): 9781804547298

Cover design: Head of Zeus

Typeset by Siliconchips Services Ltd UK

Printed and bound in Great Britain by
CPI Group (UK) Ltd, Croydon CR0 4YY

Head of Zeus
First Floor East
5–8 Hardwick Street
London EC1R 4RG

WWW.HEADOFZEUS.COM

For my lovely Rob.

One

One month to the wedding. 9th August

I screeched a final slice of Sellotape over the cardboard box and hoiked it onto the precarious stack stood ready to go. My back gave a warning twinge as I scrawled 'Travel Books' on the side with a Sharpie. It was 5 p.m. and my bum was numb from sitting too long on the floor. Everything we owned had been straitjacketed with bubble-wrap and packed with Tetris-like skill and I'd spent the past hour rereading old Christmas cards and looking through photo albums, a bottle of Merlot on the go. It was an all-the-feels flick-book through time: nestled in Mum's arms as a baby by the Christmas tree; my first and last day of school, sporting the same excited, toothy grin; clubbing with my best friend Abi in our baggy jeans and matching crop tops – we'd shared everything since we were four years old, and I vividly remembered sharing that first G&T – we'd both hated it. George and I getting engaged on graduation day and throwing our mortarboards in the air… key life moments captured forever and then hidden in cupboards.

I'd been trying to simultaneously pack and de-clutter and it had started out so well, holding each of my possessions to my heart, Marie Kondo-style, until I'd decided pretty much everything was useful *and* beautiful and the 'keep', 'throw' and 'give to charity' buckets had been abandoned. The red wine wasn't helping.

'How are you getting on?' George asked, dragging two bin bags in from the bedroom.

'Slowly,' I said. 'I love this hot weather, but it's hard work packing up the flat in the heat. An iced coffee would go down a treat right now.'

'Ooh, yes,' he said, wiping his brow. 'I'll walk down and get us one once I've finished in the bedroom.'

He was wearing his Leeds Uni hoodie and since he'd last surfaced, had added a feather boa, a pair of headphones and a sombrero to his look.

'You found the fancy dress stuff then?' I laughed. 'Watch out for the gorilla face under the bed; it always creeps me out.'

'The glow-in-the-dark one?' he said. 'That's definitely coming.'

'Does it spark joy in your heart?' I asked.

'It does,' George replied, sliding the bin bags alongside the Jenga of boxes.

'The heart wants what the heart wants.' I kissed him on the cheek and looked around at the mess. The more we packed, the worse it seemed to get. There was stuff literally everywhere.

'Shall I take this lot to the storage place to give us some room to manoeuvre?' George asked, surveying the carnage.

'As long as we haven't accidentally packed anything we'll need for the wedding or honeymoon?'

'I told you, I haven't seen the gorilla yet,' George said, chuckling to himself.

It was officially official. We were leaving London to get married and live in the countryside. We'd put all our savings down on a new-build in Surrey and bought off-plan, which George said was the smart thing to do. We were feeling smug but skint and with the wedding taking every spare penny we had, we were totally broke. Technically, we'd be 'between homes' until after the wedding, so I was staying with my parents and George would sofa-surf with friends until the big day. 24 Orchard Close would be ready when we got back from honeymoon, so it was only for a few weeks and then we'd be snug and settled in time for Christmas. Getting to know our new neighbours and starting our new life.

George heaved the last of the taped-up boxes into the car and came back for a final check, jangling his car keys and looking around.

'Right, that's everything in the car. Anything else for this run? What about that rack of wine?' he asked, nodding over at my pride and joy.

'In a cold storage unit?' I was aghast. 'Absolutely not, the temperature would ruin it.'

'Would it? A few bottles of supermarket plonk?'

'That's not plonk! I'll have you know that's my pension in disguise.'

A conciliatory miaow sounded from behind the sofa and Basil's tail periscoped its way around to see us.

'Hello, my little, tiny baby,' I said, picking him up and cuddling him tight. He wrestled his way out of my arms and lurched onto the floor, giving me a dirty look, before winding in and out of George's legs, purring rhythmically. Traitor.

'He loves you so much,' I said, smiling.

George tried to move away, brushing frantically at the white hairs left on his trousers as Basil backed him into a corner.

'SHOO. NO thank you. AWAY, please. Honestly Hols, I think I'm allergic to him,' he said, rubbing his eyes. He was being outmanoeuvred.

'You've lived here for nearly three years, George; I think you'd know by now if you were genuinely allergic. Love me, love my cat.'

We'd given long-distance a shot for a while after uni, but London to Leeds was too much of a schlep every other weekend and eventually, George had moved into my tiny flat in London. He still went back to Sheffield once a month to see his mum, but he said the work opportunities were better in London, so it made sense to live down south for our careers. Although my career was now mainly drinking wine and peeling potatoes.

'I can't wait until we move into the new house. We are going to have *so much space*,' George said, edging his way past Basil and picking up my pink pouffe.

'That can't go yet,' I said, grabbing it off him, 'I need somewhere to put my feet.'

'And this?' George asked, picking up my cardboard cut-out of Gordon Ramsay.

'Absolutely not. Gordon keeps my culinary standards in

check; he's staying to the bitter end,' I said, propping him back up in the kitchen.

'He can have his own bedroom in the new house,' George said dreamily, 'three bedrooms instead of one, a massive TV on the wall and space for my table football.'

'Hmm,' I said, taking a long look at all the character in my little flat. The sash windows, the exposed brick walls, the fireplace and wooden beams. It would be all plasterboard and plastic in the new place, but I suppose it would be safer and more secure. No more draughts rattling through the windows at night.

'How long do cats live again?' he asked, backing out the front door.

'Get used to him,' I shouted as it slammed shut.

There was a huge space where the boxes had been, and I could finally see my fluffy, raspberry carpet again. Basil curled into a white, furry ball and closed his eyes as I took a large gulp of wine, savouring the rich, heady taste of a classic Italian red, before wrestling another cardboard box into shape. I bubble-wrapped the porcelain dish I'd bought from Portobello Market, still full of angel cards, the green glass balls from Venice and the candlesticks Mum and Dad had bought me as a housewarming gift. It felt strange emptying my little flat of all its me-ness, but George was right; it would save us a month's rent and it was only for a few weeks. I hadn't planned to take my candlesticks on honeymoon, so I had to suck it up and pack it all away. We just needed enough stuff to get us through our wedding and everything else would be safe until the house was ready. I spotted our wedding blackboard on the mantelpiece and picked up the blue chalk, rubbing out the number 31 and replacing it with a nice fat 30. *Days until we say I DO*. Thirty days until our happily ever after.

Two

Four weeks to the wedding. 12th August

I carefully slid the cork out of the Pomerol Le Pin and breathed in the familiar scent of a heady French red. The undertones were so rich, they were almost meaty, and blackberries and plums whooshed happily up my nose as I gave the cork a second sniff. The table of six watched closely as I tipped a *soupçon* into the host's glass. The perfect pairing for his steak.

'The 2015 vintage,' I said, with a confident nod. 'It was their best in a decade.'

'Ah yes, of course,' the man said, his half-moon specs quivering as he swirled the thick, cherry liquid enthusiastically and watched the drips run slowly down the glass. He inhaled deeply and closed his eyes. 'Lovely, really lovely,' he said, slurping a mouthful, sucking it into his teeth and giving a delicate gargle before swallowing.

I waited for the official nod.

'Yes, yes, go ahead,' he said, his hairy fingers gripping his glass tightly as he held it out to me.

I poured the wine as Margot laid down the main courses with a smile.

'*Alors*. Tonight's *plat principal*. Wagyu beef with a Pinot Noir jus, served with dauphinoise potatoes, and freshly foraged leeks and beans from our bistro allotment.'

The combination of smells was divine, and my stomach gave a low growl as I silver-served the vegetables to the table. The pre-wedding juice cleanse was taking its toll and I couldn't remember the last time I'd had a mouthful of cheesy potatoes. George had suggested we replace breakfast and lunch with celery juice in the run-up to the big day, so I just had to hang on for a few more weeks and then the carbs would be back with a vengeance.

My first year working at Chez Margot had whizzed by. I couldn't believe my luck when I'd stumbled across it only three streets from the flat, when I first moved to London. Marylebone was full of surprises like that: streets crammed with lovely shops and pathways that led to cosy pubs with tiny roof gardens. The flat itself was more like a wardrobe than a dwelling, but what it lacked in size, it made up for with position. I could walk twenty minutes in any direction to the most amazing places. Fabulous cocktail bars on Carnaby Street, real Italian coffee right next to the train station, Selfridges, Liberty and other fantastic shops on Oxford Street. Chez Margot became a small piece of my London tapestry from the moment I saw it. Eating there turned into my payday treat and Margot got so used to me popping in for a homebound glass of wine, first with Abi and later with George, that we eventually became friends.

When I lost my job last summer, I'd made a beeline for the bistro on autopilot, and it had been Margot's shoulder

I'd cried on before telling anyone else. 3 p.m. one random Tuesday and I remember it like it was yesterday.

'Is everything OK, Holly?' she'd asked as I tinkled into the restaurant. 'This is very early, even for you?'

'Is it? I'm not sure,' I said, in a daze, 'I think I'm in shock.'

'Has something happened? Is someone ill?' She steered me to the bar and propped me against a stool. 'Let me get you a drink. You look pale.'

'No one's ill,' I replied, monotone, 'I've been made redundant.' There. I'd said it out loud. It was real.

Margot doubled the dosage and handed me a large whisky, no ice.

'Drink this and keep breathing,' she said gently, 'in for four and out for four. You just need some time. It will be OK.'

I nodded silently and gulped down the whisky, the shock of the sharp liquid bringing me back to myself as Margot busied herself in the kitchen to give me a minute. I caught my reflection among the bottles behind the bar and did a double take. My face was pinched and pale, with smudged eyeliner and hair like an orange shower pouf. What was I going to do? How would I pay the rent? Could George pay the bills for both of us? Would he? London was way too expensive to not have a job.

Margot launched herself bum-first through the kitchen door, a bottle of wine in each hand.

'So. Tell me?' she said, leaning on the bar.

'There's a restructure… they're very sorry, I'm a great employee, the cuts are unavoidable, blahdy-blah. I can't

remember the rest. They gave me this and said I could go.' I handed the letter to Margot, who scanned it quickly, then folded it in half with a nod.

'Fairly standard,' she said, 'two months' pay.'

Oh God.

'And then what?' I said, more to myself than to Margot.

'And then you'll work somewhere else. You are very employable, Holly. You'll get another procurement job in another company, and everything will be fine.'

I forced the rest of the whisky down. For the shock.

'But I hate procurement,' I said, my heart pounding in my ears, 'the thought of another procurement job makes me feel sick. This one was bad enough.'

'Ah. Then we have an entirely different problem,' Margot said, putting one bottle of wine in the fridge and peeling the plastic top off the other. 'One that needs wine.'

She glugged out two large glasses and looked at me with a serious eyebrow.

'Is there any way to see this as good news?' she asked. 'A release from your torture?'

I took a moment to process that thought, along with a mouthful of wine. The silky combination of peachy flavours distracted me momentarily as I savoured its deliciousness. Yes, my job was monotonous torture at times, but it paid the bills and meant I could afford my Chez Margot treat once a month. It meant I could live in my beautiful flat and keep Basil in luxury, fish-flavoured treats. And my wine obsession wouldn't pay for itself.

'Good news how? That I won't be able to pay my bills? That I'll have to give Basil away and start living in my car?' I said, feeling the panic rising back up.

'In for four and out for four,' Margot said, taking a deep breath in front of me.

'How will I even get another job in two months with the market like it is?'

'You've got your redundancy money to tide you over,' Margot said, pointing to my letter, 'plenty of time to have a look around. And if you hate procurement, then get a different job. Something that you like.'

'Doing what?' I replied, miserably.

Margot smiled gently. 'What do you like doing?'

I swirled my wine and stared off into space. What did I like doing? Apart from cooking and eating. And drinking. Dancing? Walking? Having a bath. I liked my commute each day. Sticking my headphones on and bopping through London to work. It took almost exactly an hour to walk to the office in Blackfriars, cutting across Soho and through Covent Garden as the market came to life each morning. Dodging the runners on Embankment as the commuter boats honked along the Thames before the mayhem of work began.

'Holly?' Margot interrupted my thoughts. 'You must know what you like? What is it that gives you pleasure?'

'Nothing that I can make a living from,' I said sadly. 'Unless I open a vineyard?'

Margot nodded slowly. 'Not impossible. You have a good nose for wine – and a qualification in it too, non?*'*

'I wouldn't go that far. We did a wine tasting course at work, and we all got the same certificate. It's nothing official, I don't know enough to get me a job.'

'But you do, Holly. You recognise a quality wine immediately,' Margot said, pointing at my glass. 'You have

a gift for it; your senses take over. You watch me pour and see the texture and consistency of the liquid. You smell the different scents and can tell the good from the bad, and then your tastebuds confirm what you already know to be true.'

She was right.

I gave a small nod. 'I do like a wine, yes.'

'And food too,' she said. 'You have an appreciation for quality ingredients and both simple and unusual taste combinations. A delicate palate should not be taken for granted.'

'Yes, of course. I also like eating food. Especially your food.'

'Don't dismiss these talents as "eating food" and "drinking wine". It is more than that.' Margot stared at me thoughtfully. 'In fact, I am looking for someone to help me here at the restaurant a couple of days a week if you are interested?'

'Really?' I said, looking around my favourite place and imagining working here. 'Doing what?'

She gave a shrug. 'A bit of everything. Prepping vegetables in the day and helping me with the customers at night. Welcoming them in, pouring the wine, bringing out the plates. I can teach you.'

I let the idea roll around in my mind for a second. Hanging out here with Margot and being paid for it would be amazing, but how could I make London-life work on restaurant wages? No. It wasn't realistic.

'Thank you so much Margot, but I'm not sure it would pay enough to cover my bills.'

She shrugged again. 'Have a think. I pay £15 an hour in

cash and the tips are good. See it as a little extra to tide you over while you look for something else?'

George had been horrified.

'But you've got a degree? Why would you take a job as a waitress? It doesn't make sense.' he said, shaking his head.

'I haven't taken a job as a waitress, George; I'm going to help run the restaurant. Putting my degree to use at last and learning a craft.'

'A craft? You've got a first-class business degree and speak fluent French and Italian; you should be using it to get into a proper company to better yourself. You'll never earn the big bucks chopping lettuce and polishing forks.'

'Stop panicking, it's only a couple of days a week and I'll still be out looking for other jobs. It'll be fun learning how to make Margot's dishes – her desserts are to die for. Sous-chef by day and hostess by night. Getting under the skin of the business.'

'Drowning in a pile of potato skins more like. Come on Holly, you're better than that. Where is your ambition? You used to be so hungry for success.'

'I still am. I'm just not interested in reaching the dizzy heights of Chief Procurement Officer in a faceless concrete tower. I'm tired of Zorbing my life away on the corporate hamster wheel.'

The nit-picking went on for weeks, but I took the job anyway. It was never going to make me rich, but it was something completely different and I knew I'd be happy working with Margot. Two days a week turned into five and with tips on top, I could just about afford my half of the bills. But most importantly, I was learning again. Learning about Michelin-star food and serving terrifyingly expensive wine under Margot's watchful eye.

The bistro looked especially beautiful tonight. Marylebone was abuzz with tourists and families making the most of the long, summer evenings, and happy couples sat at tables with cold pints and Aperol Spritz after a long day shopping. The distant whine of traffic from Oxford Street was almost entirely absorbed by laughter and chatter and the searing heat meant we could open all the windows, inviting in a soft, warm breeze. The silverware sparkled against the polished, mahogany tables and white chrysanthemums stood strong in wonky, turquoise vases, as Freya Ridings gently crooned over the speakers. It had been a year since that conversation with Margot and I hadn't looked back. I felt more at home in Chez Margot than I did in my own home. Chez Holly. Well, Chez George and Holly now, or as our wedding hashtag would have it #Geolly. With the wedding only a month away, the hashtag was one thing on our never-ending to-do list that we *had* agreed on.

'How's everything going with the wedding planning?' Margot asked as she violently whisked the Cointreau and cream together to accompany dessert. 'Are you all set?'

'Erm... not exactly. There are still a few things left to sort. My dress for one,' I said, with a nervous flutter. I'd left the dress shopping to the last minute and didn't technically have one, as such, just yet. I had three different dresses on hold, but I wasn't *completely in love* with any of them. I was building my outfit piece by piece and so far had a veil, silk underwear and a pair of Louboutins sitting next to an empty coat hanger that laughed at me from the wardrobe each morning.

'You haven't got a dress?' Margot gasped. 'But what do you mean? The wedding is only a few weeks away!' My stomach dropped. Oh God, she was right; what the hell was I playing at?

'Whaaat? No, no, yes, of course I've got a dress,' I lied, and Margot looked visibly relieved. 'I've got a few options; I just need to decide which one I'm going with.'

'Ah, well that is a different thing altogether,' she said with a little shrug. 'Wear them all. A quick costume change every couple of hours will keep everyone guessing.'

Margot sliced and diced three large oranges, layering the pieces with the Cointreau cream to build a mini stack on each plate. With one chef's table and a maximum of forty covers each night, we could take our time and give the customers our undivided attention. The oven was crammed full of lemon and pistachio tarts, which were baking to perfection, each one slightly cracked with a glossy, golden crust. I polished six crystal glasses onto a silver tray, sloshing a large shot of Tawny Port into each and adding a plump black cherry.

'Well at least your venue is sorted,' Margot said with a smile. 'The church is beautiful, and we will make the food extra special for you both.'

'I know you will and thank you again for letting us have the reception here. Chez Margot has such a special place in my heart. It will be so cosy and romantic.'

'The ninth of the ninth is a magical date, I think. With a new moon, if I'm not mistaken. A good day for a new start.'

'George has always said he wants to be married and in

his own house by the time he's thirty, so we're well ahead of schedule. Then two kids by the time we're thirty-five.'

Margot effortlessly transferred the tarts from the oven to a cooling tray and sprinkled them with brown sugar.

'And is that what you want?' she asked, as she concentrated. 'Your fiancé loves a milestone, but these expectations are imaginary. Time is a human invention, Holly; age is meaningless. Why pressure yourselves?'

'We've been together eight years,' I replied with a chuckle. 'I don't think anyone can accuse us of rushing into things.'

'Of course not. But life is not a template to complete. It's important to follow your own path.'

Margot disappeared into the larder, her words hanging in the air. She had a point, but it wasn't quite as simple as that. George and I were a team and our lives were so entwined that it was difficult to remember which part was my path and which part was his. I was trying to pinpoint the last time I'd made a decision entirely on my own, when a gentle but insistent tapping started on the back door. I pulled back the curtain to find George's face squished against the glass in a pig snout and quickly opened the door.

'George! What are you doing?' I whispered frantically.

'Been to the pub,' he said, swaying from side to side and giving off a beery waft.

'Well, that's obvious. Are you OK? Why are you here?' I glanced over my shoulder as Margot was summoned into the restaurant by the man in the half-moon specs.

'You look beautiful,' George said between hiccups, leaning in to kiss me with wet lips.

'George! You're drunk. I'll see you at home,' I said,

shooing him away. He stumbled backwards and tripped on the top step, grabbing the handrail as he slowly slid to the ground.

'Can you take me home?' George asked, using his jacket for a pillow as he lay on the floor.

'No, I won't be finished for another hour,' I whispered. 'Get a cab.'

'I can't find my wallet,' George said, his eyes closed, snuggling down as if to sleep.

'Get UP. You can't lie there, I'm at work. Oh God. Hang on. I'll get you some cash.' I shut the door and ran to my bag, rootling around for a tenner as Margot came back into the kitchen.

'We have one of those lactose intolerants in the group, asking for milk-free cheese,' Margot muttered, raising her eyes to the ceiling. 'Honestly, what do they expect me to do? Oat milk Dairylea dippers? I am not a magician.'

I hovered near the back door, desperate to give the money to George and get him off the doorstep. Margot was in a cheese-fluster, so I waited until she was in the fridge, then posted the note through the letterbox and watched as it fluttered through the air onto George's snoozing face. He snuffled around for a bit, then repositioned himself and settled back down. FFS. I needed him to wake up, notice the money, and GO. I grabbed my phone and dialled his number, dropping it into my apron, still-ringing, as Margot returned with a wheel of Gouda and a smelly blue Montagnolo.

'These will 'ave to do,' she muttered, selecting a sharp knife. 'It wouldn't be my normal choice of combination, but perhaps it can work.'

'We have some fresh figs in the larder if that would help?' I said loudly.

'Can you hear that?' Margot asked, stopping deadly still. 'Is that your phone?'

I frowned and pretended to hear it for the first time. For the love of God, why wasn't it kicking into voicemail? I heard a low groan from George outside and held my breath as Margot marched over and flung the back door open.

'What the...?'

'George? Is that you?' I said, trying to hold it together. Honestly, how would I ever be taken seriously in my professional life when my nearest and dearest were openly trying to take me down like this?

'Thanks for the cash,' George said, peeling the tenner off his cheek, 'I'll see you back at the house, shall I?'

Margot looked entirely perplexed as he pulled himself together and shuffled off down the street.

'Is this the man giving you advice on how to live your life?' Margot asked, pointedly.

'Erm... yes, it did look very much like him,' I replied, mortified.

'And which milestone is he working towards here?'

'I know, I'm so sorry Margot – he shouldn't just turn up like that.'

'Why are you sorry? You can't control George's life choices any more than he can control yours.'

Three

Three weeks to the wedding. 19th August

I'd spent the entire day in wedding dress hell and had finally got myself sorted. Dress, check, veil, check, old, new, borrowed and blue, checkety-check-check-check. I got back to the flat and immediately switched my shoes for slippers and my dress for a silky dressing gown. Basil kadunked in through the cat flap and gave a welcoming singsong of miaows, which I easily understood to mean, *What time do you call this? You're late. Feed me.*

I sent a quick message to George to see where he was. It wasn't all flexitime and long lunches; sometimes the council meetings dragged on and he couldn't get away.

Me: *Are you home for dinner?*

George: *Yes please – can we have chicken pie?*

Me: *Pie? In August? Really?*

George: *We can have it with a salad?*

George: *But ideally with mash xx*

FFS. Not again. What was it with men and P-based foods? Pie and potatoes and peas and puddings. Margot had whipped up an interesting-looking dish at the bistro last week that I was desperate to try out. Pan-fried duck with a hot red sauce, Thai-spiced vegetables and coconut rice. Duck pie with a twist, if you will. Sans lid.

I fed Basil and opened the windows to let the heat in. It was twenty-three degrees outside, which coincidentally was my go-to, year-round temperature for the flat. I couldn't stand feeling cold. Maybe it was being a winter baby; I came into the world snuggled in a blanket and zipped into a onesie and not much had changed in twenty-seven years. Soft, warm, and cosy was how I liked it.

I unwrapped the duck breasts, removing the skin and laying it flat on a tray in the freezer. Mum's voice rang loud and clear through my head as I got the rest of the ingredients out of the fridge. *Every meal starts with an onion.* I put a large pan on the hob and added half a bottle of white wine, a good slug of Chardonnay vinegar, five-spice, garlic and chicken stock.

'Alexa, play Ella Fitzgerald,' I instructed while slicing a fat Spanish onion into perfect circles. The brass band kicked in and 'Ain't Misbehavin' rang out as I scattered the onion rings across my trusty frying pan, where they hissed and sizzled, slowly turning translucent as I added cherries and beetroot.

'Alexa, volume up,' I called while chopping the celeriac julienne, neatly and precisely, just as Margot had taught me, adding it to the onion with salt and a splash of red wine over a low heat. A 2009 Bordeaux. Far too good to cook with, and almost too good to drink, but I added another glug to the pan and poured myself a large glass. I was running out of time to have nights in the flat like this and I deserved a treat. The absolute luxury of cooking a meal and relaxing with some nice wine and a bit of Ella. Basil happily curled up by the window, a cat after my own heart, always looking for the warm spot.

'We'll be alright, won't we, Basil? You're going to love the new house. There'll be so much more space for you to roam around and hang out with other cats,' I said in earnest as he silently blinked.

'Miaow,' he said, which clearly meant, *How can you know I'll love it when you haven't even seen it?*

He had a point. I seared the duck on both sides, then added some fresh chillies to the sauce and covered it with a lid to stickify. What if Basil didn't like it in Surrey? What if he was lonely in the middle of the countryside, away from all his friends? Away from London and his flat and everything he'd ever known. I stopped to take a couple of deep breaths.

The duck went in the oven to cook through, and I put the rice on. Ten more minutes and everything would be perfect.

The sound of keys rattled in the door and Basil trotted over to welcome George home.

'Hi, babes,' I called as George pinned himself to the wall, edging around Basil to avoid the dreaded white hairs. 'You're fighting a losing battle.'

'I know,' he said, making a run for it, 'I need to start carrying a lint roller.'

'Hmm, sounds sexy,' I said, as he kissed me on the forehead. I was at a crucial stage in coconutting the rice, so I couldn't let go of the pan.

The brass band were in free flow, building up to a glorious crescendo, as Ella sang her heart out.

'Alexa, off,' George barked.

'Ahhh, I was listening to that,' I said into the silence.

'Are we not having pie and mash?' George said, looking around for his P-foods.

'Not exactly,' I replied, with a smile. 'I thought I'd treat us to this amazing new recipe Margot taught me last week. 'Done right, it's Michelin-star quality, so I hope you're hungry.'

'Oh,' he said, looking disappointed.

'We can have pie and mash anytime,' I said, exasperated. 'This duck is going to be the best thing you've ever tasted.'

'I'm not a massive duck fan,' he said, as my heart sank. I finished off the rice and took the duck skin out of the freezer to fry and serve. It was too late to stop now, even if I had to eat it by myself. I placed the frozen skin in the frying pan, with a weight on top, and cooked it until it was golden and crispy. 'I was looking forward to some chicken. Sorry, Hols, you know my tastes are simple.'

'Totally. Sorry, I should've checked before doing it. I can put a chicken burger and some chips in the oven?' I said, taking the duck skin off the heat. George smiled and put his arms around me, nodding into my back.

'And some baked beans?' he whispered in my ear.

'Urgh. If you absolutely must…' I rolled my eyes and cracked open a tin.

'I can't wait to marry you,' he pulled back and kissed me on the cheek. 'Our kids are going to be so beautiful and kind with you as their mother.'

'Not for a few years yet,' I laughed, grabbing the yellow foods George had requested from the freezer and bunging them on a tray.

'You might change your mind once we're married and in the new house.'

'Noooo George, I won't. I'm not ready to have kids yet. We've had this conversation a million times.'

'But it doesn't make sense. There's no point putting our lives on hold so you can serve wine and chips every night at Chez Margot.'

I was stung by the accusation. He knew how much I loved working at the bistro.

'It's a lot more than serving wine and chips, as you well know. You're confusing Margot's with the Wetherspoons you go to with your work mates.'

'Call it Viognier and halloumi fries if it makes you feel better, but the reality is, you're wasting time waitressing when we should be cracking on.'

'What's the rush? We've got plenty of time. Can't we just enjoy the wedding and being Mr and Mrs on our own first? Before the Ballinger bambinos come along. I want to open my own restaurant and working with Margot is the best possible training I can have for that right now. I'm learning so much, but I need more time. Once the restaurant is up and running, we can think about starting a family.'

George walked over to the sofa in a huff, Basil snuffling at his heels, as the oven timer pinged to let me know his yellow food was ready.

Four

Two weeks to the wedding. 26th August

It was time to finally say goodbye to my little London flat. The place that had seen me through most of my twenties, my first real job, living with Abi while trying to make long-distance work with George. And then eventually, Abi moving out and George moving in.

George was still asleep as I tiptoed downstairs to have a few minutes alone and take it all in. One last time. The summer sun was shining bright and the apple tree that had brushed against my window and reminded me of the seasons for the last five years knocked its fruity branches in farewell on the glass. Bus after bus thundered past on the street below, speeding early-risers and late night-returners to destinations across London. The coffee shop on the corner had a steady stream of punters going in and out, laden down with cups and paper bags. I was going to miss my commuter cappuccino from there each day. The new tenants were moving in at the weekend and the landlord wanted to give the flat a lick of paint and fresh carpets, so it really was time for us to go. I stood on the stairs and snapped a couple of photos to remember the place by. The shelves where my books and plants had once sat were now bare, the floor lamps had all gone and Gordon had finally succumbed to storage. The place wasn't the same without him. Everything we collectively owned was either packed into a box or zipped inside one of the Tardis-like Ikea bags. The only things not bubble-wrapped and boxed were the kettle, a few breakfast bits, the radio, and Basil, who eyed me suspiciously from his bed. Although, when it came down to it, what else did I need for a perfect morning? I flicked the radio on and filled the kettle, taking my time to enjoy the moment. It was the last time I'd do this first thing in the morning.

'I'll have a brew,' George shouted down, breaking my reverie.

I took two cups from the cupboard and popped a teabag in each.

'And some bacon if there's any going?' he added.

'Anything else?' I called up, sarcastically, opening the almost-empty fridge and pulling out the bacon and tomatoes. My frying pan was on the hob, where it always was, as I added a knob of butter and knifed open the bacon.

'Yes, toasted bread and ketchup, not fresh tomatoes, please.'

Neanderthal.

I added the bacon and tomatoes to the pan as the water came to the boil, all the breakfast sounds kicking off at once. The bubble and steam of the kettle, the popping and spitting of the bacon, the thunk as the toast shot up. It was all go, while the stone-cold tomatoes sat quietly and tried to work out what was happening. Basil yawned and stretched before padding over and looking up at me with a miaow. He could obviously sense that change was afoot, although after me, no one loved Basil more than my mum, except maybe my dad, so he'd be getting a big lifestyle upgrade for the next few weeks.

I made two glossy teas and ran one upstairs to George, who was propped up in bed, reading his phone.

'Thanks,' he said, without shifting his gaze, as I placed his cup on the bedside table.

'Last day in the flat then,' I said, sadly, which got his attention. He clicked his phone blank and chucked it on the bed.

'I know! I can't wait to get out of here and into our brand-new house. Away from all the London pollution and living on top of one another. No more cracks in the walls or neighbours partying till three in the morning. We are moving up in the world, baby,' he said, with a smile.

'I'm going to really miss it, though, I've lived here for so long,' I said, looking at the paper light shade that Abi and I had put up together while bouncing on the bed, the brown shelves I'd attempted to paint white, but were still a coffee cream, and the curtain pole I'd had made especially as the window was an odd shape and wonky at the top.

'You'll love it when we're in the country. We're both nearly thirty, Hols; we should be married with kids on the way by now. If only you'd stuck with your job, you'd be ticking off all the boxes: career, house, husband.'

'I have got a career, George. Success doesn't have to equal

sitting at a desk, waiting for the next email to come in, you know.'

'No, but it should equal pound signs somewhere along the line,' he grumbled.

'Oh for goodness sake, is it going to be like this for the rest of our lives?' I said, exasperated. 'How much does it cost to be a member of this relationship exactly?'

'Sorry, babe. It's just I could see our future so crystal clear before and now it's more difficult, that's all… I know you love the waitressing gig with Margot.'

'It is NOT a waitressing gig.'

'It's putting plates of food down on tables and pouring wine… isn't it?'

I glared at George and was about to say something I'd almost certainly regret when the fire alarm started shrieking. I ran downstairs and grabbed the frying pan, holding it out the back door in a fury as my blood boiled. The smoky bacon was sizzled and crispy, perfect for a sandwich, but I'd lost my appetite. The alarm blared on until George appeared with a broom and gave it a hefty poke, our ears still ringing with the noise.

'Sorry, Hols, I didn't mean to snap,' he said, looking genuinely contrite in his M&S pants as he leant on the broom. 'I'm hungover and wasn't thinking. I don't like it when we argue.'

'It's not a race to the grave, George. We are allowed to enjoy our lives and our jobs and being married for five minutes before we move on to the next thing on the list.'

'I know. I just want us living our best lives as quickly as possible.'

'Can we please just focus on today for today? Leaving here is a big deal for me.'

George put his arms around me and I leant into him. The stress of packing up and going was really hitting me hard.

'I know. I'm sorry. I'll put some clothes on and get us some coffees from the corner. I know how much you love their cappuccinos.'

'Don't remind me,' I groaned. 'I can't bear it.'

'I'm pretty sure they'll have cappuccino in Surrey, Hols. You're not going to be tied up in a field. It'll be like living here, but better.'

Will it? Of course it will. I was being silly. Basil must have overheard us saying it was moving day, as I caught the wisp of his tail as he disappeared through the cat flap for one last London prowl.

Five

The wedding. 9th September

This was it then. My big day. Well, *our* big day. I didn't feel old enough to be getting married. Twenty-seven on the outside and twelve on the inside. I'd been with George for such a long time that I couldn't remember life before him. BG. Before our Leeds University days, where we'd shared everything. Our textbooks and opinions, cheese toasties and cans of cider for dinner, and that ridiculously small futon that passed as a double bed.

Eight happy years of Holly and George and today, our lives would be officially entwined together forever. I'd change from Holly Roberts to Holly Ballinger and become a Mrs. George's other half, the old ball and chain. I sat up in bed and looked over at my wedding dress sparkling in the sunlight, throwing dancing rainbows across the wall. I'd opted for a super-simple shape, full-length with a slash-neck, long sleeves and a beautiful train at the back. The top was covered in tiny crystals that twinkled as I moved, and the skirt was ivory silk and slid on like a dream. Perfectly fitted and elegant. I couldn't wait to wear it.

I got out of bed and stretched up to the ceiling, elongating my fingers as much as physically possible, then folded my body down and touched the floor. The Pilates classes were finally starting to pay off; I felt full of energy and nervously excited for the day ahead.

'Alexa, play a soothing meditation,' I instructed as my phone pinged.

Margot: *Good morning bride-to-be. We are beautifying the bistro for you. Can't wait to see you. Bonne chance xx*

The wedding was a local affair. We were getting married at Marylebone church and Margot had gifted us the bistro at cost for the reception. I'd sourced the wine from a starter vineyard in Italy and the Champagne was a gift from the local butcher. Dad's mate Jeff was wrapping his Volvo in white ribbon and donning a chauffeur's cap and the Mums were going head-to-head on the flowers having *done a course* together a few weeks back.

There was a knock on the bedroom door and Abi poked her head in with a big smile, carrying two flutes of Champagne.

'Good morninnnnng Mrs Ballinger-To-Be,' she sang. 'Feeling excited?'

'*Acknowledge your thoughts and let them go. You have nothing to do right now*,' the meditation gently lilted in the background.

I smiled and nodded, as she handed me a glass.

'Excited to see you,' I said, giving my best friend a hug, 'and terrified about the wedding part.'

Mum burst into the bedroom brandishing a perfect red rose, looking fraught.

'Holly, Lillian is insisting we put hydrangeas in every vase which I really must disagree with. My view on this – and I'm sure you'll agree – is that we stick to the classic autumnal wedding flowers of roses, dahlias, and sea thistle?' Her eyes glared with the question.

'Annabel, I don't know why you're bothering Holly with this; it's very obvious that the hydrangeas should be treated as a feature flower,' George's mum said, skidding in behind her. 'Don't you remember what Mrs Dingle said when I won the "arrangement of the week" competition?'

'Lilian, we have been over this several times: the hydrangea is a domineering flower and needs to be kept entirely separate from the more delicate flowers.'

'I think you'll find Mrs Dingle said…' Lilian started.

'*Everything is in flow. You cannot control those around you*,' the meditation continued.

'Alexa, off,' I said sharply.

'What do *you* think, darling?' Mum asked, eyebrows off the charts with stress.

'Erm… well, it would be good to use all the flowers.'

'Exactly,' both mums said at the same time, eyeballing each other.

'Mum – maybe you can do the flowers for the church and bistro, and Lilian can do the posies for me and Abi?'

They both nodded in satisfaction. Each thinking they had a superior role to the other.

'Sounds like the best idea, love,' Mum said. 'The venue will be where we spend the most time, so it needs to be right.'

'It would be my honour to do your bouquet, Holly. Something modern and fresh, avoiding the obvious.

A hydrangea-focused bridal bouquet for my new daughter-to-be.'

'Daughter-in-law-to-be,' Mum corrected, putting her arms around me.

'OK, well that's that sorted,' Abi said, raising her glass to change the subject. 'Happy Wedding Day, Holly!'

Mum hugged me and whispered, 'my little girl all grown up and getting married.'

Lilian blew me a kiss. 'Welcome to the family, Holly,' she said. 'The new Mrs Ballinger, just like me.'

My phone was pinging every other second with messages of good luck, love, and other random questions. Auntie Pam asking for directions, George's cousin had food poisoning, the girls from school were having a WhatsApping frenzy to agree a venue for prinks. It was bedlam. I switched it off and threw it in the bedside drawer so I could concentrate on getting ready. I'd showered, shaved, moisturised and Spanxed, and it was time to chill out and have my hair and make-up done. Abi was a miracle-worker when it came to slapping on the slap. She'd worked in theatreland for years and knew exactly how to optimise the female face – any face, in fact. I handed myself over to be transformed from pale-faced mannequin to cherubic-bride, sitting eyes-closed in the light as she brushed on foundation, blusher, highlighter and bronzer, and spritzed me with face-hairspray to make sure everything stayed put.

'OK Mrs B-To-Be, I think I'm done,' Abi said, spinning my chair around to face the mirror. I stared at myself for a good ten seconds, looking my whole face over in confusion. I couldn't believe it was me. My bridal face. Enormous eyes and cheekbones for the first time in a lifetime, and a lighter, brighter look about me. I was the same and different all at once.

'Oh. My. God. How did you do this? What did you...? I hardly recognise myself,' I said, hugging her tight. 'Thank you so much, I love it.'

My red bob had been pouffed up and wound around big Velcro rollers in the hope of creating a magnificent hair mushroom once it was set, and Abi was brushing my shoulders and arms with sparkly powder.

'Alright love?' Dad called, peeking around the door and giving me a big smile. 'Bloody hell! Look at you!' I jumped up and hugged him, his grey beard tickling my face.

'Look at me? Look at you! You look so handsome,' I said, brushing a speck of lint from his shoulder.

'I've got something in my eye,' he said, shaking his head and wiping away a tear.

'Wait until you see her in the dress,' Abi shouted from the en suite.

'Jeff's already here,' Dad said, looking at his watch, 'nice and early as always. We should probably leave at 11.30 a.m. to be on the safe side, so you've got half an hour.'

Ahmagadddd. It was time to put my dress on. I was a bundle of butterflies with a stomach full of Champagne. The lady in the shop said not to underestimate the amount of time it would take to do up the sixty-eight buttons. I shimmied it on and felt extremely proud as it slunk down into position. Over the past six months, I'd slowly morphed into someone else's body, and now Abi had given me someone else's face. George was getting an entirely new me. I wondered if he'd found the card I'd hidden in his blazer pocket yet. I'd written him a little message and popped in a Polaroid from our uni days, when we were fresh-faced and obsessed with each other. And the *pièce de résistance* was that the card played our song. Fleetwood Mac's 'Everywhere'. He'd love it.

Abi finally emerged from the bathroom in her bridesmaid's outfit. A vision in sparkling navy with a plunging neckline and a mermaid fishtail.

'Beautiful,' we said to each other in unison.

'Can you do me up?' I said, pointing at my back. She wiggled over and stood behind me, taking time to make sure every single pearl button was perfectly in place.

'Absolutely gorgeous,' Abi said, smiling at me in the mirror. 'Are you ready?'

'Eight years of ready,' I nodded.

We made our way downstairs to Mum, Dad, Lilian and Jeff, who were ready to go and looking immaculate. Mum and Lilian had chosen different shades of purple with Dad and Jeff suited and booted in top hats and tails. Jeff smiled at me and tipped his hat.

'Your carriage awaits, m'lady,' he said, pointing outside to his be-ribboned Volvo.

Dad held his arm out, this time with something in both his eyes.

'I'm not giving you away, you know that, don't you?' he sniffed. 'You're out on temporary loan as far as I'm concerned, and we'll see how George gets on.'

'You've had plenty of time to put him through his paces,' I said, rolling my eyes. 'We've been living like an old married couple for years. This is just the official bit that we didn't get round to.'

Mum, Lilian and Abi gave me a kiss and we had a quick selfie before they jumped in their cab.

'We'll see you up there,' Mum said with a wave.

'A beautiful bouquet for a beautiful bride,' Lilian said, handing me an elaborate lump of hydrangeas which weighed a tonne. The cab drove off with them smiling and waving, leaving me, Dad and Jeff in silence.

'Time to get this party started,' I said as Jeff opened the car door and took my hand to help me in. I passed him my enormous bouquet and slid into the back seat where Dad met me from the other side.

'Do you want this on your lap?' Jeff asked, his face covered in flowers.

'Er... not just yet. Can it go in the front?'

Jeff strapped the bouquet into the front seat like a third passenger, and the four of us set off for the church.

Six

The wedding. 9th September

I knew something was wrong as soon as the car pulled up. Mum and Lilian were caught in a tense exchange, the priest was checking his watch and Abi ran over as soon as we arrived. Dad wound down the window and she poked her head in.

'Nothing to worry about, but George is running a few minutes late,' she said.

The car clock glowed 12.05 p.m. *I was running a few minutes late*. George was running over *twenty minutes* late. Why wasn't he at the church?

'No problem,' Jeff nodded, 'I'll drive round the block and be back in ten.'

'Actually Jeff, it *is* a little bit of a problem. How long is he going to be?' I asked, my heart in my throat. 'Why is he late? Is Andy there? What's going on?' Andy was his best man.

'I think he's been trying to get hold of you,' Abi said, giving me an eye.

'Who has? Andy?' I said, thinking back to my phone, which was switched off and in my bedside drawer.

Mum and Lilian appeared either side of Abi.

'Darling, have you heard from him?' Mum asked.

'I don't know why you're panicking, Annabel,' Lilian said, 'I'm certain he'll be here any second now.'

'I'll thank you to keep out of it and let me speak with *my daughter* in private,' Mum replied, murderous.

'Jeff, let's do another loop,' Dad shouted from the back.

'Is your bouquet OK in the front like that Holly?' Lilian asked. 'It looks a little… hunched?'

'Bouquet? Dead body more like,' Mum said, completely losing it, as Jeff pulled out into the traffic. Where the fucking-fuck was George?

'Have you got your phone, Dad?' I asked, feeling sick.

'Yes, but it's bad luck for the bride to see or speak to the groom before you get to the altar. You know that.'

'It'll be worse luck if we don't get that far,' I said, taking his phone and punching George's number in. It rang out over and over and eventually clicked into voicemail.

'George? It's me, where are you? What's going on? Call me back on Dad's phone. We're stuck in traffic, driving a slow loop around the church.'

'Don't you worry love, there's always something that comes up on a wedding day,' Jeff said with a chuckle. 'When I married Marjorie, the wedding car didn't turn up and she was half an hour late. I was worried to death that she was standing me up.'

'I'll kill the little bastard if he makes a show of you today,' Dad said in stark contrast.

Surely not. I racked my brains for any clues from our

conversation last night. Andy had just arrived from Liverpool and the ushers were all in London and heading out for dinner. What had we said to each other? They were going for a *curry* and some *beers* and he loved me and couldn't wait to see me at the altar blah blah blah. Oh God, maybe he'd had an accident? Maybe he was in a hospital somewhere with Andy. Or the boys had sellotaped him to a post-box for a laugh and he was powerless to do anything. Naked and stuck tight.

Dad's phone pinged.

Mum: *He's here.*

I felt the blood rush back to my face. He was fine. It was fine. There would be a perfectly good explanation and we'd have a happily married lifetime to laugh about it.

'He's there, Jeff,' I said. 'We can go back.'

'See, I told you it would all be OK,' he replied.

'What possible reason can he have for being late on your wedding day?' Dad said, furiously. 'If there's one thing I can't abide, it's poor timekeeping.'

'Calm down, Dad, this is supposed to be a happy day, remember?'

Jeff got us back to the church in record time, screeching to a halt outside the front door. Lilian gestured to someone inside, then disappeared through the doors and Abi and Mum rushed over to help me out of the car.

'Have you seen him?' I asked, scanning their faces for information.

'Yes, he arrived with Andy just after you drove off,' Abi replied. 'He seemed fine.'

'Ah, thank God.'

Jeff wrestled the bouquet from the front seat and handed it to me.

'See you in there,' he said with a reassuring wink.

'Are you OK, darling?' Mum asked.

I nodded, taking a deep breath.

'Everyone's here and the church looks beautiful,' she whispered, hugging me tight, 'and the flowers are fabulous too, of course.'

'You've done a marvellous job, Annabel,' Dad said.

'I'll go in then and leave you to it.' She touched both our faces and gave Abi a smile as the priest waited patiently by the front door.

'Are you *really* OK?' Abi whispered as we walked into the vestibule. I shook my head and took a deep breath as she fussed about with my train, smoothing it down and fanning it out. The harpist was plucking out a Taylor Swift number, and I could see everyone seated through the crack in the curtain. Rows of gleaming mahogany pews decorated with pale-pink roses, packed with guests wearing their finest, waiting for the ceremony to begin. Candles flickered on every shelf and from all the nooks and crannies, lighting up the church and giving off a soft, romantic glow. Jeff and Marjorie, Auntie Pam and Uncle Steve, my cousins sitting together across two rows, George's school friends, our university mates, everyone happy, smiling and shining. And then there was George. My George. Tall and handsome at the end of the aisle in a sharp, navy suit, with a peacock cravat that matched his eyes. Chestnut curls cropped short, his hands clamped firmly in his pockets as he nervously shifted from foot to foot. I took another deep breath. I was ready.

I nodded at Abi and she signalled to the harpist, who stopped playing. There was a moment of silence as Dad squeezed my hand and mouthed 'I love you,' then the music kicked in and Christine McVie filled the room.

Abi pulled the curtain aside with a big grin to step out first, as George spun on his heels and walked down the aisle towards us, slipping through the curtain and pulling it behind him. There were now four of us squeezed into the tiny foyer.

'What are you doing?' I squeaked, hiding behind my dad. 'It's bad luck to see me before I get to the altar.'

'I need to talk to you,' he replied, his eyes to the ground as he walked straight outside.

Oh no. No, no, no, no, no. I looked at Abi who ushered me towards the front door to follow him.

'I'll get them to sing the first song to buy you some time,' she said.

'What the...?' Dad was turning purple.

'Hang on, Dad, let me find out what's happening.'

I suddenly felt dizzy and for a brief second, thought I might faint, but somehow managed to keep it together and put one foot in front of the other to get myself outside.

George was stood facing up to the sky with his eyes closed as I clip-clopped over in my Louboutins. He was deathly pale and taking dramatic deep breaths.

'George? What's going on?' I asked, as he continued to heavy-breathe.

Now wasn't the best time to have a breakdown, but it would at least explain things. In fact, an ambulance turning up would make the situation a lot less embarrassing if this was about to go the way I thought it was.

He finally looked at me.

'I'm so sorry Holly, I just can't do it,' he said.

'Can't... get married?' I said, unprepared to hear the words coming out of my mouth.

He shook his head as Fleetwood Mac loudly blared from the church.

'Speak to me, George. What's going on? What the hell are you talking about?' I was starting to panic. 'This was your idea? You were the one pushing to get married. I was perfectly happy as we were.'

'I was fine until yesterday, and then it hit me.'

'It hit you?' *I'll bloody hit you.* 'What hit you, George?'

'That we've had our time. Our seven-year itch, whatever you want to call it. We shouldn't get married. It's the opposite of what we should be doing. Sometimes people get married when they should be splitting up and that's what I think we'd be doing.'

'And you thought you'd tell me this now? NOW, GEORGE? Outside our wedding while our friends and family are waiting for us in the church?'

'I tried to call you earlier, but I couldn't get through.'

'Earlier this morning? THIS morning?' I hissed back. 'Well you didn't try very hard. Did you call my Mum? My Dad? Abi? The landline? Did you try the landline, George? Because I didn't hear it ring. And failing all those options, now that I understand the severity of your message, maybe you could have got in your car and DRIVEN TO THE HOUSE.'

'I know, I'm sorry, I should have tried harder or come over. Andy convinced me it was cold feet. But just then, when I was standing at the altar in front of everyone,

I knew it wasn't cold feet. I knew in my heart that my feelings aren't forever feelings, and that I can't go through with it.'

I burst into tears, ruining my new face, and George put his hand on my arm, making me jump.

'Get your hands off me. Don't ever touch me again. I can't believe you're doing this, that you're saying this,' I whispered, tears pouring down my face. The music had now switched and our friends and family were half-singing 'You've Got the Love', mixed in with a lot of collective muttering. I needed to leave and fast. I looked around for Abi and Mum, anyone in fact who could get me away from here. From the mass humiliation that was about to happen. That had already happened. George stared silently at the ground, kicking at an imaginary stone, his cheeks flushed and his hands in his pockets. The one person I would normally trust to look after me was no longer an option. He eventually looked up.

'I don't want you to hate me,' he whispered, as my heart thudded through my ears.

'Is this really happening?' I said, shell-shocked.

His eyes were bloodshot from crying. I lifted his chin so we could be face-to-face, but it meant seeing the anguish up close. This was really happening. George was leaving me. Right now, on our wedding day. He slowly nodded and I lost all feeling in my body. I couldn't breathe.

'You'll have to tell everyone,' I said, pointing back at the church and avoiding his eyes, my head was spinning, 'and sort everything out… I can't bear… I can't go in there…' My brain had gone into auto-protect mode, which hadn't happened for a while.

'I'll do it all. Of course I will,' George said flatly, devastated.

Dad and Abi were waiting in the doorway, keeping a respectful distance.

'I need to leave,' I said, rustling over to them.

'I'll get Jeff and your mum,' Dad said, quickly snapping into action.

'This way.' Abi dropped her bouquet on the floor, swept up my train and led me down an alleyway next to the church. 'What the hell is going on, Hols?'

My heart was beating so fast that I put both hands on it to physically hold myself together. My brain was on auto-scan, continuously running through the past hour, week, month, trying to make sense of what had happened. I started hiccupping in shock and faced Abi, blank and bewildered as I tried to steady myself and catch a thought on what to do next.

'Shall I go back and tell the priest,' she asked, 'so he can organise everyone?'

'No, don't leave me,' I said, gripping her hands in panic. Everything was disappearing. My whole life and future had just... gone. 'What am I going to do?'

'You don't need to do anything right now. You're in shock. You need a vodka and to be with people who love you,' Abi said, putting her arm around me.

'Why has he done this?' I burst into fresh tears. 'Doesn't he love me anymore?' The hiccupping was getting worse. 'I won't ever be able to come back here, I'll have to give up my job, oh God, I can't face everyone, I can't...'

'Vodka. Just vodka for now.' Abi hugged me tight, holding me together as Jeff screeched alongside us, Mum and Dad sitting anxiously in the back. I bundled in next to

Mum, as Dad muttered 'little bastard,' and Abi got in the front.

'One for the road?' Jeff asked, passing me his hip flask as he revved up the Volvo and zoomed off.

Seven

The day after. 10th September

Did it really happen? There was a pain in my chest where my heart used to be and my body felt weak, so it must have done. George. What had gone wrong? I needed to speak to him but I couldn't bear to look at my phone. Where even was my phone? My brain flicked back to the chaos of getting bride-ready and all the messages gushing in before I turned it off. I slid open the drawer next to my bed and there it was. Black and blank and nestled in my knickers. I had half a mind to throw it in the bin and ignore the inevitable outpouring of pity but avoiding it would only prolong the agony. Better to get it over with. I held the side button down until my phone vibrated into life and watched the screen light up like a Christmas tree, silent for about half a second before the pinging started, like an alien's laser gun. Pingggg, ping-ping-ping, ping, PING. No. It was too much. I switched off the sound, dropped it back in the drawer and buried it under a stack of bras.

'Good morningggg,' Mum's gentle voice came through

the door as she quietly knocked. 'It's nearly midday. Are you awake, my darling?'

'No,' I said, slamming the drawer shut and pulling the duvet over my head.

She came in and sat on the bed beside me, followed by a Basil-esque thud, as he snuggled down at my feet.

'Are you sure? I've made you a crispy bacon and tomato sandwich, just the way you like it,' she said, wafting the delicious smell around to attract me like a human tapeworm. It worked. I poked my head out to find Mum with a sandwich in one hand and a cup of tea in the other.

'Oh Holly,' she said, with tears in her eyes, 'my baby, what happened? What was George thinking?'

'I don't know, Mum,' I said, feeling numb. 'What am I going to do?'

'Can you still go on your honeymoon? Or can you claim it on the insurance?'

'I don't think wedding insurance covers the groom changing his mind.' I took the tea as Mum stared into space and started eating my sandwich.

'But what…?'

'I don't know, Mum,' I said again. None of us knew.

'Have you heard from him?' she asked, clearly as baffled as I was.

I shrugged. 'Probably. I'm currently incommunicado.'

I pulled my knicker-drawer open, fished my phone back out and handed it to her. I couldn't face the verdict.

'112 new messages and 15 missed calls,' Mum said, her eyes wide, '112! Well, George is bound to be one of them, isn't he?' She handed it back and I had a quick scroll. All the missed calls were from George. He'd been trying to get hold of me since 6 a.m. I went onto my messages, which were in total chaos, and could be split into three easy categories:

1. The pre-wedding, 'Good luck Mrs-B-To-Be' messages.
2. The increasingly panic-stricken, 'trying to reach you' George messages.
3. The 'Is everything OK, hun?' post-apocalyptic, non-wedding messages.

Everyone I cared about and respected, everyone I'd ever known, in fact, 'just checking in'. My school friends, our uni friends, my gran, Lilian, Margot, Jeff, EVERYONE. I burst into tears and Mum grabbed the tea as it started to spill in my lap, taking a good slurp to wash down my bacon sandwich.

'Oh God, Mum, how can this be happening? My life is ruined.'

My phone started ringing as I scrolled, and I dropped it like a hot potato. George. I was going to faint. I couldn't bear to speak to him. I didn't want to speak to him. Oh FFS. I had to bloody speak to him. My face went hot, and my heart was hammering as his name loomed large on the screen and the ringing continued. Maybe he was calling to apologise. To explain that it had all been a huge misunderstanding.

'Quick!' Mum said, unable to take action, with her hands now full of my breakfast. I was desperate to hear his voice and dreading it at the same time. I swiped the green button and held my breath.

'Hello?' I breathed into the phone.

'There you are! I thought you were never going to

answer!' He boomed his greeting with a joviality that belied the seriousness of the situation. Yes, here I was. And there he was. As if nothing had happened and my entire life hadn't been blown apart.

'Yep,' I said, flatly.

'Holly, I'm so sorry,' he said, then took a long pause. 'I kept thinking I'd change my mind but I left it way too late to tell you. Obviously. We should have had the conversation months ago.'

'The conversation...?' I parroted back. I couldn't think of my own words.

'We've both known for a long time that we aren't right for each other,' George said.

'Have we?'

'Yes. We don't enjoy the same things. I like to go drinking and party with my friends and you like to stay in and cook. I'm a big adventurer and you're more of a home bird.'

'Am I?'

Mum sat deadly still, listening intently.

'I want more out of life and you're happy where you are.'

George paused as I caught my breath. A simple home bird with no ambition? This was a very strange apology call. I was too shocked to think. What did he mean?

'But I love our adventures?' I blurted. 'We've only just come back from Venice?'

'I don't mean a weekend in Italy, Hols; I mean the big life adventure. Working in America, having four kids, travelling the world – really going places as a power couple.'

Mum put the bacon sandwich down, while her eyebrows did their thing.

'Four kids?' I repeated, in a daze.

'Yeah, maybe. Four, five? I don't want to hurt you any more than I already have, but we just aren't on the same page anymore. We don't have the same levels.'

'It sounds like you don't think I'm good enough for you?' I said, softly. 'I've got loads of levels.'

'I don't think we can make each other happy,' George said quietly.

'But I am happy? You do make me happy? Well, you did until yesterday.'

George took a deep breath and tried again. 'I'm just not sure how *I feel* anymore.'

'Oh.' I slumped against my pillow. 'I see.'

But I didn't see. My brain couldn't compute what was being said. My entire future was slipping through my fingers and I wanted to fix it quick, to say the right words to make it stop, to make him change his mind. But my mind was blank. I was so confused.

'I just… why now? I've always been the same. Did I do something wrong? Have you met someone else?'

'Of course not. I can't believe you'd even think that,' George replied hotly.

'Sorry,' I mumbled, 'it feels so sudden, yet so definite. So final. I can't believe you really mean it. We were getting married. Yesterday. Everything was planned.'

'I know,' George paused. 'I'm so sorry, Holly. I don't know what else to say.'

Neither did I. We'd had it all mapped out. Not just the wedding, but the rest of our lives.

Eight

Two months later. 10th November

I had my head under the duvet and had decided this was where I'd be living from now on. It had been raining non-stop for days and it felt good to be safely cocooned in my old bedroom, in the house where I grew up, with the heating on full blast. Hidden away from having to explain the scrambled mess that was now my reality. It had been two months since the wedding and the only indicator of days going by were Mum and Dad bringing in food at regular intervals and opening and closing the curtains with gentle smiles. Mum had taken to making me shower at least once every twenty-four hours and that was about as much as I could cope with. My new life parameters consisted entirely of my childhood bed, where my body lay both empty and heavy and my heart was broken. My phone played its familiar tune from underneath my pillow and the sound cut through the nothingness and twisted my stomach. I couldn't keep going round and round in circles on phone calls with George. He'd made his decision, for now at least, and there was no turning back. I slid my phone out to turn it off and just about stopped myself hitting the red button. It wasn't George this time. It was Margot. Oh God. She must be chasing for payment. Or maybe checking when I'd be back at work. How could I ever set foot in the bistro again? Knowing that it had been polished and preened for my wedding breakfast, lovingly decorated in flowers by my mum, a delicious, five-course feast prepared by Margot. An entire restaurant sat ready and waiting for guests that never came. To celebrate the wedding that didn't happen. Food left uneaten and bottles of Champagne left un-popped. A forever reminder of George's rejection. The thought of it made me feel physically sick. I tapped the green button and held the phone to my ear.

'Hi, Margot,' I said quietly.

'*Bonjour* Holly,' she said, '*ça va?*'

'Terrible,' I said, taking a deep breath. 'I'm so sorry, I know I said I'd be back by now, but I need more time. I haven't been out for days and I just don't think I can face walking into the bistro yet…' I held my breath as tears silently rolled down my face.

'You haven't been out? Didn't I see you in a nightclub last night on Instagram?' Margot asked, perplexed.

'Did you? Oh. That.' I said, slightly embarrassed. I must have forgotten to set Stories to 'George only'. 'No, it was me holding a glass of Champagne up to the TV. I cropped it to look like I was at a party.'

'I don't understand?'

'It was a fake post to make George think I'm living my best life instead of at home on the sofa drinking Shloer.'

'Hmph. And did he think it?' Margot asked. 'Is there any hope of a reconciliation?'

'He hasn't seen it. He's been offline for fifteen hours. I don't think there's any hope, no. He keeps calling and trying to explain himself, but it just doesn't make sense. I haven't actually seen him since the... since our...' I broke off. I couldn't say the word.

There was an audible tut and I imagined Margot's frown. Moving her hand from hip to head and ruffling her pixie curls in annoyance.

'I haven't seen him either,' Margot said.

'Has he not been in to pay? He said he'd settle up. The wine can go back but there was so much food... and the cake, oh the cake. Margot, I'm so sorry; you spent weeks making it for us.'

'You should not be worrying about these things. George has created this situation. He can apologise and explain to me about payment. *Non*, it is something else that I'm calling about. I have an idea for you, but it might be too soon.'

'Go on?' I was intrigued.

'A friend of mine from Paris, Genevieve Blanchet, is in need of some help for the winter season, and I thought of you,' she said. 'It would be doing what you do with me, working in the kitchen with the chef and as a hostess serving drinks and food in the evening.'

'In Paris?' I asked, perking up.

'*Non*, at her chalet in Verbier. The ski resort. Do you know it?'

'Erm... no,' I gave an involuntary shudder, 'I'm not really a ski-resort-type person, to be honest, Margot. In fact, I'd say I'm the total opposite. I've never been up a mountain, have zero sense of balance and I hate the cold. Although my French is pretty good, I suppose.'

More tutting from Margot.

'You don't need to be a ski-person to work in a chalet,' Margot said kindly, 'but you might like a change of scene for a while and this could be interesting?'

'Oh no, please don't send me away, Margot. I'll pull myself together, honestly, I'll be back at the bistro in no time…'

'*Arrêt*. I am not sending you away. There is no rush to come back to work. You can take as much time as you need, but I think maybe you need more than just time. A new space. New teachers. Genevieve's twin brother has an impressive wine cellar and apparently their new chef Xavier is exceptional. Paris-trained with five years at Le Cinq.'

'Is that good?' I asked.

Margot sighed. '*Oui*, it is much better than good. I'd go myself if I didn't have a business to run. Working with Xavier would teach you a more modern type of French cuisine and you can bring those talents back to the bistro in the spring.'

'I don't know, Margot; it doesn't really sound like my sort of thing.'

'Six months working with one of the best chefs in Paris? It is like free entry to the Cordon Bleu cookery school without any of the entrance exams. If you study hard with him and learn his tricks, you can come back as my head chef.'

'Really?' I said, feeling a tiny bit brighter. Learning from a pair of old French pros did sound cool, but the thought of living with them for six months didn't exactly thrill me.

'It is an amazing opportunity, but up to you of course; there is no pressure. If you prefer to stay, then your job is here whenever you're ready to come back.'

My heart nearly stopped. I wasn't ready to go back to the bistro – not yet, anyway. How could I ever look at it as my home-from-home again? It was always my treat to myself when I wanted to get away from the world. Now it would forever be a reminder of rejection. Margot was right. I'd be living with my parents indefinitely unless I made a plan, but I was too muddled to think straight. George had shattered my sense of self, and everything was a mess. I had nowhere to go. Another couple had moved into my happy little flat and every spare penny I had was tied up in Orchard Close. I was in life limbo without many options. A snail without a shell. A single, skint, nomadic slug.

'Can I think about it?' I asked, to buy myself some time.

'*Non*,' Margot said, 'I am sorry, these jobs go very quickly. Genevieve messaged this morning to ask if I knew of anyone, so I think it is synchronicity. The new moon at work. If you take time to think about it, someone else will take it.'

'OK, but I need more information,' I said, googling Verbier while Margot stayed patient. 'How much will I be paid? What are the hours? Where will I stay?'

My screen immediately filled with images of chocolate box, wooden chalets, thickly iced with snow. Big, blue skies full of sunshine and smiling faces in brightly coloured ski outfits. Maybe a few months in the mountains was exactly what I needed. A chance to hide away for a while from real life and making decisions – and duplicitous men.

'These are small details,' Margot said, dismissively. 'Genevieve will confirm everything. You will stay in the chalet. Your food and wine and ski pass are paid for. Of course there is work to do, but you will have a wonderful time.'

'But I've never been skiing before? I'm happiest either lying in the sun or wrapped in a blanket and sitting on a radiator – what if I don't like it?'

'What if? What if? What if? What if you *do like it*?'

'Hmm... that's true. I know you're only trying to help but I don't think I should be making life-changing decisions right now,' I said miserably. 'It's too much.'

'It is too much, yes. But life-changing decisions happen all the time. You either decide things for yourself or the universe conspires to make things happen. George made a decision that changed your life forever and now it's your turn. Sometimes, life unexpectedly shakes you to the core and other times, it sends you a gift.'

'You think this is a gift?' I asked.

'*Mais oui*,' Margot replied.

My natural instinct was to say no again, switch off my phone and snuggle back under the duvet. It was a comforting thought, but I could see it wasn't sustainable long-term. Besides, maybe this was a way to show George I had just as much ambition for my life as he did. That I could do travel and adventure and drinking and partying like he wanted. And maybe... that would change his mind? Would it change his mind? Please God, let it change his mind. Eight years couldn't be over just like that, could it? What other choices did I have? Go back to the bistro? No. Get another job? God, no. Stay in bed? Mmm, yes. Or try something new and go. I had no home, no money, and no George. I had to say yes. It was time for home bird Holly to fly.

Nine

Three weeks later. 2nd December

I dragged my suitcase through St Pancras station on the hunt for the Eurostar terminal. My winter clothes were all packed away in storage, so I'd made the best of a bad situation, using my honeymoon suitcase and pre-wedding outfits. It was either that or ask George for the code to the unit and I didn't want him to know I was going until I was gone. All my lovely jumpers, leggings, jumpsuits and waterproofs, everything that would have been useful for a ski resort in fact, was under lock and key somewhere, hidden in a London warehouse. Mum had bought me a couple of hats and Auntie Pam had lent me her salopettes, which were so old, they were almost back in fashion. My shoe situation was particularly dire, with only my trainers, spiky boots, flip flops and wedding shoes to get me through. I'd saved for six months to buy the gold sparkle Louboutins and there was no way I was leaving them in a shoebox to rot.

I wandered through the station as someone played a

jaunty 'Ding Dong Merrily on High' on one of the free pianos. It was 2nd December, so the world had gone into full Christmas-frenzy. A bright-blue Christmas tree made from Tiffany boxes stood in the centre of the walkthrough and a never-ending stream of different-coloured bubbles filled the air, from the top floor of Hamleys. The train didn't go until 9.45 p.m. but Dad had always taught me to arrive three hours early for every trip, no matter where I was going, and that sense of travel panic was entirely ingrained. I had no choice but to turn up at 6.45 p.m. in case of some imaginary emergency. I stood idly by for a little while, watching as another random commuter took a turn on the piano. The station had been decorated to resemble an enormous Christmas cracker, with streamers running the entire length of the concourse and oversized tat making up a bizarre installation. I was stood next to a plastic comb three times the size of the shoppers, as people rushed past on all sides, and snapped it for my Insta with the caption *Time for a snowy adventure #SoloTravel #SingleBelles #BestLife* to prove to George I wasn't moping around at home. My suitcase was too big to lug around the shops, so I bought a hot chocolate and meandered over to the check-in area to make sure I wasn't delayed. Three hours I could just about cope with; any more than that and I'd have to distract myself with food to pass the time.

I scanned the departures board and saw a muddle of different places listed. Lille, Avignon, Papignon... where was I going again? Paris, then on to Geneva. Yes, Paris, Gare du Nord – where was that then? Not on the board, as far as I could see. I knew I needed to change somewhere, but where? I scrabbled about in my handbag to find my ticket. Tissues, hand gel, lipstick, purse, where was my bloody ticket? I was about to faint with stress when I found it folded in the zipped pocket of my bag and pulled it out to check. First stop was Paris. Yes, I thought so. Right. Lovely. So why wasn't there a 9.45 p.m. train to Paris on the board? I went through the trains again, one by one, but my train wasn't there. There was one at 9.25 p.m., then one at 10.05 p.m. Oh bloody hell, was I looking at the Arrivals board? No, definitely Departures. Well, where the fucking-fuck was the train then? I spied a tall, blonde lady in station uniform and made a beeline for her.

'Hi, sorry, can you help me with something? I mean, er... *bonjour, je m'appelle...*'

'We're still English this side, my love. Have you got a ticket?' she said, smiling.

I handed over my ticket in a fluster, then added my passport for good measure.

'I'm meant to be on the 9.45 p.m. to Paris but I can't see it anywhere on the board?'

'That's because you're on the 19.45,' she said, inspecting my ticket closely and giving it a rub, 'you've got a little mark over the numbers so I can see how you've missed it.'

I felt sick. 'Have I missed it?'

She laughed. 'No sorry, I didn't mean you'd missed the train, just that I can see how you might have missed the right time.'

'Ah thank God, so I haven't missed it? It's twenty past seven now?'

'Is it? Oh, I see. Well in that case, yes, you might have missed it.'

'Nooooo!' My heart dropped. Dad would be furious. 'Have I?'

We both looked up at the board where there was a flashing red 'Final Boarding' sign next to the 19.45 departure. The security queue snaked all the way back to the entrance, so there was no chance I'd make it if I joined the back.

'Come with me, duck, and we'll see what we can do,' the lady said, ambling to the front of the Fast Track queue. 'We've got another one 'ere lads. Meant to be on the quarter to eight, ain't she?' she said, handing them my passport and ticket with a peal of laughter.

'Right, through you come, then. Suitcase up on here for checking, please,' the security guard said. 'Don't worry, plenty of time.'

I could see my dad shaking his head in despair. Absolute rookie error. It was 7.33 p.m. as they checked and stamped my passport and vaguely pointed me towards the ramp for Platform 5. They say if you have a body, then you're an athlete. Not true. I ran as fast as my pale skittle legs would carry me, up the travelator, dragging my ginormous suitcase behind me and by the time I reached the top, I thought I was going to keel over and die. Doors were opening and slamming all over the place and whistles were being loudly blown at both ends of the train. I was meant to be in Coach K but of course the coach in front of me was Coach A. I didn't have time to run down the platform, so I opened the nearest door, leapt onto the train, pulled my suitcase up behind me and collapsed into the only empty seat in an over-packed carriage. I'd made it. That was the most important thing. I was on the train and against all odds, I was on my way.

I felt three sets of eyes on me as I settled into my chair. I was in a four-seater with a table, surrounded by virtually identical teenagers. Twin girls and a boy, with white-blond hair, golden tans and matching ice-blue hoodies. The ski equivalent of *Love Island*.

'Good afternoon, madam, can I get you a drink?' An angel tinkled a wobbly drinks trolley towards me full of booze and handed me a paper napkin and a packet of peanuts. The combination of her smiling face, the free nuts and all the teeny, tiny bottles of gin was like Christmas come early. I could see why people loved the Eurostar.

'Amazing, yes please. Thank you so much – have you got any Tanqueray and cucumber?' I asked hopefully. The world had gone mad for gin – even the local Wetherspoons had twelve different types these days.

The waitress splashed my gin with a Mediterranean Fever-Tree and passed it across. Let the ski-season begin! I took a huge slurp as she moved on to the Brady Bunch.

'I'll have a red wine please,' the boy said. Very posh. I was drinking cider out of a shoe at his age.

'Can I check your passport for proof of age, please?' she said, then turned to me. 'I presume you're happy for them to drink alcohol?' As if they were *my children*.

'Er... no, they're not with me? I'm not much older than them myself,' I laughed.

'They're with me,' a voice from behind me said. A voice belonging to a man in an ice-blue hoodie. Of course they were. 'And you're sitting in my seat,' he said.

I gave a little cough and felt myself turning red.

'Am I? Ah. Apologies, I had to jump on the train at the last second... I'll move.' I quickly necked my G&T and set down the empty glass as the waitress stood frozen to the spot. She looked at me, looked at him and then looked at the posh boy cracking open the miniature red wine as I shuffled out of the man's seat and let him sit down. I'd already pocketed his peanuts. I grabbed my suitcase, but the drinks trolley was in the way so I couldn't move past. The waitress gave me a glare, so I reversed back out of the carriage and sat on my suitcase outside the loo. After she'd served the rest of the table their drinks, she huffed and puffed and eventually doubled back on herself to let me through.

'You can't just sit in First Class and order yourself a drink on a standard ticket, you know,' she said, shaking her head at me.

'I'm so sorry, I didn't realise this was First Class; I thought everyone got a free drink. I'm happy to pay?' I offered, getting out my purse and hoping it would be less than £2.80 as that was all I had.

She frowned, irritated.

'I'm not set up to take payments as everything is included in this part of the train. If you can please just take your actual seat, that would be great.'

I staggered down eleven carriages to get to my 'actual' seat, accidentally boshing a couple of innocent passengers with my rucksack along the way. The Eurostar was not designed for walking up and down with full-size luggage. Economy was a very different story, with stag and hen dos, older couples off for a week away, groups of friends sharing bottles of Prosecco and fit families en route to the alps for the weekend. My *actual* seat was next to a woman in her late fifties in a caramel, cashmere dress with bright-pink lipstick, who eye-rolled when I pointed at the empty window seat next to her.

'Sorry, can-I-just-get-to-my...' I said awkwardly, as I stashed my bags and struggled past her to sit down.

And then finally. Time to relax and enjoy the journey. I snuggled into myself and leant my head against the window watching the bleak, grey skies of London seamlessly switch out for the bleak, grey skies of Paris. Then the same bag drag through Paris following the blonde and beautiful to make sure I didn't miss the connection to Geneva and once at Geneva, I joined 'The Verbier Express', to complete the final leg to Le Châble. I took a long hard look around the train at my new tribe. These were now my people. Well, I was technically the staff, and they were technically the guests, but same, same. The ice-blue crew were a couple of tables along, so I gave them a friendly wave, but the dad stared straight through me. Obviously a big peanut fan. I was sitting opposite a lux-tanned couple who were holding hands and chatting animatedly in French. They were wearing matching black onesies, like superheroes ready to fight the evil snow monsters. My skinny jeans and Zara jumper were not going to hit the mark. I'd have to top up with a few key purchases once I got to Verbier. Hopefully, there would be a shopping centre in the village to get some basics without breaking the bank.

The train hurtled towards the slopes and the scenery finally started to shift from dull-grey winter misery to lighter, brighter winter misery. A thousand shades of green as we made our way through Switzerland, each hamlet surrounded by snow-capped mountains, with wooden chalets dotted randomly at first, then more concentrated as we approached each train station. Eventually, the snow crept more heavily into the scenery and the rest of the mountains came into view, white and bright against blue skies and sunshine. How could the sun be so blatant? Shining away here when we hadn't seen it for months back home.

My phone lit up as we emerged from the thousandth tunnel:

George: *Call me ASAP. Margot is on my back for full payment.*

Margot: *Bon voyage Holly, bisous xx*

Mum: *Enjoy your adventure my darling! Xxx*

No, I will absolutely not be calling you, George. Deal with the fallout yourself, if you're so evolved and capable. I ordered a strong coffee from the drinks trolley and knocked it back, my brain abuzz with caffeine, then took some photos from the train and posted them on my socials:

#ClimbEveryMountain #OnMyWay

I'd have to speak to George properly at some point about the house and the money and all the adulting-stuff we needed to do if it was really, *really* over. But not yet. Just thinking about it made my heart race. My brain just kept trying to make sense of his reasons. I'd thought we were so happy. I rubbed the dent where my engagement ring had sat since graduation day. Twenty-seven years old and already on the scrapheap. My finger would never be the same. That bloody dent would always remind me of George. Unless I could pay a plastic surgeon to puff it back out.

Le Châble was the end of the line and we were due in at 5.30 a.m. It had been a long journey and there were lots of tired faces, including mine, ready to go to bed. Well, *I* was ready to go to bed – maybe the hardcore ski set would be straight out on the slopes. I was exhausted. What with George and the wedding and leaving so abruptly for this job, my whole body was ready to collapse. I could have slept for a week. There was a frisson of excitement as the conductor announced we would soon be approaching our final destination and all the exercise-y types leapt up and started zipping and unzipping. Luggage, jackets, sleeping bags – it was an absolute zipfest. Ski mums and dads took sleeping children out of snuggly onesies and put them into mini ski suits, strapping them into buggies and preparing to leave the train.

First light was appearing over the mountain as the train pulled into the station and it suddenly hit me that I was in the middle of God-knows-where, with no skiing ability whatsoever. What was I thinking? I'd been having a lovely time watching the scenery change on a nice, warm train, but the thought of leaving my cosy seat to meet strangers in the cold, and then at some point having to work on top, was almost too much. The train quickly emptied as clearly everyone knew what they were doing apart from me. I lugged my enormous suitcase out of the luggage rack and decided to take it step by step. Step one – get off the train. I wasn't sure what to expect after that, other than knowing that Genevieve had arranged for Liv to collect me from the station and drive me to the chalet. Liv was the housekeeper at Chalet Blanchet and would also be my roommate. Fingers crossed she was cool and fun. And that we'd get on.

As I staggered off the train, the cold hit me in the face. It was absolutely FREEZING. Oh God, how could my body go from being so warm and cosy and sleepy one minute to so bloody cold the next? This was already my idea of hell. I took my denim jacket off and put a second long-sleeved T-shirt on as another layer. Since taking the job I'd been following all the top #instaski influencers to get some tips and according to @snoweird it was all about the layers. I had to think of myself as a beautifully complicated trifle. Lots of materials and lots of layers, the thinner and more expensive, the better. My denim jacket wasn't cutting it and my skinny jeans were doing nothing to protect my milk-bottle legs from the wind.

'Hey, are you Holly?' A girl with a strong Australian accent, blue-black plaits and violet eyes walked towards me smiling as I was mid clothes-innovation, putting a woolly sock on each hand.

'Yes, hi! How did you guess?' I gave her a wave with my sock hands, 'I'm not sure I'm totally prepared for this weather, to be honest.'

'Don't worry, I've got some stuff you can borrow; I've been out here for a while. I'm Liv,' she said giving me a big hug and taking my case. I felt immediately relieved to see a friendly face.

'That's so kind, thank you. I'm not really a skier,' I said, following her down the platform.

'No worries, are you boarding?' Liv asked.

'No, I'm staying at the chalet with you,' I replied.

'I mean snowboarding?' Liv said.

'Oh. No. Well not yet anyway,' I said with a little laugh. 'I've never been to a ski resort before. I don't really like the cold. Will I hate it?'

Liv gave me a look. 'Apparently, there's no such thing as

bad weather, only bad clothes. If you play it right, you won't get cold. Everywhere indoors is heated, so as long as you've got your kit for the mountain, you'll be fine.' Liv stopped. 'You have got proper gear for the mountain, haven't you?' she asked, looking at my high-waisted skinnies with a frown.

'Yes totally,' I said, re-thinking my Louboutins. 'I wasn't sure what the look was, so I borrowed a few bits and bobs to put an outfit together. I should probably check with you before I... er... ride though. Do you ski or snowboard?'

'Board. And if you're starting from scratch, I'd go with that. Skiing is very 1995.'

'Which was an excellent year for the vine by coincidence,' I said. 'Maybe that's why the ski lot are so into their booze. Genevieve and Luca must be loaded if they can afford to hire three of us at the chalet?'

'Getting paid a lot, are you?' Liv laughed.

'Oh. Not really, no. Bed, board, a ski pass and 50 Swiss francs a week? Is that right?'

'Yep, same as me. Don't worry, they get their money's worth. I clean the chalet and do breakfast and you'll be working 4-11 p.m. as Xavier's sous-chef in the day and serving dinner and organising the wine at night.'

I nodded, making mental notes.

'I occasionally work dinner if I'm needed or if you want to swap shifts every now and then, that's cool too. And we get Thursdays off.'

'Amazing,' I said, 'can't wait to get stuck in. I hear Xavier's pretty impressive?'

'You hear right. No idea what he's doing up here. It's not

the money, that's for sure. Must be the lifestyle, like the rest of us, I suppose.'

'The party lifestyle?'

'The mountain lifestyle. You can party if you want to or just enjoy the peace. The skiing, the food, the spas. Everything you could want is here.'

'Sounds perfect. The peace for now, but maybe some partying later.'

'Are you single? Into men? Women?'

'Very newly single,' I felt my voice catch. It was the first time I'd said it out loud and the first time I'd been single this decade. 'From a man. We were engaged. I'm in heartbreak avoidance mode at the mo' but I'll let you know when I get to the rebound stage.'

'The odds are in your favour out here. Eight men to every woman and the supply changes weekly, so you'll have plenty to choose from when you're ready.'

'Honestly, I can't imagine ever wanting to go near a man again. But good to know if I change my mind, there are options,' I said, smiling.

Liv stopped beside a Porsche 4x4 with chains stuck to the enormous tyres and easily lifted my suitcase into the boot. I chucked my rucksack and my emergency travel handbag in on top, being careful not to scratch the paint. The Porsche had that delicious, brand-new-car smell, with a dove-grey leather interior. I climbed in and squidged into my seat as Liv started the engine.

'Heated seats?' she asked.

'Ooh, yes please. As much heat as possible. Is this your car?' I asked, mouth hanging open, I was so impressed.

Liv laughed as she reversed, handing me a packet of

smoked almonds. There was half a Nutribullet of green juice sitting where I'd normally have a coffee or Coke, so Liv was getting her five-a-day in before the sun was even up.

'Yeah, right. No, it's the chalet car. We use it to ferry Genevieve and Luca about and run other errands. You'll be insured on it too. Do you drive?'

'Of course. But nothing like this before.' My mind was being blown every step of the way. 'Looks like it's time to start living the high life,' I said, popping a handful of almonds into my mouth. I'd have preferred chocolate peanuts, but they'd do for now.

Liv drove like a kamikaze racing driver up the never-ending hill towards Verbier. It was only just first light, so the roads were quiet, too early for most people to be up and about. The streets were silent, and the air was crisp and clean. A fresh dump of snow had fallen overnight, leaving a frosty layer of padding on the mountain for the holidaymakers to play in. We drove past a small, wooden church with a cross nailed to the roof and candles glowing in the window, a supermarket, a florist and restaurant after restaurant. All were dark and closed, quiet and sleeping, but this was clearly a place for the foodies and wine connoisseurs. I'd be among kindred spirits.

We eventually reached the top of the hill and Liv turned into an empty, tree-lined street and drove straight up onto the first drive, turning off the engine. This was it. This was my home for the winter. The building was chocolate-box perfect. Dark wooden slats with big windows, pristine white shutters, and a mashed potato lid. It was a Christmas house, and my insides went funny with excitement as I gaped up out of the window.

'Pretty nice, huh?' Liv said quietly, as I took it all in.

'It's beautiful,' I replied. It really was.

The front door opened and a man in jeans and a hoodie poked his head out.

'Morning,' he said, giving a bleary-eyed wave.

'That's Xavier,' Liv said, opening the boot and lifting my bags out.

Xavier the much-lauded chef? But he could only be in his early thirties? Where was my wrinkled, Ramsay-esque figure? Xavier was tall and tanned, with a mess of auburn hair and a stubbly, square jaw. I'd been expecting an old Michelin MasterChef, with a lifetime of experience.

'Morning, I'm Holly,' I said brightly. 'It's a bit early to be up, isn't it?'

'Better get used to that,' he said in a French accent, 'first lifts are 8 a.m. and sleep is overrated if you want fresh snow. Welcome to Verbier. I'm Xavier.' He swept his hair from his eyes and held out his hand to shake mine.

'Hi,' I said, taking his hand as he caught me off guard with a double kiss.

Liv passed my bag to Xavier and wheeled my case through the front door. I slapped my cheeks to force a bit of life into my face and gave my hair a ruffle as I made my way up the front steps.

'You're safe. They're not here till tomorrow,' Xavier said, as I tentatively looked around.

'And Genevieve messaged to say they won't arrive until lunchtime,' Liv added, 'so plenty of time to unpack.'

The chalet was like nothing I'd ever seen before. The front door opened into a woody dream. I was in the second little pig's house and it was heaven. Beautiful oak floors and walls met with wooden-framed windows swathed in red, velvet curtains and a soft-carpeted staircase that led to the first floor. A Christmas tree covered in fairy lights and gold baubles twinkled in the foyer and the smell of fresh coffee percolated through the air. Liv was right about the temperature; I'd gone from the hot-bottom seat of a Porsche to full-blast central heating.

'You're sharing with me,' Liv said, pointing to another set of stairs in the far-right corner that went down to the floor below.

'We're in the basement,' Xavier added.

'I imagine it's still pretty nice,' I said, running my hand along the smooth, pine handrail as the three of us made our way downstairs. Past the laundry room, the kitchen and the bathroom and finally arriving at the bedrooms. One for me and Liv, and one for Xavier.

'What's the room down the end?' I asked.

'That's the ski room and sauna,' Liv said, 'and there's a plunge pool just outside, if you're into that sort of thing?'

'No one is into that sort of thing,' Xavier said with a smile, 'except Liv.'

'Loads of people are into it actually, Xavier. And yes, it's changed my life,' Liv said, with a nod. 'Two minutes a day and it completely detoxes your body and sorts out your immune system.'

'You mean there's a plunge pool outside in the snow?' I asked, just to clarify.

Liv nodded enthusiastically. 'By the back door. You leave your towel on the bench, run out and jump in it for as long as you can bear, then come back in and use the sauna. No better way to get your blood pumping.'

'Debateable,' Xavier said, with a shudder.

'OK, well good to know it's there if I need it,' I said, knowing full well, I would *never, ever* need it.

'There are two doors into the ski room, so we can access it from down here and Genevieve and Luca can walk down the steps from the top floor.'

'The chalet is ski in, ski out,' Xavier said casually, as if that should make sense. I was going to have to get up to speed PDQ or I'd be a laughing stock. Although skiing straight into the sauna sounded very dangerous. I was hoping Liv would help me out a bit. I didn't want to look like an idiot. My palms were getting sweaty at the thought of Genevieve and Luca arriving the next day. How was I going to impress them with my basic food and sommelier knowledge? I needed Margot here to back me up.

Liv showed me into the bedroom, which was a basic twin with a wardrobe, a dressing table and a full-length mirror. The window between our beds opened out onto ground level and a selection of juices were nestled in the snow, nicely chilling in nature's ice bucket. Half the room looked like a walk-in wardrobe had imploded, with piles of clothes everywhere, all over Liv's bed, the wardrobe doors and heaped on the floor in the corner. We each had a shelf above our bed and Liv's was full of trinkets and photos, with her smiley face peering out at different ages, next to lots of other tanned, smiley faces.

My side of the room was starkly bare in comparison. A single bed with a large, feather pillow and a double duvet folded in on itself. An empty shelf screwed into an empty wall and half a tiny wardrobe to hang up my salopettes and stash my shoe collection.

'We'll leave you to settle in,' Xavier said.

'Help yourself to anything you want from my stuff,' Liv said, gesturing around at the mess. 'Sorry it's a bit, er...' She picked up a pair of stray knickers and put them in her pocket.

'No worries, I like that it's homely,' I said, side-eyeing the detritus for movement. Please God, let there not be rats.

Xavier and Liv left me to it and I collapsed onto the bed. I was here. I was really here. I'd taken the 'fuck it' pill and decided to stop deciding, and this is where life had taken me. I'd leapt, and now it was time for the net to appear.

Ten

3rd December

George: *Have you gone abroad? I know you're upset but I need to speak to you about the house. Call me.*

Should I call him? Should I? Why should I? No.

I'd miraculously managed to find a home for my clothes, shoes and miscellaneous things in the tiny spaces Liv had left me. The selection of fleeces Mum had bought from F&F were now neatly folded up in the drawer under my bed. My lucky dresses were hanging in the wardrobe and my spiky boots were polished and waiting for action on the shoe rack. Ready to get out into Verbier and see what it was all about.

I found Xavier sitting at the kitchen table, scribbling hard with a stubby pencil.

'You're awake,' he said, looking up.

'Yes, I must have dropped off for a few hours. It was quite a journey,' I said, looking around. The kitchen was immaculate. Dark-blue cupboards with old, gold handles and mahogany worktops. It was a traditional, family-type kitchen. The oven was a standard size with an island in the centre of the room for prepping the food. It was somewhere between my cubby-hole kitchen in London and Margot's more professional operation at the bistro. I'd need a few days of nosying around to work out what went where, but I felt immediately at home.

'I'm just working on the menu,' he said. 'This is the first official weekend of the season and I want it to be special.'

'What's the story with them? Brother and sister but they own this place together? Sounds a bit romantic?' I said, sitting next to him.

'They are the rich kids who got lucky in the divorce.'

'Oh wow, that's more than lucky! I wouldn't get a box of teabags if my parents got divorced.' I said, thinking of Mum and Dad back at home, harmoniously married. 'Must be a weird vibe sitting down for fine dining every night with your brother?' I said, trying to imagine it.

'It's rarely just the two of them,' Xavier said as he carried on scribbling. 'They usually have guests or friends here from Paris, so I always cater for six.' I noticed he was wearing a wedding ring and self-consciously rubbed the dent on my engagement finger to encourage the puffing out process. I'd been so looking forward to my wedding ring being a permanent feature and had zoomed in on thousands of bands before finding 'the one'. When it finally arrived, I used to try it on for an hour each day to see how I looked in the mirror as a waving wife and how I looked sending an email as a typing wife and how I looked popping out to the shops as a driving wife. I'd gotten kind of used to it. Xavier's wedding ring was too shiny to have been around for very long. Just my luck to be paired with a loved-up newlywed when I was wallowing in my own love-less misery.

Xavier looked up. 'Don't look so worried; it's just the two of them coming up tomorrow to open the chalet for the season. We won't be doing six guests for a week or two.'

'I'm not worried about a table of six. Margot and I do close to forty every day for lunch and dinner. Is there a wine merchant for the wine pairing each week, or do we order it direct from the suppliers?'

'Ohhhh, of course you won't know.'

'Know what?' I asked.

'You're in for a treat. Luca has a legendary wine cellar with every wine you can imagine, so we just need to choose and serve the wine each night,' Xavier said with a smile.

Wow. So the answers would all be in the cellar, and I could work with Xavier to make sure the food and wine worked together. I'd need to stay super-vigilant with my homework though; I didn't want to muddle up my bouquet and body in front of the French fashionistas.

'Sounds amazing, where is it?' I asked, looking around.

'At the back of the wooden staircase in the hallway. There's a door behind the green curtain. Luca will give you the official tour when he arrives; it's his pride and joy.'

'Can I go and have a sneaky peek now?'

Xavier looked up and smiled. 'No chance. That door is well and truly locked. Luca will give you a set of keys once he's shown you around.'

Xavier did a final flourishing scribble and examined his work.

'Is it looking good?' I asked, nervously.

'It is perfection,' he nodded, looking pleased with himself, 'and I've added some suggested wine pairings to help the new girl out on her first day,' he said with a smile. 'Oh, and Liv said to let you know your uniform is hanging up in the laundry room.'

'Uniform?'

'*Oui*, we've all got them. I wear chef's whites and you and Liv are in navy.'

'With a plume of red and white feathers?' I asked. 'They must have more money than they know what to do with. Why do they care what we wear behind closed doors?'

'I suppose it's to impress their guests,' Xavier said, 'make it clear that we're the staff? Are you not into dressing up?' he asked with an innocent look.

'Not French national dress, no.'

My phone lit up and started ringing off the table and *Hubbie-To-Be* appeared on the screen. Xavier looked from me to the phone and back again. I couldn't keep putting it off. I'd have to face him eventually.

'Sorry, I've got to take this,' I said, grabbing my phone and running upstairs.

I took a deep breath, my heart racing. 'Hello?' I whispered.

'At last!' boomed George's deep, familiar voice. 'Where are you? I can tell by the phone ring you're abroad?'

'I am abroad, yes.'

'Where have you gone? Your Instagram is full of snow and mountains. Strange choice for a holiday, isn't it? You can't even cope with the draught from the front door at home – you hate the cold.'

'I don't see that it's anything to do with you where I am anymore, George,' I replied.

'Don't be like that. This is hard for me as well, you know.

And there are things we need to talk about. The house, the car, the cat.' My baby, Basil. If I could have smuggled him over in my suitcase, I would have done, but I didn't want to unsettle him. He'd already relocated once to Mum and Dad's and that was enough for the time being. He was at his happiest prowling the mean streets of London, chatting to his cat-friends and terrorising mice.

'Mum and Dad will look after Basil while I'm away. They love him. You can buy me out of the car if you want it. I've no idea what we do about the house.' I felt sick about the house. I'd handed over my life savings, £12,000, everything I had, towards the deposit. 'I suppose we should just sell it?' I said, glumly.

'Unless we rent it out for a while?' George replied.

I thought about it for a moment. If we sold the house, we'd be done. We'd have no more reason to be in touch and that would be that. Maybe George was trying to slow things down? Maybe he didn't want to completely cut ties with me after all.

'Hmm… yes, you might be right; let's keep our options open. We don't need to decide today, and I'd rather wait a while than rush into a decision we'll regret. Why don't you move in for a few months until we know what we're doing? At least that'll save us paying out for storage.'

'I wouldn't feel right being in the house when you have nowhere to live,' he said.

'Don't worry about me, I'm going to be away for a while… embracing life's big adventure – as you suggested.'

'What do you mean? Where are you?'

'I'm in Switzerland. I've taken a job in a ski resort for the winter.'

'A ski resort?' He repeated incredulously, taking the news in. 'Not as a chalet girl, surely? You're far too old for that?'

'I wouldn't say twenty-seven is too old for anything George, but no, not as a chalet girl, as a chef. I needed to get away for a while.'

'Yeah right,' he scoffed. 'Seriously? That's a bit of an overreaction, isn't it?'

'Is it? Is there such a thing, when you're jilted at the altar?'

'I didn't jilt you Holly, it wasn't like that.'

'Wasn't it?' I was so confused. I didn't want to move on if George wasn't 100 per cent sure. Was there a chance we could work things out?

'We've been over this so many times. I haven't rejected you. I just don't think marriage is right for us, for *me* right now. That's not to say it couldn't be right in the future. Maybe we both just need some space?'

'I'm in another country – you can't get much more space than that. How much space do you need?' I knew I was handing him the shreds that were left of my heart to chew back over and spit back out, but I couldn't help myself. Where was my self-respect?

'Let's give it until Christmas and see how we feel then?' he offered, generously. 'And in the meantime, would you mind giving Margot a call and doing a deal on the money we owe her? See if she'll do it for cost?'

'OK,' I said sadly. I was saying yes, but I meant no. There was no way on God's earth I was going to start unravelling all the work I'd done to arrange our wedding. Taking it apart piece by piece. He'd have to find that money himself and pay up. It was the very least he could do.

'Maybe I can come out and visit and we can catch up properly?' he said softly.

'Maybe.' I replied. Was this what they called breadcrumbing? I was tired of asking the same questions over and over, but it did sound like there might still be a chance for us.

'Good. We'll stay in touch, OK? I'll come and see you. Don't hate me, Holly. I know it doesn't feel like it, but I'm trying to do what's right for both of us.' How had my life so dramatically leapt from pre-wedding nerves to no-wedding disaster?

I wandered back down to my new room to have another snooze and found Liv cross-legged in front of the mirror, straightening her hair.

'How're you doin' mate? Fancy coming out for a few drinks with me and Xavier to check the place out? Meet some of the locals?'

'Erm… I'm not sure if I feel like it, to be honest,' I said, getting palpitations at the idea of going into a packed pub and talking to strangers. Starting again.

'The orientation is part of the onboarding process,' Liv said, tossing her poker-straight hair over her shoulder. 'You can't mope around here on your first night. Get yourself together and let's go.'

OK. I could do this. I needed to get back out in the real world and start living again. Show George what he was missing. It was time to act like a sort-of-free and sort-of-single twenty-seven-year-old and oh-my-God-what-the-hell-was-I-doing-here?

Liv opened the window and grabbed a small bottle of

vodka from her snow-fridge, pouring a couple of shots into two egg cups that were sitting on the dressing table.

'*Santé*,' she said, passing one to me and downing the other. She cracked open a can of Red Bull, took a swig and offered it to me. 'We'll just go for a couple to familiarise you with the area. See it as a health and safety briefing.'

I sprayed my hair with dry shampoo and popped a roller in my fringe to give it a bit of lift. I had no idea what to wear so decided to go Christmassy, with a sparkly jumper, pleather leggings and my spiky boots. BB cream, CC cream, bronzer, eyeliner and three coats of mascara. Then a quick spritz of J-Lo Glow and I was good to go.

There was a knock on the door and Xavier popped his head in and smiled.

'Are you girls ready?' He looked like a boyband extra in his hoodie, jeans and biker boots. His eyelashes fluttered as he looked from Liv to me. Why do boys get all the good eyelashes?

'Are you ready to defy the ski resort odds and take two of us out on the town?' I asked. 'Verbier won't know what's going on. Two women, one man. What prowess he must possess, what charm he must exude, the money and influence this man must have...'

'Everything you've heard is true,' Xavier said, as the three of us set off for the main square. The wine bars and restaurants were overflowing with people enjoying dinner and the street was full of skiers and snowboarders, singing and dancing to 'Sweet Caroline,' dressed head-to-toe in their ski gear, despite it being 8 p.m.

'What is going on?' I asked, slightly bewildered.

'Après ski,' Xavier said with a smile, 'it starts around 3 p.m. and goes on all night.'

The party was in full swing and Liv was right about the ratios; I'd never seen so many men in one place. I was in an alternate social reality where women were in extremely short supply. In a sea of men, I could see maybe ten girls, dotted around. What a time to be alive. And single. I took a video and posted it to my Stories.

#PartyTime #ApresSki.

I would rather have been in bed after travelling all day, but I knew George would be watching and I wanted him to think I was having a good time.

The three of us snaked our way through the first pub to get to the bar, where it was very packed, very hot and very noisy. Xavier grabbed my hand to make sure I wasn't swept away in the crowd, and I was glad to cling onto him. I'd never find my way back to the chalet if I lost them. Liv gave us the universal sign for 'drink' and we both nodded. There wasn't really room to be specific, so we'd get what we were given. The barman saw Liv and his eyes lit up. She was served within seconds and each of us had two bottles of Desperado and a Jägerbomb to contend with. I took a photo of the table of drinks and posted it to my Stories – hope you are watching, George, I think you'll find I can party just as hard as you can. I cheers-ed Liv and Xavier and necked my Jägerbomb, hoping the quicker I drank it, the quicker it would be out of my system. I felt the syrupy liquid burn my throat as it went down the wrong way and I started to choke. Liv slapped me on the back in alarm, and I pointed to the balcony with tears in my eyes, making my way outside to cough in private. Après ski was quite something. The dancing was so enthusiastic, it was verging on violent. I took a couple of minutes to breathe in the fresh mountain air and absorb this exuberantly happy place. I was already missing home and the call from George hadn't helped, but Liv and Xavier had been so friendly and welcoming. I had a feeling I was going to really like it here.

'So, what's your story, Holly?' Xavier shouted, as I walked back in to the opening bars of AC/DC's 'Highway to Hell'.

'No story, just trying something different for a while,' I said. I didn't want to tell them my fiancé had dumped me at the altar and I was running away from real life. This was a chance to reinvent myself and be the Holly that George wanted me to be.

'It just came to you in a dream, did it? Out of the blue?' Liv said archly, not believing a word. 'What about the long-term thing you were talking about in the car?'

'Well yeah, I'm kind of mid-breakup or post-breakup; I'm not completely sure, to be honest. All I know is that I'm off the market for the time being. I'm kind of single and not-single and broken-hearted all in one. How about you two?'

'I'm trying out coupledom at the moment, and have been for a while,' Liv said. 'My current squeeze is over there.' She pointed a sharp, red nail at the DJ, who was wearing a fluorescent pink jacket and glittery Minnie Mouse ears, a look of absolute concentration on her face.

'Cool, what's her name?' I shouted over the music.

'Bella,' Liv shouted back, jumping up and down as the chorus sang out.

'And you?' I turned to Xavier, his wedding ring glinting in the disco lights.

'Bit of a giveaway,' he said holding up his hand. 'I'm married. Two years in February. My wife Christina is from London, but she lives in Paris.'

'Is that where you're from?' I asked, confused.

'Yes, and it's where she works.'

'Does she ski? Will she come out and stay at the chalet?'

'I doubt it. She runs a restaurant, so it's difficult,' he said, dismissing me and swigging his beer.

I nodded. No point pressing him when we couldn't hear ourselves think. Plenty of time for us all to get to know each other. Maybe they did things differently in France – cross-country, long-distance marriages to keep things exciting. Either way, we were in opposite camps but similar situations. He was in wedding-ring-ville with his wife in another country, and I was wedding-ring-free with my ex-husband-to-be back home.

Liv disappeared over to DJ twinkle-ears, leaving me and Xavier alone.

'Are you looking forward to getting out on the slopes?' he asked. 'Will you ski or board?'

'I'm not really sure,' I shrugged. 'What do you think I should do?'

'Board,' Xavier said without hesitation. 'I can show you, if you like?'

This was already a nightmare. I had zero sense of balance; how was I ever going to be a credible snowboarder?

'That would be amazing, if you're sure you don't mind?'

'Of course! We can get you a board and a lift pass tomorrow once the Blanchets arrive. Trust me, you'll be doing falling leaf by the end of the week.'

I'd be doing falling something.

'Can you take me on the baby slopes first? I've never even stood on a snowboard before, and I don't want to break my arm the first time I go out.'

'The green slopes are for the skiers. It's impossible to learn how to board on a flat surface. We'll have to go up the mountain to teach you on the blues, but I won't let you hurt yourself.'

'And on the wine for the first meal – you think a Champagne and a Pinot Noir are fine? What about the other courses? Do they have dessert wine?'

'You'll see. They don't drink excessively – they are the French elite. But Luca will brief you when he arrives. He'll want you to surprise him without being too surprising. You'll get the hang of it.'

'Sounds like a Christmas cracker riddle,' I said, befuddled. I was intrigued to meet Genevieve and Luca. What if they didn't like me or my style? I'd only ever worked with Margot before; what if they liked things done differently?

'You'll be fine. They are good people.'

'I just want to impress them,' I said anxiously.

'Don't worry, we work as a team, you and I. We will impress them together,' Xavier said. 'They use the chalet to entertain important clients, so it's about being attentive and thoughtful and making sure they can enjoy themselves and relax while they work.'

'I do an excellent head massage,' I said, flexing my fingers.

'Well, that would definitely relax them,' Xavier laughed,

'but they are looking to us for their food and wine. They are extremely well-connected on the Paris restaurant scene, so you will always have a job if they like your work.'

'And if they don't?' I countered, knowing the other side of that coin meant my French cooking career would be over before it started. No pressure.

Xavier left the question hanging as Liv came spinning back, dancing to 'Country Roads' with a red flush in each cheek.

'More drinks?' she asked, with a glint in her eye.

'My round,' I said, ordering the same again and downing another Jägerbomb. As long as I drank all my shots by midnight, I'd be absolutely fine for lunchtime tomorrow. I didn't want to start off on the wrong foot – serving welcome Kir Royales with the hangover-shakes, stinking of booze.

Eleven

4th December

There was a faint beeping that was getting louder and louder on the horizon. Beep, beep, beep, beep, where was it coming from? Was a bin lorry about to reverse into our bedroom? I was unconscious. I was conscious of being unconscious. I was asleep. Was it my alarm? It was my alarm. Arghhh, it was my alarm. I woke with a start, fumbled around in the dark to turn the beeping off and snuggled back into my duvet for an extra ten minutes.

'Time to get up,' Liv called, leaping out of bed and putting on her swimsuit. 'Fancy a quick plunge?'

'Absolutely not,' I mumbled, as she ran in the direction of the pool for her early-morning shock to the system. Horrendous. Much better to stay in bed where it was soft and warm and cosyyyy... zzz.

'Holly!' Liv's voice travelled across the bedroom and smacked me in the ear.

'Hmmm?'

'It's 11 a.m.' I could hear her somewhere in the back of my brain. 'Holly, it's 11 a.m., you've fallen back asleep,' she whispered in my ear more urgently, shaking me gently.

'Hmphh,' I pressed my lips together, breathing deeply.

'IT'S 11 A.M.!' Liv shouted, shaking me violently and opening the curtains wide. 'You've got to get up, they're on their way.'

What fresh hell was this? Where was I? Who were on their way? And then I remembered. My eyes flew open, and I shot out of bed, head still spinning from all the Jäger.

'Am I late?' I said, heart racing. I quickly sprayed my underarms with deodorant and started stripping off my pyjamas.

'You've got time to have a shower, but be quick,' Liv said, 'they'll be here in half an hour.' My eyes adjusted to the light, and I could see she was up, showered and looking like an air stewardess in a navy power suit. Hair in a French plait and a face full of make-up with wafts of spearmint and jasmine. The woman before me was a far cry from the Liv doing tequila headstands in The Loft Bar at 2 a.m. this morning.

Oh fuckety, fuck, fuck, fuck. I ran into the shower and sprayed myself in the face to try and wake up. My mouth tasted of bad decisions and my body ached. My arms especially. Had I been hanging from a bar like a monkey? Or doing one-armed press-ups? How had this happened? I sprayed my face again and the water went up my nose. I. Had. To. Pull. Myself. Together. I dried off, gave my hair a quick blast with the hairdryer and Liv appeared with an espresso and two paracetamols.

'You're an angel,' I said, washing the pills down with the coffee.

'Get your uniform on and I'll see you up there,' Liv said, 'Xavier has the canapés in the oven, and I'll polish the Champagne flutes. It's just a few nibbles and a risotto for now as they'll want to get straight out on the slopes.'

The clocked ticked 11.15 a.m. as I threw my bra, knickers, and brand-new stockings on. I'd stashed my uniform in the wardrobe the night before, so I had everything prepped and fresh. I shimmied on the navy dress, with my boots, brushed my hair and gave my fringe a quick curl. The uniform was a bit lacier than I'd have liked for work, but I had no choice. I had to wear it. 11.22 a.m.

'Holly!' Liv shouted down the stairs. 'They're outside.'

I took a deep breath, popped a double chewing gum and ran upstairs, past the kitchen where Xavier was piping cream cheese onto a plateful of bubbling mushroom puffs, finishing each one off with a caviar sprinkle. I stepped into the hallway as the front door opened.

'Welcome back, Genevieve,' Liv trilled, as a beautiful, swan-like woman walked in wearing a white jumpsuit and beamed at us both in delight. She was tall and elegant, and her swishy brown hair was blow-dried to perfection, brushed away from her face by oversized Prada sunglasses.

'Hi Liv,' she said, double air-kissing her and handing over her Chanel bag and gloves.

'What are you wearing?' Liv side-mouthed at me, frowning.

'And you must be Holly?' Genevieve said, looking me up and down. 'Did you bring your own uniform?'

'Er... no?' I said, panicking. 'Is this the wrong one? I got it out of the laundry room?'

'It is my nightdress, *non*?' she said, staring at the lacy frills, the corners of her mouth twitching. Oh my fucking God. Please no. My whole body went hot as I was saved by the door slamming open, a handsome French man attached to the leg that had kicked it. Presumably Luca. A real-life Gaston, with chocolate-brown eyes to match his sister's and brown hair shaved close to his head. He was already dressed like a skiing Ninja in matching navy trousers and jacket. Carrying two large bags into the chalet, which he immediately dropped on the floor, unzipping the larger one to reveal a set of traversing skis.

'Luca! Welcome, welcome,' Liv said. 'This is Holly, who will be working with Xavier in the kitchen and serving dinner in the evenings. As well as overseeing the wine, of course,' she said, presenting me to him.

'Lovely to meet you,' he said. 'Wine sounds good. Champagne sounds even better.'

'She's just getting it now,' Liv said, pushing me in the direction of the bar.

I got my brain into gear and deftly opened a bottle of Champagne, untwizzling the metal tie and ripping off the foil at breakneck speed. I splashed Chambord into the flutes Liv had polished and topped them up with Champagne, adding a blueberry and raspberry to each glass. Xavier appeared in the foyer with a platter of deliciousness and Liv was talking and laughing with Genevieve and Luca while I had a private meltdown about the fact I was somehow wearing Genevieve's *nightdress*. If I could just serve the champers without any further comments on it, I could sidle my way downstairs and quickly change. I swiftly took a tray with two glasses of Champagne over to my two new bosses.

'Kir Royale?' I offered the tray to Genevieve and then to Luca.

'*Merci*,' Genevieve said, with a small smile.

Xavier looked at me strangely. Oh Christ. It wasn't that bad, was it? The dress was knee length with a lacy frill and a crossover back, but I'd worn a vest top underneath. I mean. I get it. It could totally be a nightdress. Clearly it was a nightdress. Arghhhh. But it had been hanging up in the laundry just as Xavier had said. How was I to know it wasn't a French chalet uniform? I tucked my hair behind my ear and backed away from the love-in.

'I'm just going to er...' I waffled, as they ignored me, legging it back downstairs to double check the laundry room. It was warm and dry and smelt of lavender. Piles of green and blue towels were folded into perfect squares and bedsheets hung from the ceiling, enjoying the heat. If I was wearing Genevieve's nightie, then where the bloody-fuck was my uniform? I had a nosy round and eventually found what looked like an old school pinafore hanging on the hot pipe next to the boiler. Noooo? Surely not? I slunk the nightie off while simultaneously pulling the pinafore off its hanger to throw on.

'Are you OK, Holly?' Xavier asked, appearing in the doorway. I screamed and held the pinafore up to hide my upper thigh and under-boob, as he turned away and hid his face with his hands.

'Sorry, I didn't expect you to be...'

'I'm getting changed.'

'Probably for the best,' he said, shutting the door and

walking off. I quickly pulled the pinny on and fastened the bowtie, adding a bright-white apron with a Chalet Blanchet logo front and centre. Much more professional. I headed back into the kitchen to Xavier, to double check I wasn't now wearing Luca's dead grandmother's Sunday best, poking my head around the kitchen door to make sure the coast was clear.

'Is it safe to come in?' I asked, tentatively.

'If you're wearing lacy underwear and stockings then yes, it's very safe,' he laughed.

'You weren't supposed to see that,' I said, mortified. 'Is this convent-style get-up more like it?'

Xavier nodded. 'Sadly, it is. Now, time to impress them with your work. The risotto is nearly ready. I'll bring it up in ten minutes. They don't usually drink with their lunch, but best to go and check.'

I went back up to the dining room where Liv was armed with a breadbasket, offering Luca and Genevieve freshly baked rolls with slices of salted butter.

'Much better,' Genevieve said when she saw me.

'I'm not sure I agree,' Luca replied, and I blushed.

'I'm very sorry about that,' I said, dithering. 'I hadn't realised there were two different navy dresses.'

'Not at all,' Luca said, with a chuckle. 'You've given us some ideas on how to update the uniform.'

Genevieve tutted.

'Would you like a glass of wine with your risotto, or do you prefer to keep a clear head for skiing?' I asked, wanting to change the subject.

'I'll save myself for later,' Luca said. 'I want to get out

on the mountain. Just a beer for now and I'll talk you through the cellar system when I'm back.'

'Sparkling water for me,' Genevieve said, her gold bangles jangling.

'Of course,' I said, running back to the bar, where Liv was lifting hot bowls from the dumb waiter and polishing them with a soft cloth.

'Ahmagadddd,' I whispered.

'Don't worry, they thought it was funny.'

'I'm going to pass out with the stress of it all. And they're not even interested in the wine yet – all they want is a lager and a water.'

We sniggered.

Liv placed the empty bowls in front of Genevieve and Luca just as Xavier appeared, beating the risotto in a parmesan wheel to finish off the dish. He spooned a large portion of cheesy risotto into each bowl as Liv followed behind with a baseball bat of black pepper. I carefully placed the drinks down with a bow to complete the lunch-dance, then the three of us shrank away so they could enjoy their food. What a bloody palaver.

'Is it like that every time?' I asked once we were safely in the kitchen.

'No, we don't normally dress up in their clothes,' Xavier snorted with laughter.

'Oh God, no. I know, I'm mortified.' I sat at the kitchen table and put my head in my hands. 'Do you think I can get past it?'

'It's totally fine,' Liv said. 'I saw the glint in Genevieve's eye; she was trying not to laugh.'

'So, what do we do now? Shall I go back up and see if

they want more drinks?' I asked, anxious to please. I didn't want them to think I was completely incompetent.

'They'll be gone before you get chance,' Xavier said, as he wiped the parmesan wheel with a damp cloth and wrapped it in cling film to go back in the fridge.

'Yeah – they'll have scoffed the risotto and be out on the mountain by the time we go back up,' Liv said, 'which means I can leave you two to it and get out there as well.'

It was a relief to know I wasn't being frogmarched up the mountain on my first day. Xavier was ferreting around in the cupboard for ingredients and came back to the table with a bagful of apples and a bottle of red.

'Genevieve and Luca are out with clients for dinner this evening, but I want us to practise some dishes for another day,' Xavier said, removing six Granny Smiths from the bag and placing them on the counter.

'Laters, you two.' Liv blew us a kiss and ran off down the corridor, desperate for that feeling of freedom out on the mountain. But my freedom was in here. In the kitchen. Surrounded by food and getting ready to make magic.

'*Bonjour la classe*,' Xavier said, with a smile. 'Today, we will be making a French classic with a twist. Lamb terrine edged in green apple jelly, served with spiced brioche toast and balsamic fig jam.'

'Ooh, yes please, that sounds delicious,' I said, wide-eyed, imagining the satisfying crunch of pâté on toast.

'It is delicious. Done correctly, the terrine will have a rich, buttery taste, flavoured with apple, rosemary and mint, with hints of Bordeaux.' Xavier pulled a battered old ring-binder out of the kitchen drawer and flicked through the plastic pages until he found what he was looking for.

'*Regarde*,' he said, holding up a photo, 'this is how we want the finished plate to look, and I will walk you through the methodology as we each work on the dish.'

I felt a tingle of excitement at learning something new. The picture showed a tiny plateful of food perfection. These Michelin men knew what they were talking about. A perfect cylinder of terrine, surrounded by a smattering of green dots in different shades and sizes – presumably the apple, rosemary, and mint – interspersed with toasted crouton cubes.

'Can we make the portions larger?' I asked, taking the photo from him.

'Absolutely not. It is a starter for a reason. It is supposed to whet the appetite, not satiate it,' Xavier said irritably.

'Well it looks and sounds delicious, but I'll definitely want a double portion once we've made them.'

Xavier handed me three apples, two sprigs of rosemary and a bunch of mint.

'Michelin star food is about quality, not quantity,' he said. 'Now take this knife and follow me exactly.' I watched as he peeled the apples in perfect circles, removing the skin in wafer-thin strips. He then sliced and diced the flesh into tiny pieces, in the same way I would chop an onion. I deftly followed and he gave me an impressed nod.

'*Bien*. Keep the skin and fry the rest in olive oil, add lemon juice and then reduce.'

It was fascinating to witness and then practise the level of effort required to deliver each of the flavours in the recipe. The three apples had been reduced so much, they could now fit into a tiny jug, but they were going to a better place.

'And now the mint and rosemary go together.' He

bunched all the greenery up and put it in a mortar dish, covering the leaves in boiling water. I followed suit and we ground the herbs into a paste, the smell of spearmint, light and fresh, filling the air.

'We will also be making a rosemary jus,' Xavier said, handing me a shallot and three cloves of garlic. I knew how to make a rosemary jus, so I started chopping the onion and mincing the garlic, adding salt and pepper and lots more of the fresh rosemary. This was only a test dish, so I added a sneaky pinch of cayenne pepper to mine to add a little kick. The kitchen sounds were like ASMR to me, putting me completely at ease. The simmer of the jus, the soft pop as the apple turned to mush, the gentle scrape of the pestle and mortar. Xavier had a fixed look of concentration on his face, eyes flicking from his pans to mine, making mental notes of what had been done where.

'We will also be making our own brioche,' Xavier said.

'For the croutons?'

'For the spiced brioche toast. This is food art, remember; we don't call them croutons. Every single element on the plate has to be crafted and considered.' He was almost trance-like as he said it. 'So we need eggs, milk, butter and a little sugar,' he called out the ingredients and I ran around the kitchen gathering them from the fridge and cupboards. 'With balsamic vinegar and figs for the jam.'

'Do we prepare it all today and put it together tomorrow?' I asked, thinking the brioche and terrine will both need time to cook and cool.

'*Oui*. I have the lamb shoulder here for the terrine, and we need garlic, parsley, chives and thyme, and white wine.'

I was surrounded by a poem of ingredients.

'Which one shall I do first?' I asked, suddenly feeling muddled.

'The terrine will take the longest, so we will go terrine, brioche, fig jam and then at the very end we will do the green apple jelly. The different sauces in the pans can all come off the heat now and rest,' Xavier said.

'The rosemary jus smells delicious,' I said. 'Can I try it?'

'Of course! You are a chef! You must constantly try your food. Tasting and checking, until it is exactly how you imagine it should be.'

I dipped my little finger in and tasted it.

'NOT with your fingers,' Xavier shouted, catching me by surprise. 'With a small spoon.'

'I'm so sorry,' I said, finger still in my mouth. It was bloody delicious.

'If this was a professional kitchen, that whole pan would now go in the bin,' Xavier said. 'Think about where your hands have been, even in the past five minutes. Dirty bags of flour, touching the outside of eggs, chopping garlic. You win or lose your Michelin star on the taste of your food. Don't ever contaminate it with your body.'

'Yes, Chef,' I said in earnest. He was totally right. What would Gordon Ramsay say?

We worked quietly side by side for the next two hours, following the recipe step by step, Xavier leading the way as I copied his every move. Blending the meat with the herbs and spices to build a smooth terrine. Liquidising the apple skins and whisking them into the jelly to add an acid-green layer on top. Kneading the sweet brioche dough three times and rolling it into tins to rise and set in the laundry room.

Then finally taking the figs and adding sugar and balsamic vinegar, with a splash of Bordeaux, to make a rich and tasty jam. I knew it was tasty because I tasted it *with a small spoon*.

I gave a stretch and scrunched my shoulders up to my ears. We'd been totally lost in the cooking and hadn't stopped for breath.

'Coffee?' I asked, looking at the clock. It was 5 p.m.

'Red wine?' Xavier offered with a smile.

'Ooh yes, much better,' I said, trying to make friends. 'Sorry about the finger-licking. I'll know for next time.'

'I know you'll know,' he said, giving me a nudge and pouring out the wine. We clinked our glasses in silent exhaustion and the wine tasted all the better for it.

Twelve

6th December

'Ready for a quick plunge?' Liv loomed over me as I opened my eyes, and I instinctively shook my head. 'Come on, you have to give it a go sometime.'

I creaked myself out of bed and rubbed my eyes.

'Get your cossie on quick – ten seconds in the pool, thirty seconds in the sauna and you'll feel like a new woman.'

'What time is it?' I yawned, picking up my phone.

'Time to get up. You won't get a revenge body lying in bed.' Revenge body? Eh? What was she talking about? Liv headed for the bathroom and I had a flashback to drunkenly crying into my pillow and telling her all about George. Poor Liv. I'd rambled on and on into the darkness, sharing every last detail, until I must have fallen asleep. I had a stick or twist moment of decision on the plunge pool. What was the worst that could happen? Well, cardiac arrest. Hypothermia, frostbite... could I lose a toe? I begrudgingly put on my bikini, wrapped myself in a towel and shuffled through to the plunge pool with my eyes half-closed.

'Morning.' Xavier was already there and waiting in a pair of budgie smugglers. *Vive le France!* His body had light and shade, as if it were carved out of marble, and not a hair in sight. I clutched my towel tightly, hiding my pale potato of a body, and looked on in terror as Liv walked straight past us from the bathroom and slowly lowered herself into the plunge pool. OMFG. I was NOT doing that.

'Morning,' I replied. 'Your turn next, is it?' Liv was counting slowly and loudly to ten as she wriggled around. Then she was out as quick as she'd got in and ran past us both into the sauna.

'A masterclass,' Xavier said with a smile. 'Ladies first.'

It was now or never, and I didn't want to parade myself around in front of Xavier, so I needed to be quick. I was fully prepared to hate it, but Liv was right, I had to give it a go. I left my towel on the bench by the back door and ran to the plunge pool. It was ABSOLUTELY FREEZING from the second I got outside. The soles of my feet felt it first as I ran out, then my entire body as I held my nose and jumped in. But that cold feeling was NOTHING COMPARED TO THE PLUNGE POOL. Oh my God, oh my God, oh my God, fuck, fuck, fuck, fuck, I came up for air and my teeth were chattering and my skin was stinging and I thought I was going to cry as I flailed around and screamed. Xavier stood in the doorway laughing to himself as I wiped my hair from my face and fought to survive. My heart was thumping, and I'd lost all sense of myself.

'You can get out now,' Xavier called, holding my towel up high so he was hidden from view. Right, yes, I can get out. My shaking hands grabbed the ladder, and it was all

I could do to get myself out. Every ounce of energy was being used by my system to avoid a heart attack.

I ran to my towel which was warm and soft as Xavier wrapped it around me. He must have popped it on the radiator as I ran into the water. Thank God, thank God, I could have cried with relief as I got back into the ski room, which felt like a welcome cuddle in comparison. Liv had just left the sauna as I walked in.

'Yes girlllll!' she said, giving me a high five. 'Proud of you.'

The sauna was another level and my body prickled with sweat as I thought I might die another way instead, from overheating or dehydration. This plunging lark was a rollercoaster through the senses, that was for sure. I could only stand it for a minute, before I left the heat, crossing over with Xavier mid-run, wrapped in his towel as I headed for the bathroom.

'Xavier and I are doing breakfast and then we're taking you up the mountain,' Liv called from the shower.

Oh no. I hadn't mentally prepared myself just yet and really didn't have the capability or inclination to throw myself into the snow.

'Honestly Liv, I'm really not sure I'm ready to…' I started.

Liv popped her head out of the shower and gave me a look. 'Be ready to go at 9 a.m. It's time to show you the magic of the mountain.'

I supposed today was as good as any other. I was going to have to grit my teeth and get on with it. I took my time getting ready, with a long, hot shower then pulled out the green salopettes Auntie Pam had loaned me and lay them on the bed with my pink hat and matching earmuffs. I was confident this wasn't a sexy look, but I wasn't here to be sexy. It didn't really matter what I looked like. I piled my clothes on, thermal layer, fleece layer, enormous socks, ski suit, elasticated belt, hat, gloves and was just adding my earmuffs as the *pièce de résistance* when Liv came in, stopping in her tracks to look me up and down.

'Holy fuck, what are you dressed as?' she laughed.

Liv wore jet-black ski trousers and a rainbow jacket with a chunky silver zip. Her long plaits hung over her shoulders with her fringe swept back by a pair of mirrored sunglasses. Effortless mountain chic.

'I know, I'm so sorry, I haven't done this before,' I said, laughing hopelessly. 'I'll just stay here. I don't want to embarrass you and Xavier or slow you down – your fair-weather friend dressed as Kermit the Frog.'

'Wear it for now and I'll sort you something out in the week,' she said, putting her arm around me, 'but you'll struggle to get a man looking like that. Even out here.'

'I've told you, I'm not interested; I'm still half-taken,' I said, exasperated.

'Not now, you're not. But when the time comes, you don't want to miss out because you were dressing like your gran. Stick with me, you mad pommie.'

Xavier was sat on the bench in the ski room, goggles perched on his head as he studied the piste map. He looked up as we walked in and gave my outfit the once-over.

'Interesting,' he said, stifling a smile.

'I know. You'll have to bear with me while I work it all out.'

'I've got something that will work very well with it,' he

said, rifling around in his CamelBak. He pulled out a green hat with froggy eyes on the front. 'Shall we swap hats?'

I mean. I didn't want to be made a mockery of, but equally, in for a penny, in for a pound. I nodded and accepted the frog hat gracefully, handing over my pink beanie in return, which worked nicely with Xavier's metallic navy outfit. I wondered if I was in any way giving off an ironic vibe. I suppose I could always pretend I was in fancy dress, but dressing as a frog in a French-speaking resort was asking for trouble.

'Holly, are you down there?' Luca called through to the ski room, at the exact moment I put my earmuffs on, ready to head out and face my fears.

'Yes, I'm here – is everything OK?' I asked, hoping he might save me from the mountain.

'Are you on your way out?' Luca came into the ski room and saw the three of us suited and booted and ready to go. 'I want to show you around the wine cellar,' he said. 'Can I give you a quick tour now, before you go? It'll only take half an hour.'

I looked over at Liv and Xavier, who smiled patiently and nodded.

'Of course!' I said, excited, giving Liv my helmet and goggles and stuffing my hat in my pocket, slightly sweaty as I'd been about to step outside.

Luca marched off upstairs to open the cellar door and I followed close behind, feeling stressed and excited all at once.

'First things first, there are only two sets of keys,' he said, holding a bunch in each hand. 'Mine are the red set – which I have on my person at all times – and yours are the yellow, which you will keep for the season.' He handed me my keys like he was handing over an ancient chalice, and I received them without breaking eye contact, then zipped them into my pocket.

Luca swept back the heavy green curtain that covered the cellar door and unlocked it with his red-fobbed keys. Large and carved from oak with a small glass window in the top, he pushed it open, reaching into the darkness to switch on the light. A reverent silence hung in the air as the two of us made our way down the steps and Luca surveyed his kingdom: his wine-people. And what a sight it was to behold, with hundreds and hundreds of bottles of wine stacked high on every side. The age of the bottles immediately obvious, with the youngest at the top, getting older and dustier as the bottles went down the rack. How would I ever work out what was where?

'Some of these wines have been in my family for decades, with me adding my own private collection this past sixteen years,' Luca said. 'As you can imagine, the wine is worth a fortune, so you should look at this cellar in the same way you would look at a family vault.'

I nodded, wide-eyed as I gazed around in awe. This would be part of my little world for the next few months, these wines my personal stash. A liquid library, each bottle an encyclopaedia. Everything I needed to learn to get me from wine drinker and dabbler to professional sommelier. The wine whispered to me as I followed Luca through the dank rooms. *Drink me, drink me.*

'The wines are organised by temperature, then colour, continent, country and grape. It's a very simple system to navigate once you get your head around it,' Luca said. I found that very hard to believe. There was a small brass plaque near the first batch of reds with *South America* written on it and then another that read *Argentina*. It was SO organised.

A light flashed from the climate control system showing twelve degrees for the bottles of Beaujolais and Pinot Noir, sixteen for the Malbecs and Merlots and eighteen for the Shiraz and Cabernet Sauvignon varieties. The white wines were at the far side and went from Albarino to Zinfandel. And finally… the Champagnes. Both white and pink of varying quality and cru from all the big houses in Epernay and Reims. Moët & Chandon, Pommery, Mumm, Bollinger – I was staring at an absolute fortune.

'Xavier will work with you to pair the wine with each course for our evening meals and then serve them to the table, along with the food.'

I was both delighted and terrified at the thought of picking through these beautiful bottles of wine, popping them open and cocking them up. I hadn't touched any of them and didn't intend to until I had some white gloves and a very reliable corkscrew. I had visions of snapping corks into rare bottles of wine worth thousands. What had I got myself into?

'Got it. And do I trial the wine myself, to er… check it?'

Luca gave me a look. 'Studying what we have and extending your personal repertoire and taste will go hand in hand, but I'd say you are looking at 2 per cent taste versus 98 per cent study and selection.'

'Got it,' I repeated, slightly less enthusiastically.

'The wine temperatures are carefully managed through a climate control system as you can see; the reds are always ready to serve but the whites need overnight refrigeration, once selected, for optimum taste,' Luca said, picking up a bottle of Bodega Chacra Chardonnay and wiping the dust from the label.

I surveyed the Italian whites and the Spanish reds like a kid in a sweetshop. 'Do I spy a Vega Sicilia Único?' I asked, taking a closer look at the bottom row.

'You certainly do. Their flagship. Impressive knowledge,' Luca said. 'My father bought a case in Seville a couple of years back. What gave it away?'

'My ex and I shared a bottle with our anniversary dinner last year – it has a very distinctive etching on the neck,' I said, as Luca nodded his approval. My heart gave a sad little ping at the memory. 'Are there certain sections I should avoid? Presumably, you don't drink Dom Perignon every night?' I smiled.

'Stick to the top two layers; they are the newest wines, but all should be excellent. I'm happy to give you some pointers while you are with us. Margot said you were keen to develop your nose.'

'That would be amazing Luca, thank you.'

'Sorry for the delay guys,' I said as I re-joined Liv and Xavier.

'No worries. What the boss says, goes,' Liv replied.

Xavier and Liv picked up their snowboards and we trudged through the main drag of Verbier, stopping off at Intersport to sort me out a board and some boots. We were swept up in a sea of skiers and snowboarders enthusiastically chatting their way towards the lift. The clickety-clack of ski boots walking in rhythm through the snow, as skiers held their skis aloft and swayed to an unheard beat, their snowboarding counterparts crunching slowly alongside them, cumbersome planks of wood in their wake.

Three pairs of boots and two boards later, I was suited and booted and ready to go.

'On the Chalet Blanchet account,' Xavier said to the cool kid serving me, as I went to hand over my credit card. He nodded and handed me a receipt.

'Really?' I said, surprised. 'That's so kind of them.'

'All part of the deal.' Xavier replied.

We queued for half an hour to get on the gondola, shuffling like penguins every thirty seconds or so until we eventually reached the front. The three of us pressed our bodies and lift passes against the scanner and bleeped through the turnstile, as the people behind us surged forward, knowing they were finally next in line to get on the lift. Skis and snowboards were slotted into the holes on the outside of the cable car, poking out precariously from all sides. I shoved the snowboard I'd had for all of twenty minutes in with the others and hoped for the best, quickly following Xavier and Liv into the cable car as people squeezed in around us. When there was finally nowhere else to squeeze to, the doors sighed shut and the cable car bobbed gently for a few beats before taking a running jump into the air. I was so close to Liv and Xavier, I had to hold my breath.

My stomach lurched as we creaked further and further up the mountain and Verbier gradually disappeared into the distance. We were walking-in-the-air Snowman style, the pine trees tickling our toes as we flew along. It was a beautiful, sunny day so I had zero excuse not to give snowboarding a go. Apart from fear of death, permanent maiming and/or pneumonia due to my frog outfit being very old and no longer fit for purpose. As we neared the top of the mountain, the penguins started to shuffle again, anxious to get their snowy hit. They peeled away in a dance-like state the second the doors opened, collecting their kit and clomping off into the distance. In short, everyone knew what they were doing apart from me.

'Don't forget your board, babe,' Liv said, nodding backwards, her pigtails swinging.

I stepped off the cable car and stumbled on the springy plastic floor, steadying myself to get my bearings, as my snowboard carried on its journey, bouncing off beyond my reach. Luckily, Xavier was well ahead of me and grabbed both our snowboards simultaneously, tucking one under each arm as he crunched his way to the exit.

Oh fuck, oh fuck, they were going to make me strap that bloody thing to my feet and throw myself down the mountain. This was the last time I'd walk on my own legs as a free woman. Intensive Care, here I come.

'We are at the top of a very easy blue run, Holly. I think you are going to like this one very much,' Xavier said. Without a glimmer of a smile. I mean, that seemed highly unlikely.

'Get your board on and we'll show you what to do,' Liv said, stamping her feet together and somehow clicking her boots straight onto her board, while I undid every single one of my bindings, put each boot into position and slowly winched the straps back together, securing my feet in place. The struggle to bend down and reach my feet was challenge enough. I dragged it out for as long as possible, but the time for dilly-dallying was done. I pushed myself up to stand

and tried to balance on the board, wobbling about for five seconds before falling backwards onto the snow. Xavier slid his way over to me, his snowboard and size 10 boots enormous next to mine.

'We can bum-shuffle to the edge of the mountain together, OK? Follow me,' he said, caterpillar-ing along the floor to move himself from where we were to where we needed to be. This must have been highly embarrassing for him, as a virtually professional snowboarder, but I followed suit. Liv couldn't bear it and zoomed past us on her board, blowing candyfloss vape in our direction.

'See you down there, yeah?' Liv called over her shoulder, putting her headphones on.

'You have to trust the mountain,' Xavier said earnestly as people whipped past us on both sides. 'You've got a piece of wood strapped to your ankles and the only way is down. The mountain and the snow will get you down the piste; you've just got to learn how to start and stop.'

'What if I can't do it?' I said panic-stricken, suddenly very conscious of being at the top of a mountain, with an afternoon tea shift starting in three hours.

'You can,' Xavier said.

Liv was already halfway down the run, waving up at us, and I looked behind me at the one-way traffic coming in our direction. It was too late to back out now; snowboarding down was my only option. I dug my heels into the snow and made a second attempt to stand up. As I wobbled my legs straight, my board promptly slid from underneath my feet and I fell back again, onto my coccyx – my bum wasn't Kardashian-enough for this.

'Take it nice and steady,' Xavier said, easily standing

on his board and flipping himself round to hover in front of me. He must have unbelievable core strength, of which I had zero. I briefly thought about the level of travel insurance I'd gone for and whether this day trip was going to end in a helicopter airlifting me off the mountain. Or me flying down the run in a body bag on the back of a skidoo. Both options were terrifying. Speedy and embarrassing at best, expensive and excruciatingly painful at worst. Xavier put out his hands while seemingly levitating in front of me. I took them both and attempted to wrestle myself up to standing, pulling Xavier down on top of me in the process.

'S-s-sorry,' I stammered, mortified, 'I have no control over my centrifugal force.'

Xavier stared at me thoughtfully and tried a different tack.

'OK. Instead of trying to stand up, turn your whole body over and wedge your board into the mountain, like this,' he said, flipping himself over again and balancing at an angle while holding onto the ground. This is where I was going to die. This man had no idea what he was up against. I couldn't stand up, let alone start Cirque de Soleil-ing along the snow.

'Don't worry Xavier, I'll work it out. You go and have a… er… ride with Liv, I don't want to hold you both up,' I said, scrabbling with the snow to roll myself over. The boots and board were so heavy. My body could twist but my legs weren't strong enough to follow. I was stuck mid-turn in the snow and struggling like an upside-down baby turtle, when I felt my board lift up and turn over.

'There you go, now bend your knees, and lean into the

mountain. You can do it; you can't fall anywhere but back on your face.'

'You say that as if it's a good thing?' I laughed, balancing my body out and pushing my board into the mountain as if my life depended on it. Which it did. And then I was almost, kind of, sort of UP. The wrong way around of course, but my shaky legs were up, nonetheless. I held my hands off the mountain and beamed at Xavier to show him.

'*C'est tout!*' he said, slapping me on the back and nearly pushing me back down. 'Now just relax into it and let yourself go.'

Xavier started to slide towards the left and held my hand to encourage me to do the same. I was frozen to the spot, terrified I'd cock it up, fall backwards and break my leg.

'Jiggle yourself along with me. Move your body and the board will do the rest.'

Skiers and snowboarders whooshed past us left, right and centre, including some very small children doing trick shots as they threw themselves down the mountain. Jiggle along, he said. Couldn't be that hard, could it? I was frozen through and about to have a full-blown panic attack, so I had to do something. I did a small jiggle and nothing happened. A tiny bit more jiggling and the board started to creak. My knees were absolutely killing me, so I had to make myself move somehow. I shifted the angle of the board from nine o'clock to seven o'clock. I needed to get some traction, or I'd be wedged into the mountain all night. That did the trick. The board started to slide to the left, slowly at first. I gave Xavier a smiley thumbs-up as the board shifted further round to six o'clock. Was that an over-jiggle? The sliding gathered pace. Oh no. My smile dropped. Xavier hadn't told me how to stop. Or slow down. Or steer. My weight was on the back of the board as I careered down the mountain, silently praying I wouldn't shoot off the edge. I whizzed past Liv, who looked on in shock as I gathered pace, going faster and faster down the piste. I was thundering along, the wind in my ears and my heart in my mouth as I reached the gentle part of the slope just before the bottom of the run. A neat line of toddlers were enjoying a ski lesson and I started to panic. There was no way to avoid them and no chance they'd be out of my way in time to be avoided. I had no choice but to press the ejector button, so I threw myself forward and fell in the direction of a huge dump of snow, piling into it head-first.

'Ugh.' I stayed still for a few moments then rolled onto my back and scooped the snow off my face, as Xavier swooshed alongside me, his cheeks bright red.

'Are you OK?' he called, worried. 'What were you thinking? You can't go off on your own like that; it's not safe.'

'Well thank you very much for that life lesson. I wasn't on a pleasure cruise. I thought I was going to die.'

'When you face directly down the mountain, you go at the fastest possible speed.'

'Again, information that would have been useful ten, or even five minutes ago.'

'Are you hurt?' he asked with concern, as Liv skidded to a stop, spraying snow in both our faces.

'Nice fly-by babes,' she said, 'respect.'

'All cool,' I said, unbuckling my board. On a positive note, we were almost at the bottom of the mountain, which meant I'd survived lesson one and could head back to the chalet for cake.

I slid down the last part of the piste, half running, half skidding, as Liv and Xavier cruised calmly ahead of me and into the village. It had taken me an hour to do one run, twenty-five seconds of which were spent actually snowboarding. If you can call it that. Not ideal. Après ski was kicking off all over the resort, and the music cranked up as the sun shone bright on the horizon. Après ski was definitely more my thing than pre-ski and during-ski. I could happily live in the mountains and wear the outfit if I could just skip the life-endangering part of proceedings and go straight to the part where we drink beers at altitude.

'It doesn't need three of us to serve tea and cake for two,' Liv said. 'Normally, it'll just be you two, but I wanted to introduce you to Rachael, the legendary *pâtissier* of Verbier.'

'She is amazing,' Xavier agreed, kicking snow along the pavement as he walked. 'We come to her for specific special occasion cakes. Genevieve and Luca love them.'

The three of us walked in unison past the party bars and coffee shops, as the slopes started to empty out and everyone wound down for the day. There was no way we could miss Rachael's *pâtisserie*. It was wrapped in fairy lights and stood out like a beacon of calorific pleasure on the main drag, with a permanent queue of people waiting patiently for their sugar hit. The smell of chocolate and cinnamon made my mouth water and lured us straight into the shop where there was every type of cake you could imagine on show. Huge chocolate tortes covered in truffles and drizzled in white chocolate, enormous slices of black forest gateaux with turrets of fresh cream and cherries on top, a lemon meringue cheesecake decorated in tiny orange segments and iced buns piped full of toffee sauce. My hips widened slightly as I took it all in. A flurry of people served behind the counter, placing perfect cake after perfect cake into cardboard boxes and tying them with red ribbons, but one person was clearly in charge. Rachael was petite and elegant with a neat, blonde ponytail, fixed in place with a red, velvet bow to match the decor. Her eyes were constantly scanning the shop, looking for the next customer, the next job. She clocked Liv and Xavier and gave them a smile.

'*Bonjour* my friends,' she said, thumbing a handful of notes into the till.

'How ya doin' mate?' Liv said, nudging me forward. 'Meet the latest addition to the family – Holly.'

'Hi,' I said shyly.

Rachael smiled, her green eyes sparkling. 'Well, you couldn't be in better hands than with these two,' she said. 'Welcome to the team.'

'That's good, as I'm new to all this. I need a bit of looking after.'

'She nearly killed herself on the mountain earlier,' Xavier said, 'scared us both to death. We haven't got time to keep recruiting new staff.'

'We need one of your lychee and coconut cheesecakes to help us through the shock,' Liv added, 'and to show Holly what you're made of.'

'Good job you ordered one yesterday then, isn't it?' Rachael said, grabbing a beautiful box covered in red and pink bows and passing it over the counter. 'Another one for the tab?'

Thirteen

7th December

'Holly?' Xavier hollered down the corridor, as I scrabbled to put my knickers and jeans on.

'Just coming,' I said, to keep him at bay. Where was my bra? I scanned the bedroom, as Xavier opened the door.

'Argh, sorry, I thought you said you were coming,' he said, retreating quickly and slamming the door before I could cover myself up. For God's sake, couldn't I tell a small white lie without paying the price of full-frontal nudity every time? I spied my bra hanging on the wardrobe door handle and slipped it on, with three long sleeved T-shirts, a cardigan, and my pumps. I hadn't quite mastered the footwear situation, but I was getting better at the layers. I opened the bedroom door to an empty corridor and made my way upstairs to a sheepish Xavier.

'What is it with you bursting in on me getting changed?' I said, crossing my hands over my heart.

'You said you were ready?' Xavier shrugged, slightly pink.

'I said I was coming, which is a good five minutes before I'm ready.'

'Next time, say "I'm naked" and I'll know,' Xavier replied, a smile on his lips.

Genevieve padded into the hallway in a cloud of perfume, wearing coral ski pants and a forest-green jacket with matching headband.

'*Bonjour*, Holly,' she said, swooshing her silky hair. 'How are you settling in?'

'Very well so far. Thank you for having me here at such short notice.'

'Of course. As it happened, we *needed* someone at short notice, didn't we Xavier?'

Xavier looked uncomfortable and gave a half-nod as Luca ran down the stairs, hair like velvet, brown eyes shining. 'It's not Xavier's fault Rose left us in the lurch,' he said. 'Don't make such a big deal of it, Genevieve. She tried her best and it didn't work out.'

'Fern, Rose, now Holly… we're building quite the bouquet,' Genevieve remarked, as Luca rolled his eyes, his muscles visible through his jacket.

'Ah Xavier, *bonne matin* my friend,' Luca said, clasping Xavier's hand.

'*Bonjour*,' he replied, zipping up his jacket and heading for the door. 'Holly and I are off to the farmers' market to buy ingredients for this evening.'

'Ooh la la, enjoy!' Genevieve called after us. 'Don't let them tempt you with too many tasters. The cheese stall is dangerous.'

Xavier and I headed out into the frosty air, my white pumps immediately proving themselves unfit for purpose, exposing each of my toes to the cold. My jeans were also unfit for purpose. And so were my knickers. Not a good start to the day.

'Luca's cellar is unbelievable, isn't it?' I said, as we walked towards the village. 'I think the challenge will be less about the wine pairing and more about finding the right bottle in time to serve it. There must be a trick to it?'

'Oh yes, it's very simple. Didn't Luca mention the app?' Xavier said. 'It's all in there.'

'Really?' I said. 'Ah thank God, that is *such* a relief!'

Xavier laughed. 'Sadly, *non*. I have no idea, I'm afraid. It's a total maze to me too.'

'You had me going then. I was imagining typing B4 into the app and an enormous robot hand picking out the right bottle for me.'

We trudged up the hill to the market, my socks already soaked through. I needed to get better at dressing. This was a disaster.

'Are you not cold?' Xavier asked, looking me up and down. 'No snood?'

'A little bit, yes,' I said miserably. The layers were working but what I really needed was a sheepskin and some wellies. And a balaclava.

'Take this,' he said, unwinding the red knotted wool from his neck and wrapping it around mine. I felt instantly warmer and comforted by the musky smell of his aftershave.

'Thanks,' I said, shuddering as the heat hit my body.

The farmers' market loomed large as we reached the top of the hill, beckoning us in with its colours and smells. The happy hustle and bustle of market traders selling their wares was music to my ears and a treat for my nose. Ripe, juicy fruits, apples, pears, grapes and kiwis, each one polished and perfect. An ice-cream van had been transformed into a wheel of Edam with 'Le Grand Fromage' emblazoned on the side. You could smell the cheesy deliciousness wafting through the crowds and a short, round man in a red apron and matching hat was surrounded by clutching hands as he offered free samples. Rachael's cake stall stood proudly in the centre of the market in all its sugary glory, alongside the butcher, the fish man, the baker and there was probably a candlestick maker in there somewhere too. Shopping was going to be an absolute treat and just when I thought it couldn't get any better, a whole other section of the market appeared, dedicated to cooked dishes. An enormous tartiflette bubbled on an outdoor barbeque, where slices of potato and chunks of slow-cooked gammon were rigorously flipped by a strong-armed man in a chef's hat. Next to him, a cauldron of French onion soup gave off a deliciously sweet smell, as the ribbons of onion simmered in scalding liquid. Queues of people criss-crossed around the market, and I was *beside myself*. I had officially arrived in foodie heaven.

'Pretty cool, huh?' Xavier said softly. 'It's here every Wednesday and Saturday, and there are a couple of people I want to introduce you to. Rachael has quite a lot of sway, so she makes sure we get what we want.'

'She has a market stall as well as that ridiculously busy *pâtisserie*?'

'I know. She never stops. She knows everyone and everything.'

'I don't know what to do first. Can we spend the day here, eating?' I asked, shiny-eyed.

Xavier laughed. 'Sadly not, we've got food to cook.'

'Maybe we can do both? Buy food, eat half of it, and serve up the other half?'

'Hmm, maybe,' Xavier smiled. 'I've decided to serve our terrines as starters tonight, as they turned out so well, followed by a traditional Bouillabaisse.'

'And for dessert?' My favourite part.

'Caramel profiteroles with whipped cream,' Xavier said.

'That sounds amazing! OK, so I need a couple of nice whites and a cheeky dessert wine up my sleeve, in case they want to triple it up. I should go and introduce myself to the wine man, on the *Vin, Vine, Wine, Everything's Fine*, stall over there.'

'We don't have a budget for more wine. Every wine you can possibly imagine is already in Luca's cellar,' Xavier said, spoiling my fun. I wouldn't get any freebies with that attitude.

'I still need to get to know the locals,' I said, dragging him over.

'Hi there! I'm Holly,' I said loudly to the tall man with the goatee beard holding a small glass of red.

'*Bonjour*, David,' Xavier said.

'*Bonjour*, my friend,' David smiled and put his arm around Xavier, patting him heartily on the back.

'Oh. You know each other?' I said, surprised.

'Of course. We all know each other,' Xavier replied, looking around. 'David is part of the furniture, specifically Rachael's furniture. David, this is Holly, who has just joined us at Chalet Blanchet. She wanted to meet you, even though you won't get any business from her.'

'We'll see about that. You never know when I might be able to offer something irresistible. Holly is right to want me on speed dial. *Enchanté*,' he said, holding his hand out for mine and kissing it. 'I am at your service day or night. If you need wine,' he gestured to his sign, '*everything's fine*.'

'Lovely to meet you,' I said. 'Can you source rare wines, or is it more the standard stuff?'

'I can source *an-y-thing*,' David whispered, leaning in close. 'In fact, this glass of red I'm sampling is a Saint-Emilion Premier Grand Cru from Chateau Ausone. I'm looking to order two cases for a private household on the east side of the mountain. Would you like to try?' He wafted his glass under my nose and gave me a nod that was half question, half confirmation.

'Ooh yes, why not?' It was only 11.30 a.m., so 10.30 a.m. in London, but it was nearly Christmas, so time didn't count.

'It's a bit early for me,' Xavier said, holding his hand up.

David poured me out a snifter of the red and topped up his own glass before clinking it with mine. We nosed our wine in unison, breathing it in deeply while staring at the richness of the liquid as it clung to the glass in tiny waterfalls. I gave mine a good swoosh before rinsing it around my palate and sucking it through my teeth. The flavours were intense: cherry and orange mixed in with an earthy sediment. I swilled the mouthful round a couple more times for good measure and just at the point you're supposed to spit it out, I swallowed.

David had his eyes closed and was slowly nodding to himself while savouring the flavour. 'Yes,' he simply said.

'Delicious,' I agreed, holding my glass out in the hope of a bit more, 'very chewy.'

Xavier gave a bemused smile. 'Is it?'

'I agree. Rich and full-bodied. It is so full of flavour, my tongue is still tingling,' David said, closing his eyes again.

'Go on then, you've convinced me,' Xavier said, watching us both closely.

David took the bottle out and filled the three of us up. It was 11.42 a.m., so closer to reasonable as we repeated the performance, Xavier enjoying the eye-wateringly expensive red for the first time. And then we had another glass as there was no point leaving a quarter of a bottle when we'd come this far.

'So, Holly, do you board or ski?' David asked, as he twirled and swirled his glass.

'Neither yet,' I said, honestly.

'I took her out boarding yesterday,' Xavier said. 'She has a lot of potential.'

'Thanks a lot,' I laughed.

I let the red wine flow through me and felt a small hit of happiness as I looked around. This beautiful food haven, in this beautiful ski resort, on this beautiful mountain. What a bloody beautiful time to be alive. If I'd married George, I would never have known it existed. A sting of rejection hit me as I thought about it. I pulled my phone out to distract myself from the feeling and took a quick video. The food, the people, the mountains, the snow; I wanted to remember this moment forever. George had unknowingly given me a gift and I had to embrace it. I never would have known this magical place if it hadn't been for him. I posted the video to my Stories but didn't tag the location. Let George see that his home bird was more than capable of life's big adventure. It was OK. I was going to be OK. My life had been turned on its head, but I was still standing and taking bigger breaths each day.

'Holly, we need to get the foods for dinner,' Xavier said, handing his glass back to David and shaking his hand. '*Merci*.'

'Thank you so much, David,' I said, writing my number on a serviette. 'Can you let me know if you get anything special in?'

'Take my number also,' David said, handing me a bright-white business card. 'Us wine pros need to stick together, *non*? And take this Sicilian Fiano to try. It is from a vineyard in Etna and tastes of the volcano. Impossible to get around here. If you need anything, just call.'

I felt warm and lightheaded as we did the rest of our shop. I left Xavier with the fish man while I bought another warm baguette from the *boulanger*. I threw my hand into the fromage melee to grab a couple of cheese samples and ripped off the end of the bread to make myself a mini cheese sandwich.

Rachael spotted me scoffing and waved across the market. I nodded and smiled with my lips pressed together to keep my mouthful in, speed-chewing as I walked towards her, to try and swallow it down.

'Has Xavier been by? We need some of your caramel profiteroles with whipped cream for dessert later.'

'I only sell the profiterole pastry shells, so he must be planning some sort of deconstruction with caramel sauce.

How many do you need? Will twenty do you?' Rachael asked, pulling a tower of plain profiteroles out of the fridge.

'Did I hear my name?' Xavier appeared, with a bag of wet fish and a basket of fruit and veg. 'What happened to the bread?' he asked, looking at the baguette I'd decimated.

'Erm… I had a small piece with my cheese sample,' I tried.

'I'll get another one and then we need to get back,' he said, exasperated. Rachael handed over the box of profiterole shells, beautifully packed in a red box.

'There you go. Take a pic when they're done; I'd love to see them.'

I wandered back to the baker via the cheese man and tried for another sample.

'You have already had some free cheese, *non?*' Le Grand Fromage said in an accusatory tone.

'*Non?*' I said, innocently, clutching onto my bread.

'*Oui*,' he said, with irritation, passing a sample to someone over my head. I turned around and it was Xavier, with a fresh baguette in his basket.

'*Merci*, Laurent,' he said to the big cheese man, steering me out of the market with our foodie wares. I felt happier than I had in months. What a place. And I could come here twice a week for the next four months. Xavier gave me his free cheese and I mushed it into another wedge of French bread and popped it in my mouth. Is there anything better in the world than the right cheese with the right bread?

I put my work pinafore on and straightened my hair. The red worked well with my blue uniform, so I didn't completely hate it. Liv was lying on her bed reading a magazine, still fully dressed in her snowboarding gear.

'Are you not boiling hot?' I was overheating just looking at her. 'At least take your helmet off?' Liv flicked her eyes up at me and released the catch on her helmet to reveal two sweaty plaits. She untangled them one by one and gave her head a rub.

'I can't stop reading this article about a woman who married her horse,' she said, pouring herself a green juice and taking a swig, before pulling her foot in to give it a massage. Liv's legs seemed elasticated as she put her feet on her thighs to knead them while reading *Take a Break*.

'Are you ready for your first dinner then?' Liv asked, eyeing me up and down. 'The uniform suits you. You've got that sexy nurse meets serial killer vibe going on.'

'Have I?!' I said, peering at myself in the mirror. 'I didn't know that was a vibe.'

'Hmm… and don't let Luca put you off; he can be quite aloof. Don't worry if he ignores you, that's kind of his thing.'

'OK, good to know, thanks.'

Liv half nodded and went back to reading about the bride and horse groom.

The kitchen was a-bubble with Bouillabaisse and Xavier was perfecting the terrines, with tiny green dots of the mint and rosemary paste, the apple jelly, and the rosemary jus.

'There's some extra brioche to go with the starters over there,' he said, pointing at a basket full of crispy breads, 'and the balsamic fig jam is in the fridge. You can take it all up when you go.'

'No problem,' I said, gathering everything together.

'Which wine have you chosen?' he asked.

'It took me forever to decide, but I eventually settled on a 2001 Chardonnay.'

Xavier nodded. 'Very nice.'

I opened the wine cooler to grab it and show him, but there was something wrong. I felt the bottle all over like a sick child; it wasn't anywhere near cold enough.

'Is everything OK?' Xavier asked, sensing my panic.

'The wine isn't chilled?' I said in alarm, 'I don't understand. I put it in here yesterday lunchtime.'

Xavier stopped mid-sprinkle and came over, putting his hand in the fridge and checking the other bottles.

'They are all the same,' he said with a frown, 'that's very strange. You didn't switch the under cupboard lights off at any point, did you?'

I stared at him for a few seconds, trying to understand what he meant.

'These lights are on the same circuit as the wine fridge and the dishwasher,' he said, pointing to the string of lights that lit the kitchen counter.

'Yes, I switched them off on my way to bed last night. I was worried about the heat on the meringues that were cooling.'

Xavier nodded. 'That'll be what's happened then. We have to keep those lights on 24/7. I'm so sorry Holly, that's my fault, I should have told you as part of the kitchen briefing. There isn't time now to get this bottle chilled and serve it with the main course.'

'I'll work something out,' I said, grabbing the brioche and jam and legging it up the stairs. I skidded at the top and crashed head-first into Luca.

'Hey, hey, hey... is there a fire?' he said, looking down at his shirt, where the jam had conveniently landed.

'Oh no, I'm so sorry,' I said, handing him the basket and grabbing the tea towel tucked in the back of my apron to wipe it off. Luca was defenceless against me cleaning him and frustratingly, the tea towel had a scrap of terrine on the spot I'd decided to use. Luca watched in horror as I smeared meaty paste on top of jam on his beautifully tailored shirt.

'Do you want to stick a piece of toast on there while you're at it?' he asked.

'Oh my God, I'm SO sorry, you must think I'm a total idiot. Why don't you take it off and I'll put it in the wash? Liv's downstairs, I can ask her to soak it.'

Luca gave me a look. His dark eyes were a mixture of annoyed and bemused. 'Don't worry about it. I've got hundreds of shirts,' he said, slowly unbuttoning this one to reveal a perfect six pack – or was it an eight pack? A multipack.

Genevieve chose that moment to walk down the stairs.

'What is going on?' she gasped. 'Luca, put your shirt back on immediately.'

He laughed and ran past her, appearing seconds later in a fresh shirt. He was still pressing the studs together as he walked down the stairs.

'Shouldn't you put that jam where it won't do any more damage?' he said.

'Yes of course, apologies Luca, I mean Mr Blanchet, *monsieur*. I'm so sorry,' I said in a fumble.

I went into the dining room, where I'd laid the table earlier. The cutlery was polished to gleaming and my glassware was shining and ready to go. I placed the basket of brioche next to the jam on the table and lit the candles that were dotted around the room. It was the perfect setting. If only there was some wine. Genevieve was sitting in the lounge with the newly dressed Luca.

'Can I get either of you an aperitif?' I asked.

'Champagne for me, darling,' Genevieve replied.

Luca nodded in agreement.

I popped the cork on a bottle of vintage Moët to kick the night off.

'And what wines are we having with our dinner tonight?' Luca enquired.

'Welllll,' I said, quickly, panic-thinking, 'erm... for the wine this evening, we haaave Champagne as requested with the lamb terrine starter.'

Genevieve and Luca stared at me, barely blinking.

'And thennn to accompany your main course of Bouillabaisse, which is a traditional Provençal fish stew...' Think, think, think. My mind flicked back to the bottle of wine David gave me earlier. Yes, that would be perfect. 'We have a Sicilian Fiano.'

'...which will pair perfectly with the fish,' Xavier interjected, appearing in the doorway with a lopsided grin. 'We have a delicious menu prepared for you which will be ready in around five minutes.'

'Thank you, Xavier, that sounds perfect.' Genevieve toyed with the long, gold pendant around her neck and smiled. Then turning her attention back to me, 'Excellent choice, Holly; I adore Fiano.'

I smiled, backing out of the dining room and serenely closed the doors, legging it downstairs with Xavier as soon as we were out of sight. 'Good thinking,' he said as I ran back to the bedroom and retrieved the Fiano from our window-ledge-fridge where it was nestling in the snow among Liv's fresh juice and vodka selection.

'Everything OK?' she asked, still reading in bed.

'So far, so good,' I said relieved, kissing her sweaty head and running back upstairs. Genevieve and Luca were quaffing their Champagne and laughing together as I ran back down to the kitchen to get their starters. This was WAY more running than I was expecting.

Xavier had both plates under a closh, which he whisked away as I went in.

'*Terrine à deux*,' he said, 'I've saved you some for later as well.'

Food was the last thing on my mind. I just wanted to get through this shift without any irreversible disasters.

I put on my most winning smile and took the starters upstairs, placing them down gently in front of Genevieve and Luca. My hands were shaking, which was absurd. It was two small plates. I wasn't doing heart surgery. Just carrying two small plates up some stairs and putting them on a table. Well, I'd managed to do it successfully, without throwing anything down Genevieve's red silk dress, so I'd take that as a win.

'Your starters are served,' I said, stating the obvious. 'Lamb terrine edged in green apple jelly, served with spiced brioche toast and balsamic fig jam.' They both nodded and stared at me as I stood back. I didn't know what to do, so I decided on a curtsy.

'Is there… anything else?' I asked, cautiously.

'More Champagne?' Luca asked with a smile.

'Oh, yes, of course!' I said, whipping out the bottle

from the fridge and topping up their glasses. Slowly nose-breathing to calm myself down. I was a nervous wreck.

'*Merci*, Holly,' Genevieve said smiling, as Luca gave a dismissive half-nod.

I quietly left them to it, retreating back down to the kitchen where Xavier was lost in his own world, violently playing air guitar to 'Livin' on a Prayer', briefly stopping when he saw me, until I picked up a spatula and head-banged with him through the ah-ah-oh-ohs.

'I love Bon Jovi!' he said, when it finished. 'Do you like rock music? You have a wild streak, I think?'

'Really?' Did I? I'd been one half of #Geolly for such a long time that I'd forgotten who the Holly part of that equation was. Was she wild? Would she like to be?

He nodded, giving me a cheeky look. 'Right, go and clear the starters and I'll prepare the main courses.'

I went upstairs and collected the plates, then retrieved the wine from the fridge, which was chilled to perfection.

'We have a wine straight from Etna to accompany your main course,' I said, peeling back the aluminium at the top of the bottle and easing out the cork. 'It is from a small, family-run vineyard on the east-side of the volcano. They only produce a small quantity of bottles each year, so we are incredibly lucky to have this one to taste.'

I poured a small amount into my own glass to check David wasn't playing a trick on me – it would be just my luck for the wine to be disgustingly vile and astringent, after bigging it up to Genevieve and Luca. I swirled the honey-coloured liquid into a spin, gave it a good sniff and tipped it back. It was good. It was very good. Nectar from the Gods. I wasn't sure I wanted to share it, now I'd tried it. I closed my eyes and savoured the taste. Then poured them out two glasses.

'A very light and soft wine, with a gentle aroma. Peaches, apples and a hint of volcanic soil on the palate as an aftertaste,' I said, nodding. Margot would be so proud of me. 'Should be perfect with the Bouillabaisse.'

'Delicious,' Genevieve said, nodding with approval.

'Where did you get it?' Luca asked, clearly impressed. 'I thought I knew all the winemakers in Sicily. It is one of my favourite places. There is a whole section in the cellar dedicated to Sicilian wines.'

I laughed, 'I can't start giving away my sources in week one. How will I stay one step ahead to impress you otherwise?'

He nodded thoughtfully. 'Well, you've impressed me tonight. This is delicious,' he said, snaffling it down and holding out his glass for more. I topped them both up as the kitchen bell pinged.

'That'll be your main courses. Excuse me while I get them for you.'

I ran downstairs, giving myself a teeny tiny fist bump on the way. Thank fuck for that.

Xavier had the Bouillabaisse in a huge bowl that was destined to spill all over the floor if I had anything to do with it.

'I'll take this upstairs,' he said, wisely.

'I think that's best,' I said, picking up the ladle and dishes for serving and going ahead of him. We paraded into the dining room and placed the bowls and stew on the table. Xavier took the lid off and a steamy cloud of fishy deliciousness poured out. He ladled a large serving into each bowl while I topped up the breadbasket with thick slices of baguette. Hot chunks of white fish, prawns and scallops, with garlic croutons and a hint of orange coming through in the sauce.

'Xavier, you have outdone yourself this evening,' Genevieve fluttered. 'You are SO talented.'

'The starters were superb,' Luca said thoughtfully. 'The spicy rosemary jus was divine with the terrine. Is that a new recipe?'

'Holly and I made them on Monday,' Xavier said. 'It shouldn't have been spicy?'

'Mine wasn't spicy,' Genevieve added, perplexed.

'Oh. Yes, I added a little something extra to the one I made,' I said, blushing.

Xavier looked surprised.

'Well, whatever it was, it worked. I can't get the taste out of my mind,' Luca said, with a smile. 'Bravo, Holly. Looks like we've now got two brilliant chefs in the chalet.'

Xavier smiled. 'She definitely has a talent. I hope this Bouillabaisse tastes as good.'

'You know it will,' Luca said, looking at me and tapping his glass for a refill. I poured another two large glasses of Fiano out for them and looked around the table.

'Is there anything else we can get for you?' I asked.

'*Non*, you can go,' Genevieve said, dismissing us.

Xavier and I backed out of the room, and he closed the double doors with a flourish. I wasn't really sure how to behave yet. Were we servants, or kind of cool friends-slash-housemates who did all the cooking and cleaning? Xavier definitely felt more like the latter. Maybe I would too once I got to know them better.

'I didn't realise you were experimenting on the terrine,' Xavier said. 'Great work.'

'Thank you. I'm sorry, I thought they were test dishes for us to eat and I always like a bit of spiciness with my food.'

'No apology needed, you'll have to show me what you did so I can taste it for myself.'

'I'm just so relieved my first dinner has gone well. David saved the day with that Fiano. We can finish it off if they don't drink it all.'

'I doubt there'll be any left,' Xavier said. 'Unless they eat their mains incredibly fast and we can get them onto dessert. I have built a miniature croquembouche of profiteroles and it is magnificent, even if I do say so myself.' He opened the big fridge to reveal what looked like a wedding cake. Rachael's profiteroles were stacked high, each one piped full of Chantilly cream and stuck in position with caramel sauce. Xavier fired up the stove and poured half a bag of brown sugar and a carton of whipping cream into a hot pan. He added a good slug of vanilla extract and gently stirred the ingredients together for hot caramel sauce. He was like a wizard casting a spell, breathing in his brew while adding a pinch of sugar here and a stick of cinnamon there. The smoky concoction immediately smelt good, and he put a blue jug into the oven to warm as I went back upstairs to clear.

'How was everything?' I asked, looking at the empty plates.

'Terrible,' Luca said with a toothpaste-ad smile.

'Compliments to the chef or should I say *chefs*. I'm only sorry we didn't finish it,' Genevieve added, pointing at the near-empty cauldron of Bouillabaisse.

'You've done your best,' I said with a smile, clearing the table and taking everything back to the kitchen. Including the remaining dribble of Fiano.

'Xavier, I don't have a dessert wine to go with the profiteroles. I was thinking, well, hoping really, that the chef might recommend a liqueur to go with the dessert instead?'

'But of course,' he said, putting his arm around me. 'Do not worry, we are on the same side. A warm spiced rum is the perfect accompaniment to this mountain of calories. Let me heat some up and we'll take everything up together.'

I felt my shoulders relax, the tension draining. George would never have pulled me out of the fire like that. He would have forgotten the ingredients for dessert and put it all on me to sort out. I watched Xavier as he poured the warm rum into a small carafe, putting the caramel sauce and spicy liqueur side by side on a tray. The mini croquembouche was a masterpiece, and one I hoped we wouldn't destroy between us en route to the dining room. Xavier carried the profiteroles up the stairs with poise and balance and I followed closely with the tray and two crystal tumblers for the rum.

'Ooh la la,' Genevieve said as we came into the dining room, 'this is amazing, Xavier. Your talent is wasted on us.'

Xavier beamed and Luca gave a delighted clap, repositioning himself on his chair like a child, in anticipation of his dessert. Xavier placed the tower in the centre of the table and poured the caramel from a height, letting the delicious goo tumble slowly down, pooling at the bottom of the plate. It was all I could do not to grab the top profiterole and shove it in my mouth.

'*Bon Appetit*,' Xavier said, as he gave a little bow. I poured half the spiced rum out and left the carafe on the table. This meal felt too special to just be an ordinary, Thursday-night dinner. Was this how the other half lived? Every night was like Christmas Day. Thank God I wasn't rich; I'd weigh a hundred stone.

'*Merci*, Xavier,' Luca said as he smashed his spoon into the tower, knocking it down. A thing of absolute beauty, decimated in the blink of an eye.

'We'll leave you to it,' I said, backing out of the dining room once again and pulling the doors behind us. I closed my eyes and breathed an audible sigh of relief.

'One night down, four months to go,' Xavier smiled. 'You did well; they like you.'

'Do you think?' I said, relieved. 'I couldn't read them at all.'

'They are both good fun. We were at school together, so I've known them for years. Luca and I also played rugby in Paris.'

'Classmates and teammates – and now you work for him on top?'

Xavier nodded with a chuckle. 'I was captain of the rugby team as well, and I'm not sure Luca ever really got over it, to be honest. He doesn't like being told what to do, that's for sure, but now it's his turn to call the shots, so equilibrium has been restored.'

'Shall we eat?' I asked, eyeing up his Bouillabaisse as we walked back into the kitchen.

'Definitely,' Xavier said, rubbing his hands together. 'I'm starving. Take a seat and get ready to enjoy my famous fish stew.' He ladled it out into two hand-painted bowls and sliced up the last of the crusty bread, as I poured us two tiny glasses of Fiano. What a feast.

'You still haven't told me your story, Holly,' Xavier said lightly. 'What brought you to Verbier? Adventure? Love? Heartbreak?' His hair fell into his eyes as he chased a prawn onto a piece of bread.

'You're right, I haven't,' I said, misty-eyed. 'All of the above, I suppose, but mainly heartbreak. My fiancé called our wedding off a few months ago.' The panicky feeling started again, so I gulped down some wine to get rid of it, drinking my feelings away.

Xavier went quiet, contemplating his food, 'I'm sorry to hear that,' he said eventually.

'I know. Not quite the happy ending I was expecting, and all my money is tied up in the house we were buying together. The house we *have* bought together.'

'What kind of man proposes unless he is absolutely certain?' Xavier said angrily. 'What was his reason?' His visceral upset restored a flickering of a glimmer of hope in my faith in men.

'He was my university boyfriend, so we'd been together a long time.' I shrugged. 'I don't know. He said we… grew apart – well, he grew apart from me – and I didn't notice.'

'He sounds like a selfish child,' Xavier said, shaking his head. 'You can't just discard those you claim to love when things get tough. A relationship is about the good times and the bad. You've had a lucky escape.'

'It's been pretty awful,' I said, 'and he's been constantly in touch ever since. Trying to justify why it happened on the day.'

'It happened on your *wedding day?*' Xavier was incredulous.

I nodded miserably, as the shame came flooding back.

Xavier frowned as he ate, his forehead crinkling in concentration as he enjoyed the different flavours of the stew. The cogs in his brain almost visible in considering how it might be improved. He dipped his bread into the white wine sauce and crunched through it, slowly nodding to himself.

'It's delicious,' I said, nodding wholeheartedly in agreement. 'I'm going to be in trouble if this is the kind of food I'll be eating every day. Not much chance of them leaving any of the profiteroles, though.'

'Don't worry about that,' Xavier said, opening the fridge to reveal four perfectly plump profiteroles, oozing with cream, next to a small jug of caramel sauce. I could get used to this. George's speciality dinner was a potato waffle cooked in the toaster, served on a bed of baked beans.

'What about you?' I asked pointedly. 'How did you end up here?'

'Through Luca,' Xavier said pensively. 'I'd been working on the restaurant scene in Paris for a while and had my own restaurant which was going well – and still is – and then... well, let's just say things got complicated and I nearly lost everything. Luca stepped in and helped me out and thank God he did. He suggested I work for him here until things settled down.'

'That's quite a change?' I said, surprised.

Xavier shrugged. 'The idea works well for us both. Luca likes to impress important restaurant owners and wine producers and I like to be behind the impressing. And it's only six months of the year – the rest of the time, I'm in Paris.'

'How romantic! Whisking you off to the mountains on his private plane. Luca must really like your Bouillabaisse,' I said, trying to imagine having that much money.

'He does,' Xavier said, running a hand through his hair. 'And I like the peace out here. I can do my own thing without anyone bothering me.'

'And what about your wife? It must be awful spending so much time apart. Why didn't she come with you?' I asked.

'Christina runs the restaurant in Paris. She's a chef, that's how we met, so we are dividing and conquering to make things work for now. It won't be forever. She's the only person I trust to run the restaurant while I'm here in Verbier.' The kitchen lights bounced off Xavier's wedding ring as he twiddled with his napkin.

'Sounds like couple goals. Working hard together towards your dreams.'

He stood up and whipped away our empty plates. 'We're working hard, that's for sure. Which reminds me – I need to give her a call.'

Fourteen

10th December

Christmas was just around the corner, and I had to admit I couldn't have chosen a more perfect place to spend it; Verbier gave off Christmassy vibes every day. If only Mum and Dad (and Basil) could be here to celebrate it with me. Liv, Xavier and I walked through the village on our way to the lift, enjoying the buzz of activity as people busied about. The chocolatier icing fondant gifts, the baker handing out fresh loaves of bread, Rachael arranging her shop window into a Christmas tree of macarons. How different it would have been if the wedding had gone ahead, and I was still with George. I'd have been decorating 24 Orchard Close in glitter and fairy lights and getting our beautiful home ready for our first married Christmas as Mr and Mrs Ballinger. I felt a pang of loss for the future I thought I'd have. I'd imagined it all so specifically. Having everyone over. My parents, his parents, his sister and her boring, ruddy-cheeked husband. Wrestling the turkey into shape and cooking up a feast, with three types of potatoes and two types of stuffing. I'd wanted it all. To play wife – to *be* a wife. Hadn't I? I thought back to that awful moment with George and a chill ran through me; *my feelings aren't forever feelings*. I still couldn't believe it had happened. That my life had crumbled so quickly and now I was here. Living in this funny little winter wonderland. The village was a-sparkle with Christmas cheer, gold and silver baubles hung heavy on the pine trees and multi-coloured fairy lights were strewn across the street. The farmers' market had taken it up a notch, with the traders wearing big-eared elf hats, and selling food with a Christmassy spin; giant pretzels, buttery stollen and hot turkey sandwiches. David was giving the cheese man a run for his money as people enjoyed samples of chocolate liqueur, port and Champagne, exchanging crisp notes for beautifully wrapped bottles as they stocked up for the big day.

The three of us dragged our boards along, making tracks in the fresh snow as it fell.

'Ready to get out there?' Liv asked.

'Not really, but I'll do my best,' I said, slightly terrified at the thought of another public faceplant and possible broken wrists in time for Christmas.

'You have been improving?' Xavier said it as a question. It was questionable.

'Well, they say every day's a school day.'

'Do they?' Liv asked.

'Who are they?' Xavier added.

We crammed onto the gondola and were whisked off, high above the village which glinted and glowed in the wintery light. Genevieve and Luca weren't planning a visit this weekend, so we had the whole Verbier playground to ourselves. The cable car came to a juddery halt as we shuffled out, squished between the crowds. I was still sporting Auntie Pam's salopettes, which weren't doing much for my street cred, but then neither were my terrible attempts at snowboarding. The three of us walked to the top of the blue run and sat down to strap on our snowboards. At least I could now do this part.

'See you down there,' Liv shouted, shooting off down the slope without a backward glance.

'I'm fine!' I shouted after her.

'Don't worry, I'll help you,' Xavier said, already stood up and wiggling along like one of Andy's soldiers in *Toy Story*.

'I don't want to hold you up, honestly, you go on with Liv,' I said, staring down the run ahead of me and once again asking myself how the fuckety-fucking-fuck I'd managed to get myself into this situation.

'I'm not going anywhere. First rule of the slopes: know where your friends are. Second rule: don't worry about the people behind you; worry about the people in front of you. Third rule: don't be tempted to bin bag down the mountain if you can't find your board.'

'Ahhh, thank you, Sensei. Wise words indeed. I certainly won't be climbing inside a bin bag to shuttle down the mountain, I can assure you. I value my bones.'

Xavier manoeuvred himself out in front of me and took my hands to help me stand. I had very nearly almost got the standing up part of this sorted, so progress was definitely being made. My knees wobbled as I felt the snow under my board, and I tried to ground myself by pushing into the soles of my feet like the pros repeatedly say to do on YouTube. Xavier was standing perfectly still, steady as a rock, like it was no trouble at all. Between his helmet, his snood, his goggles and his liquorice-black outfit, there were just two slivers of Xavier on show: two tiny stripes of skin on his cheeks. I couldn't see his eyes, but no doubt they were staring at me intently.

'OK?' he asked with a questioning nod.

Absolutely not. I was so not OK.

'Yep,' I said, nodding back.

Xavier let go of my hands and shuffled backwards, staying in front to protect me as I made my way down. *If I made my way down.* I sort of knew what to do but I didn't want to do it. Would this ever be fun? I tipped myself slightly over the edge, digging my heels in with all my strength. I heel-slid forward and to my delight, started to slowly scrape down the mountain. Very slowly, but it was happening. Xavier gave me a thumbs up and spun round to board alongside me and do the exact same thing. Yessss, I was doing ittttt. Was I doing it?

'Is this it?' I shouted to Xavier.

'Yes,' he shouted back, 'it's called falling leaf, but you won't be able to stay on your heels for too long; your knees won't like it.'

'What do I do next then?' I shouted, while sliding at a snail's pace down the piste, my whole body clenched in fear.

Xavier smoothly swivelled on his board to face me, spraying snow on an innocent skier as he turned. Show off. He must have the thigh muscles of a prizewinning ox.

'Switch onto your toes,' he said, holding both arms in the air and spinning around. Easier said than done. I sat down with a thump as my legs gave way and swung my snowboard around to face the mountain. Then continued my embarrassingly slow descent but this time on my toes.

'Looking good, Holly,' Liv shouted, as she flew past for the third time. Xavier was slowly carving alongside me and gave a double thumbs up. I was glad my most uncool life moment to date was being so closely witnessed. I slowly chipped past a family of four eating sandwiches on the side of the piste and eventually made it to the bottom of the slope where Liv was vaping and scrolling through her phone.

'Verrry nice babes,' she said, in a cloud of bubblegum. 'Tightly controlled.'

'You're doing great, Holly,' Xavier said. 'Think how far you've come in a week. You are doing falling leaf down the mountain on heels and toes. Next step is joining them together and then it is just practice.'

'I'll never look as good as you two,' I said, disheartened. I looked up at the slopes as people swooshed down on all sides, skidding to a halt for a quick beer before carrying on. I was cold, wet, and miserable. The snow was not my thing.

'Coming back up?' Liv asked.

'You two go on; I think I'm going to have a break,' I said, pulling off my gloves and my wrist-guards and unbuckling my helmet.

They didn't need telling twice, running off towards the lift to get a few runs in together.

'I'll save you a seat,' I shouted after them. Honestly, how was I ever going to work this out? Maybe I needed a few days on my own, practicing sliding about.

The restaurant at the bottom of the piste was bustling with activity. A beautiful wooden chalet, with rows and rows of trestle tables, stuffed with smiling people eating sandwiches and fries and drinking tiny beers. There was a circular ski-up bar serving cheese and ham toasts for those on the go and a sunbathing section where the less-active holidaymakers snoozed in deckchairs. I trudged into the main restaurant on the hunt for a Mars Bar and the place was teeming with people balancing trays of various foods and confidently walking in different directions. There didn't seem to be a queue, or system of any kind and I wasn't sure how to navigate the chaos, so I followed a ski instructor who seemed to know what he was doing and copied his every move. I was standing behind him in the queue, waiting to pay for my glühwein and apple strudel when I felt someone tweak my pigtails.

'*Salut*, Holly,' Rachael said, her tray laden down with two bowls of mushroom risotto and half a bottle of red wine. A much more nutritional effort than mine.

'Hiii, how are you?' I said smiling and adjusting my hair, it had been a stretch to pull together the tiniest pair of pigtails, but I'd just about managed it.

'Better for having the afternoon off and remembering what it's all about. David's just got here too if you want to sit outside with us?'

We paid for our trays and I followed her out into the sunshine where it was weirdly hot considering it was less than two degrees. The sun was beating down on the mountain and the DJ had just started. As soon as the clock struck 12 p.m., people began gearing up for après ski and the drinks orders switched from hot chocolates and coffees to alcohol. Glasses of apple and pear schnapps with chunks of fruit on cocktail sticks would appear alongside large beers on trays. Two ten-foot speakers were already pumping out 'Mr Brightside' and the party vibe was underway.

'David! How have you made it up here so quickly? You were surrounded by a crowd of winos on the market when I saw you two hours ago!'

'I like to make hay while the sun shines,' he said, 'but the most important thing is to enjoy the mountain.'

'That's why we're all here,' Rachael agreed, cracking open the red wine.

'I'm glad I bumped into you. I wanted to thank you for saving me last week with that delicious bottle of Fiano,' I said.

'Did I?' David replied, looking rightly baffled.

'Accidentally. It ended up being the only wine I had for my first night at the chalet and luckily it was absolutely spot on.'

'Ah I see! Well, good, I'm glad. I've only seen excellent produce coming out of that vineyard, so you can't go wrong serving wine from there. I bet Luca couldn't place it?' David said with a smile. 'Always nice to get one over on his well-travelled nose.'

I laughed. 'Exactly. You helped me impress him and Genevieve on day one, so I'll be coming back for a few emergency bottles in case I need them in the future.'

'And if you don't, you'll just have to drink them yourself,' Rachael said, tucking into her risotto.

'Worst case scenario, of course.' I laughed.

I eyed the two of them with their matching meals. A quiet camaraderie as they comfortably chomped away. David in khaki green and Rachael in metallic purple, the two of them looked great together.

'Are you up here on your own?' David asked.

'God, no. I came up with Liv and Xavier, but I've left them to it. I'm way too slow still, so they're getting a few fast runs in together.'

'Everyone was a learner once. Xavier taught himself a couple of seasons ago in fact, so it doesn't take long,' Rachael said.

'Really? I assumed he'd been snowboarding for years?'

'No, he's a city boy,' Rachael replied. 'He'd never been to the mountains before he came to work for Luca.'

'We've never really got to the bottom of what he's doing here. His restaurant in Paris is world-renowned,' David added.

'He told me he was building his network out here, working hard to impress Luca's contacts?' I said.

'There must be more to it than that,' Rachael said. 'The best place to network with the French foodie elite is in Paris. No need for him to be hiding away here in Verbier.'

'Luca has managed to convince him otherwise somehow…' I replied.

'He can be very persuasive when he wants to be,' Rachael said. 'Nothing gets between him and his food.'

'He has a nose for wine and a mouth for food, that's for sure,' David said. 'I'll dig you out a few unplaceable bottles to keep him guessing when I get back.'

'We won't need too many; one or two will be plenty for back up. Have you seen his wine cellar? It's bigger than my parents' house,' I said.

'I haven't, but Xavier has told me all about it. Luca's wine cellar is the stuff of Verbier legend. He has some of the best wine in the resort squirrelled away down there, which is why I like the idea of you serving him up a few randoms. Throw him off.'

Rachael laughed. 'Whatever floats your boat, my love,' she said.

'You two have got this place sewn up between you. With booze and cake, what more do people need? Have you been out here long?'

'I've been holidaying here since I was small and always loved it,' Rachael said, 'so I decided to open a shop a few years back. Then I met David and the rest is history.'

David beamed. 'And I started out as a wine merchant, working across *Les 4 Vallées* and decided to settle in Verbier when I met Rachael.'

'We both know Liv through my sister, who met her travelling in Oz,' Rachael said. 'She decided to give the mountains a go and followed me out here last season.'

'Ah, I didn't realise you were connected to Liv as well,' I said.

'Everyone is connected out here,' David replied, 'like a beautiful snow spider's web.'

Xavier came hooning towards the table, stopping himself just in time to look almost casual, removing his goggles, helmet, and gloves in one fell swoop.

'Hey hey,' he said, giving Rachael and David a nod.

'Where's Liv?' I asked, looking behind him.

'Still going,' he shrugged. 'I've had enough of that run for today.'

'What happened to rule number one?'

'Liv is a lone wolf. She waits for no one,' he said, throwing his stuff on the table and heading into the restaurant.

'He's got that right,' Rachael said with a chuckle.

'Are you out in town later?' David asked.

'I'm not sure. Genevieve and Luca are in Paris this weekend, so we have the place to ourselves.'

'Any chance of a private tour of his wine cellar?' David asked hopefully.

'Erm...' I said, immediately nervous at the idea, 'I'm not sure I'm allowed. Luca has been pretty clear that no one goes down there apart from the two of us.'

'I thought as much,' David replied glumly. 'I can but dream.'

Xavier returned with two large beers and placed one in front of me.

'Dreaming again, David?' he asked, sitting back down.

'David is trying to coerce Holly into a tour of Luca's wine museum,' Rachael said, piling her plate onto David's and handing them both to a waiter.

'Not this again?' Xavier said, raising his eyebrows. 'I've told you before, the place is like a bank vault. It wouldn't surprise me if there are cameras hidden in the barrels.'

'Can't I just have a quick look on Christmas Day? Genevieve and Luca are away, and Holly has the keys. I won't touch anything, I promise,' David said, with a cheeky smile.

'He'd find out somehow. Luca has a sixth sense when it comes to his wine.'

'Are you guys at the chalet for Christmas then?' I asked. 'That's lovely news. I'd kind of assumed we'd all be working.'

'Orphans Christmas all together,' David smiled. 'The Blanchets are having Christmas in Paris, so Xavier has offered to cook for us.'

Rachael and David started putting all their bits and bobs

back on. Helmets first, then goggles, gloves, and tightened snoods.

'Better get back to it,' David muffled at us. They double waved as they walked back to their snowboards, leaving Xavier and me cradling our beers.

'I'm not sure I deserve this after today's poor effort,' I said, taking a good swig. Beer tasted so much better in the mountains: light and fresh and way too drinkable.

'Every time you try again is worth celebrating,' Xavier said, holding his glass out to clink mine. 'You are better today than yesterday, and tomorrow, you'll be even better.'

He was so solid and certain. What must it feel like to have such absolute belief in yourself? The sun was shining through the droplets in Xavier's hair that had started life as snowflakes. A message pinged on his phone. He picked it up, read it, then shoved it in his pocket.

'Is everything OK?' I asked tentatively.

'Yes, just sorting some stuff back home,' Xavier smiled.

'In Paris? The food capital of the world sounds so glamorous. Do you miss it?'

'I miss the city buzz sometimes, but not often. I miss being on top of the latest food innovations and learning new things from the team,' he replied.

'I didn't realise your restaurant was so big?'

'*Oui*. One of my old chefs is now working at Le Rouge, at the top of the mountain. We should go up and see him sometime; I hear he is doing interesting work with the raclette.' He stared hard into his beer and traced his thumb in a circle around the Amstel logo before snapping out of his reverie and taking a long drink.

'You've lived so many lives already,' I said. 'Classically

trained chef, five years at Le Cinq, five years with your own restaurant, two years here – how old are you again?'

Xavier smiled. 'Only thirty-four, but some days I feel fifty-four.'

'I don't know what I've been doing with my time. Procurement has a lot to answer for. Your wife is very good to take care of things in Paris while you work out here.'

He nodded. 'She loves to cook. It is her life passion. We met at Cordon Bleu, and she is an amazing *pâtissier* – one of the world's best.'

'I'd love to live in Paris,' I sighed. 'Maybe that should be my next step.'

'Nothing to stop you,' Xavier said.

'Apart from that little thing called Brexit.'

'Yes, the rules are incredibly hard to navigate,' he replied.

A waiter went past, balancing a tray full of shots and I stopped him and bought six. Xavier looked at me with alarm.

'Two each for us and two for Liv when she shows up,' I said.

I gave the clear liquid a sniff. I'd presumed it was schnapps, but on closer inspection, it was schnapps' hedonistic older brother – Sambuca. I gave Xavier a smile to try and get one back and clinked my glass with his before downing it. The liquid burned my throat, and the aniseed fumes consumed my mouth, breathing their way out through my nose. Yuck.

'Oof, I'd forgotten how strong that stuff is,' I said, slightly reeling.

Xavier wasn't fazed at all; the shot glasses looked like thimbles in his spade-like hands as he drank them one after the other. I posted a picture of the remaining four to my

Instagram then pushed them to the side *for later*. I didn't like drinking shots.

#ShootYourShot #Chasers

George was always the first to look at my Stories and this one was no exception. He seemed to be keeping a close eye on me, so maybe he did care what I was up to.

'Thanks, I feel better for that,' Xavier said, putting one of his hands over mine. I put my other on top and he put his other on top of that like an NFL 'hands in' and then we broke it off. His big, cat-like eyes were sad, but kind and he was really kind of hot.

'Hey, hey, hey, what's going on here then?' Liv said, skidding up to the table on her board, while lifting her goggles. Her plaits were like two icicles stuck to her shoulders.

'Sambuca's going on,' I said, handing her two glasses, which she promptly poured down her neck.

'Whose is that one?' Liv asked, pointing at my second shot.

'I ordered the wrong thing,' I said, eyeing the Sambuca cautiously.

'I'll have it,' Xavier replied, saving me from myself. He gave me a wink and drank it. Rather him than me, a six-foot man can handle three shots. At five-foot-four-and-a-half, I could just about manage one. The music shifted up a gear and a few people were already dancing on the tables. Liv unzipped her jacket to reveal a tight-fitting turtleneck to match her turquoise boarding pants, leaving me looking like her very uncool older sister. The three of us ordered another round of beers and sat in the sunshine, enjoying the music and the alcohol buzz. The feeling of freedom. No pressure, no deadlines, no worries.

'Shall we board back to the chalet?' Liv asked.

'Definitely not!' I said. 'I'm getting the lift down.'

'We're all getting the lift down,' Xavier said. 'We've had a lot to drink. I stopped counting at four beers.'

'Nooooo,' Liv said, staggering towards her snowboard, but Xavier got there before her and snatched it up.

'Yes,' he said, smiling. 'No drinking and boarding Liv; it's dangerous.'

Getting the cable car down in the dark was a different kind of magical. The lift was virtually empty as those brave enough to ski down had already taken the kamikaze route home. Floating through the sky back to Verbier, I felt light and giddy. The weight on my heart was starting to lift. The three of us watched as the village got closer, transforming from a sparkly speck in the distance into a magical fairyland of chalets, bars and restaurants encased in Christmas trees. It had been three months since the dreaded 'I don't' but I was somehow excited for the future again. New kit, new skills, new friends and a new start. If I'd told my duvet-hiding self back then that by Christmas this would be 'future me', I'd never have believed it. Thank God for Margot and her synchronicity. The ink-blue sky was full of stars, and the resort was abuzz with chatter as we danced off the lift and half-ran back to the chalet.

It was such a joy to kick off my sweaty, snowboarding boots and rub my aching feet. They'd been scrunched up all day, doing their best to heel-toe me down the mountain, and needed a yogic stretch. I got into the shower while Xavier and Liv faffed about, still buzzing from the last round of tequila shots. The hot water stung my cold body, and I had a moment of pure happiness for this freezing cold adventure and these new friends who had so unexpectedly come into my life. I threw on my teddy bear onesie and sat happily underneath the hairdryer, enjoying the heat as it dried my hair, and occasionally blasting hot air down my top.

'Spirulina nightcap?' Liv mouthed over the noise, offering me a bright-green shot.

'Interesting colour,' I said, tasting it, 'is it mixed with nuclear waste?'

'We're out of that. I had to use pineapple juice and ginger instead.'

Liv had a gift for combining the most bizarre drinks but getting the balance just right. It was bloody delicious. I drank it down as my phone rang and a photo of me and Abi drinking margaritas appeared on the screen.

'Hols!!! I miss you! How are you getting on?'

I nearly burst into tears hearing Abi's tinkly voice. I could just imagine her wandering through Marylebone on the way home from work and was desperate to give her a big hug.

'Abs? Oh my Goddd, it's so good to hear your voice. I miss you too!'

'Are you enjoying it out there? Are they looking after you?'

'Yessss. Really good! Well, kind of, you know. It's been a lot but…'

'Of course it has. This whole year has. Have you been out on the slopes?'

'Yes, loads. I've been learning to snowboard – well, falling on my face mainly, but God loves a trier, right? When are you coming out to see me? I want to see your face.'

'Me too… I was hoping to come in early Jan, but I've got a three-month theatre gig so not sure I'll be able to now. Pencil me in for next winter instead.'

I laughed. 'I'm not sure I'll be out here next year as well. How are things at home? Have you seen Margot?'

'Yes, I was in there for dinner last night – she misses you, but she's totally fine. I wasn't sure whether to tell you that I also bumped into George, but you sound really happy, so maybe you'd rather know?'

My stomach dropped. 'Why? What was he doing? Did you speak to him? Did he mention me?'

'He was certainly enjoying himself, so I'm glad you are too. Drinking shots and laughing his head off with some girls. He didn't look like an almost-got-married man.'

'Sounds very much like a single man. He's probably glad to have me out of the way.'

'He didn't look wracked with guilt and indecision, put it that way. I wanted to slap his smug, smiling face.'

'He's stopped commenting on my Insta Stories, Abs. He still looks at them but doesn't message me anymore. Which is a message in itself, I suppose.'

'I'm so sorry, Holly. He didn't deserve you. Let's not waste any more time talking about him.'

Six hours later.

I pressed my eyelids down tight and tried to go back to sleep. Shhhh, sleepy-sleep, dream, sheep, think of nothing, nothingggg. No. It was no good. I needed something to help me settle and some earplugs to block out Liv's snores. I crept out of bed as quietly as possible and tiptoed to the kitchen, pushing the door open to find Xavier stood barefoot in his dressing gown, stirring up a pan of hot milk.

'Oh,' I said, self-consciously zipping my onesie up to the neck, 'sorry, I wasn't expecting anyone else to be up.' I glanced at the clock. It was 4 a.m.

'I couldn't sleep. I tried for a while then gave up.' Xavier pulled two cups out of the cupboard.

'Same,' I said. 'What are you making?'

'It's an old grandad-drink my mum used to make when we were little called Ovaltine. I have a secret stash of it for when I can't sleep.'

'No way!' I said and laughed. 'My mum used to make that for me too, except now I always add a Baileys.'

Xavier stepped to one side to reveal a bottle of Baileys on the counter.

'Same,' he said with a grin. 'So what's keeping you up? Too many thoughts?'

'Always,' I said. 'I think these past few months have shaken me up more than I realised. I spoke to my friend Abi earlier and it seems George is getting on with his life as if I'd never existed. Out of sight, out of mind.'

'I'm sure that's not true,' Xavier said. 'How can he not have regrets? For his behaviour at the very least. Losing you must have left a huge hole in his life.'

'Doesn't seem that way. I thought being out here would help me forget all about it, but it's hard to make peace with knowing my old life is just carrying on without me. I miss my mum and dad and my friends… and my cat.'

'Of course you do,' Xavier said, adding several chunks of dark chocolate to the pan, 'it's only natural.'

'The bistro I worked at in London is so beautiful, the food is gorgeous, and my friend Margot is such a wise old owl. It's a lot to lose all at once. I'm worried I've made too many changes, too quickly.'

Xavier nodded, whisking the chocolatey milk into a bubbly froth and adding the Ovaltine. 'I know how it feels to leave your whole life behind,' he said, pouring out two mugs and topping them with cream. 'You know the restaurant Luca is helping me out with back in Paris? When I said things were complicated, it's because my ex-business partner Chantal is also my ex-fiancée.'

'Really? I didn't know.'

'I didn't mention it before as it's still hard to talk about, but I know exactly how it feels to build a life and a future with someone and have it blow up in your face.'

'I'm so sorry to hear that, Xavier,' I said, really wishing I wasn't dressed as a teddy bear.

'Luca bought Chantal's half of the business when we split.'

'I did think it was strange that a top chef like you was working in a chalet solely to build his network.'

Xavier smiled. 'It's taken me three years, but this is my last season at Chalet Blanchet and then I'll be the owner of my restaurant again. I'll have my business back. I'm going to mark the occasion by giving the restaurant a new name.'

'What's it called at the moment?'

'Lavedrine et Lapointe. Chantal and my surnames together. But I'm going to rename it Lavedrine X. I want her name off.'

'Crossing Chantal out of your life?'

'X because the restaurant is in the tenth arrondissement, and for Xavier. I'm looking forward to finally being able to put it all behind me. Luca did me a huge favour paying Chantal off. I was a total mess when she left.'

'What happened?' I asked, softly.

'She cheated on me with one of our biggest-paying customers. A man I considered a friend. I found them together one night at our flat. I was supposed to be working but left early with a migraine and came home to find them there.'

'That's so awful,' I said, putting my hand on his arm.

'It was a huge shock. The restaurant was my dream, Chantal and I built it together, but it was my idea and my vision. I put every single penny I had into it, as well as my heart and soul, working around the clock to make it successful. I trusted her completely and she betrayed me in every possible way. And once I found out, everything around me crumbled. We called off the wedding, Chantal wanted out of the business, and I wanted her out too. Out of the business and out of my life. I could barely look at her.'

'It must have been awful for you. Trapped in your own life, like that,' I said.

'The restaurant was doing well but not nearly well enough for me to buy her out. I had lost my fiancée and I was about to lose my business, and that's when Luca stepped in. Chantal was at school with Luca and me and the three of us were close, so it was a way for him to help us both out at the same time. Luca bought Chantal's stake in the business so I didn't have to sell, and Chantal got the clean break she wanted.'

'Sounds a lot like my George situation,' I said. 'How can people be so selfish and cruel? I feel like I'll never be able to trust anyone ever again.'

'It's hard to open yourself up again when something like that happens, that's for sure.'

'But you did it! With Christina, right? Success is the best revenge and now you're married and you have your business back.'

'Christina is an angel. She is the most supportive, kind, lovely, generous…'

'Alright, alright,' I laughed.

'I wouldn't be where I am today without her. She took it all on her shoulders and stepped in as head chef to keep things going while I paid off the loan and got myself together.'

Xavier stared quietly into his Ovaltine before taking a long drink. He seemed lost in thought so I followed suit to cover the silence. It was delicious. Part Ovaltine, part hot chocolate with a cream lid and a dash of cinnamon. The perfect cure for insomnia.

'Luca must really like you to help you out like that?'

'Luca likes to play the hero when he can. Don't get me wrong: if Luca hadn't stepped in, I'd have had to sell the restaurant and start again, but I've known him long enough to know any act of kindness always has a price. There's always something in it for Luca too. He has been expanding his restaurant portfolio for some time now. So I got an affordable loan and he got the hottest chef in Paris to impress his clients and help build his network.'

Xavier pulled a chair out and sat down, yawning into his fist. He looked exhausted.

'I suppose he has so much money that it's easy for him to be generous,' I said.

'Luca knows a good investment when he sees one,' Xavier replied. 'I've paid him every penny back with interest, but he likes to refer to himself as a co-owner, which was never the deal. I'll be glad to have the business back in my name. He's made his money and had me as his personal chef for the past three years. It's time to let me move on.'

Fifteen

14th December

'Luca was so excited for Xtreme that he's already gone, so I have officially finished work for the day,' Liv said with a smile, sprinkling chia seeds on her porridge.

'Is he entering as well?' Xavier said, with a smirk, pulling a tray of warm croissants out of the oven and piling them onto a plate. The smell was divine.

'Of course he is,' Liv said, 'you know he can't resist an opportunity to prove himself.'

'To show the world he's a winner,' Xavier said, rolling his eyes.

'Are you entering too, Xavier?' I was already impressed.

'Yep,' Liv interjected, 'and me.'

'Really? You're all competing? What do you have to do?'

Xavier ripped open a croissant and dolloped on a teaspoon of raspberry jam.

'You have to jump,' he said, 'the higher the better.'

'They've been building the kicker all week,' Liv said, 'it's a huge lump of snow and you've gotta try and get over it.

Come up and watch; we could do with a cheerleader. Unless you want to enter too?' She nudged me and we laughed.

'Yeah right. If I can toe it down as a leaf.' Eddie the Eagle Edwards I was not.

We finished breakfast and got ready to go up the mountain.

'You can't keep wearing those God-awful pants,' Liv said, pointing at my salopettes, 'they're fine occasionally as an ironic nod to the past, but not every day, mate. You can borrow these until you get your own.'

She threw me over a pair of her boarding pants, and I had to admit she had a point. I stroked the silky material of my froggy trousers one last time, then folded them into a big marshmallow and shoved them under the bed. Liv's white boarding pants were much cooler and MUCH warmer. Almost as if they weren't full of holes. I layered myself up with thermals, a purple fleece and a waterproof zip-up, split my hair into tiny bunches and mascara-ed my invisible lashes. I was starting to look the part.

'There ya go, mate. Looking like a boss,' Liv said, impressed. 'Just gotta get you linking up those turns and we'll make a snowboarder of you yet.'

I didn't want to be a snowboarder. I wanted to sack off this nightmare endurance training and sunbathe in the Champagne bar with a drink in my hand. And I wasn't the only one – a lot of people were doing this, day after day. 'Going skiing' seemed to be code for 'day drinking'. Which I could absolutely get on board with. I just needed to find my people.

Xavier appraised me from the doorway with a smile. He was dressed in black with a pair of red goggles loose around his neck.

'Getting there,' he said, thoughtfully. 'What's that saying of Rachael's again, Liv?'

'Looking hot to trot?' I offered, putting my hands on my hips. 'Too cool for school?'

'All the gear and no idea?' Liv shouted from the bathroom.

'That's the one,' he said, smiling.

'Thanks a lot,' I laughed. 'Well, at least I *look* like I know what I'm doing. I'm halfway there.'

The three of us made our way out of the chalet and through the village. Xtreme Verbier had brought a carnival atmosphere to the village, with flags lining the street and party music playing even though it was only 10 a.m. The good vibes were flowing and there were people everywhere.

'The place is buzzing,' I said, as we made our way through the crowds to the lift.

'Yeah, this is one of the season highlights,' Liv said as we squeezed between two 6 ft boarders chatting away in German. There was a collective intake of breath as the lift doors closed, then everyone relaxed and shuffled about a bit to settle in for the journey. When we reached the top of the mountain, it felt like we'd *really arrived*. The lift doors opened, and we entered another world. The piste was cordoned off into sections, with crowds lining the course, cheering and waving oversized scorecards as contestants made their way down and attempted the big jump. A booming voice on a microphone announced each would-be winner before the Klaxon sounded and they set off down the run, while Team Xtreme circulated with clipboards to sign people up.

'Fancy your chances?' a beardy teenager asked, nodding at the jump. Clearly the outfit was working.

'I'll think about it,' I said with a knowing smile. Knowing I absolutely wouldn't.

'Sign us up,' Liv said, dragging Xavier behind her.

Beardy gave them both a number and pointed them towards an enormous queue.

'Oh great,' I said, 'I'll see you sometime tomorrow then.'

'It'll go quick,' Xavier said. 'I'll listen for your cheering when I come down. Number 540,' he held up his number, 'the winner.'

'I don't think so, mate,' Liv said, sticking her number on her chest, 'the glory is going to 541.'

'Good luck guys,' I said, giving them both a quick hug, 'be careful coming down; it looks icy out there. Don't break a leg.'

They headed off and I wandered over to the hot drinks stand. There were happy faces everywhere, the sun was shining, and Ed Sheeran was blasting from the speakers. My hot chocolate came with a healthy dollop of fresh cream, and I made my way over to the deckchair area to enjoy it while soaking up the atmosphere.

'And next to compete in Xtreme Verbier is Luca Blanchet. All the sevens, lucky number seventy-seven. Luca is wearing traversing skis and is competing at the top of the pops in the highly competent category.'

A sarcastic 'Oooooooohhhh,' erupted from the crowd as a tiny dot started flying down the mountain. Skiing at breakneck speed, Luca approached the jump, sailing high into the air, somersaulting twice and landing on his feet to rapturous applause.

'Wowsers, look at him gooo,' bellowed the commentator. 'That had the look of a pretty perfect run from number seventy-seven, but let's wait and see what our judges thought…'

Luca skied to the holding pen to wait for his score, and I made my way around the edge of the crowd to give him an encouraging wave.

'The scores are in ladies and gentlemen and the judges *are ready*. We have eighteen, seventeen, nineteen, nineteen and seventeen. A total of ninety out of a possible one hundred and an excellent score for Luca Blanchet, putting him easily in first place.'

The crowd cheered and whistled as Luca's name and number pinged into the top space on the leader board. He gave his million-dollar smile and waved, giving a champion's clasp on both sides before skiing out of the competitors' area. He was busy unhooking his skis and locking them together, so I waited until he was on the move before casually wandering past, but he kept going towards the bar without noticing me.

'Luca?' I called, spinning on my heels to follow his long strides. He didn't stop so I trotted after him, repeatedly calling his name. Why was he ignoring me?

'Luca? LUCA?' I shouted. Eventually he stopped at the circular bar, and I tapped him on the shoulder enthusiastically. He jumped and turned round, pulling out his AirPods.

'What the…? Holly? You gave me a fright!' he said.

'I'm so sorry,' I said, out of breath, 'I didn't realise you were listening to music.' I silently kicked myself as he paused Spotify and pulled out a packet of cigarettes, shaking one loose and offering it to me. I shook my head. He put the packet to his lips to take it for himself and lit it with a Zippo.

'Are you here competing?' he asked.

'Definitely not. No plans to break any bones today,' I said, horrified at the thought.

'You can't jump?' he smiled, taking a long drag of his cigarette.

'Not exactly. I like to keep my feet on the ground.'

'Well, maybe we can change that,' he said, with a twinkle in his eye.

The barman pointed at Luca, ready for his order.

'Amstel *et*... what is your drink?' he asked gesturing towards the bar.

'Oh no, I'm fine thanks,' I said, shaking my head.

Luca stopped in surprise. He wasn't used to the word 'no'.

'But you must have a drink?' he said, waiting for my order. Oh God, I was bound to make some huge cock up if I talked to him for more than five minutes. I'd just stay non-alcoholic and make my excuses after one.

'Yes, sorry, of course, that would be nice. A lemonade would be great, thanks.'

Luca frowned. Were fizzy drinks uncivilised?

'With lime?' I added, trying to please him. His frown deepened as if that made even less sense. 'And vodka?' Third time's a charm. He shook his head in despair.

I could see people looking in our direction as Luca's name remained at the top of the leader board and skiers and boarders flew down the piste on a mission to beat his score. There was a lot of bravado as people launched themselves onto the kicker. One boarder attempted a forward flip and landed on his face, another jumped and grabbed her board but somehow launched herself backwards. It all looked very dangerous to me, but the crowd continued to ooh and ahh as the numbers ticked on.

'I saw you land that jump,' I said, side-eyeing Luca. 'It was pretty cool.'

'You liked that, eh?' he said, smiling. 'Is very simple stuff, really; a child could do it. In fact, I did do it as a child.'

'You've been skiing a while then?' I asked.

'*Oui*. Before I could walk,' he said wistfully. 'The chalet has been in the family for five generations, so we are all skiers.'

'Do the rest of the family still come out here?'

'My grandparents have passed on and my parents don't speak. It's just Genevieve and I that use the chalet now. But hopefully we'll have our own families one day and can re-start the tradition.'

'Well five generations would be very proud of that jump, and you're still in the lead,' I said, pointing up at the enormous scoreboard. Luca squinted his eyes and put his arm around me as he saw his name in shiny lights. He smiled modestly.

'For now,' he nodded.

'You never know,' I said, feeling suddenly lightheaded, 'no one's beaten you yet.' Was it the vodka or the feel of a non-George arm around me? Something was making me wobbly.

'More drinks, *s'il vous plaît*,' Luca said, gesturing to the barman.

'Isn't the final later today?' I asked in alarm. I didn't want him drunkenly breaking his neck and somehow blaming me.

'I won't make the top three,' he said, draining his beer. 'Besides, these beers are small. I am French. We do things differently to you English.'

He was right, it was me on the vodkas feeling woozy. He seemed fine.

'How are you finding Verbier?' Luca asked.

'Cold,' I said, zipping my coat up tight.

He laughed. 'The skiing wouldn't be quite so good if it wasn't. But you are enjoying it? We are looking after you?'

'At the chalet, you mean?' I said, smiling as he stared at me. 'Yes, Liv and Xavier have been very kind. Apart from forcing me to cold plunge every day.'

'Ah, you have been having ice baths?'

'Unfortunately, yes.' I said, shuddering at the thought of it.

'It is very good for you though, *non?* And a luxury, I think?' he smiled. 'To have a plunge pool and a sauna. Not many London homes have that.'

The word 'luxury' felt very much at odds with my own feelings and experience. It was actually the last word I'd use to describe it. *Hellish* sprang to mind. I couldn't see Londoners popping themselves in a wheely bin of ice before hitting the tube each morning, whatever TikTok said.

'That's for sure. It's so different here from my London life. I sometimes feel like a fish out of water, but I'm trying my best to get up to speed with everything.'

'Well, apart from the London fashion *faux pas*, I think you are settling in well.'

I blushed, thinking about that bloody nightdress debacle. What must I have looked like? 'Xavier has clearly been impressed with your skills in the kitchen, and he is a hard taskmaster. You have also chosen some excellent wines this week.'

'Really? I'm so pleased to hear that! It means a lot coming from such a wine pro.'

'You clearly want to learn and have a good eye,' he said.

'I do, but there is so much I don't know. I'm fascinated by your cellar and would love to understand the wines better. Margot speaks so highly of your knowledge and excellence.'

'I'd be happy to teach you,' Luca said with a smile, stubbing out his cigarette.

The music cranked up a notch and a saxophonist appeared at the end of the bar, playing along to the happy house pumping out from the speakers.

'Passion for work is not easy to find. Xavier has it too.'

'And what do you do for work?' I asked, realising I had no idea. 'What kind of job lets you spend half your life in Paris and the other half up a mountain?'

Luca gave a proud smile. 'I invest in restaurants. Mainly in Paris but one or two elsewhere in France. It allows me to indulge my two great loves of food and wine.'

'Oh yes, of course – you invested in Xavier's restaurant, didn't you?'

'That one is slightly different; we are partners,' Luca said.

'Well, if you ever need a spare pair of hands in any of them, keep me in mind.' I could happily eat away my days, julienning carrots and pouring wine, flitting from restaurant to restaurant.

Luca gave me a lazy smile and shook his head, pulling out another cigarette. 'I wouldn't give you to someone else,' he said, sparking up again. 'You work for me now.' He gave me a smouldering look as a cloud of smoke puffed out of his nose. I held my breath to stop myself choking.

The commentator's voice boomed over the microphone loud and clear. They were finally up to 540 and introducing Xavier to the crowd. I was glad of the distraction.

'Xavier and Liv are up,' I said, looking to the top of the mountain and seeing Xavier start to make his way down to the enormous jump. He carved left and right, going faster and faster until we could finally recognise him. He flew up the kicker, jumped, grabbed his board, spinning 720 degrees and miraculously landed on his feet. The crowd went wild, and I joined in with a cheer, while Luca enjoyed his cigarette.

'I had no idea Xavier was so good,' I said, clapping my hands in delight. 'I've only ever seen him on the blue runs. He must be bored to death hanging out with me.'

'I'm sure Xavier has his reasons for sticking to the blues,' Luca said with a smile. 'I noticed he'd been going out of his way to show you the ropes on the slopes as well as in the kitchen.'

'Making sure I don't fall off the edge,' I said.

'He clearly likes you,' Luca replied with a wink.

'Does he? I mean we are friends, of course!' What was he implying?

'*Oui, oui*, of course,' Luca said, his brown eyes glinting, 'just *friends*.'

The cheering was still going as Xavier's scores came in, with the sound of cowbells ringing all around the arena. He was close on Luca's heels with an overall score of eighty-five, as Liv started hurtling down the mountain. She had no fear. I watched fascinated as she slid along the rail at the top of the jump and launched into the air, grabbing her board into a neat forward roll and landing easily. I stood up and screamed along with the rest of the crowd. Another amazing jump. Legend.

'How cool was that?' I whooped, as Luca gave an unimpressed shrug. I couldn't believe I'd been out on the slopes with these two pros, and they'd been humouring me so kindly. I needed to get some lessons in so I could at least graduate onto the red runs. No wonder Liv always went on ahead – she was probably going off-piste to stretch her legs. Liv's score came in at eighty and there were some boos from the crowd in reply. She pinged into eighth place on the leader board with Xavier third. I dropped them a pin and, when they were close enough, waved them over for a well-deserved drink.

'Congratulations!' I shouted, the vodka well and truly taking over. 'You were both brilliant. I am so proud to be your friend and protégée.' I pulled them in for a double hug. 'And look who I found?' I said, pointing at Luca, who high-fived Liv and shook Xavier's hand. I was clearly the uncool one in the mix.

'*Quatre bières et quatre Poire Williams*,' Luca called to the barman.

'I take it we aren't working later?' I whispered to Liv as we sat down. Slightly awkward question given the company, but better to check before I had my fifth drink.

'Nah,' she said, 'no chance Genevieve is coming out today, is there Luca?'

'You never know with her,' he shrugged, 'but let's assume you have the night off.'

Xavier held his beer out to cheers, and we happily clinked glasses, settling in to watch the remaining competitors as they zoomed down the mountain, spinning and jumping as they went. We booed as Liv eventually slid out of the top ten, but Xavier and Luca were firmly locked into the final, which was coming up. They wouldn't be able to see straight at this rate.

'Guys are you sure you'll be alright on your final run after all these beers?' I said in alarm. They both laughed.

'The beer is only loosening us up. It is oiling my knees, Holly, don't worry,' Xavier said, putting his arm around me and smiling.

This was obviously where I was going wrong. Way too sober at 10 a.m. and relying on turbo-powered coffee to get me through. If I had a hip flask full of schnapps, it might get my snake hips moving.

'You'll see our optimum performance after all this preparation,' Luca said, raising his glass, 'although my first jump was pretty optimum, wasn't it, Holly? You missed it, Xavier?'

'I saw it, my friend,' Xavier said coolly. 'Very impressive, but it's the final that counts.'

'We saw you on the big screen at the top of the mountain,' Liv said. 'I'll film you both coming down this time.'

'I can show you how it's done, eh?' Luca said, putting his arm around Xavier.

'Let's see, shall we?' Xavier replied, with a smile.

'Well, there we have it, ladies and gentlemen. Each of our competitors have shot their shot and we can now confirm the top ten for the final. If your name is on the board behind me, then please make your way back up the mountain for the *Xtreme Home Run*.'

Luca was sitting pretty in second place and Xavier had

just made it through in tenth. They finished their beers in unison and stood up to go. Luca held his hand out to Xavier, who shook it heartily.

'May the best man win,' Liv said, raising her glass, 'and please don't kill yourselves.'

'Yes, be careful,' I said nervously. 'You are both winners, remember.' There was no doubt a chest-beating contest was about to commence but the vibe didn't seem to be about the home run. The boys zipped up their jackets and pulled on their gloves. Xavier gave a wave as he headed to his snowboard and Luca clicked on his skis to glide over to the lift. His tanned skin in sharp contrast to the bright-pink stripes on his cheeks. A modern-day Tarzan.

'Good luck,' I said, and he gave me a sultry half-nod.

'Alright, alright, stop staring at them,' Liv said, ruining my daydream as I watched Luca head off after Xavier.

'I'm not! Well, maybe I am a little bit. I'd forgotten what it feels like to check out a man,' I said, giggling, the alcohol taking over my brain and mouth.

'Don't worry, it'll come back to you in no time, babes; it's animal instinct.'

'I still don't know how it will play out with George, but either way, I've got a lot of making up to do.'

'Look around you, mate; there are literally thousands of men here – *thousands*. Choose whichever one you like,' Liv said, pointing at the sea of men surrounding us. She was right, there were men as far as the eye could see. French, English, German, blond, bald, short, tall, fit, fat. You could design the exact man you wanted and find him somewhere in the crowd. Yet that conversation with Luca had sent me a bit funny inside. Was it his devastating good looks, his limitless wealth, his skiing talent, his air of entitlement? Was it any of those things? Or just the look he gave me that sent me off kilter? It was the first time in a long time a man had looked at me like that. He would be the perfect revenge boyfriend. That'd show George. When I was hanging out with the Blanchets, jetting in for a weekend at the chalet. Luca was everything George wanted to be. Imagine how annoyed he'd be if I ended up with the fully-fledged version, having nearly married the wannabe prototype.

'Our competitors are now ready to go. Are *you* ready to watch them flyyy?' the commentator shouted. The crowd cheered and rang their cowbells as the guy in first place skied down the mountain, casually spraying snow left and right, until he hit the jump and spun like a helicopter, effortlessly delivering a classic 1080. His landing was soft and relaxed as he lifted one leg in the air and gracefully ground to a halt. What. A. Pro.

'Now *he's hot*,' Liv said. 'Go and chase after him?' We watched as he skied to the barrier to wait for his score and kissed his boyfriend on the lips.

'Looks like he's taken,' I said.

Luca flew out of the starting blocks and bulleted down the mountain for maximum speed. He was going to kill himself. He hit the jump at a frightening pace, flying off the front and flipping himself backwards, followed by a clean 360 before landing sharply and swooshing to a stop. It was unbelievable. The first guy had been awarded ninety-two points, but Luca's performance earnt him ninety-four, putting him straight back into the top spot.

The next seven competitors came down, one by one, performing various jumps and grabs. One faceplanted and another was stretchered off with a dislocated knee. Xavier was up last, and I hoped he hadn't seen the medical van beeping into action; we needed him to stay strong and not be spooked. There was only one snowboarder in the top ten and Xavier moved differently to the others as he snaked his way down the mountain, carving up the snow. He was doing little jumps as he went, to get into position for the big jump at the end. He hit the kicker and flew into the air, rolling like a gymnast as he bent forward and held onto his board. He went so fast, I couldn't count the turns, but the commentator was quick to confirm.

'Wowwww, that was Xavier Lavedrine, with an impressive 1440 in mid-air. I've never seen anything like it! Let's hear it for him, ladies and gentlemen!' The cowbells jangled as Xavier unstrapped his board and walked out to the exit, punching the air as he went. There was a much longer pause ahead of Xavier's score being announced and the crowd had started a disgruntled slow clap.

'The final score is in and it's going to disrupt things, as number five-four-oh, Xavier Lavedrine, has been awarded a total of ninety-five from the judges. It's a mighty win for the snowboarders today,' he boomed, dragging Xavier over and holding his hand in the air.

Liv and I were standing on our seats and cheering.

'Go on Xavier!' Liv whooped.

'Wooohoooo, yes, Xavier! Winner!' I shouted.

We ordered a round of celebratory beers and Jägerbombs, but the boys took ages to come back, so we had to drink ours followed by theirs while the awards ceremony took place. Xavier took his position on the gold podium, with

Luca winning silver and a ballerina-esque woman winning bronze, and then they eventually made their way back to us.

'Congratulations!' I shouted, hugging Xavier first and giving him a big kiss on the cheek. 'You were amazing.'

'Thanks,' he said, going pink.

'Awesome,' Liv said, hugging him after me as I made my way over to Luca and kissed him on both cheeks.

'We won some kit as well, so it wasn't just a trophy,' Xavier said. '500 Swiss francs of North Face vouchers.'

'Please,' Luca held his vouchers out to Xavier, 'take mine too. I only wear Salomon.'

Liv raised her eyebrows and gave me a funny look. The power-play was still power-playing. Xavier gave a charming smile and dismissed the offer with a wave of his hand.

'*Non*. They are your prize for second place,' he said as the testosterone batted back and forth.

Luca gave an accepting nod and tossed them on the table. 300 Swiss francs for second prize.

'If you don't want them, we can take Holly shopping and get her some new gear,' Liv said, 'then she can stop borrowing mine.'

'But I love your clothes so much! I especially love your boarding pants,' I said, kicking my leg out to demonstrate them to everyone. There were so soft and comfortable.

'SO DO I,' Liv replied.

'Yes of course,' Luca said, 'take them.'

'I can drive you to Le Châble this weekend if you like?' Xavier offered.

'*Non, non*, don't you remember you are seeing your wife this weekend, Xavier?' Luca said, putting his arm around me with a smirk. 'I'll take you shopping in Le Châble, Holly, no problem.' Luca was staring at Xavier strangely and I was stuck in the middle of their weirdness so I signalled to the barman for a final round of beers. It was nearly 3 p.m. and we'd been sitting around drinking and cheering all day. The sun was starting to slump in the sky and we had time for one last drink before the mountain lost its glow and turned grey and cold.

'Did you get a video?' Xavier asked, hopefully.

'Sure did, mate,' Liv said, pulling out her phone so Xavier could zoom in on himself and re-enact the run. 'I got you too, Luca; I'll show you after.'

Luca sidled over while Xavier and Liv huddled over her phone.

'Congratulations,' I said, 'your jump was amazing.'

'As the Nike ad says – you don't win silver, you lose gold. I'll do better next time. You should give jumping a go on your skis,' Luca said, giving me a friendly nudge, 'it's fun.'

I laughed, 'Oh well, I'm not actually a…'

'I prefer women on skis. So much more elegant than the snowboarders.'

Oh God. I didn't like to correct him.

'Hmm, yes, well, I'm really a very basic beginner at the moment, so I won't be trying the jumps any time soon,' I said. Or indeed, ever.

'I was going to ask if you could help me with something tomorrow? I need a second opinion on a Champagne bar I'm considering investing in, another nose alongside mine to taste the Champagne and review the overall experience.'

'Really? Wow! Of course I will. I'd love to.'

'The business is doing incredibly well by all accounts, but I want to sample it for myself and get another point of view.

We will be mystery shoppers: observe how busy it is, the type of clientele the bar attracts and whether the experience is worth the effort.'

'Undercover noses. Sounds good to me.'

'Excellent. We have to ski there, so let's go tomorrow after breakfast. It is down an easy blue, so you'll be fine as a beginner.'

'Oh. Erm... really? Ski there on our skis, you mean?' I said, like an IDIOT.

'Yes Holly, on our skis,' Luca said, looking at me oddly.

'Do we need to visit it so soon?' I said slowly, to buy myself some thinking time.

'*Carpe diem.* Seize the day. The skiing route is straightforward, and I can give you some pointers if you get stuck.'

I'd need a lot more than pointers, having never put a pair of skis on *in my life*. How to start, how to stop and how not to fall off the edge would all be very welcome information to start with. My mountain prowess was pretty much zero. I was the seasonaire equivalent of a child clinging to the edge of the swimming pool while the rest of the class learnt butterfly.

'I really want to help and it's so kind of you to offer on the skiing tips, but I've actually got an appointment tomorrow lunchtime that I can't miss...' I said, flailing desperately, in a bid to put him off.

'At the weekend then?' Luca said, throwing his skis down and clicking his boots in. 'It's no problem.'

No problem for him. I needed to get on YouTube and watch some tuition videos ASAP.

'Right. Well, I suppose that could work,' I said, feeling

queasy. That would give me three days to prepare and have several *appointments*. AKA beginner's ski lessons. I couldn't throw myself down the mountain on skis without an ounce of experience.

'Good. Let's meet at the top of the lift on Sunday at 2 p.m.,' Luca said, giving me a double kiss, before turning to the others. 'I am going down to the village; I have a few things to do,' he said. 'Congratulations again, Xavier. Send me the videos, Liv; I'd like to see how I can improve.'

He gave us all a final nod before skiing off. He'd left his North Face vouchers on the table, under his empty glass. 300 Swiss francs was two months' wages out here. It was criminal to discard them like rubbish.

'Shall I take them back to him?' I said, wiping away the ring of condensation Luca's beer glass had left.

'He doesn't want a reminder of second place,' Xavier said with a smile. 'Take them for your shopping trip, Holly.'

'I can't, I feel too cheeky,' I said.

Liv laughed. 'Why? He said you could have them – money means nothing to him.'

'Keep them with yours for now,' I said, pressing them into Xavier's hand. His touch was warm and soft as he wrapped his fingers around mine and smiled.

'Fine, I'll take them, so they don't go to waste, but they're not for me to spend.'

Sixteen

15th December

Oh God. Today was going to be the day I died. And my friends would not say *at least she died doing what she loved* – they would all be aghast at the idea I'd died careering off a mountain, having barely skied before, trying to impress a boy. *What was she thinking?* they'd say. *She didn't even have a freezer*, they'd say. Oh God, oh God. I'd booked myself a beginner's ski lesson as soon as the phone lines had opened and now three of us were stood with an instructor on the green run, eager to learn. Me, a grown woman of twenty-seven, in my bodged-together ski gear, and twin teenagers in matching mint outfits, whose alpha parents had dropped them off with big smiles and waves, before whizzing off towards the grown-up runs.

'Good morning class, my name is Alice and I'll be teaching our beginner's ski class today. Have any of you done any skiing or snowboarding before?' Alice was tall, with cropped, white-blonde hair, brown eyes, and an accent I couldn't place. She was wearing a nice pair of green salopettes, which put me instantly at ease. Unless she was doing it ironically.

I tentatively put up my hand. 'I've done some snowboarding, but I'm in no way an expert,' I said, faux-modestly.

'Excellent. And you girls?'

The twins shook their heads in unison.

'This is the first time…'

'…we've ever been skiing.'

They shared the sentence, then giggled.

'OK, so we might have a difference in capability, but let's see how we get on,' Alice smiled. I very much doubted there would be any difference in capability and silently kicked myself for suggesting I had experience. I would no doubt be worse than hopeless.

'The first step is to get you all up the mountain, so follow me,' Alice said.

She used her poles as leverage to get her skis moving forward and the three of us copied her exactly, like ducklings behind a mother duck. The sliding along bit was surprisingly easy; maybe it wouldn't be that bad after all.

And then we reached the button lift. A terrifying machine propelling metal seats on thin wires up and down the mountain at speed. The seats whirred aggressively around as innocent skiers and boarders attempted to grab one and jump on, taking their lives in their hands. The button slowed for no one. It was like entering the Labyrinth through a monster's chomping mouth. You had to choose your moment.

'OK girls, you will go first, and I will follow.' Alice walked us to the front of the queue, and I ignored the dirty looks as the man in charge unclipped the rope and let us through. The man gestured at twin one to stand on a cross on the floor as the first button hurtled towards us. He wrestled it into order and simultaneously placed her hands on the wire, and the button between her legs, allowing her to elegantly sit down as the lift slowly dragged her up the mountain. Twin two did the same thing, making it look entirely effortless.

My helmet was so tightly fastened, I could feel my heart beating through my ears as I stepped onto the cross for my turn and waited. My metal button clanked around the corner, swinging dangerously towards me as the man grabbed it and slotted it into position. I held on for dear life and the slack in the wire eventually went taut as my skis started sliding up the hill. YES. I was doing it. I edged slowly up the mountain, and it all seemed to be going well until one of my skis wiggled off the smooth path the skiers had made and into the powder to the side. I could feel my leg being left behind as the ski wedged itself further and further into the snow, and the button took the rest of my body up the mountain.

'Let go, Holly!' Alice shouted from the button behind me. 'Let it gooo!'

Alright, Elsa. My legs were doing the splits up the mountain as I pulled the metal seat out from between my legs and inadvertently fired it towards twin two. I fell face-first into the snow, rolling to the side to save my stuck leg. Skiing wasn't going to be my sport. I clicked off the ski on my free leg and watched it shoot down the mountain before I could grab it, hitting some poor bloke who was trying to eat a croissant in peace. I gave him a wave to claim it as he angrily looked around. I'd retrieve it once I'd retrieved my leg. I inched myself backwards so I could dig my other ski out, carefully clicking it off my boot and wedging it into the snow next to my poles. I was running out of time to be Luca-ready for a casual ski on Sunday.

'Holly? Are you OK?' Alice swooshed over to me, knocking my second ski over and sending it flying down the mountain after the first, hitting the croissant-man again, mid-bite. I gave him another wave.

'Yes, just a nice stretch,' I said, giving my inner thigh a rigorous rub.

'You nearly got to the top of the mountain, so bear with me and I will bring the girls down here to start our lesson.' With that, she swooshed off down the mountain, grabbing my skis from the croissant-man and hopped back up on the button lift to collect the twins. I couldn't imagine ever being that confident on the slopes. She was zipping up and down, navigating the mountain with a nonchalant ease. I'd packed one of Liv's protein flapjacks to enjoy should a moment present itself, so I unwrapped it and took a bite, bum-shuffling towards the piste, to be well clear of the button lift swinging past. I put my goggles on my head and lay back in the sun, enjoying the sweet taste of honey and nuts. There was plenty of time. I just needed Alice to teach me how to hoon it down a blue run by 2 p.m.

The three amigos came snowploughing towards me at a tortoise-pace, so I saw them coming a mile off. Alice gently pushed my skis over to me, making sure I caught each one and didn't send them careering down the piste a third time. I clicked them on and was ready to start.

'OK. So that was a snowplough. Very good work, Tina

and Gina. Holly, I will show you too and you can practise with us by following me.'

FFS, I only had three days. I couldn't snow-plough next to Luca while he was doing Olympic-level double flips; I needed to learn proper skiing and quick. Nonetheless, I followed Alice, Tina and Gina in an embarrassingly slow four-woman snake down the side of the mountain. We eventually got to the bottom and I side-eyed the button lift which was clunking and clicking as it dangerously circled innocent skiers.

'We will get the lift back up the mountain now. Holly, you go first, and I will wait until all three of you are at the top before I follow.'

I had no choice. The very least I needed to be able to do as a skier was get to the top of the mountain. I navigated my way to the side of the queue where the man gave me a look, took a deep breath, and let me through. This was going to be a very simple, mind-over-matter exercise. The lift transported thousands of people up the mountain every day. Those fourteen-year-old twins did it first time. The button would not defeat me.

I stood in position and watched as my allocated button jiggled towards me, swooping in fast and then slowing down as the man did his thing and I grabbed it with both hands. In seconds, I'd been scooped up by the lift and was once again making my way up the mountain, clinging on with everything I had, but this time mindful of keeping my skis facing forward and following in the tracks of all the button-lift success stories that had gone before me. And it worked. It was working. Every muscle in my body was clenched tightly and I was holding my breath, but it was working, I was successfully snailing my way up the hill. I didn't move, other than to adjust my skis when they occasionally went rogue, and as I reached the top, it felt like a new day was dawning. I was euphoric.

'Let go,' the man shouted at me, as I continued to cling to the button and slowly went around the top section of the lift. I wasn't sure how to get off so I held on with a vice-like grip.

'What are you doing? Let go of the button!' the man repeated in alarm, as the wire continued dragging me up and I rose into the air. I started to panic. If I let go now, I'd fall, but every millisecond I clung on meant I was going higher and higher. The man had run over by this point and was wrestling the button from me. He released it into the sky with a jolt as I fell in a heap on the floor.

'*Vous êtes folle!*' he said in disgust as I caterpillar-ed myself to safety. Tina and Gina had already dismounted and were standing neatly to the side. I managed to get myself up as if nothing had happened by the time Alice skied off the lift and came over to us.

'OK girls, we are now going to go down the mountain very slowly, using the full width of the slope for our practice. You need to keep your knees bent but soft and stay grounded in the soles of your feet. *Allez?*'

We all nodded and followed her lead down the mountain. It was unusually quiet on the piste, so we could take our time and go extra slow, which suited me just fine. If I could get it right going painfully slow, then it was just a matter of practice.

Alice gradually built us up over the course of the lesson to use slightly less of the mountain to traverse from left to right, but it was still the very basics of the basics of beginner's skiing. It wasn't going to cut it with Luca. I'd have to take a few risks when I met him on Sunday but at least I was getting direction from a professional teacher. It was one thing self-learning with Xavier by my side, but quite another when I was trying to blag the boss.

As I slowly swooshed along with the sun on my face, I took a moment to appreciate the magic of nature and actually enjoy myself. I was starting to see why people were into it. Skiing down a mountain was certainly something I never *ever* saw myself doing, but maybe it wasn't all freezing cold lifts and wet bums after all. There was something about the fierce concentration needed on the slopes that resulted in pure, unadulterated freedom. A genuine break from reality, from social media rabbit-holes and the frenetic pace of life. There was no time to think about anything else but getting down the mountain safely. I slowly arrived at the bottom of the slope just behind Tina and Gina, who were giving each other a high five.

'Excellent work, all of you,' Alice said, smiling around at us. 'I see lots of natural talent amongst you. It is just practice now you have the basics.'

'Thank you so much…' Tina said.

'…we've really enjoyed it,' Gina said.

'Are we safe to practise on blue runs, do you think?' I asked tentatively.

'Not yet,' Alice said, shaking her head. 'You work here, don't you?'

I nodded.

'Do the greens for a couple of weeks until you are comfortable, and then onto the blues. Girls, if you are only here for a week, I suggest you stay on the greens and get as much practice as possible. Maybe try a blue on your last day with your parents if you are feeling confident.'

If I spent the next three days practising on the green runs then I'd be fine on a gentle blue by Sunday. I smiled and nodded at Alice, about to completely ignore her advice.

'Time for me to go then, girls, but you have all done a wonderful job today. Remember, head up, stay confident and worry about what is in front of you, not what is behind you.'

Good advice – for life, in fact.

'Thank you, Alice,' I said, as I clicked out of my skis and scooped them up. 'Nice to meet you two, go safe,' I said to Tina and Gina as they waved and headed back towards the button.

No, thanks. I was going back to the chalet for some hot chocolate and cake and to gather myself together for Xavier's next lesson.

'Remind me of the menu again?' I stood still in the kitchen doorway, trying to remember the starter that had sounded so good.

'I've already told you once, Holly,' Xavier seemed annoyed as he read from his notepad. 'Savoury crème brûlée to start, cassoulet with parsnip gratin for main, and Reine de Saba to finish.'

'That's it. Crème brûlée is my favourite,' I said. 'So what's in a savoury one?'

'You're about to find out. We are cooking them together today,' Xavier said, his cheeks slightly pink. 'This recipe is my own invention, and it is *perfection*.'

I was excited already.

'Eggs, of course,' he continued, 'goat's cheese, brie, leeks, pink peppercorns, and a small amount of onion.' He kissed his thumb and forefinger together, then busied himself gathering the ingredients.

'Sounds amazing, let's do it,' I said, flicking the radio on and tying my apron, ready to get to work. 'Any word from Lord and Lady Blanchet?'

'Yes. Genevieve messaged to say she's arriving tomorrow lunchtime. She wasn't sure what Luca was up to, but she said not to worry about him. Do you know where he is?' he asked.

'Me? Of course not. Why would I know what he's up to?'

Xavier gave a half-shrug. 'I thought he was taking you shopping sometime?'

'Oh right, no, nothing yet and no idea if he even will. He was probably just saying it to be nice.'

'Well, no doubt he'll be here in the next few days,' Xavier said, handing me a box of twelve brown eggs. 'The crème brûlées are quite simple but we have to be precise and quick, otherwise they will flop.'

'OK, where do I start?' I asked.

'First you need to separate the yolks,' Xavier said, putting a large glass bowl in front of me. I carefully cracked open the eggs, extracting each yolk from its gooey counterpart and plopping all twelve into the bowl.

'Now for all the other ingredients,' Xavier said, handing them to me, 'finely slice this leek, like this…' he cut the leek into microscopic ribbons, 'roughly chop this onion and blend together a slice of goat's cheese and a slice of brie.'

I set about the leek with a sharp knife and took a painfully long time to chop it. How did Xavier do it with such speed and precision? I put the cheeses in a bowl and tried to paste them together, but more of it was sticking to the spatula than anywhere else.

'Warm it in a pan,' Xavier called, one eye on me as I tried to work it all out.

I eventually had all the different ingredient elements ready to go.

'Good,' Xavier said, impressed, 'now whisk the egg yolks with half a litre of milk and some salt and pepper, then gradually fold the other ingredients in.'

'Got it,' I said, enjoying the gentle vibration of the whisk against the bowl.

'That's it,' he said, his eyes fixed permanently on the mixture, 'now keep whisking while I get the peppercorns.' He went over to the larder and started rifling through the shelves, moving things around at speed. The mixture was already light as air, so I gave it another blast of the electric whisk for luck, then set it to one side, going over to see if I could help.

'The pink peppercorns are next to the spices,' I said to his back. Xavier turned around with a jar of gherkins in one hand and a bag of sugar in the other.

'You're supposed to be whisking!' he said, rushing over to the bowl.

'I've already done it,' I said proudly.

'You don't stop halfway through! You have to continuously blend the mixture until it goes into the oven,' Xavier said in alarm.

'Oh right! Sorry!' I said, picking up the whisk and turning it back on.

'It's too late now,' he said, 'you've left it too long. It will taste like a quiche.'

'But I was only a few seconds. Are you sure?' I said, examining the whisked mixture, which seemed perfectly fine.

Xavier gave me an irritated look. 'Yes. I'm sure,' he said, taking the bowl from me. 'In fact, by way of demonstration, we will cook these as well as a correctly prepared batch and then you can see and taste for yourself.' He silently ground a handful of peppercorns in the mortar and pestle and added them to my mixture which I poured into the eight white ramekins sat waiting. I then repeated the whole process, this time continually whisking as Xavier instructed, adding the peppercorns at the very end, and filling another set of ramekins, ready to cook. All sixteen went into the oven as Xavier clashed about with the washing up and I tidied everything away.

'Sorry, Xavier. I didn't do it on purpose,' I said eventually, breaking the silence, not sure why it was such a big deal.

'You have huge potential, Holly, but you have to listen,' he ranted. 'This is the difference between an average chef and one with a Michelin star.' He shook his head.

The oven timer went off and we pulled the two trays of crème brûlées out for cooling. They all looked identical as we transferred them to the wire rack, so only time and the taste test would tell.

'Now they rest for half an hour, and we finish them with honey and sesame seeds to refrigerate overnight. The top needs to crack in the same way a crème brûlée dessert would crack. The honey gives a delicious sweetness in contrast to the sharp taste of the goat's cheese.'

'What would be wrong with a quiche-like texture here?' I asked, genuinely curious.

'There's nothing wrong with it. It just doesn't give the delicate smoothness that we want. It is the difference between serving a rough-chopped terrine and a smooth pâté.'

I nodded. 'So either could work, but not for what we want to do?'

'Exactly. And because we are serving with homemade granary toasts, we have the texture of the seeds and nuts in the bread and the saltiness of the butter to consider.'

I nodded again.

'You need to think about the entirety of each dish in relation to all the elements, as well as all the other courses.' It felt like Xavier was being unnecessarily cross with me and I wasn't sure why.

'Of course, sorry. I didn't realise stopping blending would make such a difference.'

Once the brûlées were cool enough, we drizzled a thick layer of honey onto each, sprinkled them with sesame seeds and put them in the fridge to set.

'I'm desperate to try one,' I said, looking at them longingly as Xavier slid the tray into the fridge.

'That's enough Chef School for today,' he said abruptly, taking off his apron and hanging it up. His phone started ringing and *CHRISTINA* flashed up on the screen. He pressed the green button and her face appeared: alabaster skin with a neat, black bob and big, red lips. Of course she was gorgeous. Gorgeous and talented. They were quite the power couple.

'*Bonjour, Cherie,*' she breathed happily into the phone.

'*Salut*,' he replied, turning his back on me and walking down the corridor to his bedroom, leaving me stood in the kitchen alone.

Seventeen

17th December

I snuck around the back of the chalet to the ski room to stash my skis and boots. I'd been for another early morning ski lesson and didn't want any tricky questions from Liv and Xavier while I was being snow-ambidextrous.

'Have you been out already?' Xavier asked as I padded into the kitchen.

'I have,' I said, swiping a slice of ginger cake from the platter he was preparing and rearranging the other pieces to hide the gap.

'*Non, non, non!* They're going upstairs,' he said, shooing me away with a tea towel.

'Sorry, I need sustenance,' I said, taking a big bite, 'I need to recoup some calories.'

Xavier was stirring a large pan of simmering milk while slowly pouring in chocolate sauce. The smell was delicious.

'I'll make you a hot chocolate,' he said, gesturing at the kitchen stool next to the counter. I watched as he whisked the liquid into a froth and the hot chocolate started to thicken. My mouth watered as he poured it into a round bowl, lumped cream on top with chocolate sprinkles and placed it in front of me.

'No marshmallows?' I asked, hopefully.

'Pfttt! Absolutely not. Hot chocolate doesn't need anything extra to sweeten it. What is it with the English and Americans turning hot drinks into desserts? Keep it simple.'

The bowl had no handles. This was how the French served their hot chocolate. Boiling hot and impossible to drink. I'd have to just enjoy the sweet, chocolatey aroma until it was cool enough to pick up. Lapping at it like a cat wasn't really an option. I watched as the cream melted into a pool in the middle of the hot liquid, leaving a greasy film.

'This looks nice and cosy. What's going on?' Liv asked, bursting into the kitchen, dressed in her uniform.

'Xavier's sorting me out,' I said, biting into my ginger cake.

'Course he is,' Liv said, swooping in for a piece of cake herself.

'No more cake, you two! The platter is starting to look paltry!' Xavier said, sprinkling raspberries in the gaps Liv and I had left. He chopped up some strawberries as additional garnish and added them to the subterfuge.

'What are you up to this arvo?' Liv asked, grabbing the platter of cake and a flask of hot chocolate to take upstairs. 'Boarding practice?'

'Er, no, not today. Luca has asked me to go with him to check out a Champagne bar he wants to invest in.'

'Has he?' Xavier frowned. 'He doesn't usually need a second opinion on these things.'

'Ooh, look at you out and about with the big boss,' Liv said, nudging me.

'I think he wants me to test the quality of the Champagne?'

'What kind of line is that? Sounds a bit suss, babes,' Liv said.

'Does it? I couldn't say no though, could I? He's the boss.' I had to assume it was all above board. Luca had given me no reason to think otherwise. 'What are you guys up to?'

'I'm heading back to Paris for a few days,' Xavier said.

'You must be desperate to see your wife,' I said, grabbing a couple of strawberries, 'I hope you'll be wining and dining her after all this time.'

'Something like that. I need to sort out some stuff at the restaurant too, but I'll be back on Thursday,' Xavier said.

'Well enjoy it. Don't worry about us – Liv and I have everything under control.'

'The menus are written out here.' Xavier pointed to the noticeboard where the next three days of menus were scribbled out and pinned up. 'I have absolute faith in you to look after things while I'm away.'

I gave them both a wave, biting into a strawberry as I retraced my steps to the ski room and reluctantly stuffed my feet back into my tight-fitting ski boots, still damp from my morning lesson. I picked up my skis and poles, ready to go again.

'Holly?' I turned to find Luca stood in the doorway. All six foot of him.

'Ah! *Bonjour*, Luca,' I said, wanting to be professional.

'Are you on your way to meet me?' he asked, putting his size twelves into his made-to-measure ski boots and zipping up his jacket.

'Yes, I just popped back for some lunch,' I said. 'Shall I go on ahead and see you up there?'

'Not at all, wait a minute and we can go together,' he said, pulling his snood across his nose and mouth and clipping his helmet into position. Oh God. I was going to die snow-ploughing next to him. At the very least of embarrassment. We left the warmth of the chalet and crunched out into the snow, walking in amicable silence through the town towards the ski lift. Rachael was in the *pâtisserie* and gave us a wave as we walked past. I shook my ski poles at her like a seasoned pro and as we approached the lift, instead of joining the back of the queue like everyone else, Luca walked straight to the front and the liftman waved us through and into the bubble.

'Life is too short for queues,' he said, giving me a slow smile. 'We go up the mountain here and meet my guide at the top.'

Oh God, I was definitely going to die.

'Your guide?'

'I have a guide who escorts me around the mountain,' Luca said, as if it was obvious. 'He will drive us to the ski area which links to the Champagne bar.' He was sitting so close, I could feel his pulse pounding through his thigh. Or was it mine? 'Your appointment was OK on Friday?'

'Was it?' He'd lost me again.

Luca looked at me strangely. 'You said you had an appointment?'

'Oh. Sorry. Yes... no... I had to have my skis adjusted,' I said quickly.

'Sharpened? So you can go faster?' he asked.

Oh fuck. That didn't bode well. Was there such a thing as getting skis blunted to slow them to a virtual standstill? 'No, just the bindings,' I said, throwing words out and hoping he wouldn't ask anything else.

Luca nodded, giving his reflection an approving eyebrow in the window behind me.

The lift swung into the station and we waited for the sea of people to drain out. The two of us were the last to leave, boinging off towards the exit. Again, as I went to go right, Luca turned left and beeped his wrist through a black steel door.

'Another short-cut?' I asked, delighted, as Luca held the door open for me. It led straight onto a travellator that took us through the middle of the mountain. Instead of the bun fight I normally encountered with Xavier and Liv as we wrestled through the crowds, Luca and I swept along a well-lit tunnel, with The Killers blaring out on all sides. Another couple were coming the other way and waved as they passed. The woman looked like a film star and was dripping in gold necklaces with gold and black ski goggles to match. I suddenly felt a bit self-conscious in Liv's Roxy pants as we approached the end of the travellator and Luca bleeped us through a second door out into the blinding sun.

'*Bonjour, bonjour*.' A small man in a dark-orange jacket and black trousers welcomed us with two glasses of Champagne.

'*Salut*, Charlie,' Luca replied, taking one, 'this is Holly, who joins us today.'

'Good morning,' he said brightly, handing me the second glass which I readily accepted, taking a large gulp. For my nerves.

'Hi, nice to meet you,' I said, easily finishing it with a second and third mouthful.

'Are we ready for *Taverne à Champagne*?' Charlie asked, smiling at us both, his black curls making a bid for freedom from under his headband. My knees were knocking at the thought of these two pros anywhere near me on the piste.

'I should flag that I'm very much a beginner,' I said, smiling, 'and I'm not being modest; I've literally only skied a few times before.' Three times. But who's counting?

Luca and Charlie exchanged looks.

'Not a problem, Holly; it is a short, easy ski to the bar,' Charlie said cheerily, slapping Luca on the back. 'Now come along the two of you. I take your glasses back.' We handed him our empty flutes which he somehow folded into his jacket. 'Follow me just along the slope here and yes… Holly, please…?'

Charlie led us over to a brand-new skidoo that looked more like a luxury speedboat than the knackered old go-carts I'd seen taking people up and down the mountain. Smooth, metallic black paint with oversized skis on the front and a caterpillar track at the back. We'd be like royalty travelling in this. Charlie took my hand as I stepped up and over to sit in the back and Luca slotted in next to me.

'Do you like it?' he asked.

'Champagne and short-cuts? What's not to like? And we haven't even done any skiing yet – the best bit!' I was hoping if we faffed about for long enough, we'd only have time to do the bare minimum of skiing and could come safely back in the skidoo.

'Plenty of ski time when we get there, don't worry about that,' Charlie said, jumping on the front like a plasticine Wallace and starting up the engine.

'You look very chic in your ski gear,' Luca said, as we kadunked up the mountain, being thrown from side to side.

'Do I?' I blushed, knowing full well I had mascara goo in my eyes and frozen snot up my nose. Why was I getting all hot and flustered at Luca giving me the smallest amount of attention? His body pressed against mine as we sat tightly together in the back of the skidoo. This was supposed to be a work visit, so why did I feel like I was on a date that I wasn't prepared for? Probably because Luca was a prize-wagyu-beef-level hunk. His dark eyes sparkled as he stared at me, adding to the date vibes, but it had been so long since I'd been on one, maybe I was misreading the situation. Were the smouldering looks just a French thing? I wasn't sure if I should try and smoulder back or laugh it off.

He put his non-George arm around me to steady the impact of Charlie riding the skidoo like a jet-ski and I breathed in his expensive, musky scent. The higher we went, the more bones I anticipated breaking when we eventually reached our destination and had to start making our way back down.

'Here we are,' Charlie said, finally shuddering to a stop. Luca and I dismounted.

'My friends, the plan today is to stay on these few pistes and enjoy ourselves,' Charlie said, gesturing out at the snowy playground before us. 'We can go up and down until we get fed up and then...?' he stopped and looked at me, questioning.

'The Champagne bar?'

'*Mais oui*. Champagne,' he said, delighted, 'Luca – we can go off-piste a little later if you want to go higher into the mountain?'

'*Non*, Holly and I will be staying here to ski,' Luca replied. Would we? Oh God, this was going to be the most humiliating day ever. I gave him a quick smile and clicked my skis on. Into the valley of death.

Charlie had driven us to the top of the mountain and the Champagne bar was at the bottom. I slid carefully forward on my skis and peered over the edge. Three ski slopes finished in a bowl of snow at the bottom and were overlooked by the bar. We were on top of the world, with mountain peaks all around: the ultimate playground for the rich.

'What is this place?' I asked with wonder, staring at all the glamorous people launching themselves down the piste. Women in big fur hats, leather ski-suits, oversized sunglasses, and dark lipstick. I felt like the work experience girl on a film set.

'It is only reachable by private skidoo and helicopter,' Luca said, 'so it is much quieter than the public pistes. Very good if you are learning.'

I watched the skiers and snowboarders hurtling down the three slopes and couldn't see anyone who looked like they were 'learning'. We should all be forced to wear red helmets and L plates until we've passed a basic ski test to prove we aren't a danger. I wondered what kind of learner Luca was expecting me to be.

'Are you ready?' Luca asked, nestling his goggles into position.

I nodded. I was not ready. Luca threw himself down the mountain and slalomed his way out of sight. OK. I counted to ten and put myself into the snow plough position, gently taking off and following a huge, snaking loop, like Alice had taught me. The slopes were nice and empty, and it wasn't too steep, so there was plenty of space to spread out. With the afternoon sun on my face and that lovely feeling of freedom on the mountain, it was almost like I was enjoying myself. Maybe there was something to this skiing lark after all. Charlie shlooped quietly behind me, lurking in case of emergency, as Luca whizzed past for the second time, head down and skis straight, going like a bullet.

'Follow your arm and lean into the loop like this,' Charlie said, skiing out ahead of me with his hand in the air, then lowering it and using it to steer. I followed exactly what he was doing and through some wizardry, my baggy loops became a smidge smaller. I was becoming a pro skier by osmosis. I did three very gentle runs on the easy blue and was done. Luca zipped past me five times then quickly graduated onto the black and was up and down it like a sewing machine, getting his Olympic-level practice in. Thank God skiing was such a singular sport. Once you're on the mountain, you're kind of on your own. Unless you've got Charlie on your tail. Or Xavier. He didn't leave my side on that first day out together. I stopped at the bottom and signalled to Charlie that I was done, unclicking my skis, and locking them up with my poles next to the bar.

'You don't need to worry about them being stolen.' I

turned to find a very sweaty Luca behind me, red-faced from his intense ski session.

'Are they not cool enough for this set?' I asked, turning the Intersport barcodes over. I was probably the only person this side of the mountain with rented skis.

'I can't imagine there are many thieves up here, but I suppose you never know,' he said, propping up his designer skis and poles, monogrammed with inter-looping Ls and Bs.

'Time for a break?' I asked.

'I'm done skiing for today,' Luca said, much to my joy and delight.

'Really? That's a shame. OK, well, tomorrow is another day,' I said, in faux disappointment.

'Don't let me stop your practice,' he said, gesturing back up the mountain, 'make the most of it.'

I quickly backtracked. 'No, no, I've had lots of practice today. I don't want to overdo it.'

We left our skis and walked towards the bar. A large wooden sign with *Taverne à Champagne* in individual, battered gold letters creaked gently in the breeze, welcoming us into a bar area sculpted from ice. It was a feast for the eyes, with pyramids of glasses decorating the shelves, flanked on all sides by bottles of Champagne from every one of the French houses. Bollinger, Moët, Pommery, Cristal, they were all represented with bottles of all sizes on display. The regular bottles and magnums looked tiny in comparison to their older siblings – the eight-bottle Methuselahs and sixteen-bottle Balthazars – both of which seemed extremely lavish until I spied a couple of forty-bottle Melchizedeks on the bottom shelf. There were tables and chairs covered in sheepskin rugs and people quaffing Champagne everywhere.

'*Bonjour*, hello, welcome.' A beanpole-esque waiter appeared as we approached the bar. 'Follow me, please.' We walked past a huge firepit and were seated in a polished wooden booth. I sank into the cosiness of the red, velvet cushions as the waiter hovered over us.

'Would you like to order some Champagne?' he asked, handing us both a menu.

'Is there anything else?' I laughed.

'Water?' Luca smiled.

'I actually would like some water, but Champagne sounds good too,' I said.

The waiter gave a nod and scurried off leaving us to peruse the enormous selection of Champagnes. This was *definitely* one for my socials. I held the menu up and took a surreptitious snap, blocking Luca's face but catching his muscley arm and the Rolex on his wrist.

#ChampagneValley #ChampagneLifestyle #HowIRolex

That'd piss George off.

'Have you decided?' The waiter returned and filled our water glasses and Luca gestured at me to choose. Eek – I hadn't properly looked.

'Are we getting a glass or a bottle,' I asked quietly. The prices were eye-watering, so if I was in any way expected to pay, I'd be sticking with the water then skidoo-ing it home.

'Whatever you like,' he said. Ahmagaaddd, that made the decision harder.

I ordered two glasses of the Moët rosé and there was the faintest nod from Luca to confirm I'd made a good choice.

'Moët's rosé is far superior to its white,' he said.

We settled into our seats, which were heated from within, and the waiter handed us woollen blankets to keep us extra snug. There were heaters above us and the firepit crackled quietly in the corner, keeping us warm, despite being surrounded by snow. I took my ski jacket off to reveal Liv's low-cut, red top and Luca stripped down to a long-sleeved purple thermal and put his sunglasses on. Oozing confidence, his arms and legs all over the place as he lounged comfortably in his chair.

'This is the first *Taverne à Champagne* and they are looking for investment to expand,' Luca said.

'It's pretty impressive,' I said, looking around, as Luca's ski boot rested against mine under the table. Maybe he couldn't feel that I was there through his boot. I moved my foot away and a few seconds later, he moved his to rest back against mine. 'Are we here to test out the service or the vibe?'

'Both,' Luca replied, 'and the Champagne, of course.'

'In case they are serving Prosecco?'

'*Non*, for our own pleasure.'

'Well, it seems excellent so far. They must make a fortune?' I said as a waiter walked past with a magnum of Premier Cru Mumm and 4 glasses.

Luca laughed. 'That's the idea,' he said.

The waiter reappeared with a half-bottle of rosé, an ice bucket and two glasses. He peeled back the pale-pink foil, popped the cork, and expertly poured, the bubbles fizzing with excitement to have escaped their prison.

'Cheers!' I said, holding my glass up and clinking with Luca.

'*Santé*,' he said, 'to us.'

'To us, making it back down the mountain alive,' I laughed, as I took a sip of my Champagne. Which. Was. Delicious. I took another sip to be certain, but it was like no rosé Champagne I'd ever tasted before.

'What is this?' I asked, taking a closer look at the pink liquid in my glass and reaching for the bottle.

'They only serve the very best in this bar,' Luca said, amused. 'The standard rosé is the Moët Grand Cru, and the quality goes up from there. Your palate is so impressive.'

WTAF. I really hoped there was no expectation of us splitting the bill – this sort of quality was probably £100 a glass. It was too late to put it back in the bottle now.

'It all goes on the chalet tab,' Luca said, reading my worried face. 'We are here working, remember.'

'Ah, well that's very kind.' I breathed a sigh of relief and turned my sips into mouthfuls, enjoying the *exceptional* taste. A far cry from a few drinks in the local pub with George. The closest I got to a fizzy pink drink with him was a pint of Kopparberg. This was the life I was meant to live. Vintage Champagne paid for by hot, French men. I just needed to up my skiing game, so Luca invited me again.

'You are quite fascinating, Holly. Somehow both professional and scatty, with a good instinct for wine, but you seem a little lost. The mountains aren't your territory and you're too old to be a seasonaire – what brings you out here?'

'That's quite the CV summary,' I laughed. 'I thought you knew?'

Luca shook his head and lit a cigarette.

'Wellllll… I was engaged until a few months ago.' The words still didn't sound right. 'And when that didn't work out, I thought I'd try something completely different. A new chapter, a new challenge. A new me.'

'An interesting brief,' Luca said, his eyes still on me.

'It is. So I've started with a new job in a new country.'

'You have. Which is going very well.'

'And taken up a new sport,' I said, breezily, gesturing out at the mountain. 'What can I say? The transformation is in progress.'

Luca laughed. 'I saw you wriggling along the piste like a caterpillar, so that makes sense. I look forward to seeing you emerge as a butterfly.'

Eighteen

25th December

'Merry Christmas,' I whispered to myself, as I opened my eyes. I lay looking up at the ceiling for a few seconds and made my Christmas wish, in the same way I'd done every year since I could remember. *I wish I didn't feel so alone*. I glanced across at my wall of Blu Tacked photos and felt a pang of sadness. This was the first Christmas I'd ever spent away from my family, and I missed them. Mum had sent a box of presents and cards that were waiting for me under the bed and I blew a kiss to the photo of her and Dad, then one to Abi and one to Margot as I took a moment to reflect on what this day should have been. My first Christmas as a married woman. Maybe I'd never have one of those now. Liv's empty bed was a visual reminder, if I needed one, that I was the only single person in the chalet this Christmas. Rachael and David would be coupled up and here for lunch. Liv was spending the day with Bella, and Xavier would have been in Paris with his wife but was saving his holiday to spend New Year's Eve with her instead.

Me: *Merry Christmas Mum! Miss you all so much xx Give Dad and Basil a kiss from me and I'll call you later xx*

Me: *Merry Christmas Abi!! Sending you a Christmas cuddle! Xx*

Me: *Joyeux Noël Margot. Bisous xx*

I fired out a few pre-emptive WhatsApps in the hope of getting some back. I was in two minds about sending one to George but decided not to. He hadn't looked at any of my Stories since the Champagne bar with Luca, and if he really cared, he'd message me.

My phone pinged, but it wasn't from George.

Liv: *Happy Christmas Holly!*

I replied to Liv and tried to forget about George, opening the curtains to my first White Christmas after a lifetime of hoping for one. The same cosy snow scene I'd been looking at for the past month. A winter wonderland. I cracked open the window and there was absolute silence. The lifts were closed, and the air held that sacred quiet that only happens on Christmas morning. That collective peace on earth for one day only, or a few hours at least, when the world stops.

'Morning, Holly,' Xavier called from the doorway, wearing red pyjamas covered in tiny toy soldiers, 'Merry Christmas.'

'Merry Christmas!' I replied, giving him a double kiss. It was nice to see his face.

'Do you fancy helping with the food today? I know it's technically your day off, but…'

'*Oui!* I mean yes. I'd love to,' I said, relieved to have something to keep me busy.

'It's just us for breakfast,' he said, 'and I like to do Eggs Benedict with muffins on Christmas Day – sound good?'

I nodded. 'Have they got a Christmassy twist?'

'Not really, but I can add a sprig of holly to your plate if you like?'

'Er... no thanks, I've got enough Holly going on,' I replied.

Xavier was the perfect combination of solid and manly, with his bed head and morning stubble, and soft and festive in his cute pyjamas and green elf socks. His wife was missing an absolute treat. I'd worn my traditional reindeer onesie to make me feel more at home. Dad had bought the matching set a few years back: Mummy, Daddy and Rudolph for me. Snuggling into it on Christmas Eve always signalled the start of the festivities. Xavier launched into action as soon as we got to the kitchen, wrestling the turkey out of the fridge and unwrapping it to rest at room temperature, then going back for the ham for breakfast and filling a pan with water to poach our eggs.

'*Plan du Loup* eggs I presume?'

'They're the best!' he replied, with a smile.

I put a Christmas playlist on Spotify, and Wham's 'Last Christmas' kicked in.

'Is this the sort of thing you listen to at home?' I asked.

'*Oui*, but in French.'

'Oh yes, of course,' I said, turning it up. 'It feels so strange not to be at home for Christmas morning. This is the first time I've ever been away. It must be even weirder for you, to not wake up with your wife?'

'*Oui*, but the restaurant is fully booked in Paris, so it's how it must be this year.'

'Have you FaceTimed?' I asked.

'We've had a few messages this morning.'

'A few messages? Bloody hell, Xavier, don't overdo it on the romance, will you?'

'Don't worry.' He smiled. 'I'll call her later and we'll see each other on New Year's Eve.'

Oh God. Another bloody single milestone to drag myself through. I'd have to knock myself out with some brandy and try and sleep through it.

The muffins popped out of the toaster and Xavier buttered them generously, adding the eggs and the ham, then going back to vigorously whisk the hollandaise sauce before pouring out two generous portions. I was mesmerised by his breakfast dance, slowly moving from one thing to the next as he brought everything together.

'Coffee?' he asked, jolting me from my daydream.

'Yes please, but I'll make it,' I said jumping up to help.

'*Non, non*, relax,' he said. 'Eat it while it's hot.' He put the two breakfast plates on the table, poured us both an orange juice and filled the cafetière before sitting down to join me.

'This is quite the Christmas treat, *Monsieur Lavedrine*,' I said. '*Merci beaucoup*.'

'You're very welcome,' he said, with a big smile. 'Here's to a Holly jolly Christmas!'

My eggs were perfectly cooked, bright-orange and runny, with thin, crispy ham covered in rich hollandaise sauce. The ham had the salty tastiness of gammon, contrasting perfectly with the eggs and buttery muffin. It was the definition of food porn.

'This is exactly what I need. Can't I just eat this and go back to bed? What better way to celebrate Christmas than with a delicious breakfast followed by a film in bed and a bottle of Baileys?'

'Sounds good,' Xavier said, as if it were an invitation, 'but we have guests, remember?'

'I don't mean together, obviously,' I said, blushing to make it obviously, obvious.

'Obviously,' Xavier replied with a Christmas twinkle in his eyes.

'So, what's the plan with the food?' I asked, looking forward to the cooking chaos. 'I'll be your willing sous-chef – as always – just tell me what you need.'

'Rachael and David aren't coming until 2 p.m. so we have plenty of time,' Xavier said, easy and relaxed. 'We take our time over breakfast, we get ready – maybe a Christmas day plunge to get the blood pumping, and then we start cooking around 12 p.m. to eat at 4 p.m.'

'4 p.m.?' I said, incredulously. 'That's almost the end of the day!'

'It's a dinner-lunch. Dunch.' Xavier replied.

I savoured the final mouthful of my breakfast, sad to see it go. This was going to be quite different to every other Christmas cooking experience I'd had. The adrenaline rush of speed-chopping vegetables while Jamie Oliver reassured me on timings from the TV. George would only eat PAXO stuffing, his mum didn't eat peas but loved green beans, his dad liked a Yorkshire pudding but only if it was Aunt Bessie's, whereas Mum liked hers homemade. Dad wasn't keen on turkey, so I always did him a steak and George's sister was a vegan, so her stuffed mushrooms had to be cooked away from everything else. It was quite the bloody effort. I was used to running around non-stop, smeared in olive oil, checking everyone was okay. Always the last to get dressed, without a scrap of make-up on for the Christmas photos. I fleetingly wondered who would be cooking for George and his family this year.

'Dunch sounds good,' I said, 'but I'll give the plunge pool a miss.'

'Come on Holly – it'll make you feel alive,' Xavier said, loading our plates into the dishwasher and heading down the corridor.

'Honestly, I just don't…' *like it*, I finished silently. In fact, I hated it.

'You might not get another chance to plunge first thing on Christmas Day,' Xavier called, disappearing into his bedroom.

Good. I didn't want to experience any more freezing-cold moments in that pool of hell.

'I'll see you in the kitchen in ten,' I shouted after him. 'Enjoy!'

I jumped in the shower and felt perfectly alive enjoying the hot water thundering down on my head. I didn't need an icy shock to get my blood pumping. I felt clean and healthy and my skin was flushed and fresh. I put my Christmas outfit on – I'd bought a traditional Swiss jumper in navy and paired it with my jeans and trainers. We weren't officially working so we could cook in our real clothes like normal people. My bob had grown out and my hair was nearly to my shoulders, so I tied it up in a ponytail and took my box of presents from Mum and Dad into the kitchen. Xavier was already in there wearing the red version of my jumper and looked up with a smile.

'Do you feel better for it?' I asked.

'I'm not sure,' he said, looking pained, 'I feel like I might keel over at any moment.'

I put my present box by the door as a reminder to put it under the tree upstairs.

'Ah, Holly, how thoughtful, *merci*! I have a little something for you too,' Xavier said, rooting around in the cupboard and pulling out a beautifully wrapped present.

'Oh. Wow, thank you,' I said, taken aback. 'I'm so sorry, this isn't for you, actually; it's a present from home for me.'

'Of course,' Xavier said, slightly pink, 'I didn't mean you should have…'

'I did get you a little something, though,' I called, as I legged it back to the bedroom to grab the tiny presents I'd bought for Xavier, Liv, Rachael and David.

'*Non, non*, please, don't worry,' Xavier shouted after me.

My gift was embarrassingly small in comparison. 'I hadn't realised we were buying for each other properly,' I said, apologetically, as I carefully opened the pillow of a present Xavier had given me, the gold foil crinkling between my fingers. A North Face ski jacket sprang out from the wrapping, and I was almost too shocked to speak.

'Xavier! You can't buy me a ski jacket; it's too much!' I said, slightly overwhelmed.

'Not at all. I used the vouchers, so it was no trouble. I don't think Luca took you shopping?'

'No, he didn't.'

'Of course he didn't. He is all talk and no trousers. Or no jacket, in this case. Your jacket isn't warm enough, so it's important.'

'I can't believe it!' I threw my arms around Xavier and kissed him on the cheek. 'It's perfect!'

'I'm glad you like it,' he said, with a shy smile.

I tried it on over my Christmas jumper and ran to the

bathroom mirror. It was gorgeous. Deep purple, warm but not too padded, long enough to cover my bum, but chic and tight and flattering. I ran back to the kitchen to show Xavier again and do a twirl.

'What do you think?' I asked, putting my hands in the pockets and freezing as if on a catwalk.

'Very nice,' Xavier laughed. I changed pose and shaded my eyes pretending to look into the sun. 'Yes, yes, you look like a member of the Olympic ski team.'

'Do I?' I said, doing a few ski moves at my reflection in the oven and checking myself out. I loved it so much. If I wasn't starting to sweat, I'd have kept it on to cook.

'I've never met anyone like you, Holly. You find the joy in every moment. I'm going to miss you when the season ends.'

'We've got loads of time before then,' I said, genuinely touched. 'This is such a thoughtful gift Xavier, thank you so much.' I didn't think it would happen this year, but Xavier's present had given me that warm, fuzzy Christmassy feeling inside. That feeling of home.

'You're welcome. Shall I open mine?' Xavier asked, holding up my present.

'Yes of course, but it's really just a token,' I said. He tore open the packaging to reveal an elaborate wooden X on a leather cord, carved with intricate patterns which reflected in the light. He held it up and stared at it for a few seconds, watching it spin in the air.

'It's just a Christmas decoration,' I said, feeling like a massive cheapskate. 'I saw the X and thought you might like it for your new restaurant. In the tenth.'

Xavier looked at me strangely.

'It's only small, I hadn't really…'

'Stop apologising, Holly. It's perfect – thank you.'

'Is it…?'

'I love it,' he replied, hanging it on the kitchen notice board. 'I'll keep it here to remind me of my promise to myself. Merry Christmas, Holly.'

'Merry Christmas,' I replied, watching him stare at the X as it twirled in the light.

'I better take this coat off,' I said, cheeks hot and flushed, 'and then we can get cracking with the turkey.'

I gave him another hug and held on tightly; his big arms felt warm and strong. There was something so solid and safe about Xavier and I found it difficult to let go.

Nineteen

31st December

Christmas Day flew by in a flurry of eating and drinking. David and Rachael brought wine and cakes and Xavier and I went to town with the turkey and *all* the trimmings. My eyes had been opened to an entirely new world of stuffing, with a failsafe pork sausage and horse chestnut recipe that was an entire meal in itself. George's PAXO had been holding me back for way too long. Twixtmas had been a funny old blur as it always was. The twins had been back for a few days skiing but one by one, everyone had disappeared off to get themselves in position for New Year's Eve. Genevieve had gone back to Paris on the same flight as Xavier earlier in the week and Luca had left an hour or so ago, leaving just me and Liv in the chalet.

'New Year's Eve,' I said out loud, while I deep-cleaned the kitchen, Lady Gaga blasting from the radio. 'We are finally at the end of this shitty, shitty year.' I gave the counter another spray and looked up to see Liv stood in the doorway.

'You alright, mate?' she asked, rightly concerned at me talking to myself.

'Nearly finished in here,' I replied, 'but I'm absolutely knackered. It's been like running a restaurant with the number of covers we've done between us this past two weeks.'

'Now you see why they need three of us,' Liv smiled.

'They weren't joking when they said they like to entertain. I've never worked so hard in my life! How many friends can two people have?'

'Well, we're finally free for a couple of days, so you can let down your hair tonight.'

'It's been such a strange year – I can't wait to see the back of it,' I said, feeling sad.

Liv came over and gave me a hug. 'You're doing great. One day at a time is the only way with these things.'

'I know,' I said, hugging her back. 'I'm not even sure it's George I miss, really; I just feel a bit lost. So much of my future was made up of things we were planning to do together and now I have to work out what I want to do for myself, you know?'

'You'll be fine, babes. Just look out for the moments that make you feel happy and do more of them.'

'That's a good way to look at it,' I said, thoughtfully.

'Bella is DJing at Le Rouge tonight if you fancy it? I'm heading up there now and she's on at 10 p.m.'

I wasn't always sure what did make me happy, but I was pretty clear on what didn't. I'd had enough of nightclubs and drinking for a while. I wanted the exact opposite in fact – some solitude and peace.

'Thanks for looking out for me, but I'm going to have

a quiet one. I've spent this entire year either drinking or hungover and I want to start next year right.'

'New year, new you, is it?' Liv laughed.

'That's the one. Live, laugh, love and all that.'

'No worries, you know where we are if you change your mind.'

I wouldn't change my mind. New Year's Eve was always a milestone moment, but this year it was more than that and tonight felt like an important hurdle in moving on from George. I hadn't been alone for more than five minutes since I'd arrived in Verbier, and it was too easy to go from distraction to distraction. I needed a few hours to myself. I finished off the kitchen then went back to my room to write out a list of New Year's resolutions:

1. Get a handsome new boyfriend to show George what a mistake he's made.
2. Sell the house and get my money back.
3. Become an excellent chef.
4. Develop my wine nose and become a master vintner.

I opened a can of sparkling apple juice and poured it into two Champagne flutes. The sun was starting to set as I took them outside and propped them on the edge of the plunge pool. It looked like an idyllic jacuzzi, pre-bubble. No one needed to know it was only 7 degrees and I was... alone. I took a photo and opened Instagram, typing *#DoubleBubble #ChampagneForTwo #TooBlessedToBeStressed* but as I looked at my picture-perfect post, I realised it was beautiful but fake. Maybe *New Year, New Me* meant being more honest with the world... and myself. There was no shame in being out here on my own – I was living life's big adventure, wasn't I? The apple juice sparkled beautifully, lit by the orange glow of the sun, so I took another picture with just the one glass, as a gust of icy wind blew across the water. I ran inside and posted:

Starting the New Year right. #ChampagneHighLife #HotTub #AllTheBubbles

I didn't need to pretend there were two of us sipping Champagne in a jacuzzi, toasting the New Year. I'd just pretend I was in there drinking Champagne on my own. Little steps.

I put my phone away and bolted the door. I had the whole place to myself and I was looking forward to a bit of me-time. Making a nice dinner and putting on *Jules Holland's Hootenanny* to see the New Year in. I walked through to the kitchen, taking a drink from each glass as I went.

'Holly?' I turned mid-slurp to find Luca stood on the stairs with his ski bag slung over his shoulder. 'I didn't think anyone was home tonight,' he said.

'Neither did I,' I replied in panic. 'I thought you'd gone back to Paris?'

'I tried. The last ski-train was cancelled because of the snow and now I'm stuck here.'

'Oh no! Although, there are worst places to be stuck, I suppose?'

'I was meant to be having dinner at Madame Brasserie, in the Eiffel Tower, so I have somewhere much better to be,' Luca said, looking irritated.

That shut me up. To think some people actually spent

New Year's Eve up the Eiffel Tower, rather than scrabbling last-minute plans together, or watching fireworks on the TV.

'Drinking already?' Luca asked, staring pointedly at my two flutes. 'Is someone else here?'

'Oh. Er, no, just me. They're both for me.'

Luca frowned.

'It's not Champagne, it's fizzy apple,' I said, to explain myself.

Luca's frown deepened. 'We can do much better than that,' he said, going back upstairs. My New Year party for one was now officially ruined, so I had to make the best of a bad situation.

'I was planning to make Steak Diane if you'll be here for dinner?' I called after him.

'*Merci*, I will. That sounds good.'

I wasn't sure if that meant I'd have to wear my uniform and serve him in the dining room, or if we could keep it casual. I hoped for the latter, put my apron on and drank the rest of the Appletiser, taking two fillet steaks from the fridge and tenderising them with a small wooden hammer. I sliced two Spanish onions into perfect circles, followed by a punnet of button mushrooms, enjoying the rubbery squeak as the blade cut through. Dijon mustard, a splash of cognac, double cream and some Worcestershire sauce to spice it up. I washed, peeled and sliced a bag of potatoes into chips, then fried them to crispy, sizzling the onions and mushrooms in another pan and gradually adding the other ingredients for the sauce. Jules Holland provided the background music as I checked on the steaks, my mouth watering just looking at them. I was lost in thought preparing the food when Luca re-emerged half an hour later.

'This might be nice to try?' He stood in the kitchen doorway, holding up a dusty bottle of red. 'It's a Chimere Chateauneuf du Pape.' He'd changed into jeans and a soft wool jumper, his hair still damp from the shower.

'We can't open that, can we?' I said, looking at the bottle in awe. 'I mean, obviously you can, but I won't have any.'

'Of course you will! We are seeing the New Year in together,' he said, easing out the cork and pouring two glasses. I eyed mine cautiously – it was supposed to be *New Year, New Me*, but I couldn't say no to vintage red wine. I'd just have one glass. Or maybe I could drink until midnight then start the *New Me* as the clock struck twelve.

'*Salut*,' Luca said, holding his glass up.

'*Salut*,' I replied, taking a sip of the red, which was bloody delicious.

'Medium rare for your steak?' I asked.

'Is there any other way?' he replied. It was a good point. 'What's this?' he asked nodding towards Jules on the TV.

'Oh… I suppose you don't get it in France. It's the *Hootenanny*,' I said with a smile.

'The Hooter Nanny?' he repeated, enjoying the sound of it.

'Yes, we always watch it on New Year's Eve.'

'Your family?'

'No, me and George… my ex, we used to watch it,' I said, feeling my heart sting. Not anymore. It would just be me watching it on my own from now on. I gave the sauce a stir and ruffled up the chips, throwing the steaks on to cook.

'Shall I put it on in the lounge and we can eat in there?' Luca asked.

'Lovely,' I said, 'and er... should I put my uniform on?' Better to ask than get it wrong.

'Of course not. Unless you mean that slinky number from your first day?' he said raising his eyebrows.

My cheeks flushed. 'No, not that one.'

I sizzled the steaks, both plump and juicy, cooking them to perfection, then served everything up. *Steak frites* in front of the TV with a hot French man, va va voom! I just had to remember he was the boss and to stay professional at ALL times. I checked my reflection in the tiny kitchen mirror, tucked my hair behind my ears and put some lip balm on. The plates were hot as I carried them into the lounge, where Luca had laid the table, and the red wine was aerating. Jules was all smiles on the TV, introducing Adele. Perfection.

'*Merci beaucoup*,' Luca said, taking his plate, 'this looks delicious.'

'It was easy,' I replied with a shrug.

'Even more impressive,' Luca said, taking his first bite and closing his eyes to savour the taste.

We ate our dinner on the coffee table and watched as band after band performed a combination of old classics and new music. The steaks were perfect and sitting on the sofa, drinking expensive red wine with Luca was a definite upgrade on last year's *Hootenanny* – and strangely comfortable.

'Did they find someone to take your place at the Eiffel Tower dinner?' I asked.

'It wouldn't have been hard,' he said with a shrug, 'but to be honest, it's a relief not to have the pressure of a big night out. I so rarely have a night in. This is... nice.'

'You can't beat a good bottle of wine and a steak,' I said, not wanting to misinterpret his words. He looked gorgeous sitting there on the sofa in the candlelight, but it was just an accidental night in together, wasn't it?

I took our empty plates down to the kitchen while Luca decided on some Champagne for midnight. There was a chocolate mousse in the fridge, so I served up two portions, with chopped berries and clotted cream.

'I thought we'd go with the Dom Perignon?' Luca said, popping it open and pouring out two glasses.

New Me would have to wait until tomorrow morning.

He handed me a glass as Jules started the countdown to midnight. I felt the tension of the past year start to slip away. It was time to let it go. Out with the old and in with the new.

'Seven – six – five – four…' I held my glass out to Luca who clinked it and smiled. 'Three – two – one! Happy New Year!' The TV screamed, party poppers exploded, and gold confetti covered everyone in the studio as they cut to the fireworks. Luca was sitting so close to me, our legs were touching and I was starting to feel slightly flustered.

'Happy New Year, Holly,' he said, and before I knew what was happening, he leant in and kissed me gently on the lips.

I was pretty sure this wasn't allowed as I kissed him back, breathing in his unique scent of cigarette smoke and expensive cologne. Was I allowed to kiss him back? What was happening?! It had been years since I'd had a first kiss and I was suddenly very conscious of my body and what was where. Luca's nose touched mine as I pulled myself away and looked at him. Not bad at all.

'Happy New Year to you too,' I said, trying to play it cool but feeling totally panicked. I sat forward on the sofa and started stacking the dessert plates, grabbing Luca's fork and spoon and accidentally knocking the salt on the floor.

'It's only a kiss, Holly, no big deal,' Luca said, leaning back lazily as I fussed about.

'What? No, not at all. Absolutely *not* a big deal,' I said. Oh God. I wish I smoked.

I looked down at the plates I was clutching and headed for the kitchen, pausing in the dining room to clear my head. Breathe, Holly, breathe. It doesn't mean anything. I mean, that's just what the French do, isn't it? *French kiss?* And everyone kisses at midnight on New Year's Eve. But then suddenly, I felt Luca's body behind me, his mouth hot on my neck. I breathed in his smoky cologne as he pulled me back into his arms and kissed me again, then stopped for a few seconds to catch my breath. This was definitely not a New Year kiss; this was a real kiss. Before I had time to organise my thoughts, I heard the sound of a closing door.

'Helloooo? Holly, are you up there?' Liv's voice echoed through the chalet, as I stood up sharply and adjusted my clothes.

'We're in here,' I called, as Liv walked into the lounge and took in the cosy scene.

'Ah, sorry I didn't realise…' she said, '*bonsoir*, Luca.'

Luca nodded curtly. '*Bonsoir*,' he replied. 'Would you like a glass of Champagne?'

'Happy New Year!' I said, hugging her. 'How come you're back so soon?'

'I was worried about you moping around here on your own so I thought we could see the New Year in together. But looks like you're OK,' she said, with a surprised look.

Twenty

1st January

'Hey, Holly is that you?' I heard the voice but couldn't place it or see who was speaking. Skiers in the mist. I was running back from the market and the snow was falling thick and heavy. I looked around and couldn't see anyone, then felt an arm around my waist and jumped. This would be the perfect time for a serial killer to strike.

'Guess who,' a voice said in my ear.

'The Abominable Snowman?' I guessed, trying to wriggle free.

'Close,' the voice said as Luca appeared in my eyeline. Ah, thank God. I lived to fight another day.

'Oh hey,' I said coquettishly.

'Happy New Year,' he said.

'I thought we'd said all that last night?' I blushed thinking of our 'no big deal' kissing. The first time I'd kissed someone fresh since Fresher's Week.

'Well, today is the first official day of the New Year,' he

said, 'so we can say it again. I've been skiing all morning. Fancy a late breakfast?'

'You've been skiing in this?' I said, looking at the white-out on top of the mountain.

'It's not this bad everywhere. Charlie always knows where to take me,' Luca said, sparking up a cigarette as we hurried down the street.

'I can make you some Eggs Benedict back at the chalet?' I said. 'Or the banoffee pancakes Xavier has on the menu to serve when he gets back?'

'I wasn't asking you to *make me* breakfast, I was asking you to *join me* for breakfast.' Oh. He wants to take me for breakfast. OK, well that's cool, stay calm. But what does that mean? I can't be seen out in Verbier eating breakfast with Luca. Whatever next? Liv serving me eggs and bacon while I'm sat on his lap? I needed to get some control on this situation.

Luca stopped mid-step and took a sharp left, grabbing my hand and dragging me behind him. We ran past Rachael's *pâtisserie*, where she did a cartoon double-take as she recognised Luca's ninja outfit and had a nosy out the window. We skidded up to the Verbier Grand Hotel, then gathered ourselves together and went in like a civilised breakfasting couple. The hotel was spacious and calm, with the gentle sounds of quiet chatter accompanied by the clinkety-clink of cutlery. The dining room had huge ceilings, big windows, and large mirrors on every available wall. Crystal chandeliers hung down in the centre of each section with a two-way roaring fire in the middle of the room.

'*Pour deux, s'il vous plaît.*' Luca took charge and got us a cosy table close enough to the fire to stay warm – but not so close as to risk my highly flammable outfit going up in flames. Was this a business meeting, a friends thing or a date?

'I take it you didn't like the sound of my Eggs Benedict?' I said, lightly, to test the conversational waters. What do you talk about on a date with your boss?

'*J'adore* your cooking, Holly, but I thought it might be nice to eat together. No stress, you know?' Luca said with a twinkle in his eye.

'Some cornflakes?' I asked, smiling.

'Or the crunchy nuts?' he said.

I scanned the prices on the breakfast menu and had an internal panic. I hadn't paid for anything up to now, so it felt like the right time to at least offer. I didn't want to spend our entire breakfast-date worrying that Luca would gesture towards me when the bill arrived, like George used to. I could afford to pay for breakfast, surely. I'd just have to organise a quick payday loan to cover the fresh unicorn milk he would no doubt order and pour freely into his coffee.

'I'll have the fruit bowl please, and a latte,' I said to the immaculate waiter stood to attention next to us, who scribbled and smiled.

'Full breakfast, with orange juice and coffee. Two eggs, both poached, and brown toast with butter,' Luca added, snapping the menu shut.

'Quite the appetite,' I said.

'No body-shaming please,' Luca replied, flexing his muscles in my direction.

I laughed. 'None intended. And please, it's my treat today, after the wine and Champagne last night.'

'Certainly not.' Luca looked horrified. 'You are here as my guest.'

Damn. I should have ordered the smoked salmon.

A flurry of waiters appeared and did a synchronised serving dance, placing two baskets of tiny pastries down as if a mirror separated them, followed by fresh toast, a fruit platter, water, juice and our coffees. I was mesmerised by their graceful efficiency, working at pace like a pit-stop team in their pristine, white tuxedos. I smiled and murmured, 'thank you' as they nodded, disappearing as quickly as they'd arrived.

'Are you thinking what I'm thinking?' Luca said, leaning in.

'That this looks delicious?' I replied, my mouth watering.

'No, that you and Liv could learn a thing or two from those guys,' he chuckled.

'Hilarious – I bet they get paid a lot more than we do,' I said, picking up an apple and custard pastry and trying to decide if I could get away with putting the whole thing in my mouth. It didn't seem very ladylike if this was a date. These blurry lines were very confusing. I decided to cut it up with a knife and fork to be on the safe side. Luca watched me with a bemused smile as he rested his leg against mine under the table.

'So why are you having breakfast at lunchtime?' I asked.

'I missed it first thing,' Luca said, buttering a slice of toast then drizzling it with zigzags of honey before taking a satisfying bite. 'Breakfast like a king, lunch like a prince and dinner like a pauper.'

'I'm not sure lobster and fillet steak are on the menu for paupers these days,' I replied, watching him wolf down a second piece of toast, followed by a banana. 'Dinner like a sumo wrestler, more like.'

'I have to keep my strength up,' he said. 'Skiing takes a lot of energy, as you know. How are you feeling after your visit to *Taverne à Champagne*?'

'Great! It was such a treat – thank you for taking me up there. I'd never have known it existed otherwise,' I said, putting a cleanly-cut square of pastry in my mouth.

'I was wondering if you might like to go with me to something else?' he said, eyeing me as I chewed.

'Sounds ominous,' I replied. 'What is it?'

'I know it's last minute, but I've got this spa voucher that I need to use by the end of next week and... I wondered if you might like to come with me?'

'Do we have to ski there?' I asked, cautiously.

'No skiing, just spa-ing,' he said.

'Well that sounds much more my kind of thing,' I said, feeling excited. There was no question that this was a romantic gesture. Did he think we were seeing each other? I wasn't sure how the French did things. Or if I was even interested. I didn't want to give him the wrong idea.

'Excellent. A week tomorrow then,' Luca said with a smile, as a large plate of eggs and bacon was placed in front of him.

It was hard work, but someone had to do it and I couldn't very well say no to the boss. This year really was *New Year, New Me*. All the way from here on in.

Twenty-One

9th January

The helicopter whirred loudly as Luca and I arrived on top of La Vallée. Charlie had collected us from the chalet and we'd been escorted to the Helipad by the hotel concierge, who Luca rewarded with a discreetly delivered 50 franc note. I'd had no idea this place even existed; it was mind-blowing. I'd dressed up as much as I could, with my new jacket and Liv's red boarding pants. Mum and Dad had sent me some cash for Christmas, so I'd treated myself to a ridiculously large pair of Chanel sunglasses which were also helping with the vibe. Bit by bit, I was transitioning from London Holly to Verbier Holly, jumping from the grubby pages of the *Metro* to *Vogue: Winter Edition*.

It was a perfect winter's day: bright-blue skies, not a cloud in sight and the sun was already up and shining. The air was cold and fresh as I took a deep breath and surveyed the situation. Hot French man, private helicopter ride, off to a spa for the day, no work and no worries. Life was good.

'Wonderful to see you again, Mr Blanchet, welcome on

board. And to you too, er…' The pilot shook Luca's hand and turned to me with a pause.

'Holly,' I said, shaking his hand a little too heartily. 'Holly Roberts.'

'A pleasure,' he said with a respectful nod. 'My name is Claus. Have you flown in a helicopter before, Ms Roberts?' he asked, handing me some headphones, which I popped on. I shook my head. He said something else which I couldn't hear. I nodded and smiled as he frowned. Luca lifted my left earphone.

'The headphones don't go on until we sit down,' he said, smiling.

'Ah, right. Sorry,' I shouted as I took them off, wrapping them around my neck.

'Ready?' Luca shouted back over the deafening drone of the propellor. I gave him a double thumbs up and he nodded with authority at Claus, who opened the door to the helicopter and waved us in. Luca helped me up the steps as I pointed to my bag which was still on the floor. He dismissed me with a shake of his head, jumping into the seat next to me. The interior was spotless cream leather and smelt brand new, with bottles of mineral water for the two of us and a folded-up copy of *NZZ* in case we fancied perusing the latest business news. Definitely not. The pilot shut the door behind us and put our bags in the back. This was officially the most glamorous thing I'd ever done.

'Good morning, Mr Blanchet and Ms Roberts, this is your captain speaking,' Claus came through loud and clear, while flicking numerous switches and doing his final checks. 'We are locked and loaded and ready for take-off. If you can ensure your seatbelts are secured and headphones are in position, we will be on our way.'

I smiled at Luca and leant back into my heated seat. He was so effortlessly comfortable in this environment, with his daddy-long-legs crossed and his headphones on, flicking through the newspaper. The engine started and I found my hand clasping his in fear as we took off into the sky. Music blared through the headphones as we flew off up the mountain, high above Verbier where the morning skiers went from colourful ants, to dots, to flecks as we climbed higher and higher into the sky.

'So where exactly is the spa?' I asked, as we dipped over the top of the mountain and started to head down the other side.

'You'll see,' Luca said with a smile, 'it's not far – you can just about see the water through the trees.' He pointed into the distance as the helicopter swooped down and my stomach dropped. I dug my fingernails into Luca's hand, making him jump as a tiny square of blue on the horizon gradually got bigger, expanding into twelve blue circles as we approached the hotel.

'I can see them now,' I said, pressing my face against the window.

'Those are the spa pools,' he explained, 'each one a different temperature and a different pressure. The combination is heavenly and *that* is where we will spend the day.' The engine changed tone as we started to descend, hovering over our landing spot for a few seconds before Claus slowly lowered the helicopter into the snow.

'Welcome to Le Mirador,' a tall lady with a beehive called out to us, as we made our way down the steps. She handed

Luca and I hot towels to freshen up after our arduous, half-hour flight.

'Thank you,' I said, cleaning my hands and patting my face with the flannel before placing it back on the silver plate she was holding.

'Mr Blanchet, we have your favourite suite all ready,' she said, with a beaming smile. His favourite suite? Why would we need a suite? We were only here for the day? Oh God, what was he expecting? A kiss was one thing, and I had barely wrapped my head around that, but what happens in a suite was a different proposition altogether. Did I want something to happen? Was I even ready? Kissing someone other than George had been a welcome distraction, a *really good* distraction in fact, but I wasn't sure I wanted anything else just yet.

'Espresso?' asked the voice of the beehive, holding out a small tray with two tiny coffee cups, interrupting my increasingly panicked thoughts. I dutifully knocked mine back. I was getting used to the bitter taste of an espresso in the mornings as part of my lady-of-the-mountains transformation. The large hot chocolates with whipped cream and marshmallows would have to wait for my days out with Xavier.

She handed a key to Luca with a leaf attached as a key ring. An actual leaf.

'Would you like me to show you to your room?' she asked.

'I'll take it from here,' Luca said, popping the leaf in his pocket. He took my hand and marched us both towards the hotel entrance, which was made entirely of glass. It was so spotlessly clean, that the mountain reflected back as we walked through the automatic doors and into the glass lift.

'Here we are,' Luca said, unlocking a door with *Penthouse* etched into the wood.

I froze. I couldn't just smile and waltz in there without saying something – I didn't want to give him the wrong impression.

'Luca, before we go into the, er… bedroom… I wanted to say thank you so much for bringing me here – the helicopter ride was unbelievable, and this spa is honestly the most beautiful place I've ever seen.'

Luca looked at me uncertainly, waiting for me to finish.

'I wouldn't want you to get the wrong idea, or should I say I hope *I haven't given you* the wrong idea… it's just that since George, I haven't actually been with another…'

Luca frowned, confused. 'The suite is just so we have somewhere private to get changed, Holly. The bathroom is through there.'

The suite was bigger than my London flat, which put my new life into sharp focus. Floor-to-ceiling windows gave us a 360-degree view of the mountain, with a private pool on the balcony and the jacuzzi already bubbling. Both the bedroom and lounge had open fires, adding a lovely, smoky smell to the space. A fully stocked mini-bar with Champagne, beers and snacks, and a walk-in wardrobe, which I wouldn't be using. The bathroom was more like a spa than any bathroom I'd ever seen – a whirlpool bath for two, an enormous shower with different temperatures, scents and pressures, and a mini sauna. I could quite happily have stayed in the bathroom all day, going from bath to shower and back again.

'It's so beautiful,' I said, turning to Luca. 'I've never seen anything like it.'

'We have it all day, so we can get changed and relax,' he said, his spicy aftershave making me feel slightly woozy as he wafted across the room and unzipped his bag. 'I thought we could start with our own jacuzzi, before we head down to the others?' he said, nodding out at the balcony.

'Sounds good. I'll just get my bikini on,' I said, running to the bathroom to change.

Luca sploshed into the jacuzzi with two glasses in one hand and a bottle of Champagne in the other.

I hadn't thought this through at all. I wasn't body-confident enough to be running around in a bikini all day. I covered myself up with one of the dressing gowns and walked through to the balcony, gingerly stepping outside. Ahmablaaadygoddd. It was freeeezing. Luca watched me from the jacuzzi, looking deliciously hot and inviting. I didn't want to take my dressing gown off in front of him, but I didn't have much choice. I couldn't stand around being indecisive, so I shimmied out of my robe and flumped myself in.

Luca laughed and handed me a glass of Champagne.

'What's so funny?' I said, staying low in the water, like a hippopotamus.

'Very elegant, Holly,' he said. Oh God. I knew I wasn't. I just smiled serenely and waited for the moment to pass. I needed to acclimatise so I tipped my head back into the water to wet my hair, channelling my inner sexy shampoo-ad model and we polished off the Champagne. Luca's swimming trunks left nothing to the imagination, as he stood proud, letting it all hang out, like an oven-ready poussin.

'Shall we have some lunch and then we can relax in the pools?' Luca asked. I nodded enthusiastically. Yes, I was ready for heaven, thanks.

We got dressed with lots of layers for temperature-management and packed a day bag to take down to the spa. The lift took us to the second floor, where the pools were nestled into the side of the mountain, each one connected to two others via a mini water-corridor, apart from the slightly larger pool in the middle.

'It's very quiet here, isn't it?' I said, as we walked through to the restaurant.

'Exactly as I like it,' Luca replied. 'The bustle of people in the village is a distraction.'

'I like the peace and quiet too, but I haven't seen another person yet, apart from the staff?'

'You can only get here by helicopter, so it keeps most people away,' he said, with a shrug. Luca seemed quite satisfied with that, but it was a shame such a beautiful place was sitting here quietly with no one enjoying it.

A waitress with a long, blonde plait approached us with two menus and a smile.

'Good afternoon, Mr Blanchet, Ms Roberts,' she said, nodding politely at us both. 'We have a lobster linguini special today, with scallops and caviar, and a pulled pork ravioli starter with a stewed apple sauce. Can I get you some drinks?'

'*Oui*,' Luca said, scanning the wine list. 'Champagne?' he asked me, peering over the top. Not again. I was starting to get heartburn.

'Erm… how about a nice Semillon?' I ventured with a smile.

Luca's brow furrowed, and the waitress looked from me

to him and back again, not sure what was happening. She was obviously used to his suggestion being final.

'Yes, the Semillon,' he said, snapping the wine list shut and handing it to her, 'and some sparkling water.'

'And some still water too, please,' I added, as she scribbled away on her notepad, giving a decisive nod before walking off.

I felt Luca's foot under the table and looked up to find his brown eyes on mine.

'The food here is delicious,' he said, scrutinising the menu. 'The chef isn't as good as Xavier, but very close.'

'You know it well, then?' I asked innocently, pretending to focus on the starters.

'I try to come once or twice a season. It is so peaceful and luxurious,' he replied. 'Genevieve and I used to come with our parents, so we know it well.'

'Wow, you're so lucky. My parents only ever took me to the seaside in England. A place like this is a dream in comparison.'

'My father likes to throw money at problems instead of facing them,' Luca said, 'so we had a lot of luxury distractions as children.'

'And as adults,' I said, looking around.

'*Oui*. You might say we are still quite distracted. My father made his fortune through property and gave us everything we ever wanted and more and now I want to build something for myself. Prove I can do it too.'

'Through investing in restaurants?' I asked.

'Yes. I want to broaden my portfolio in France and then beyond. Culinary excellence, paired with the very best wines from around the world.'

The waitress returned with a bottle of Semillon and presented it to Luca, who gestured at me to try it. She opened it and poured a splash and a half into my glass. I gave it a sniff and took a small sip. Perfect. A nice crisp glass of white was exactly what I wanted. I gave the waitress a smile.

'Delicious, thank you,' I said and put my glass back down to be filled.

We ordered our food and clinked cheers for the third time that day. The hotel was positioned on top of the mountain, so there were snow-topped peaks all around and the spa pools steamed and bubbled, calling out to us while we enjoyed our lunch.

'This ravioli is amazing; would you like to try?' I asked, holding out my fork to Luca, not really wanting to share it.

He shook his head and didn't offer any of his king prawns in return. Maybe that wasn't the done thing among the mega-rich. I was half minded to take a piece back for Xavier to inspect and pull apart. But maybe that wasn't the done thing either. I'd have to savour the taste and report back as best I could.

Luca ordered two aniseed oysters to enjoy when the starters were cleared and as they were set down in front of him, he passed one to me.

'Oh, I'm not really a big fan of...'

'An aphrodisiac, *non*? Oysters are the food of the gods,' Luca said, squeezing chilli sauce onto his shell as the slimy slug in front of me glistened in the sunlight. I wasn't sure I could do it. I looked around surreptitiously for somewhere to throw it.

'I'm not sure I need an aphrodisiac, to be honest,' I said. I could see my oyster watching me as I took another mouthful of wine. Luca wasn't taking no for an answer and was ready to shuck, so I picked mine up to mime along. I added the chilli sauce just as he had and clinked shells with him, doing all the actions without opening my mouth, followed by the post-oyster face. Luca gave me a huge smile, clearly pleased I'd gone along with his initiation test. I smiled back and discreetly placed the full shell at an angle on my side plate, so Luca couldn't see the chilli-covered snot ball still sitting there, untouched.

We devoured our lobster linguini and decided against dessert, taking yet another espresso with us into the spa pools. I was on a permanent caffeine high. The air was bitingly cold, but the sun was hot on our faces, so it was a strange dichotomy of hypothermia standing outside the pools and sunburn sitting in them. I slathered my face in factor 50 and put on a sun visor, spraying Luca's cheeks and nose before getting into the first pool, which was a gentle pulsing bubble at a medium heat.

'You know we can do some of these pools naked?' Luca said, coyly. 'That's how the Romans meant for them to be experienced.'

'Oh, really? I think I'm OK in my bikini for now,' I said, terrified I'd be forced to hand over the three tiny scraps of material keeping my dignity in place. I hadn't pictured my spa day having naturist vibes. Or Luca as an exhibitionist.

Luca drank his coffee and lit a small cigarette as we bobbed about in the water.

'Do you still hear from your ex-fiancé?' he asked. George's face flashed through my mind and my heart stopped for a second at the thought of him.

'Not really, but we need to sell the house we own together, so sooner or later we'll have to be in touch about that,' I said. 'But our relationship is over.'

'And are you glad of it?' His questions were abrupt, but they did make me think. Was I glad of it? Eight years for nothing.

'I'm not sure *glad* is the right word. It was a shock, and it was humiliating to be so close to getting married and not see it coming. To think I'd have married a man who didn't even love me, and I hadn't noticed. But now I'm starting to realise that this has been the absolute best decision for me too. Have you ever been close to getting married?' I asked, deflecting.

'Yes, of course. I have been engaged three times, but only in love once,' Luca said, casually, as if that was entirely normal.

'And none of them worked out?'

'Not yet,' he laughed.

'Third time is supposed to be a charm,' I said with a smile, 'that's a British saying, like third time lucky, does it translate?'

'Three is the magic number, *non*?' he said. 'Yes, I know it. You have two more to go then.'

'God, no thanks,' I said. 'I don't think marriage is for me.'

'Lovers are much more interesting,' Luca said, inching towards me. 'It keeps things hot, you know? Sexy.'

'Hmm,' I thought about a lifetime of staying sexy and wasn't sure I could be bothered with that either. George wasn't the answer, but maybe the jury was still out on Luca? Surely I could enjoy his glamorous lifestyle while they deliberated? He finished his cigarette and swam over to me, swooping in for a kiss as I wrapped my legs around him under the water. He pushed me up against the edge of the hot tub, kissing me harder, then pulled back to look me in the eyes. There was a fire I hadn't seen before as he picked me up without breaking eye contact and twirled me around, kissing me in circles and making me dizzy.

'Ready for the next one?' he asked, pointing at the circular pool in the middle, with a much bigger whirl to it. 'It's twelve foot deep and has no steps – we have to jump in. It's part of the experience.'

'Good, because it's bloody freezing out of the water, so the faster I'm in the next pool, the better.'

Luca pulled himself up onto the steps and I quickly followed, attempting mind over matter to not feel the bitter breeze the second I stood on the side. *Think warm thoughts, think warm thoughts.* It didn't work. Luca held my hand.

'We can jump together?' he said and I nodded. 'One, two, three…' I held my nose as we both jumped and the second I hit the water, I realised it was a plunge pool. The air disappeared from my lungs and my body felt like it was shutting down. I swam to the top, gasping for air like a terrified carp, where Luca was laughing.

'*Tres bien!*' he said, his hands out of the water clapping. 'I know you like to plunge! This one is very good for your circulation.'

'You tricked me,' I spluttered through chattering teeth, as I clambered out of the icy water, wet hair all over my face. The cold air felt suddenly warm, and my entire system felt discombobulated as my body shook from top to bottom.

Luca casually pulled himself out of the pool, using his

big arms and tight abs to effortlessly slide up and out. This was obviously his idea of a good time. Not to be fooled again, I dipped my toe in pool three, which was reassuringly hot, and slithered in, feeling the delicious water wrap itself around me and soothe my shaking bones. Luca wasn't far behind, still chuckling to himself.

'That was not funny!' I said, feeling much better about the situation now I was warm again.

'But you look so much more vibrant and invigorated now,' he said with a smile. I'd already forgotten the uncivilised shock of the cold water, so I was all for basking in the post-ice-bath glow.

'Are you going to join me in the naked spa pools?' Luca asked.

'Which ones are they?' I replied, peering out at the remaining nine pools around us.

'That section over there,' he said, pointing to an area separated by large bamboo screens. He'd obviously done this before and clearly enjoyed teasing me.

The waitress appeared with two glasses of Aperol Spritz, filling the air with a citrussy zest. We hadn't even ordered any drinks, but this was exactly what I wanted. She placed the cocktails down next to us and was accosted by Luca.

'*Bonjour*. Can you please reassure my friend that the two pools over there are for naked swimming, and she won't get into trouble for removing her costume?' he said.

Friend? God, this was confusing.

'Yes, the area is clothes-free,' she said, pointing at a small sign tacked onto the bamboo, of a man and woman in swimming costumes crossed out with big red marks. The message seemed to be *death to those who refuse to expose themselves*. Despite this reassurance that we wouldn't be arrested, I just didn't feel relaxed enough to strip off and jiggle around with my bits out. Luca was imagining some cool, sexy time, but there would be nothing attractive about my boobs floating on top of the water like inflated airbags.

'See?' Luca said with a lascivious wink.

'I do see. But I'm not sure it's me,' I said, taking a long drink of Aperol Spritz and feeling instantly happier. 'Maybe I'll feel differently after one or two of these.'

Luca did a circling signal to the waitress to bring another round and we both laughed.

'It's alright for you with your biceps and your cheese-grater abs,' I said, 'I'm not used to swinging around naked. I'm English; we are a civilised nation.'

'Very civilised. Beans on toast for dinner, for example?' he shrugged. 'Don't be so uptight.'

He had a point. Maybe running around naked for a few hours would do me some good. Oh God. But what about the airbags? I'd have a couple more drinks and think about it.

'I'm not uptight *actually*,' I said, dragging myself out of the pool and striding forcefully over to the naked area. I pulled on the bow at the back of my bikini to prove I meant business and removed my top in one quick motion, holding it in the air like a prize with my back to him. Luca couldn't get out of the pool fast enough, scrambling onto the side and chasing me into the clothes-forbidden oasis. Was I meant to take my bottoms off right here? In the middle of the spa? I needed a newspaper or a pineapple to stand behind. I draped my bikini top over one of the screens and sidled into the pool to whip off my third triangle of dignity. Luca was already naked and swimming around like a happy little seal. I had a flash of feeling brave, which quickly subsided – it just didn't feel right to be swishing my bits around in the water and Luca's toad in the hole kept bobbing to the surface, putting me off. On a sexy scale of one to ten, this was a maximum of two. It was not doing good things for the attraction levels. For me, anyway.

'Sorry Luca, I've changed my mind,' I said, apologetically, grabbing my top.

'Eh?' Luca said, jumping out of the naked pool and putting his trunks back on. 'Is this you not being uptight?'

'Naked swimming just isn't for me,' I said, stretching myself out for a swim in one of the fully-clothed pools, which was perfectly nice. I didn't need to be naked to enjoy myself. Roman perverts. Why else would they make it mandatory to be naked – constantly having orgies, so they had an excuse for endless sex. It's a miracle they got round to building any roads.

Luca slid in and swam alongside me with a conciliatory smile. 'No worries,' he said. 'I didn't mean to push you.'

'It's still lovely here,' I said, 'and being in a bikini is exposing enough for now.'

'True, true,' he pulled me over to the side and kissed me. I could feel how excited he was getting and could see how easy it would be to get carried away in this paradise. Maybe I didn't need to know where this was going; maybe I just needed to enjoy it for what it was and let go.

It had already gone midnight when Charlie pulled up outside the chalet. He ran up the steps to unlock the front door, then back to the car to help us out. A gust of cold air slapped me in the face as I bundled myself together and ran in behind Luca, with Charlie following closely, carrying our bags.

'What an amazing day,' I said, glad to be home. 'It's been like experiencing a little piece of heaven.' I pulled my coat around me as Luca shut the front door.

'*Oui*, it has been fun,' Luca replied.

Charlie came running down the stairs. 'That's all the bags in your room, Monsieur Blanchet,' he said.

'Oh. My bag doesn't...' I started as Luca held up his hand.

'*Merci* Charlie,' he said, handing him 20 francs, '*bonsoir*.'

'*Au revoir*,' Charlie replied. 'See you soon, Holly.' He swung the heavy front door behind him, leaving a charged quiet in the air as Luca and I stared at each other.

'I better get my bag,' I said, slightly freaked out as I hardly ever went upstairs. I had no reason to, as the food and wine were very much at ground and basement level.

'Follow me,' Luca said, taking my hand. I was so tired, it was all I could do to put one foot in front of the other and carry myself up the stairs. 'This one is mine,' Luca said leading me into the first room on the right, decorated in mint green and gold flock wallpaper. It had a four-poster bed with a huge feather duvet and was covered in enormous pillows.

'Oh wow! This looks cosy,' I said, spotting the Nespresso machine on the side and a mini fridge full of cold drinks. Charlie had placed our bags on the powder-pink chaise lounge.

'It does the job,' Luca said, lying down on the bed. He tapped the space next to him. 'Try it out for size.'

I honestly couldn't resist. I slipped off my trainers and lay down next to him, my body sinking into the mattress and my head into one of the fluffy pillows, totally exhausted. Luca turned towards me, resting his head in one hand.

'You enjoyed it?' he asked, knowing the answer.

'Of course? How could I not? Thank you.'

'Favourite day in Verbier so far?' he pushed.

'Sure,' I replied. I didn't have the strength to think of any comparisons. Luca leant over and kissed me gently on the lips, then sat up to look at me. I smiled before closing my eyes. I was sooo tired. We'd had an amazing day and now I just needed to snooze for a couple of minutes and I'd be on my way. I was starting to drift off when Luca kissed me again. This time a little more passionately. I kissed him back, slowly. He was firm and sexy and teasing, and I was breathless under the weight of him, enjoying the tickle of his stubble as he moved down to kiss my neck, unzipping my top as he went. I had goosebumps down my back and the primal urge Liv had promised me would return, kicked back in, full force. I put my hands above my head and surrendered as he pulled the lacy edge of my bra back with his mouth, shuddering involuntarily as he slid one arm underneath me and pulled me close.

I hadn't expected things to escalate so quickly and still wasn't sure how I felt in my heart. I knew how my body felt as I clung to Luca and kissed him, but I didn't want things to go too far, in case there was no way back.

Luca finished unzipping my hoodie and pulled it open, his free hand now under my T-shirt, stroking me softly. Oh God, I was tingling all over, maybe I could… He kissed me again, his breath hot and excited. No. It was too much. I put my hands on his and gently untangled myself.

'I'm so sorry,' I said, suddenly very aware that I was lying in his bed. 'I can't. I just don't think I'm ready...'

'Wait, what? Of course. Sorry if I misread the signs; I thought you wanted it too,' he replied, hands immediately in the air, rolling back to his side.

'You didn't and I do, it's just such a big step for me,' I said. 'I haven't been with anyone other than George for such a long time.'

'I understand. It is hard. The French way is very different,' Luca said. 'You have to get straight back on the horse, *non*?'

'I might feel differently tomorrow, when we've had some rest?' I said, as my eyes closed. My mind filled with horses as I drifted off to sleep. Could it be time to try another horse? A French Stallion, perhaps?

I woke with a start. Shit. I'd only meant to rest my eyes for a few minutes and now it was the middle of the night. I looked over at Luca, open-mouthed and snoring happily, and quietly peeled the duvet back and grabbed my bag. I crept downstairs and then downstairs again to my bedroom and thanked my lucky stars that Liv wasn't home, so I could noisily strip my clothes off and snuggle into my own bed for the remaining few hours until morning.

Twenty-Two

10th January

'Oh. My. God,' Liv was shaking me awake, waving her red ski trousers in my face, 'look what I've just found in Luca's room! These are mine! Luca has been wearing my trousers?'

I opened my eyes blearily and tried to focus.

'Oh, sorry. I borrowed them,' I said, rolling over onto the cold side of the pillow.

'What?' she said, bouncing on my bed, shaking me awake. 'You borrowed them?'

'Yes, sorry, I didn't think you'd mind.'

'But I just found them on Luca's floor? In a pile by his bed? *On the floor*, Holly?'

'I must have left them there, sorry,' I said, jumping up and grabbing them off her.

'You must have left them there? HOLLY?' Liv shouted, wide-eyed with her hands on her hips. 'What do you mean?'

'When I took them off, I must have left them on the floor,' I said, flustered.

'You're sleeping in *his bed* now?' Liv asked.

'Nothing happened, just a couple of…'

'Pairs of trousers on the floor?' eyebrowed Liv. 'Hmmm?'

'Alright, alright, yes – trousers were removed. I must have taken them off in my sleep.'

'And not just any trousers – *my trousers*,' Liv said, holding them over me with two fingers, 'or as they shall henceforth be known, *your* trousers.'

'Sorry, sorry, thank you.'

'No problem. That's 70 Swiss francs,' she said.

'For what?'

'They're no use to me now, I'll have to burn them! God only knows what they've caught from Luca's bedroom floor. And if I might offer a small word of advice from a dabbling-with-Luca perspective… I wouldn't go any further with it,' Liv said, sharply.

'Why not?'

Liv pulled on her thermals and plaited her hair. 'You're still getting over one nightmare of a man who screwed you over, and I hate to say it, but Luca will highly likely be another.' She sat on the edge of my bed. 'Look we're not really supposed to talk about it, but he's got a bit of a reputation for hooking up with the staff. Something happened between him and the last girl that was here, Rose. She was supposed to come back this season but didn't turn up for work. Xavier and I weren't sure what was going on. There was some kerfuffle between Genevieve and Luca, and then a week later, you turned up.'

'I didn't know that,' I said, getting back into bed and putting the pillow over my head, 'but there's hardly anything going on. Honestly.' I absolutely did not want to become an accidental notch on Luca's belt, if this is what he did with all the chalet girls.

'I'm just saying that it's all cool and fun while there's trousers on the floor, but it won't be his life that changes if things don't work out.' Liv leant over and gave me a hug.

'Thanks for the heads up. I appreciate it.' I mumbled into her ear.

I sighed into my pillow, roly-poly-ed the duvet around me and went back to sleep.

Xavier was sitting at the kitchen table with his menu notebook, brow furrowed and pencil hovering by the time I got up. He half-nodded as he saw me and carried on writing.

'Heyyy, when did you get back? How was Paris?'

'Good,' he said curtly, not meeting my eye.

Liv walked in and grabbed an apple, biting into it and joining Xavier at the table.

'Welcome back,' she said, giving him a double kiss.

'*Merci!* I missed you,' he said. 'What's been going on?'

'What hasn't been going on? There's been all sorts of chalet excitement since you left,' Liv crunched gleefully. 'You'll never believe it, but *our Holly* had a lovely time yesterday, being treated to a spa day by *our*... Luca!' How the hell did she know about the spa?

'Yeah, I heard about that,' Xavier replied soberly.

'I didn't realise it was public knowledge?' I said, feeling myself blush.

'Charlie's one of the gang, Hols; there's no secrets in the inner circle,' Liv said. 'So, what's going on? If you start dating, will me and Xavier end up working for you?' Liv wasn't going to let it go, but how could I tell them what was going on when I didn't know myself? Especially when Xavier looked so disappointed in me.

'It was nice, you know, standard spa stuff, hot and wet. It was just an old voucher of Luca's that needed using up, so no big deal.'

'Course it was,' Liv said, 'that sounds very much like Luca. Out of date vouchers he needs to use up.'

'Very unlikely,' Xavier scoffed.

'Mixing work and pleasure is a recipe for disaster, Hols, trust me,' Liv said.

'Alright, alright, I didn't realise you were doubling up as the HR department. Is there a policy on workplace relationships that I've contravened?'

'We're just trying to look out for you,' Xavier said with a shrug.

'And I appreciate it, but I'm a big girl. I can work things out for myself.'

Xavier shrugged again and stood up abruptly, making his way over to the fridge.

'Anyway, let's talk about something else.... What's the brief for the wine later?' I called, desperately trying to change the topic.

'Luca is entertaining a wine merchant tonight, so it's just the two of them. I'm keeping it simple with steak frites and salad. I imagine he'll want an impressive red to balance it out. Should be easy.' Xavier said, still refusing to look at me. This was ridiculous; what was his problem? Maybe I should have told him what was going on, as a friend; I was just about to go into the fridge and try and speak to him when Luca marched into the kitchen in smart trousers and a shirt.

'*Bonjour*, Xavier. I heard you talking about dinner this evening. I have a second person joining me, so we will be three.'

'No problem,' Xavier called from inside the fridge, rattling things about.

'Liv – can you lay an extra setting please, and I'll need you to work tonight.'

'Oh no, it's fine,' I said, jumping in. 'Liv has plans this evening. I can lay the table and serve the three of you.'

'I'm afraid that won't work, Holly, as I'd like you to be the third guest.' I felt my cheeks go instantly pink. 'I am entertaining a very influential vintner who is in Verbier for the weekend – Henri Thienpont – and I want to impress him.'

'Oh, of course. What do you want me to do?'

'Well, we'll all need to play our part,' Luca said, 'Xavier will impress him with amazing food, you and I will entertain him over dinner and impress him with some fabulous wine and conversation, and Liv will impress him with her sparkling wit and exceptional service.'

Liv was clearly furious.

'Honestly Luca, I can talk about wine while serving it. I don't need to sit down at the table with you both.'

'I insist,' Luca said. 'You two don't mind if Holly eats with us, do you? I need it to not feel like a business meeting.'

I mouthed 'sorry' at them both.

'Of course not,' Liv said, seething.

'Makes no difference to me,' Xavier said, popping his head around the fridge door and trying to look nonchalant.

'*Bien*,' Luca said, and left as Xavier disappeared back inside.

'That's just GREAT,' Liv said. 'I was supposed to be seeing Bella for date night. I'll have to cancel now, thanks to your new boyfriend!'

'Honestly, that's the first I've heard of dinner tonight. And he's not my boyfriend! We're just… he's not my anything,' I said, feeling terrible.

'I'll do it, Liv; you go out with Bella,' Xavier called from the fridge. At least he was still alive in there.

'I can't now he's asked me to work it. Urghh!' Liv stomped out of the kitchen in a rage.

'I can suggest we eat at 6 p.m., no starters and just a really quick steak,' I called out to Xavier. No reply. This was so unfair. I'd only just found out about the bloody dinner myself. There wasn't much else I could do, so I left them both to stew on it. I'd do my best to make dinner as short a shift as possible and sort it out with them later.

I decided to wear one of my old London outfits seeing as I didn't have to go 'out' to be 'out out' and could safely wear heels without worrying about breaking my ankle. I put a dark-green jumper dress on with my purple tights and boots. It felt strange to go into the dining room without a uniform on. Forbidden territory.

Luca was already sat down with Henri talking quietly when I walked in, and I couldn't help but notice how closely he fit the archetypal perfect man. Tall, fit, French, rich, into wine, smelt nice. Not as funny as Xavier, but he tried his best.

'*Bonsoir*, Holly,' he said, holding a glass of red wine out to me, 'please meet Henri Thienpont from Chartreuse Wines.'

'Lovely to meet you,' I said, taking in the small, thin man sat next to Luca.

'Henri, this is Holly Roberts. Holly works at Chez Margot in London and is working with us for the winter season. She has an excellent nose and is an equally talented chef – she has been supporting Xavier on the food *aussi*.'

'*Enchanté*,' Henri said, kissing my hand. It was quite the intro.

'I've opened the Pomerol if you would like some?' Luca said, smiling over at me.

'Lovely,' I replied. He poured it out and handed me a glass. I felt like a massive imposter and wasn't sure what I was supposed to be doing to impress Henri. I took my glass from Luca and sloshed the wine about, sticking my nose in to enjoy the fruity smell. The blackberries and blackcurrants were coming through nice and strong; the aroma was divine, and it tasted even better. I savoured my first mouthful, slowly exposing it to each of my tastebuds in turn.

'It is good, *non*?' Luca said smiling, watching me enjoy it.

'SO good. Where did you get it?' I asked.

'This is one of Henri's,' he said, taking another sip.

'Ah, fantastic,' I said, turning to him. 'Congratulations! This is quite something.'

Henri beamed with pride. 'We have had the vineyard in Bordeaux for several generations and are extremely proud of the Le Pin produce.'

'It is a king among Merlots,' Luca said, 'that is certain.'

Liv slipped quietly into the dining room, wearing a fixed smile on her face. I was *so in trouble*, but it wasn't my fault. She wouldn't even speak to me so I could tell her my speed-eating plan to get her out of here ASAP and off on her date with Bella.

'Good evening, Luca, Henri, Holly,' she said, fake-smiling at us all. 'Dinner this evening is a fresh crab and avocado toast, followed by steak frites with grilled mushrooms and tomatoes and a light chocolate mousse with a grapefruit and orange sponge.'

'Sounds delicious,' Henri said, smiling, '*merci*.'

'It really does. Thank you,' I said as Liv avoided eye contact.

'Medium rare steak for you, Luca. How would you like yours cooked, Henri?'

'Rare, *s'il vous plaît*,' Henri replied.

'Holly?'

'Medium rare as well please, or whatever's easiest,' I said blushing. This was excruciating.

'I'm sure Xavier can manage two medium-rare steaks,' Liv said officiously as she strutted off back down to the kitchen.

'Shall I top up the wine?' I whispered to Luca, uncertain of my role and mindful of our glasses getting low.

'Allow me,' Luca replied, glug-glugging us back to a reasonable level, as Xavier appeared with our starters. He placed them delicately in front of us.

'Your starters are served. Crab fresh in this morning from Devon and avocado from our sustainable farm out in Verona. There is a very light crayfish sauce served on the side which I would highly recommend trying and the toasts are half rye, half raisin. I hope you all enjoy.' I kept trying to catch Xavier's eye to make him laugh but he was such a consummate pro, there would be no deviation from the script.

'Thank you so much, Xavier; this looks delicious,' I said, desperate to get his attention.

'*Merci*,' Luca dismissed him with a wave, resting his arm on the back of my chair.

'*De rien*,' Xavier said with a funny little bow, backing out of the dining room and leaving us to it. How depressing. It was such a shame he and Liv couldn't join us for dinner so we could all have a laugh together.

The crab was unbelievable.

'Luca doesn't exaggerate, so you must have a gifted nose for wine, Holly?' Henri said, crunching into his toast.

'I'm very keen to develop it, and I enjoy all the practice,' I laughed, swirling my glass.

'You're very welcome to come and visit our vineyard, if you are ever in Bordeaux,' he said. 'I'd be happy to show you around.'

'I'd love that,' I said, excitedly, feeling happy inside. I think this was one of those moments Liv had told me to look out for on New Year's Eve.

Henri pulled out his wallet and gave me his business card.

'Please,' he said, 'call me any time, it would be my pleasure.'

Liv silently took our plates.

'Thanks Liv,' I said as she nodded, smile still stuck in position.

Luca ignored the activity around him as the starters were cleared and Xavier served the steaks. This was his world:

where Charlie drove him around, and Liv made his bed, and Xavier cooked his food, and I poured his wine. How would he cope if he had to do everything for himself like the rest of us? But that would never happen.

'I've made a selection of fresh sauces to accompany your steaks,' Xavier said, putting three gravy boats on the table, 'Béarnaise, peppercorn and blue cheese. And of course, your *frites*.' A platter of hand-cooked chips was laid out in front of the three of us. It was the dinner to end all dinners.

Henri's phone vibrated in his pocket, and he reached for it apologetically.

'It is my wife,' he said, looking at the screen, 'I should take it.' He walked through to the reception area, leaving Luca and I alone.

'Is it going well?' I asked, anxiously.

Luca smiled. 'Very well. I'm thinking of partnering Henri's vineyard with one of my restaurants, so it is more of a social meal than anything else. Having a third person takes the pressure off the conversation, so thank you for eating with us.'

Henri came rushing back into the dining room in a fluster.

'*Je suis désolé*, Luca, I am going to have to go,' he said, panicked, 'my wife has locked herself in the garage and I need to get back to her.'

'Not at all, please go, do what you need to do,' Luca said.

'You are very generous to understand. I am so disappointed not to get to the main course with you both. My apologies to you too, Holly; it was lovely to meet you. Perhaps I'll see you again and the four of us can go out for dinner?' he said, double kissing me goodbye.

'Er... yes, that would be lovely,' I said, unsure what else

I could say. Did he mean a double date? Luca saw him out, then came back through to eat his meal.

'His poor wife!' I said, 'I hope he gets back to her quickly.'

'He lives half an hour away, so she'll be stuck in there for a while.'

All this distraction was making me hungry. The steak was cooked to perfection, pink and tender and delicious. I piled together a piece of steak with a chip and dipped it in some peppercorn sauce and had just shoved the whole thing in my mouth when the double doors to the dining room opened and Genevieve stood staring at us, with her jewellery clients Mimi and Frank in tow.

'*Bonsoir*, Luca and, er… Holly. *Ça va?*'

Luca jumped up from the table and double kissed his sister, then Mimi and Frank in turn, just as I was getting a taste for the steak. FFS. This was hands down the best steak I'd *ever* eaten, and I wasn't going to miss out. I quickly cut myself another piece and popped it in my mouth as Genevieve eyeballed me furiously. I slow-chewed, smiling at her to say hi. I looked over at Liv, who was on tenterhooks, her eyes flicking from Genevieve to Luca, unsure what to do.

'Ah! *Salut*, Gigi,' Luca said, scratching his neck, bright red, 'I didn't realise you were here this evening?'

'Clearly not. I am sorry if I've interrupted your… private dinner?' Genevieve replied, but she didn't seem sorry at all, clocking the near-empty bottle of Pomerol, 'I messaged Liv to expect us, but not for food. I thought you were in Paris with Fern?'

Luca cleared his throat. 'Change of plan. Henri came over for dinner and I asked Holly to join us, as part of her… learning.'

'I see,' Genevieve said, taking it all in, 'Well, we should let you finish. Mimi, Frank, darlings, let me show you to your room and perhaps we can meet down here in twenty minutes for a drink?' The question was directed at Luca.

'Of course,' he said.

The three of them gave a final snooty look around and left us to it. I realised I'd been holding my breath and let out a huge sigh. Liv had scarpered and rightly so, the sneaky minx.

'That was awkward. I thought Genevieve liked me, but she looked really annoyed – we were only having dinner?' I said. Luca looked anxious and nauseous all at once and pushed his plate away.

'Genevieve doesn't like us to blur boundaries with the staff,' he said, pointing between us.

'Really? Are we the staff? She's never called us that before.'

Luca looked distinctly uncomfortable.

'Who is Fern?' I asked.

'Our aunt. She's not well and I was supposed to visit her this weekend.'

'Oh, I see. I'm so sorry to hear that,' I said, as Liv re-appeared.

'Liv, did you know Genevieve was due this evening?' Luca asked sharply.

She shook her head. 'My phone has been dead all day, so I haven't been getting messages. Sorry, Luca. Shall I clear the table?'

Luca nodded, standing up. I'd only eaten half my steak, but I lay down my knife and fork so Liv could take my plate. I'd have to finish it in the kitchen. I eyed up the last of the Pomerol. That wasn't going down the sink either.

'I should probably catch up with Mimi and Frank,' Luca said, distracted, 'would you mind serving the drinks? And you... er... should probably put your uniform on, you know, with Genevieve being here.'

Oh. I felt like I'd been slapped in the face. Two large glasses of red wine and half a steak and I was being dunked back in the plunge pool. It was a rhetorical question, but I nodded. I looked over at Liv, expecting her to be all *I told you so* but her eyes had softened, her fixed smile gone. This was so humiliating. I didn't reply.

'Thank you,' Luca said, leaving me at the table alone and going upstairs.

'I'm so sorry, babes,' Liv said, rushing to my side.

'He didn't even say anything to them. He just completely ignored me.'

'I'd tell him to stick his drinks,' she said. 'I can serve them for you, don't worry.'

'No, he's asked me to do it, so I can't say no. I do work here after all.'

I helped Liv clear the rest of the table and wiped it down ready for Genevieve and her guests to have drinks. Spritzing orange air freshener throughout the downstairs to get rid of the meaty smells. To erase any memory of Luca and I having dinner. It all seemed slightly dramatic; we were two consenting adults, what was the big deal? I went back to my room and put my uniform on, ready to assume my alter ego, swinging by the kitchen to finish my steak before I went up.

'Dinner was amazing Xavier – well, what I managed to eat of it,' I said.

'Good. That steak is the best,' he replied.

'Is the rest of it here somewhere?' I said, sniffing about

and seeing my plate on the side. 'It would be a crime against beef for it to go in the bin.' I sliced it up and transferred it onto a clean plate with a baguette and some butter. Xavier handed me the Dijon.

'Perfect,' I said. 'I need to soak up all the red wine before I get back to work.' I pulled the bread apart, which was still warm from the oven. Layered on the butter and a tiny bit of mustard, before piling in the steak and chomping down on it. Nothing better.

'I'm sorry your dinner got cut short,' Xavier said, softly.

I shrugged. I was more embarrassed at being told I couldn't eat at the master's table, than upset with Luca. Maybe Genevieve coming home early was a blessing in disguise. The last thing I needed was another man who saw me as somehow inferior to him. I'd been so confused about the whole Luca situation anyway – maybe now I had my answer. I finished my steak sandwich and washed up my plate.

'I suppose the chocolate mousse is off the cards?'

'You can have whatever you like,' Xavier said, opening the fridge to reveal the three untouched desserts.

'Amazing. They look delicious. I'll save mine for later as a reward for getting through the next few hours. Once Verbier-ella has done all her chores.'

Xavier put his arm around me. 'You'll be alright,' he said.

I took a deep breath and made my way back upstairs to the bar, but I could hear Luca and Genevieve having a heated discussion, so I hid behind the door so as not to disturb them.

'What were you thinking? Have you no standards?' Genevieve said angrily. They were arguing in French, so

I had to click my brain into gear to understand what they were saying.

'It is nothing, it was just dinner,' Luca replied.

'Just dinner? It's a disgusting show of immorality. Can you not control yourself?'

'Of course. Please, Genevieve, you're over-reacting. I was simply being friendly.'

'Fillet steak and Pomerol is more than friendly. Do you need me here to watch your every move? To stop you making life-altering mistakes?'

'Not at all. I hear you. It stops today.' Luca was bright red and flustered.

'I should think so. We can't keep losing staff to your indiscretions and we won't find anyone else this far into the season. Can you keep it civil?'

'Of course I can.'

Well, that was it then. I'd been played by a player and stitched up like a kipper. I considered packing my bags and getting on the first train home. Liv and Xavier didn't like me anymore and Luca was clearly ashamed of me. I wasn't up to his 'standards'. I hadn't realised I was so low-level. Was I not rich enough or classy enough? I wasn't sure what was wrong with me, but I'd been put in my place. It was time to paint on a smile and get back to serving the drinks.

I cleared my throat and bustled noisily into the bar as Mimi and Frank walked down the stairs.

'*Bonsoir Mimi, Frank, qu'est que vous voulez boire?*' I asked in my most professional voice. Mimi looked me up and down, clearly bemused at the switcheroo from diner to server.

'White wine? Champagne?' Genevieve added. 'Anything you would like.'

'*Gin-tonic?*' Mimi said.

'*Moi aussi*,' Frank agreed.

'And two glasses of Champagne,' Luca said, looking straight through me.

I nodded and made the drinks, chopping lemons and zesting the glasses, adding ice and stripy straws, popping yet another Champagne cork and pouring two glasses of Bollinger. I just needed to get through this weird shift and then I could decide what to do.

'Can you ask Xavier to bring us up some *amuse-bouche* please, Holly?' Genevieve asked. 'And perhaps prepare a few snacks?' Mimi and Frank nodded enthusiastically.

I bowed at them, like Liv had taught me to do, and once I'd slowly exited the dining room, I legged it down to the kitchen to Xavier's smiley face.

'Do you have any amusing bouches?' I asked.

'Mini pasties already in the oven,' he replied. 'I thought they'd want a little something as soon as the drinks started flowing. Next up will be the snacks and then... your chocolate mousse.'

'Noooo!' I was aghast; it was the only thing keeping me going. I had half a mind to quickly scoff it to stop any redistribution efforts later. 'Genevieve did actually ask for some snacks as well.'

Xavier pulled some pre-rolled dough out of the fridge. 'I knew it. I'll rustle up some pizzettas,' he said, scattering some flour on the counter and tearing the dough into small sections for kneading. I watched him as he danced from fridge to cupboard and back again, chopping, rolling and grating to gather the different ingredients for the pizzas. A bell rang upstairs as the oven timer sounded and Xavier plated up the mini pasties and handed them to me. Lucky I wasn't hungry, or a couple might have gone missing en route to the dining room. I carried them upstairs as the bell tinkled a second time.

'Where have you been?' Genevieve said in irritation. 'We need more drinks.'

'Apologies, here are your *amuse-bouche*. Mini pasties – we have mushroom, these ones are chicken and these are spinach and cheese,' I said, pointing each of them out. 'Would you like the same drinks again?' Four heads nodded in my direction, so I made another two gin and tonics and topped up the Champagne. Luca had barely looked at me, but I was desperate to get his attention and speak to him. I wanted him to know that I'd heard his conversation with Genevieve and was nobody's 'low standard' option. I kept staring at him, but he didn't look over at me once. In fact, not one of them looked at me for the rest of the evening. I was completely ignored and treated as staff – there to serve them and that was it.

Post-pasties, post-pizzettas and post-my-chocolate-mousse, the four of them were finally satiated and got up to go. I was stood behind the bar area, polishing glasses to gleaming, ready and waiting in case they wanted anything else.

'*Merci*, Holly,' Genevieve called behind her as she led Mimi and Frank out of the dining room and up the stairs. Luca was at the back of the group and shook my hand, using his tip-palming skills to pass me a secret note. He mouthed 'sorry' as he left. Sorry for what? Sorry for ignoring me? For pretending to like me? For humiliating me? I should have mouthed 'fuck off' back at him but I wasn't quick enough. I unfolded the piece of paper which said *I'll make it up to you* in tiny black letters, with his phone number scrawled next to it.

Luca: *I'm sorry about earlier, it was rude. I'm home to Paris tomorrow morning, so let's talk when I'm back.*

Me: *It's fine, don't worry. There's nothing going on with us anyway, it's no big deal.*

Luca: *Let me make it up to you.*

Twenty-Three

17th January

'Are you out skiing on your own?' Xavier asked, looking around in surprise as I slid my way over to him and Liv at the edge of the mountain.

'She's too important to ski with us now,' Liv said snidely.

'What? Noooo! I love skiing with you guys. I wasn't sure if I was welcome anymore, so I thought I'd practise on my own.' Liv had been giving me the pseudo-silent treatment all week, and although Xavier had picked me up after Luca blanked me, things didn't feel quite the same between us. I couldn't put my finger on it, but rather than mope around the chalet, where Genevieve seemed permanently cross with me, I'd decided to put my energy into skiing and get a few runs in.

'Of course you can still come out with us,' Xavier said, stiffly, kicking the heel of his left boot into the snow.

'Come on then, let's see ya,' Liv said, giving me her first smile in days, scraping along the snow in front of me and gesturing down the piste. Unbeknownst to the two of them, I was almost a reasonable skier, having snow-ploughed my way through half a season. I set off in earnest, swooshing gently down the empty slope. It had just turned 12 p.m. and the early risers had already stopped for lunch, leaving plenty of room on the piste to manoeuvre. Xavier came bombing down behind me, then slowed to a gentle carve while I did awkward but acceptable turns all the way down to the bottom.

'Those private lessons with Luca are really paying off,' Xavier said, with a hint of sarcasm.

'Not bad at all,' Liv said, giving me a begrudging thumbs up.

'My only *private* lessons have been with the beginner's ski school, but I have been getting a lot of practice in,' I admitted, thinking of the *hundreds* of times I'd forced myself up and down the piste so as not to immediately die when skiing with Luca.

'You should stick to that rather than getting arrested for crimes against snowboarding,' Liv said, with a laugh. 'You're way more in control.'

'And less likely to break something,' Xavier added, as the three of us were scooped up by a rickety old chair lift and launched into the sky, back to the top for another run.

'I'm going to do a few runs off-piste,' Liv said, sliding under the *do not enter* tape and bunny-hopping backwards towards the edge.

'Whattt?' I said, alarmed. 'Careful Liv, you're not allowed to go…'

She gave us a double salute, flipped her board round and disappeared into obscurity.

'She's getting good,' Xavier laughed, as we shuffled over to the nice, safe blue.

'We'll probably never see her again,' I said, worriedly looking out for a red dot haring through the trees. 'Sorry Xavier, don't feel you have to hang out with me, when you could be letting loose with Liv.'

'Not at all. Liv tries to kill me when we board together,' he said, positioning his goggles on his nose, ready for action.

'One extreme to the other,' I said, taking off gently, every muscle clenched tight as I slowly skied to the right, then slowly skied to the left, tracing an oversized zigzag into the mountain.

Xavier was boarding smoothly alongside me, so relaxed he could have been smoking a cigarette and swirling a late-night brandy. Why did everyone else always look so cool and I still felt completely out of my depth? I looked over, irritated, as he wiggled his board playfully in the snow, jumping and spinning as he went. It was easy to forget this was supposed to be fun, day after day, piste after piste, trying to stay alive. I was hunched over and concentrating hard, but somehow still managed to hit a mogul and shot towards the edge on one ski, throwing myself on the ground and faceplanting. Again.

'Holly? Are you OK?' Xavier called, speeding across to pick me up. He rolled me over, my face full of snow. 'You were doing so great.'

'I still can't do it,' I said, wiping the slush from my eyes and looking up at the sky. 'No matter how many times I practise, I still end up falling on my face.'

Xavier leant over me, concerned and it was nice to feel like he didn't totally hate me anymore. It was also quite nice lying down on the snow in the sun. Maybe a little snooze was in order.

'I know what will help,' Xavier said, sitting down. He pulled out a flask from his inside pocket and gave it a shake.

'Coffee?' I asked, disappointed.

'Red wine,' he replied, holding the flask out to me.

'Red wine in a thermos?' I said, taking a swig. 'How uncivilised!'

'My apologies. We should respect the wine,' he said, pouring some into the lid and drinking it with his pinkie out. He seemed to be back to his old self again, which was a relief; I didn't want there to be any awkwardness between us.

Xavier looked so at home on the mountain. Goggles on his forehead, his charcoal pants just the right amount of loose, with the matching jacket to complete the look. We sat on the side of the slope, completely at ease with one another, not needing to say anything. This is what I wanted. Was it too much to hope that one day I might find the companionship I shared with Xavier with a man of my own? Lucky Christina had him all to herself. How could she bear being away from him so much? Why are all the good ones always taken?

Mine and Xavier's phones pinged in unison, and I unzipped my pocket to pull mine out. It was Liv on the group chat:

Liv: *Sorry guys, I took a wrong turn and ended up in Bruson. Don't wait for me xx*

The ski lift hurtled to the top of the mountain, rattling as it lurched to an almost-stop, allowing us to get off and glide to the side. Xavier nodded over to the restaurant to signal the end of piste practice and the start of us ordering our bodyweight in cheese. We slid our way over to the front of Le Rouge and Xavier tucked my skis in with his board, wrapping everything up together with his lock.

'Safety first,' he winked.

'Absolutely,' I replied. 'You can never be too careful with the rented kit. Shall we try and get a table inside?'

Xavier nodded. 'Actually Holly, before we go in, I wanted to apologise for the past few weeks. I know I've been a bit off with you. I've had a lot on my mind with Luca and the restaurant and everything, but I shouldn't have brought that into work.'

'Is it anything I can help with?'

'Not really. And to be honest, it feels weird talking to you about it now that something has happened between you and Luca.'

I was about to explain that nothing had really happened between me and Luca when the calm was disrupted by a snippy voice behind us.

'Why can't you go back and get it?' she snarled.

'Because it'll take ages and the snow under the lift is up to my waist, so it's dangerous. You can buy another pole in the village.'

'But those poles were a present from Daddy; he won't be happy when I tell him you left it behind. It won't take long – I can wait for you in the bar?'

'It wasn't me that dropped it though, Pippa, was it? If you want it so badly, go and get it yourself.'

That voice sounded painfully familiar. Could it be…? Surely not…? I slowly turned around, knowing the voice but not believing for a second it could possibly be him. But it was. It was George, shaking the snow off his skis and clicking them together with his poles as he bundled them in with the rosy-cheeked brunette's. I stood very still, in complete shock. How could it be him? What was he doing here and who was she? I wasn't sure whether to go over and speak to him or get away ASAP. I spent too long frozen in indecision and George looked directly up and into my eyes, as he clicked his padlock into place. I quickly looked down, burying my face in my snood as I turned and walked away.

'Holly?' he called out, in disbelief.

I stopped and slowly turned around. Seeing George here in the flesh, in my magical new world was too much to compute.

Pippa stopped and looked from me to George and back again.

'Pippa, this is…' George said, not taking his eyes off me.

'Your ex-fiancée,' she said, with a glint in her eye. She took great care to emphasise the word *ex*, holding out her hand to shake mine. 'I recognise you from George's Instagram. Nice to meet you.'

I was just about to ask who she was and where the hell she'd come from, when Xavier appeared at my side. He smiled at everyone.

'Hi,' he said, shaking hands with George and Pippa, 'I'm Xavier. Are you friends of Holly's?'

I half-nodded, hesitating to introduce them. 'George and I are… were… at university together,' I said, struggling to articulate what we now were to each other. 'I've not met Pippa before.' I took in her shiny ponytail and big, blue eyes. She looked fresh out of uni herself, with her clear skin and pouty lips. No wonder he'd stopped looking at my Stories and commenting on my posts.

'It was a bit more than university, wasn't it Hols?' George said, puffing out his chest.

'George and I work together,' Pippa said, linking arms with him territorially, 'sort of. Well, George works for my dad at the council, and I occasionally work there too, as Daddy's assistant.' Oh. *That* Pippa. He'd always referred to her as Philippa. Philippa Anders. Daughter of our local MP. And he'd always described her as the triple B: brat boss baby.

Xavier looked over at me and I smiled flatly, trying to communicate with my eyes. He clocked that something was wrong and tried to move us along.

'What are the chances of you all meeting like this on the slopes? Shall we get out of the cold?' Xavier said charismatically, leading the way. 'We can walk and talk.'

'Are you on holiday?' I asked, confused. It was baffling to me to see George on a piste; he'd never been skiing in his life. He was probably thinking the same thing about me. George nodded and smiled at Pippa.

'Pip... I mean Pippa fancied a week away, so we came over last minute. We're staying at a little place called the Verbier Grand Hotel,' George said, very pleased with himself. 'Do you know it?' His supercilious expression quickly changed as I nodded. I knew it and I doubted George was paying for it. Or Pip, for that matter. Pip's Pop was clearly a generous man.

'I know it well,' I said with a nod. 'The breakfast is to die for. Xavier and I live out here, so we know all the hotels.' *Take that, George.*

'You're living out here together?' George asked.

'Yes,' I said, looking fondly over at Xavier as he leant in to talk to Pippa. He was out of hearing distance, and we did live under the same roof, so it wasn't a total lie. 'I told you I was working out in Switzerland?'

George suddenly looked sick. Obviously disappointed my life hadn't dissolved into nothing the second he'd ditched me.

We got to the door of Le Rouge, and I was desperate to shake him and Pippa off. Xavier was already at the front desk conferring with the Maître d' and George went over to join him, while I awkwardly waited with Pippa.

'Ballinger for two at 12.30 p.m.,' he said as the Maître d' turned to him.

Xavier looked back at me and I shook my head at him. His eyes narrowed slightly as he tried to understand what I was saying.

'I don't have a Ballinger down for today,' he said, looking through the list. 'Please join the queue and I'll seat you as soon as I possibly can.' The walk-in queue snaked all the way out the door and halfway back to the chair lift.

'Hang on just a minute, I think you'll find...' George said hotly, pulling out his phone and speed-scrolling, 'I definitely booked us a table for today. I have the confirmation here somewhere.'

'You're very welcome to join Holly and me for lunch?' Xavier said. Oh God, no.

'Lovely,' Pippa smiled as I walked over to Xavier and whispered in his ear.

'That's my ex-George. The one I was going to marry.'

'I figured,' he whispered back. 'Let's have a bit of fun

with him. Show him what he's missing.' I had no idea what Xavier was playing at but it was too late to back out now.

'We can share their table, George,' Pippa snipped. 'I'm NOT joining that queue.'

'It's no problem,' Xavier beamed.

'We'd love to, thanks,' Pippa switched to a smile, while George carried on scrolling.

The Maître d' bustled on ahead. 'This way, please. Anything for Monsieur Lavedrine. Here we are, a table of four.' George stood hovering, not sure whether to sit down, but the Maître d' was insistent, and it was starting to cause a scene.

'My friend Maxim is the head chef here, so they've sorted us a table,' Xavier explained with a kind smile. 'It saves you guys queuing and will give you all a chance to catch up.'

'Sit, sit, sit,' insisted the Maître d' as George and I looked at each other in awkward horror. He sat down with Pippa, opposite Xavier and me. What the fucking-fuck was going on? I'd unexpectedly slipped into the twilight zone. We ordered drinks, and a mountain of bread and olives appeared on the table while we chose our food.

'Shall we share a raclette?' Xavier asked the table, taking charge. 'I would highly recommend the five-cheese option if you're up for it? By all accounts, it is excellent.'

'If it's cheese, bread and potatoes, then count me in,' I said, snapping my menu shut.

'*J'adore raclette*,' Pippa said, eyes shining in Xavier's direction. George harumphed his agreement as the waiter wrote everything down with a flourish.

'So where do you live?' Pippa asked, popping a stuffed olive in her mouth.

'Chalet Blanchet. It's a ski-in at the end of Blue Eight,' I said, 'not far from the church.'

'It's been in the family for years,' Xavier added, giving me a nudge under the table.

'We have a family chalet in Val d'Isère, but I fancied a change this time, you know?' Pippa replied. 'Maybe we can do a chalet swap next time?'

She laughed and clinked her glass with Xavier, as George watched the exchange with a frozen smile.

'He's amazing,' I whispered, nodding over at Xavier, 'and his body is to die for,' I added conspiratorially, knowing George was conscious of his love handles.

'Good to know,' he said. 'And you're skiing now too? I thought you hated the cold?'

'I hardly ever get cold out here. There's no such thing as bad weather, George, just bad clothes,' I said. 'Yes, I've been learning to ski with Xavier and my Australian friend, Liv.'

'Is she in the Australian Olympics team?' piped up Pip. 'I heard they were out here training?'

'Are they? Er… I'm not sure she's on the official team,' I said.

'Olympic Team? Who's that?' Xavier asked as the raclette arrived and saved me.

'*Regardez-vous*, the five-cheese raclette with brie, camembert, chevre and gruyere.' The Maître d' placed the large metal grill on the table with a tiny pan for each of us and a platter of cheeses to choose from. Bowls of boiled potatoes, coleslaw, tomatoes, sliced red onion and sweetcorn all served with warm French bread and salted butter.

'And what is it that you do, Xavier?' George asked pointedly.

'I'm a chef,' he replied.

'Ooh, very fancy,' Pippa laughed.

'It can be,' he said with a smile. 'Holly and I work together.'

'Where did you train?' Pippa asked.

'Cordon Bleu,' Xavier replied, 'and then under the head chef at Le Cinq.'

'And now you just cook at one of the chalets?' George tried again.

'He's not just a cook, George,' Pippa said, looking embarrassed. 'Cordon Bleu is the best culinary school in the world and Le Cinq is the best Michelin star restaurant in Paris. Daddy's been on the waiting list for ages. Xavier must be a huge talent if he worked there.'

'Something like that,' Xavier smiled, letting his answer hang for a beat before returning the question. 'And your job?'

'I head up PR for one of the MPs at Westminster council,' George mumbled.

'Very cool,' Xavier said with a nod.

'How is everything going with work and… er… home?' I asked, grilling a piece of raclette to drizzle onto my carb-fest of a dinner. So far, it was a potato sandwich with some salad on the side.

'Not bad,' George said, 'I moved into the house as you suggested, for security reasons. No point paying the mortgage and leaving it empty.'

'It's absolutely gorgeous,' Pippa said, with a smile, 'so smart and clean.'

'Are you living there as well then?' I asked and she nodded. George went very quiet.

'Sorry, have I said the wrong thing?' Pippa said, putting

her arm around George and smiling brightly. The man who should have been my husband. The house that should have been my home. 24 Orchard Close had been destined to be Chez Geolly and was now seemingly Chez Gippa. I'd been so stupid thinking he was holding onto the house because he was holding onto us, when he'd already moved Pippa in and was actually holding onto her.

'Pippa and I have only just started seeing each other,' George said quietly, 'in case you're thinking she had anything to do with...'

'About six months now, isn't it?' Pippa shot back. Xavier's eyes flew from Pippa to George and then finally to me, as he realised what that meant. He gave me a pained look which I returned with a fraction of an eyebrow.

'We met six months ago, yes, but...' George started.

'And what a night that was!' Pippa said with a snort. 'Not sure I'll ever look at a cucumber in the same way, if you know what I mean.' She gave Xavier a double eyebrow-raise and laughed. I was torn between eating a forkful of cheesy potato and forking George in the eye. The food had it by a gnat's whisker. I quickly did the maths. George and I were still together six months ago. July. A month before we moved out of the flat and two months before George said, 'I don't'.

My mind was whirring. 'Moved in quite fast then?' I said, feeling empty as I remembered everything George and I had planned for that house together. Eight years of imagining our future.

'I could say the same about you two,' George retorted, as Xavier reached over and stroked my cheek, sending a shiver down my back.

'Holly and I are very much in love, yes,' he said, pulling me into him. Thank God he was playing along. 'It felt right for us to be together, didn't it, my love?'

I looked at him staring at me intently and felt my heart catch.

'It did,' I smiled and held my breath as he leant in and kissed me, his warm lips firm and sensual. His arm around my shoulder, softly stroking my wrist, giving me goosebumps. George and Pippa sat silently opposite, George glaring furiously.

'Maybe we should change the subject though, *non*?' Xavier said, raising his glass and putting his hand on mine. 'A toast to old friends and new,' he said, as we all clinked glasses. I eyeballed George equally furiously. I'd speak to him about Pippa's timeline when we were alone. No point ruining a good potato sandwich.

'*Excusez-moi? Un autre bouteille de Semillon, s'il vous plaît*,' I said to the waiter as he scurried past.

'You're using your French then?' George said, clearly impressed.

'*Un petit pois*,' I said. Joking in French went over George's head, but Xavier smiled.

'I speak fluent French as well, George,' Pippa said.

'I know you do but I didn't realise Holly's French was still so good,' he said, tearing off a big hunk of bread and slathering it with butter.

'You only ever know someone as well as they want you to,' Xavier said, clear-eyed, holding his stare.

George looked at me thoughtfully, adding bubbling brie and onions to his plate.

'*Mesdames et Messieurs*. Le Rouge will transform for

après ski in half an hour. If you have not been here before then you are in for a treat. Le Rouge is where the party happens in Verbier so get your dancing shoes on, or if you prefer a quiet end to the day, we will bring you your bill and you can escape before the chaos begins.'

'Are you a party person, Pippa?' I asked, hoping she wouldn't mention the cucumber again.

'Yeahhhh!' she said, downing the rest of her Semillon.

'George?' Xavier asked.

'Hell no, we won't go,' George chanted in reply.

Hell was right and it was set to continue. I squeezed Xavier's leg as a signal for us to leave and he squeezed mine back in reply. FFS. I'd have to grab him once we were alone.

'More drinks?' Xavier asked as the waiter appeared.

'Why not?' George smiled. 'If that's cool with you guys?'

I glared daggers at him, making it 120 per cent clear that it was absolutely not cool. 'Sure,' I said, smiling sweetly. What was he playing at?

'Great. We'll take four large beers and four shots of tequila, please,' he said to the waiter, as the music started cranking up.

'Bloody hell George, that's a lot of booze!' I said alarmed.

'Money doesn't count when you're on holiday,' he said with a wink. Oh yes. That was one of his life rules.

'Time to partyyyyy!!!' Pippa loosened her ponytail and shook out her hair en route to the ladies as Xavier disappeared into the kitchen to thank Maxim. I could finally speak to George without any airs or graces.

'Alone at last,' he said, moving to sit next to me and draping his arm along the back of the chair.

'Do you mind,' I said, promptly removing it. 'What

are you doing, George? Is it not bad enough that you abandoned me on our wedding day; now you're waving your new girlfriend in my face while *my* new boyfriend pays for all the drinks?' I was livid.

'He is your boyfriend then? Replaced me pretty fast, didn't you?' George said, teasing.

'Not as fast as you, by Pippa's cucumber calculations.'

'Nothing happened that night. We just got talking. It was a superfood-themed dinner that work put on and the desserts were made from cucumber.'

'I don't care about the details, George,' I said, holding my hand up. 'You dumped me on our wedding day and said there was nobody else. It seems a bit of a coincidence that Pippa was on the scene the whole time and now you're out here on holiday together.'

George put his hand on my leg and shuffled towards me, giving me his signature, sorrowful look. The same curly-haired face I'd seen say sorry a million times before. His hand felt both familiar and alien as I moved my knees to the side and batted it away.

'What are you doing? Can you keep your hands to yourself, please,' I said.

'Don't be like that. I'm sorry, Holly. I admit I wasn't wholly innocent, but it wasn't just Pippa. I was scared of the commitment. Getting married didn't feel right.'

'I imagine it did feel strange if you were knocking off the Triple B behind my back.'

'Don't call her that.'

'I don't call her that. YOU call her that. That is literally your name for her.'

'It was and it was childish of me. Don't you think it's

weird that we've bumped into each other here? Like fate or something? Is the universe trying to tell us something?'

Was this some kind of surreal joke? He was so cavalier about people's feelings. Mine and now Pippa's, casting us aside to suit himself. How had I not seen this side of him before?

'Yes. I think the universe is trying to tell me that I nearly made a terrible mistake,' I said, moving away as George leant in. 'I'm not interested anymore, George. Did you think I'd be forever waiting until you clicked your fingers? Xavier is three times the man you are.'

Pippa returned just as the waiter appeared with the drinks, passing them to us and placing Xavier's on the table for when he came back.

'Cheers!' Pippa said, holding her tequila up, in celebration of God knows what.

'Cheers!' George replied, kissing her on the lips, as they both downed their shots, leaving me with no one to clink. I felt a reassuring hand on my shoulder as Xavier cheers-ed me out of nowhere and mirrored George, kissing me full on the lips. My whole body tingled as his lips found mine. I leant in, wanting the kiss to carry on, then caught myself and slowly pulled away, knowing it was all for show, that he was only doing it as a favour. He was happily married and there was no room to have even the smallest of feelings. I couldn't do that to another woman. Even so, we locked eyes slightly breathless as we both drank our shots. I glanced over at George, who surreptitiously winked while Pippa wasn't looking.

'Can we get out of here?' I said as Xavier supped his beer. I couldn't bear the idea of a full après-ski session with

Winky McWinkerson and Pippa. They'd already outstayed their welcome as far as I was concerned.

'Of course,' he replied, taking concerted gulps to get his lager down. 'So that's the George you were going to marry?'

I felt my whole face flush at the thought of it.

'Yeah...' I said, 'what are the chances, eh?'

'Don't worry, I'll get us out of here,' he said, gesturing at the waiter for the bill.

George and Pippa were already on the dancefloor as we stood up. I waved over at them and pointed to the door as Xavier put on his coat. *Goodbye George, forever.* Duran Duran was playing loudly, so it wasn't worth shouting goodbye and I thought giving him the Vs was a bit harsh. George pushed his way back over to us, through the dancefloor. Honestly, just take the hint and GO AWAY.

'Are you guys heading off?' George asked, as Xavier put his arm around me.

'Yes, we have a few things we need to do,' he said, squeezing me protectively.

'OK, well leave the bill to us,' he said.

'Already settled. Drinks are on me,' Xavier said nonchalantly, 'and my friend treated us to the raclette.'

'It was great to see you,' I said, lying through my teeth.

'You too,' he said, with a smile. 'Maybe we'll bump into you again?'

'Maybe,' I said, 'but I hope not,' I muttered as we waved again to Pippa and made our way to the door.

I couldn't wait to get away. I needed a shower to wash George off. How could I have thought I'd be forever happy as Mrs Ballinger, when he was still so obviously such a little boy?

The sun had already set behind the clouds and the air was cold as we queued for the lift.

'Thank you for saving me in there,' I said, feeling completely discombobulated, 'I hope it doesn't get you into trouble with your wife.'

'Not at all, that's what friends are for. Christina understands that more than most,' Xavier said with a smile.

Twenty-Four

24th January

'It was so nice to see him again. No one knows more about French-Swiss fusion than Maxim,' Xavier said fondly. 'He was always coming up with brilliant new dishes at Le Cinq. We all hated him for it.'

'Charming,' I said.

'In a loving, fiercely competitive way of course.'

'His raclette last week was delicious, so I'm looking forward to meeting him.'

The gondola clunked its way up through the pine trees, as birds swooped and dived alongside us. It was 2.30 p.m. and nearing the end of the skiing day, so only a handful of people were in the lift, and it was strangely quiet. The weather was pretty awful, and I would 100 per cent have been in the spa or be eating something cheese-based if I was on holiday. Xavier and I didn't have any of our snow kit with us and were wearing matching blue jeans with thermal layers for warmth. I felt so much lighter and freer without my wrist-guards and knee support and helmet and goggles. It was a relief not to have to keep tabs on it all.

I wiggled myself about a bit to check the outfit was working – it was paper-thin yet tight and cosy. The thinnest of thin thermals with leggings under my jeans. I felt warm and totally comfy. The lift rocked about as it went up the final hurdle to Le Rouge, rolling us about like meatballs in a tin can. The restaurant was at the very top of the resort, so we'd switched lifts three times to navigate our way this far. The snow was gushing down on all sides as we eventually ground to a halt and got out.

'Finally,' I said, jamming my hands in my pockets and nosing my face into my snood, 'that took forever. I'm assuming Maxim doubles up as Santa Claus and that we are now in Lapland?'

'He might do if you ask him nicely. The best things in life are worth waiting for,' Xavier said.

'I thought the best things in life were free?' I replied.

'Not when it comes to food. *Alors.* We need to stay focused. We have ninety minutes to watch and learn from Maxim and then we'll get the last lift down,' Xavier said, as the snow swirled around us. The sky was now a dreary grey haze and even my yellow lenses weren't helping with visibility.

'Got it. In, listen, learn, out,' I said, with a nod.

'The last lift – it is 4.30 p.m., *oui*?' Xavier called over to the man in the small glass office, operating the lift. He gave a wiggle of his curly eyebrows and nodded. The lift was right next to the restaurant, so we could seamlessly move from warm lift to warm lift station and through the warm walkway into the warm restaurant. Just how I liked it.

'*Bonjour, bonjour*,' a twenty-stone Frenchman thundered his way over to us, embracing Xavier overzealously. 'You must be Holly?' he said, shaking my hand enthusiastically, then double kissing the air.

'*Bonjour*, Maxim,' I said, smiling.

'Please, call me Max,' he replied.

'Where is everyone?' Xavier asked, looking around the half-empty restaurant. An elderly couple were cradling their coffees in one corner, next to a tall, blond man with a gaggle of blond children eating chocolate brownies, and the other three tables had already finished and were waiting to pay the bill.

'The weather is putting people off,' Max said, with a shrug. 'Perfect timing for your visit as I am not so busy, eh?' He led us through the tartan-filled restaurant and into the kitchen where a flurry of chefs buzzed about.

'Quiet please,' Max called, commanding the attention of everyone in the room. 'I would like to present to you all the excellent Xavier Lavedrine, a chef friend of mine from Paris. We worked together at Le Cinq.' They each smiled or waved in welcome, and Xavier went pink.

'And this is his latest protégée, from Chalet Blanchet in the village, Holly Roberts.' They seemed less impressed as I smiled my hello. Robin to Xavier's Batman, his affable but ultimately less interesting sidekick.

'You can all finish up for the day. The restaurant is empty, and I don't think we'll have a rush with the weather as it is.' The kitchen cleared almost before he'd finished his sentence and Max grinned warmly at us both.

'First, a drink? What can I get you? A coffee? Beer?'

'Espresso please,' I said, even though I wanted a beer.

'*Deux*,' Xavier nodded, and Max called it through to the bar.

'Thank you for having us over to teach Holly some of your tricks,' Xavier said, slapping Max on the back. 'You are a legend in the village. I told Holly your chocolate fondue is to die for and now she's seen first-hand how far people travel to come and see you, I think she finally believes me.'

'You are too kind as always, Xavier. You know me, a little of this, a pinch of that. Bringing French excellence to the masses using the local gastronomy. As you say... my latest smash hit has been the chocolate fondue. All French chocolates of course, with macarons for decoration and a type of cake for dipping.' Max pulled out a tray of fondue vases made with choux pastry and sugar paper, each one a different colour. He fired up the hob and clanked out three small saucepans from one of the drawers, adding double cream to each.

'Is it all edible?' Xavier asked.

'But of course,' Max replied with a smile, breaking large slabs of dark, milk and white chocolate into small pieces and putting them into the individual saucepans.

'Is there anything I can do to help?' I asked, my mouth already watering at the thought of this creamy, chocolatey feast.

'You are here to learn, *non*?' Max said, pulling open the drawer once more and pointing to the saucepans. 'We will work side by side. Copy me exactly.'

I pulled out a heap of saucepans and put them on my side of the hob, trying to catch up. Xavier watched as we worked, eyes shining. 'We can make this back at the chalet for Luca and Genevieve,' he said.

'*Absolutement!* It is very simple of course,' Max said, pulling out two punnets of strawberries and passing one to me. 'It is as much in the presentation as the ingredients.'

'All the best dishes are,' Xavier agreed.

Max took a plump strawberry and deftly sliced it into a wafer-thin fan, sprinkling it with sugar and pepper and placing it on a tray of parchment paper. He went through the punnet as I tried to keep up, treating each strawberry with the same hushed reverence, until there was a full tray of sugared strawberries ready for crisping under the grill.

'I do strawberries, bananas and pineapple, but you can use any fruits you wish,' Max said, passing me a banana and repeating the process, but this time cutting the fruit into wedges for dipping.

I followed as quickly and as closely as I could.

'That is the healthy side of the clock,' Max said, laying the crispy sugared fruit on the plate from 12 p.m. to 6 p.m. 'Now it's time for the naughty side.'

He pulled out some pre-made dough and handed me a lump as he turned on the fryers.

'Donuts?' Xavier asked.

'Churros?' I guessed.

'Yes and no,' he said with a beam. 'I serve the fondue with madeleine-shaped donuts to bring in the French fusion element.'

He cut his dough into quarters and smoothed each piece into a plastic madeleine mould, sprinkling all four with sugar, then popping them straight into the fryer.'

'*C'est tout*,' Max said with a flourish.

'*C'est très facile*,' Xavier exclaimed.

'It's our best seller and people come for miles to try it. That and my signature dish, of course,' Max said.

'Your raclette?' I asked tentatively.

'*Mais oui*. I switch up the cheeses each week so there is always a different version for the customers to try. Give them a reason to keep coming back, eh?'

'Genius, my friend.' Xavier slapped him on the back.

The madeleines gave off a sweet smell as Max tipped them out of the fryer onto a wire cooling tray to recover from the heat. He handed me three of the edible pastry vases for my platter, one red, one white and one sporting the Swiss flag, then decorated his own platter in the same way. The vases were placed in a triangle, as he fastidiously poured the dark, milk and white melted chocolate into them and I followed suit. I was desperate to dip my finger in and have a taste but had to hold myself back.

Xavier looked over and gave me a smile. 'I couldn't choose between them,' he said, very generously, as my madeleines were full of holes.

'You forgot the sugar sprinkles on your tray,' Max observed, as he placed his perfectly-finished madeleines onto his platter. Both fondues looked beautiful, but Max's was clearly the best, no matter how closely I'd tried to copy.

'Bravo,' Xavier clapped, as the two of us stood back from our plates as if we were on a TV competition. 'I can see why the customers keep coming back.'

'Can we eat them now?' I asked, ready to drink the white chocolate sauce.

'Of course,' Max said. 'Let's take them into the restaurant and enjoy them with the view.'

The smell of the cake combined with the fruit and

chocolate was divine and I was looking forward to having mine with a nice coffee, overlooking the mountains. Max led the way, his plate held aloft, Xavier carried my plate and I carried myself, which was work enough. I heard it before I saw it; Max gave a low whistle and Xavier stopped in the doorway as I walked into his back. I peeked over his shoulder at the 360-degree view of the mountain, which was now entirely hidden by a snowstorm. The skies were completely white and it was impossible to differentiate between the storm and the mountain. The restaurant was empty and the staff had taken Max at his word and gone home. We'd been engrossed in making our chocolate fondues and lost track of time, with no idea the storm had whipped itself into such a frenzy. Max slammed his fondue down and ran towards the walkway.

'Let me check the lifts are still running,' he called over his shoulder. The clock on the wall had just turned 3.55 p.m., so we had half an hour to eat our desserts. I couldn't wait any longer. I dunked one of my madeleines in the dark chocolate sauce and took a bite. The custard cream in the centre mixed with the bitter chocolate tasted amazing, I dunked it again and offered it to Xavier, who bit into it hungrily, his lips grazing my fingers as he snaffled it into his mouth.

'Delicious,' he said, with the same wonderment I felt.

'I know. What is it? Why is it so different to our chocolate sauce?'

'The rum.'

'Oh. Yes, of course, that makes sense.'

'Booze-fuelled chocolate sauce is always a winner,' Xavier said, putting a teaspoon into the sauce and tasting a mouthful.

'This storm doesn't look good, does it?' I said, watching the wind blow layer after layer of snow across the piste. 'I'm not sure I fancy getting the lift down in that.'

'Uh, judging by his face, that might not be an option,' Xavier said, nodding at Max as he ran back into the restaurant, wringing his hands.

'The liftman has gone! He normally tells us if there's a problem to give us time to get the customers out and down the mountain.'

'Maybe he did,' I said looking around the empty restaurant.

'He didn't look very far if he didn't get to the kitchen,' Max said angrily.

The wind rattled through the windows as the snow fell around us. It had already settled up to three feet and looked like it had no plans to slow down.

'Shall I message Liv? We won't be back for 6 p.m., will we?' I said, ever diligent.

Xavier smiled. 'I very much doubt it. Unless you want to take your chances on skis?' I gave him an eyeroll and WhatsApped Liv on the group chat.

Me: *Xavier and I are stuck at Le Rouge in the storm – eek!*

Liv: *Are you OK? Shall I call the mountain police?*

Me: *We're with Xavier's friend, Max, but the lifts are closed till tomorrow morning, so we won't be back till then.*

Liv: *Stay safe babes, don't worry – I'll cover things here xx let me know if it doesn't get sorted tomorrow xx*

Max picked up his phone and punched in a number, looking like he wanted to punch someone's lights out.

'What will we do?' I whispered to Xavier, staring out

the window and starting to understand the seriousness of the situation. The wind howled through the chimney as I perched against a radiator.

'My flat is upstairs, above the restaurant,' Max said, overhearing, 'so there is nothing to worry about; you will be safe here, you can stay with me. It is small, but we will make it work.'

I turned to Xavier. 'That sounds OK then, doesn't it?' I was relieved we had that option at least. 'As long as we've got food and a bed for the night.'

'Not ideal,' Xavier said, 'but better than being stuck on the mountain.' I dunked my second madeleine; this time into the white chocolate sauce and this time, I wasn't sharing. It. Was. Divine. It couldn't just be the rum; there was foodie witchcraft baked into it. I didn't care if I was stuck up here forever – as long as we could keep making, dunking and eating these chocolate-covered madeleines, I'd live a happy life.

'*Zut alors*,' Max cursed, 'The lift staff are all on the ground – they saw all the chefs leave and didn't realise we were still up here. Idiots.'

'Don't worry, my friend; we are not trapped in Alcatraz. This is a pretty cool place to be stranded – we will be fine,' Xavier said.

'I only have two bedrooms in the flat and not much of a lounge,' Max said, 'so I'm afraid the two of you will have to share a bed.'

I glanced awkwardly at Xavier. We didn't have much choice and I didn't want to appear ungrateful.

'That's so kind of you Max... Thank goodness we are stuck up here with you,' I said.

The snowstorm blew heavy around us, but we had electricity and heating and enough food to feed a small army. Maxim and Luca worked together to prepare a beef bourguignon in red-wine gravy as I shelled peas and made a pan of buttery mash. Three chefs cooking to pass the time, as the weather got worse before it got better.

Maxim's phone rang and he had a heated conversation in French before hanging up.

'They think the storm will pass overnight and first lifts will be back open at 8 a.m.,' he said, 'so I will see if I can find you both something to wear in bed.'

We went up to the flat to settle in for the night. Maxim hadn't been exaggerating: his flat was tiny. The double bed in the guest room filled the bedroom entirely, leaving only a few inches around the edge in which to manoeuvre. Xavier lay down on the left side, fully dressed.

'Is that your side?' I asked.

'I don't have a side,' he replied, 'I'm flexible.'

'You and your wife don't have a side? You switch it up every time?' I asked with raised eyebrows.

'Well, we tend to…'

Max gave a sharp knock on the door and walked in with two enormous T-shirts and two brand-new toothbrushes. 'It's the best I can do, I'm afraid,' he said.

'It's plenty enough,' Xavier said, taking them from him. 'Thank you, my friend.'

I went into the bathroom to change, folding my clothes into a neat pile on the toilet seat as I shimmied on Max's T-shirt. It was wide and long and went well over my knees, but I felt strangely exposed with my legs out. Thank God I'd shaved them this morning. I was nervous about sharing a bed with Xavier; it felt too close, too intimate somehow. How would I ever fall asleep with him lying next to me? I brushed my teeth and carried my clothes into the bedroom, holding them against me to cover myself as I crossed paths with Xavier. I got into bed, while Xavier used the bathroom, shuffling myself to the edge so as not to encroach on his space. I was sooo exhausted; I couldn't wait to close my eyes. Xavier got into bed next to me and I could feel the warmth of his body only inches away. I tried to keep as close to my side as possible. Because I did have a side. I thought it would feel strange having a different man sleeping on George's side, but with Xavier there, safe and secure, it was somehow OK.

'Are you alright?' he asked, pulling the duvet up to his neck.

I looked over at him and nodded. 'We'll be able to leave tomorrow morning, won't we?'

'Of course we will, don't worry. We'll go down in the lift as soon it's safe. Try and get some rest. You've had quite a week, what with bumping into George and Pippa and now this.'

'I know. Thank you again for helping me out with that whole situation. You went above and beyond with that kiss.'

'It was my pleasure to help out. It must have been strange to see him again after all this time?'

'I thought I was imagining it to start with. George crashing into my new world. But maybe it was the closure I needed – to see him here with another woman like that. I can't believe I came so close to marrying him.'

'Hindsight gives a new perspective,' Xavier nodded, 'but it was a totally different you that was set to marry him. That Holly doesn't exist anymore.'

'I thought it would ruin marriage for me forever, but I still believe in love. I still want to share my life with someone and build a life together. Like you and Christina.'

'Don't worry, Holly Roberts, you are a special person. You just need to find someone as special as you are. Someone who recognises and appreciates your talents and treats you like you deserve to be treated. Goodnight Holly,' he said, giving my arm a little squeeze.

'Goodnight,' I said sleepily, feeling warm inside.

I woke to the sound of loud snores. It didn't sound like Liv though, so who...? I blinked at an unfamiliar wall and it all came rushing back. Le Rouge, the storm, the kiss with Xavier... what a week. I closed my eyes again to push it all away. Xavier had somehow managed to wrap himself around me and was holding me close, playing big spoon, his arms lying loose across my body. I tried to untangle myself but he snuggled me back in and I could tell from his breathing that he was in a deep sleep. I didn't want to scare him by waking him suddenly, so I lay still for a few moments enjoying the feel of his big arms around me; his wife was a lucky woman.

Maxim's snores reached a crescendo and he woke Xavier up with a particularly loud snort. I quickly closed my eyes as he rolled over to stretch.

'Morning,' he whispered.

'Morning,' I said. 'Can you have a word with your friend, please? That level of snoring is unacceptable.'

Xavier smiled. 'Was I sleep-cuddling you?'

'I think so. I'm not sure how it happened. I'm so sorry,' I flustered.

'There's nothing to be sorry about; it was me. I'm used to having the whole bed to myself, don't worry about it,' he said.

'I just don't want to create any problems with Christina.'

'Honestly, it's no big deal,' Xavier said, getting out of bed.

Twenty-Five

28th January

There was a loud chime as the doorbell went, making Liv and me jump.

'They're early,' I said, glancing at the clock, 'like, really early?'

'Can someone answer that?' Genevieve shouted down the stairs. I pulled the front door open with an overzealous smile, ready to welcome Mimi and Frank in for dinner *again* – honestly, they may as well move in – only to find George staring up at me with my red snood in his hands.

'George! What are you doing here?' I asked, glancing behind me to make sure Genevieve didn't see.

George gave a low whistle as he took in the chalet and the Porsche on the drive.

'Wow! Pretty sweet place to live,' he said, putting his nose over my shoulder and taking a good look inside. 'Landed on your feet here, didn't you?'

'Rather than in a heap on the floor, you mean? Yeah, I guess I did.'

'You left your scarf behind in Le Rouge last week, so I thought I'd drop it over,' he said, handing me my red, woolly snood, which was wet and raggedy and looked like it had been chewed by a cow.

'Did someone spill beer on it?' I asked, taking it from him with two fingers and holding it in the air. 'Thanks for bringing it over… I think.'

'I thought, you know, since it's the one I got you at uni on our first date, you might want it back…?'

'God, no, that one's long gone. Abi sent me this one for Christmas. It was brand new.'

Xavier appeared in the doorway, resting his chin on my shoulder and hugging me from behind. He felt so strong and warm and his George-radar was finely-tuned. I'm not sure I'd want him behaving like this with another woman if he was married to me. Although his wife was always so friendly, she didn't seem like the jealous type. It must be a French thing.

'Everything OK here?' he asked. 'Oh, hi George, didn't see you there.'

George gave him an uncomfortable nod.

'What brings you over to see us?' Xavier asked, giving him a cool stare.

'I just wanted a quick word with Holly before I fly home tomorrow,' he said, looking at the ground, 'and to bring her scarf back.' George pointed to it in my hands.

'Ahhh! She's been looking everywhere for that!'

'Glad I could be of service,' George replied archly.

'Cool. I'll leave you two to it then. Mimi and Frank are due in half an hour, Hols, so don't be too long.' Xavier said with a smile, then kissed me on the cheek for extra show and disappeared. It felt nice to know he had my back.

'Thank you for coming all this way to give me my scarf,' I said wrapping it around my arm, 'I'd invite you in but we've got important clients coming for lunch.'

'I wasn't sure if you left the scarf on purpose?' George asked.

I frowned. 'Why would I have done that?'

'I don't know,' he shrugged, 'to give us chance to talk together, alone?'

George looked at me with a half-smile, clearly hoping I had dropped my modern-day handkerchief for him to leap down and retrieve. That I'd left a red, woolly breadcrumb trail that would lead him to my chalet door. I could hear Liv and Xavier clattering around in the background, getting ready for Mimi and Frank, and didn't really have time for a heart-to-heart.

'I'm not sure there's much more to say, is there?' I asked softly.

'Well, we promised to give each other some time,' George said, 'and I can see now that I was wrong. That you have got the spirit of adventure I always thought you had. That you can party like the best of them, just like we did at uni...'

Oh God. Where was he going with this?

'I'm really not a big party person at all George, honestly...'

'You are, though. I've seen your Instagram posts since you've been out here: all the après ski bars, the Champagne lifestyle. The sort of life I'd imagined. The world I wanted for us – that I still want for us.'

'What do you mean...?' I was too stunned to say anything else.

George shuffled about in the snow and pulled something out of his pocket. A black, velvet box. My beautiful wedding ring – the one I'd chosen after hours and hours of research. A simple gold band decorated with a shower of tiny diamonds.

'I'm saying I'm an idiot and I'm sorry and I think maybe it was cold feet after all. I was flailing about, looking for something I already had.'

I couldn't believe it. George stood shivering on the chalet doorstep, offering me my old life back. Holding out the ring I'd worn a hundred different times as I'd imagined my life as Mrs Ballinger. I had no words.

'I've missed you, Holly. I've missed us. Your funny little ways, our breakfasts in bed – even Basil's fur attacks when I walk through the door. Is there any chance you can forgive me? I know it'll take time for you to trust me again – but can we try?'

'What about Pippa?' I blurted out, taking the box from him, my wedding ring twinkling in the sun.

'Pippa is a nice distraction,' he said, 'but she hasn't got any substance, you know? She gets given everything by her parents. She's not like me and you, Holly; she's never had to work for it.'

I thought of Pippa, waiting at the hotel, while George performed this Romeo scene, oblivious to his betrayal. How could I have ever seen a future with him?

'I'm sorry, George,' I said, taking one last look at my wedding ring before snapping the box shut and handing it back. 'I took some time too and realised you were right to call it off. We want different things. We both want life's big adventure, but my version is very different to yours.'

'But it's not too late, Holly. We still have the house. We don't need to get married; let's just get you home, settle Basil in. There's still time to see how our life was meant to turn out.'

He was starting to sound desperate.

'Maybe it's not too late for you, George, but it is too late for me. I've seen a new life for myself. A new future. And it isn't living in Surrey with you, defending my career choices, apologising for my love of cooking. It's over, George. You know it and so do I.'

George nodded to himself. 'I thought so, but I wanted to give it one more shot. Time to sell the house then?'

'Yep. Time to sell the house and move on with our lives,' I said.

'Worth a try though, eh?' He smiled, opening his arms out for a hug. I leant in and gave him a big squeeze.

'Worth a try,' I nodded into his shoulder.

Twenty-Six

5th February

'Happy Birthday, Holly!' I woke up to a bed full of colourful balloons and Liv and Xavier blowing paper horns in my face. Xavier held out a stack of blueberry pancakes and Liv had a cup of tea in a 'Happy Birthday' mug. A small candle flickered wildly in the centre of the pancakes, to remind me that I'd hit the big two-eight.

'Make a wish,' Xavier said, holding the candle close to my morning breath.

I closed my eyes and blew it out, wishing to be a skiing-pro or any kind of snow-pro before the season was over. Progress was still embarrassingly slow.

'Thank you so much, guys, this is a lovely surprise,' I said, taking the tea and the pancakes and stifling a little yawn. 'What time is it?' I looked around for my phone.

'7 a.m.,' Liv said.

'Is it?! What the hell? Why have you woken me up so early?' I said, enraged.

'Because we are working breakfast and then you have

your girls' day out, so I probably won't get chance to see you,' Xavier said, handing over a squishy present, wrapped in red paper and tied with silver ribbons.

'It's from both of us,' he said, and Liv nodded.

I ripped the paper open to find a gorgeous pair of boarding pants rolled into a soft, padded sausage.

'Nooo? A pair of my very own?' I said, unfurling them sleepily and shaking them out. 'They must have cost a fortune!' I put them on over my pyjamas and they were a perfect fit – a pair of snuggly, leg duvets to keep me warm on the slopes.

'We used the rest of the Xtreme competition winnings from your generous benefactor,' Liv said with a wink, 'so don't feel too bad about it.'

'Those vouchers have dressed me from head to toe. I absolutely love them. Thank you so much – both of you.' I gave Liv a big kiss and Xavier a cuddle. 'Auntie Pam's salopettes might have to be permanently retired.'

'I think that would be for the best,' Xavier said.

'Yeah, and I can get some of my clothes back,' Liv laughed.

'Absolutely not,' I said. 'I love your clothes too.'

'We've got to go to work but eat your pancakes and we'll be back later to top up your tea,' Xavier said, jumping up off the bed.

'Yeah, laters, mate – we're going out at 10 a.m., so get your ass up and be ready. Rach is meeting us at the lift.'

The two of them left and I checked my phone for birthday messages. It was a bit early for people to be awake and thinking of me, but there was already a *Happy Birthday Darling* from Mum and a *Bonne Anniversaire* from Margot.

I scoffed my pancakes, set my alarm for 9.30 a.m. and went back to sleep. A 7 a.m. wake-up call on my birthday was outrageous.

Liv burst in at 9.34 a.m., switched off my alarm and shook me awake.

'Come on lazy bones, you've gotta get up and at 'em,' she said.

'Morning, again,' I said, dreamily. 'Was Luca at breakfast?'

'Yup. And the lady of the house. Both now on their way back to Paris,' Liv said, stripping off her uniform and putting her snow gear on.

I checked my phone again. One new message:

George: *Happy Birthday Hols! The house is on the market. I'll keep you updated on any offers. Enjoy your birthday xx*

Seeing his name on my phone again caught me off-guard. I'd almost forgotten we co-owned a house. Strange to think how differently I now felt about him. I'd done a complete 180 on the man I was all set to marry. I jumped out of bed and ran into the shower, about to break my record for getting mountain-ready.

'Xavier has done you a birthday picnic with the works,' Liv said. 'Home-made bread, a charcuterie, cheeses, grapes, chocolate-dipped strawberries, madeleines. I've never seen anything like it.'

'Sounds amazing. Can't wait to get up there and eat it,' I said, laughing. 'I might sack off the skiing today, for a birthday treat.'

'You're still not in love with it then?'

'It's hard to fall in love with it when I spend so much time on my face.'

Liv and I speed-crunched through town to the lift, where Rachael was waiting for us. I was twenty-eight years old. Nearly three decades on earth and what had I got to show for it? Well, a nice ski outfit and two new friends for starters. That wasn't so bad.

'Happy Birthday, beautiful,' Rachael said, giving me a hug and pointing to her backpack. 'I've got a little something in here for you, and David sends a birthday kiss.'

'Thank you both.'

'Where are your skis?' Rachael asked, waggling my rucksack, as we joined the queue, following Liv's lead.

'I thought I'd take the pressure off and mark the occasion with food instead.'

'That's the spirit,' she said, laughing. I longed for Luca's queue-jumping nod as we huddled together, waiting for the crowd to shuffle forward. Life was so much easier when you had money. We stayed on the gondola for three stops up to the viewing platform next to Le Mouton Noir. It was one of many places in Verbier that felt like heaven. We walked across the rickety metal walkway as clouds swirled around our feet and took a thousand selfies. An innocent passer-by got roped into doing a full-length photoshoot and I posted the pictures on my Stories.

Turning 28 feels pretty great #OnTopOfTheWorld #HeadInTheClouds #HighOnLife

We made our way to the bar, where people were sitting, eating and drinking in the sunshine. Rachael commandeered one of the picnic tables and Liv laid out a red and white chequered tablecloth, giving us each a linen napkin.

'This is fancy,' I said, fluttering it over my lap.

'You ain't seen nothing yet,' she said, pulling out the spread that Xavier had prepared.

It was an absolute feast. Fresh-made quiche, still warm, mini pots of pâté with melba toast, five different types of cheese and different-flavoured crackers to go with each. Cold meats with cornichons, the largest stuffed olives I'd ever seen – the delicacies just kept coming.

'This is unbelievable!' I said, as Liv brought out dish after dish.

'I have a little something as well,' Rachael said, carefully placing a strawberry and red velvet cheesecake on the table. 'It took me forever to spell out "Happy Birthday Holly" as the strawberries were so small.'

'That looks amazing, thank you so much,' I said, giving her a hug.

'So, what's the story with you and Luca?' Liv asked, biting into a wafer-thin cracker laden with goat's cheese. 'One minute you guys are going to a spa together and the next, you aren't even speaking.'

'I'm not sure there is a story,' I said. 'He goes hot and cold. From Champagne bars to ignoring me completely. I thought that was it the other week when he blanked me at dinner, but then I think of all the special moments we've had, and I want to give him the benefit of the doubt.'

'What did he get you for your birthday?' Rachael asked, eyes gleaming. 'A horse?'

I laughed. 'Hardly. I haven't even had a text.'

'Details, details,' Liv said, rolling her eyes. 'He's bound to get you something hugely extravagant to show off.'

'An ice sculpture of your face?' Rachael laughed.

'As long as Genevieve doesn't see it,' I said. 'Can't let his twin sister know he's fraternising with the scullery maid.'

'Maybe it'll be a vodka luge and he'll drink shots off your nose.'

'Weird thought, Rach,' Liv said. 'If he could choose to slurp vodka off any part of her body, I doubt it would be her nose.'

'He's just so different to any man I've ever met before,' I said. 'When I'm with him, life feels glamorous and easy, but then he'll go back to Paris and I won't hear from him at all. That dinner last month with Henri Thienpont was ridiculous, wasn't it Liv?'

She nodded.

'What happened?' Rachael asked.

'Genevieve came home while the two of us were still eating and Luca jumped up like we were having a sordid affair. He wouldn't even look at me in front of her.'

'Hmm, sounds like it could get messy,' Rachael said, popping a grape in her mouth.

'Then just as I'm thinking we should keep it 100 per cent professional, he'll do something completely unexpected like taking me to that beautiful spa, or opening an amazing bottle of wine and I'll feel special and looked after, you know? He's so thoughtful.'

'But no text?' Liv said.

I checked my phone again.

'Not yet,' I said, feeling slightly embarrassed. He must have completely forgotten. Was it a French thing? It couldn't be, as Xavier had remembered. Was it a selfish bastard thing? Couldn't be that either as George had sent a message.

We had a dream day on the slopes, lazing in the deckchairs

in short sleeves and sunglasses, while drinking red wine and grazing on our picnic. It got to 4 p.m. and final lifts were calling, so it was time to call it a day.

'I'm going to stay up here and hang with Bella for an hour or two,' Liv said, giving me a hug goodbye.

'And I'm skiing down Red Twelve to meet David,' Rachael said. 'He's very excited about a Vermentino he's discovered, and he needs me to try it urgently.'

'A wine emergency – God, you guys have the best life!' I said, laughing. 'I want a kindred spirit like David.'

'They always appear when you least expect it,' Rachael replied.

'Get your glad rags on and we'll head out for dinner later,' Liv said. 'Bring Xavier too. Bella is DJing at The Edge and can get us on the guestlist if you fancy it?'

'Sounds good,' I replied, giving her a big hug.

The sun had gone down on my twenty-eighth birthday and it was time to get the lift down the mountain. Nobody ever got the lift down. Well, occasionally you might see a model in a ballgown and heels, or a pair of OAPs, or a member of staff on their way home. But not an ordinary, ski-jacket wearing twenty-eight-year-old with no excuses. And I wasn't even sorry. I wasn't going to fake a limp, I walked on with my head held high and took a seat as the entire resort skied down the mountain in the sunshine, as they'd paid thousands of pounds to do. I bounced home in an empty lift, through the pine trees towards the twinkling lights and happy buzz of Verbier. I crunched my way back to the chalet and could see the foyer and dining room all lit up. Xavier must have invited some friends over for dinner.

I punched the code into the keypad for the ski room and

walked straight through to the kitchen to thank him for the gorgeous birthday picnic. He was such a thoughtful soul – even down to the flask of Irish coffee to finish off the lunch. I'd been dreading spending my first non-George birthday alone, but twenty-eight felt good. The kitchen was full of cooking. Something delicious was bubbling away on the hob and a bright-blue Le Creuset pot sat snug in the centre of the oven. But no Xavier. I made my way upstairs and heard him before I saw him, arguing loudly in French.

'No, Luca, that was not the deal. I've paid your money back with interest and you've had three years of my life. Now sign the papers over.'

'I'm sorry, Xavier, but the restaurant has blossomed under our partnership, and I want to keep a small stake. It's the least you can do.'

'There is no stake for sale. I want full control back of my restaurant and that was always our agreement.'

'Be reasonable, Xavier. We are joint owners now. I currently own 50 per cent but I'd be happy to agree to 10.'

I got a little closer to the dining room and the creaky floorboards gave me away.

'Hello?' Luca called out and sharp footsteps sounded before he flung the doors open.

'Hi guys,' I said, waving to Xavier in the back, 'what's going on?'

Luca was stood smoking a cigarette, while Xavier balanced on a chair, pinning a 'Happy Birthday' banner to the wall. The table was set for two, with a dark-red tablecloth, crystal glasses and enough silver cutlery for four courses. A vase of pink peonies bloomed next to a silver candelabra. The dining room had been transformed into an intimate French bistro.

'*Bonjour*, Holly,' Xavier said, 'Happy Birthday!'

'Thank you,' I said looking around.

'Ah, *oui*,' Luca joined in, double kissing me enthusiastically, '*Bonne Anniversaire* and... surprise!' he added, pointing to the banner.

I took in the whole scene: the candles, the flowers, the polish. I couldn't believe it. Had Luca gone to all this trouble for me? He started singing a shonky 'Happy Birthday' and Xavier eventually joined in. I clutched my hand to my chest in delight and confusion and gave a little laugh.

'What is this?' I asked, looking at them both.

'It is your birthday, *non*?' Luca took my hand and pressed it to his lips. I looked over at Xavier, who gave me a funny half-smile.

'I thought you were in Paris for work this weekend?'

'Me too,' Xavier added, staring oddly at Luca.

'And miss your birthday? Never,' Luca smiled easily. 'We have arranged for all your favourite foods and wines, to celebrate your birthday in style.'

'We have indeed,' Xavier said, glaring at Luca and storming off to the kitchen. Their argument clearly unresolved.

'Really?' I had tears in my eyes. I couldn't believe it. This was the most thoughtful thing anyone had ever done. I'd already spotted the Sicilian Fiano chilling in the corner. Luca was wearing jeans and a soft, wool jumper with his lace-up boots. He looked much more Paris than Verbier.

'I thought you'd forgotten?' I said, almost speechless.

'Of course not,' he replied, tapping his cigarette into an ashtray. 'I said I'd make it up to you, didn't I?'

Xavier came back in with a tray of roast lamb, truffled macaroni cheese and buttered peas: all the foods I missed from home. He looked at me and smiled, taking in my overwhelm. 'Happy Birthday' he mouthed over Luca's head.

'Thank you, Xavier. Luca, this is *amazing*,' I said, beaming.

'*Oui, oui*,' he said, doing prayer hands at Xavier to dismiss him. He nodded at me one last time and left us to it. I hadn't eaten alone with Luca in the dining room since that night with Henri and it felt like forbidden behaviour. I was half-expecting Genevieve to burst in and drag me downstairs.

'Are you sure it's OK for me to be eating in here?' I asked, nervously.

'It is my chalet as much as Genevieve's, so we can do whatever we like,' Luca said, 'although we should probably be discreet when Genevieve is here. She can get a little sensitive as you know.'

I sliced off a piece of lamb steak, still steaming hot, juicily roasted on the outside and perfectly pink in the middle. Xavier must have marinaded the meat in redcurrant jam and the balance of flavours when I put it in my mouth was just divine. The boy had a gift. Followed by a forkful of truffled mac 'n' cheese, I was in food heaven.

'It is good, no?' Luca said, holding up the Fiano. 'My turn to pour tonight. Would madam like to try the wine?'

I took the glass and sloshed it around a bit, took an exaggerated sniff and gave him a slow, considered nod, followed by a big gulp and a thumbs up.

'*Merci!* An excellent choice. What is the vintage?' I asked in faux interest.

Luca looked stumped as he side-eyed the bottle. 'I believe it is 1997,' he said.

'Ah yes, a very good year. The year I started school,' I said, with a smile.

Xavier discreetly appeared and cleared our plates. I looked up at him and tried to catch his eye. I didn't want Xavier serving me; it felt wrong. He wouldn't look at me, so I started collecting the plates to help him.

'I can bring the plates down, Xavier?' I said, in a final bid to get his attention. He looked up sharply and shook his head silently.

'No need to do anything,' Luca said, patting me down, 'Xavier has got it.' Why did it feel like I was in the middle of a chest-beating contest?

Once Xavier had gone, Luca stood up and put an Etta James record on, adding a smoky siren vibe to the evening. He held his hand out and pulled me up to dance. The mixture of white wine, the massive amount of food I'd eaten and being up the mountain all day was making me feel sleepy. I rested my head on Luca's shoulder and closed my eyes, his hands resting on my bum. By the time the song had finished, Luca was gently shaking me awake. Xavier must have slipped back in and out unnoticed as there were two gingerbread crème brûlées on the table waiting for us, one with a gold spiral candle. Luca whipped out his Zippo lighter, adding a whiff of fuel to the air, and melted half the tiny candle as he lit it.

'Make a wish,' Luca said, holding it out to me, singing 'Happy Birthday' again in his deep French accent. This time I joined in. Despite the odds, it *had been a happy birthday*. When George called off the wedding, I thought at least the next few birthdays would be a misery, living in the past and remembering this time last year, and this time two years ago. But no. Today was a new beginning. A fresh new year that George had never been in. And Luca had been so lovely and thoughtful – what a fabulous birthday surprise. I'd never felt so special, so considered, so thought about. Luca was an enigma; every time I thought he was one thing, he proved to be another. This birthday year was for me and only me – and it was time to start indulging myself. I blew out the candle and made my final wish of the day: *to run my very own restaurant and find a man who feels safe in a storm*. My very first indulgence – two wishes.

Twenty-Seven

14th February

The sun had already set behind the clouds and the air was cold as we queued for the lift. There was no Charlie to escort us home this time, just me and Luca getting the bubble down the mountain on our own. Since my birthday surprise, I'd seen Luca in a totally new light. Up until then, I'd been convinced he was superior and spoilt, but I couldn't get over the level of thought and effort that had gone into organising that meal. Every last detail had been considered and thought through and all my favourite foods and wines included – even down to the gingerbread crème brûlée. It made me feel funny inside just thinking about it. That this strange little dalliance with the boss might actually turn into something real. And that wasn't the only post-birthday miracle to happen as my skiing was finally starting to improve as well. The yellow bubble clunked its way around to us, and we poked our skis in the outside holes and jumped in. We sat back on the seat and put our feet up, waiting for the doors to shut and the lift to catapult us into the night. Just as the doors twitched to swing inwards, a ski boot wedged itself in and David's face appeared.

'Hey guys, I thought it was you,' he said, climbing in with his snowboard and sitting next to Luca. 'Hope I'm not interrupting?' The doors slammed shut and we started to descend.

'We'll never know now, will we?' Luca said, pulling out his phone in a huff and looking out the window.

David sat directly opposite and gave me a big smile.

'Good day skiing?' he asked, stomping the snow off his boots.

'Yes. Perfect T-shirt weather, and I've finally progressed from embarrassingly-slow, wide turns to embarrassingly-slow, slightly narrower turns,' I said, laughing.

The cable car boinged through the mid-station, shuddering as it dropped us down a level towards Verbier. Luca had his feet on the seat next to me and occasionally tutted or smiled as he scrolled through his phone.

'I need to swing by Rachael's on the way back and pick up a cheesecake for Xavier. Are you going that way too?' I asked David as the bubble started to slow down and approach the exit. The three of us clattered out, grabbing boards, skis and poles, trying not to fall over as we made our way across the conveyer belt.

'Can do. Doesn't hurt to walk my better half home after a long day,' David smiled.

'I need to get some cigarettes from the kiosk,' Luca said, heading in the opposite direction, 'so I'll see you later.' No kiss or PDA in front of David. Just a quiet look of longing and disappointment.

'OK, byeee,' I called after him. I'd have to pick him up

a little treat from Rachael's on the way back, if there was anything left. David and I walked to the *pâtisserie* through the slush, which the sun had melted but would turn back to ice overnight.

'Hey Rach,' David called as we tinkled into the shop, 'nearly finished?'

Rachael was dressed head to toe in traditional Swiss costume, with icing sugar streaked through her hair and on her nose. She was pouring bright-green jelly into holly moulds and adding redcurrants in the corners to set overnight.

'They look awesome,' I said. 'Where are they going?'

Rachael ignored us both as she concentrated, then once all the moulds were full, she wobbled the tray into the fridge to set and turned and gave us her full attention.

'All… done,' she said with a smile and a flourish. 'Now, what have you two reprobates been up to?'

'Nothing reprobatish, sadly,' David said, giving her a kiss on the cheek, 'although I might have ruined a moment in the bubble between this one and Luca just now.'

'What?! Not at all! There are very strict rules about fraternising with the staff in Chalet Blanchet as you both know. Nothing going on between me and the notorious Luca-B.'

'Mm-hmm,' Rachael said.

'You could cut the sexual tension with a knife,' David said, arching an eyebrow.

'I'm actually here on instruction from Xavier, to pick up a cheesecake,' I said, 'and possibly a little treat or two to take back to the chalet?'

'I can go one better than that and give you Xavier's cheesecake, a box of cream donuts and another cheesecake that needs delivering to Luca,' Rachael said, putting the cheesecakes in a bag and adding a red beribboned box.

'Strange – he didn't mention anything,' David commented.

'Did Luca order it?' I asked, confused. There must be a mix up with the one Xavier ordered. Why would we need two cheesecakes?

'No idea, one of the girls took the order. One lemon sherbet and one berry dream,' Rachael said, writing X on one box and L on the other. She switched off the kitchen lights and put her pale-pink coat on, with her raspberry hat and matching earmuffs.

'You look like a human marshmallow,' David said, giving her a squidge.

'Very on-brand Rach,' I said, breathing in the sugary smell of the *pâtisserie* and putting my own earmuffs on, ready to head back to the chalet. 'Thank you for these. Put it on the tab if it's not already paid for and we'll sort it out at the end of the month.'

'Will do, bye Holly.' Rachael and David gave me a couple's wave as they turned the shop sign round and locked the front door. I headed back to the chalet with my bakery booty in one hand and my skis in the other, kicking the wet ice along the ground as I went. The village was alive with après ski as the bars competed for customers. Queen belting out from The Farm and Lady Gaga blasting from Mo's. I could drop the cakes back and see if Xavier and Liv fancied coming out for a drink. If they were still speaking to me. It had all been so weird lately; I couldn't keep up. I carried my skis, poles and the cakes into the ski room and released my feet from their two tiny prisons, shaking the sludge from my boots and hanging them on the heaters.

I wiggled my toes back to life with a little massage; the poor things had been cramped up all day and were freezing cold. The warmth of the chalet hit me, and I scrunched up my face, enjoying the feeling of being back inside, taking my ski jacket off, unzipping the bottoms of my trousers and hanging up my helmet. I caught myself in the mirror as I walked through to the kitchen and my cheeks were flushed, but my eyes were sparkling and happy. It had been a good day.

'Hey, Holly,' Xavier called as I padded into the kitchen, my boarding pants dragging along the floor. 'I'm just on to Christina,' he said, waving his phone at me.

'Let me see her,' I heard her say. He rolled his eyes, turning the screen round to show me his smiling wife.

'*Bonjour*, Holly,' she said, waving, 'it's so great to finally meet you! Xavier tells me wonderful things.'

'Hiii! Yes, you too!' I replied. She was even more stunning up close, radiating joy through the phone. Xavier stepped into the corridor to finish his call, as I lifted my bags onto the counter.

'She's lovely, Xavier, just as you said,' I heard Christina say. It felt good to know that he'd said nice things.

'*Oui, oui. Alors, bonne chance ce soir*. I'll call as soon as I know, hopefully with good news.'

Xavier reappeared, fresh-faced and smiling. 'Good day skiing?' he asked.

'Amazing!' I trilled. 'Blue skies, gorgeous sunshine and my turns are finally improving. The practice is starting to pay off. I bumped into a friend on the mountain for drinks and ended up at Rachael's with David. So, I have caaaake!'

'Oh yeah, thanks for picking that up,' Xavier said, taking

the bag from me and lifting it up as if to weigh it. 'That's a lot of cake?'

'The donuts are for you and Liv,' I said, quickly changing my story, 'as a little treat.'

'Hmm, the perfect gift for a chef and health-conscious girl,' Xavier said, 'calorific food.' He had a point.

'There's still more in here than I...' He frowned, peering into the bag. 'I only ordered one cheesecake? Is this the lemon sherbet?'

He pulled out the box with the L marked on top to find a pretty-in-pink berry dream nestled inside: one of Rachael's specialities. A buttery biscuit base covered in whipped raspberry mousse and dollops of fresh cream. Decorated around the edges with tiny shortbread hearts and sugared strawberries, a scrawl of chocolate sauce in the centre:

To Luca, my darling Valentine! I love you so much and can't wait to be your wife, love always, Fern xxx

A shocked gasp escaped from my mouth. What the fuckety-fuck-fuck-fuck was this? I read it again. And again. *Love always, Fern.* Valentine? Wife? Who was Fern? My brain flicked back to Genevieve asking Luca why he wasn't in Paris with Fern. He'd said she was his auntie. Oh God. She wasn't his auntie. Unless he was MARRYING HIS AUNTIE? He wasn't marrying his auntie.

Xavier closed the lid silently and opened the other cake box.

'Ah. Here it is. The lemon sherbet for tomorrow,' he said, taking it to the other side of the kitchen. I flipped the lid back open on the Fern-cake and tortured myself one more time, pulling out my phone to snap a photo and sending it to the WhatsApp group I shared with Liv and Rachael.

How could he be engaged? I couldn't believe what I was seeing. I snapped the lid shut and stuffed one of the cream donuts into my mouth, blinking back tears.

'Any idea who Fern is?' I asked.

Xavier shrugged. 'Luca embraces the French way, *non*?'

'I didn't know he was engaged?' I said. 'Is he?' I felt my cheeks burn with the humiliation of it all.

'I think it would be best to ask him,' he said, looking at me sadly.

'You must know if he's engaged. Why won't you tell me?' I was beside myself.

'We all have secrets. He doesn't tell mine and I don't tell his.'

I swallowed a mouthful of cream donut, nodding at Xavier and jumping down from the kitchen stool. I needed to go for a walk and clear my head.

Twenty-Eight

14th February

I stormed through the town past all the happy vacayers, drinking and kissing and laughing. How was this happening to me *again*? Publicly dumped for the second time in six months and this time by cheesecake. FFS. I'd never felt so miserable. I don't know if it was being made to look like a prize idiot by Luca or the sad look on Xavier's face as I'd left. I stopped at the boozy hot chocolate stand and ordered their special.

'With Tia Maria?' the man asked, his droopy moustache belying his smile.

I nodded, catching my breath as the shock hit me again.

'Glitter marshmallows? Cream?'

'Yes, everything,' I said, handing him 10 francs and waving away the change.

I slurped the creamy froth as I turned round and bumped straight into Genevieve.

'Oh, sorry…' I tried to smile and walk past, but my eyes gave me away.

'Holly?' she touched my arm kindly. 'I've been looking for you. Are you OK?'

'Yes, I'm fine,' I said, mortified. 'I just needed some air.'

'Xavier told me what happened with Luca,' she said, signalling to Droopy for a coffee and steering me to a table by the fire. 'I know you know about Fern. I'm sorry, Holly. I told him not to play around with you.'

'He said Fern was your aunt?' I said, eating a spoonful of glitter marshmallows.

'*Non*. Fern is his fiancée in Paris. And I know her through friends,' Genevieve said, pulling a crisp, white tissue out of her Chanel handbag and waving it at my increasingly blotchy face. I blew my nose as her espresso arrived. 'I told Luca he had no moral standards and should finish things with you immediately. Fern would be devastated if she found out and it wasn't fair of him to lead you on.'

'Is that what you meant by standards? I heard you talking and thought you meant…'

Genevieve paused. She understood. 'That you weren't good enough for him?'

I nodded quietly.

'Not at all, Holly. You are a lovely person. Liv and Xavier have been delighted to have you on the team. I didn't want another tricky situation with Luca to stop you working with us.'

'Did that happen before?' I asked, already knowing the answer.

'Yes, with Rose last season. Luca played the same silly game with her and then got bored. She didn't show up for work the first week back. When he got engaged, I told him there must be no more relationships, other than the perfectly good one he has.' Genevieve pulled out a packet of cigarettes from her fur coat, lit one and inhaled, closing her eyes to really enjoy it.

'I feel like such an idiot,' I said, licking the chocolatey dregs off my teaspoon.

'I had no idea he was being unfaithful to Fern, otherwise I'd have said something sooner. Le Mirador was my engagement gift to them last year and I had an email to say the voucher had been activated. I knew Luca had gone there with someone and I was with Fern at the time, so I knew it wasn't her. It didn't take me long to get it out of him.'

Shame spread through me at the thought of being topless, however fleetingly, with another woman's fiancé on their engagement spa break.

'That is so awful,' I said, mortified. 'I didn't know.'

'Of course you didn't,' she said. 'I know my brother well enough. If anything, I thought something might have been going on between you and Xavier.' Genevieve took another drag of her cigarette.

'Xavier? But he's married.' I was so confused. Why would she say that? What kind of den of iniquity was this?

'Yes,' Genevieve said. 'It is a little complicated though, I think.'

'Complicated or not, marriage is a sacred vow. I don't understand.' Did monogamy and honesty mean nothing to people these days?

'*Non*, you don't understand, and it is not my place to explain. Xavier is a dear friend and I won't break his confidence, but I think there is something he should tell you.'

'Is it best if I go home?' I asked, a wave of shock riding through me. The thought of being back in London job-less, man-less and money-less was beyond devastating.

'*Zut alors, non*,' Genevieve said. 'Luca has made his bed and now it is time for him to lie down in it and sleep.'

'As in…?'

'He goes back to Paris. He had his chance. My brother is very well indulged, Holly, as you can see. Time to face up to his responsibilities.'

'Are you sure? Wouldn't it be easier if I went instead?'

'You haven't done anything wrong. Leave him to me.'

I wasn't even sure I wanted to stay out here anymore. Liv and Xavier were being off with me and if Xavier didn't want to teach me anymore then what was the point in staying at all? I'd lost all sense of what I was doing with my life and now the back-up for the back-up was falling through.

My phone vibrated as both Rachael and Liv replied:

Liv: *Oh babes!*

Rachael: *So sorry Holly, I should have taped the box shut.*

Me: *Did you know he was engaged?*

Rachael: *Not until the order came through this morning. I was going to tell you, but it didn't seem right to do it earlier with David there.*

Liv: *I'm back at the room if you want vodka?*

Me: *No. I'm going to have it out with him.*

Liv: *Not sure on that one. Come for vodka first xx*

Genevieve's phone rang and she dismissed me with her cigarette-laden hand, which was fair enough. I still worked for her, after all. I took my cup back to Droopy.

'*Merci*,' he said, with a kind, downward-facing smile. Maybe I could go out with him instead.

I walked back to the chalet with a sense of dread. Would Luca be back, and what would I say if he was? Should I pie him in the face with the cheesecake? I could leave it in his bedroom with a Post-it – *Third time lucky with your Aunt Fern?* I needed to think of a suitably smug but mic-droppable response. A smattering of snow feathered down from the sky, and I wrapped my arms around myself as I trudged home through the town. I decided to be bold and walked in through the front door of the chalet, knowing Genevieve wasn't home, and wanting to take Luca by surprise. Let him see me in my full power.

'Hello?' I called as I pushed the door open, feeling the emptiness around me. I was all fired up and ready for a row and no one was home. I sent Luca a message in frustration.

Me: *I need to ask you something.*

Luca: *Yes?*

Me: *In person. Where are you?*

Luca: *Out for a while.*

I suddenly felt overwhelmed with exhaustion. George and Pippa, Fern, Luca, Genevieve. It had all been too much for one day and I needed some sleep. I went downstairs and walked past the kitchen, where Xavier was chopping up a pineapple.

'Still here?' I said, spying the two cheesecakes on the side. I could just chuck Fern's berry dream in the bin and carry on regardless. Luca wouldn't be any the wiser.

'Pineapple practice,' Xavier said, sculpting a perfectly proportioned star from the centre and holding it aloft.

'That is amazing,' I said, truly impressed.

'Very useful too,' he said, 'you never know when you might need to whittle a shape out of a fruit.

'So true,' I said. 'Can you make me something out of this?' I handed him a banana from the fruit bowl, which he eyed with caution.

'It's just pineapples today,' he said, putting it back. His arms were looking strong through his chef's whites, his floppy, auburn hair in his eyes.

'Am I a total idiot?' I asked, embarrassed. 'Is it a French thing?' I wondered at Genevieve's suggestion that Xavier's marriage might also be open to offers.

'*Non*. Luca likes to play games,' he said, staring at me. 'He's the total idiot.'

'He is what?' called a voice from the stairs. Luca's voice.

I picked up Fern's cake and lifted the lid.

'I thought you were out for a while?' I called as I walked out of the kitchen.

'I was. And now I'm back,' he said with a cheeky smile. He'd obviously had a few drinks and was struggling to navigate the stairs. He eventually gave up and sat down on the bottom step, his head in his hands.

'I picked something up for you from Rachael's,' I said, lowering the cheesecake to his face so he could read the message.

'You didn't have to do that,' he said, looking visibly touched. I followed his eyes and watched them change.

'I wish I hadn't,' I replied. 'It's not from me.'

'I can see,' Luca said, putting his head back in his hands.

'It's from Fern. Who I'm guessing isn't your auntie?'

He shook his head in his hands, then looked up in irritation.

'You shouldn't have opened my private gift.'

'I think you're missing the point. And I didn't open your private gift, I just brought it back to the chalet.'

'Well, someone did. The cheesecake was for me. Who opened it?'

'I did,' Xavier poked his head around the kitchen door, right on cue. '*Pardon*, I thought it was the dessert I ordered.' He gave Luca a faux-apologetic look with prayer hands, before retreating back into the kitchen.

'So, you're engaged?' I asked.

He waved his hand as if swatting away an imaginary fly. 'I'm always engaged to someone. It doesn't mean anything,' he slurred.

'Then what have you been doing with me?' I asked, dreading the answer.

'I am French,' he said shrugging. 'We do things differently to you English.'

He'd said that before.

'Well, I'm not French,' I said, storming off down the corridor and slamming my bedroom door. I'd had enough of his bullshit. Could I force-feed him fish and chips and say it's a British thing and continuously shrug like, duh, JFDI Luca? Thank God I hadn't slept with him. Maybe I'd played it well? Living his luxury lifestyle for a couple of months and moving on before I had to add him to 'my list'.

Liv was in bed with her eyes closed and headphones on

as I crashed through the door. She must have been listening to her meditation app as she gave me a trance-like half nod and didn't detect my anti-Zen vibes as I got changed and went angrily to sleep.

Twenty-Nine

22nd February

'She has to go, Genevieve; she has become clingy and unprofessional. It's for the best. We don't need the extra help anyway. Xavier can manage by himself, and no one knows more about wines than me.'

I froze on the stairs, listening in, as Luca whispered frantically in French to Genevieve, the doors to the dining room slightly ajar. I was early for my shift as I'd decided – well, Liv had strongly suggested – some notable effort was required on my part, to go full-blown consummate professional. I had to accept there had been a cultural misunderstanding (*due to out-and-out lies from Luca*) and it was time to either crack on and enjoy what was left of the season or go home. Seeing George had given me the flashback I needed to discount the second option, so I just wanted to get on with my job, and the less I saw of Luca, the better.

'Don't be ridiculous, Luca. I'm not sending another member of staff home because of your indiscretions. Pull yourself together. Maybe it is time for you to go home instead?'

I heard a quiet 'boo' in my ear and Xavier appeared beside me.

'Who are we hiding from?' he asked.

'Luca wants me fired,' I whispered, nodding towards the dining room.

'It is not only your decision, Genevieve. We both own the chalet and we both make the decisions. Just because you are a minute older than me, does not mean you are in charge.'

'Well then, we can toss a coin to decide,' Genevieve said, as Xavier and I looked at each other in horror. 'Heads she stays, tails she goes.' There was a tinkle of coins, a moment of silence and the slap of a hand. And then nothing. The dining room door burst open and Luca ran upstairs to his bedroom, making Xavier and I both jump. I wasn't sure if he'd seen us lurking in the corner, but we immediately leapt into action, walking into the bar together as if we hadn't been listening in.

'*Bonsoir*, Genevieve,' I said, grabbing a sharp knife and a couple of lemons from the fruit bowl as Xavier faffed around with the hostess trolley.

'Ah, *bonsoir*, Holly, Xavier,' she said. 'Holly, do you have five minutes? I need to speak with you about something.'

I nodded. *Tails she goes*. Fuck. I followed Genevieve into the lounge anxiously. I'd never been fired before. I took a deep breath and mentally prepared myself. The teal, velvet sofa was brushed and immaculate, its acid-green cushions perfectly plumped and sitting to attention. It was too good to sit on, so I hovered at the edge.

'Holly, I want to apologise to you on behalf of my brother and let you know that he will likely be returning to Paris this week.'

'Oh right,' I said, confused. 'OK. And is he not planning to tell me this himself?'

'He doesn't know yet and it might happen quite quickly, so I wanted to give you, what do they say? A heads up. I didn't want you worrying about what was happening.'

'Thank you, Genevieve, that's very thoughtful of you,' I said, as she stood up, her cashmere wrap trailing on the floor. She opened the door to call for the others.

'Xavier? Liv? Can you come in here please? I am calling a team meeting.'

The two of them came in and sat next to me, looking edgy in different ways. Xavier was clearly ready for a fight while Liv still had her headphones on and looked half-asleep.

'Genevieve, before you say anything, I'm sorry but I couldn't help but overhear some of your conversation with Luca earlier…' Xavier started. I shook my head and tried to shut him up with my eyes. Oh God, this was excruciating.

'*Merci*, Xavier, our conversations are no concern of yours,' she cut him off firmly.

'Understood, but Holly has done nothing wrong,' Xavier said, 'and on principle, if she goes, then so do I.'

'And me,' Liv nodded.

I looked on in shock. Were they really willing to give it all up for me? Nothing says I love you like a staff walk-out. I nudged into Liv, who knocked into Xavier, and gave them both a big smile.

'Holly is not going anywhere, but it is good to know where your loyalty lies,' Genevieve tutted. 'And please try and *help yourself from overhearing* private conversations in the future.'

'Apologies, Genevieve,' Xavier said, smiling back at me.

'And me,' Liv nodded. I think she was still asleep and being remote controlled.

'I wanted to ask the three of you to start thinking about our end-of-season party,' Genevieve said, looking at each of us in turn. 'Chalet Blanchet has always been legendary for its finale dinner party, and I want this year to be no exception.'

'No problem,' Xavier said. 'Is it a sit-down meal?'

'Platters of food, Champagne and fine wine, a DJ and dancing, maybe some fireworks – use your imaginations to make it fabulous.'

'Can Bella DJ?' Liv asked.

'Of course, if she's available – she's the best DJ in Verbier.'

'I'll speak to David about the wine and Rachael about the cakes,' I said.

'And I have a fabulous menu in mind,' Xavier said with a glint in his eye.

'Excellent,' Genevieve said smiling, 'I knew I could rely on you all to finish the season with a bang.' She flounced out of the lounge, leaving the three of us perched on her perfect sofa.

'Wow guys, I can't believe we're already planning the end of season party. It feels like I've only just got here.' I looked around at the art-directed shelves, the magazines that hadn't been opened, the candles that hadn't been lit. It was the beginning of the end and somehow, I didn't really feel like I'd even started.

*

George: *Hi Hols, good news – we had an open day on the house and 15 couples viewed it. We've had 3 offers already, so I'll email the details over and we can decide if we want to accept one or hold out for more xx*

Me: *Let's wait a week to see if any other offers come in, then accept the highest x*

Thirty

29th February

The alarm went off and I could already see Liv at the bottom of the bed, fully dressed in her boarding gear. She put her finger to her lips as I switched off the loud honk coming from my phone. My bed felt so snuggly and warm. I'd been mid-dream, racing Basil in a triathlon and had just made it onto the bikes. I closed my eyes briefly, to rest them and...

'Hols?' Liv whispered. 'Come on, get up.'

I slowly opened them again. Was I in some sort of alternate reality? I hated getting up early, I hated the cold, and I could just about get down a blue on skis without breaking my neck. A moonlit ski was a triple-threat bad idea, but Liv was beside herself with excitement and I didn't want to ruin her buzz.

'Give me five minutes,' I said, closing my eyes again.

'Noooo,' Liv pulled my duvet back and threw my thermals at me, 'it's now or never – Xavier is already in the ski room.'

It didn't *feel* like never was really an option, so I switched my pyjamas for thermals, slid into my ski pants and layered up with two extra fleeces, a balaclava, and a pair of under gloves. Now I had to get outside before I overheated and fainted. Silence was the best communication from this point on. I felt like a baby who had just been born and hadn't quite realised they were out in the world. I didn't want to think about going outside, so probably best to just deny it was happening until absolutely necessary. We walked to the ski room in our socks, where Xavier was waiting patiently. He yawned and waved as Liv and I grabbed our boots and pulled them on. The three musketeers were ready to ride or die. Literally. We stepped outside, quietly shutting the door behind us, straight onto the piste where we started crunching our way up the freshly hoovered snow. The piste bashers had cleaned the snow carpets, giving us a perfectly flat path to the top of the mountain. The moon sat golden and bright in the sky, lighting the way, while the floodlights stood dark and useless, watching us through the gloom. We weren't the only night-time skiers, and several small groups of pilgrims trudged their way up the mountain ahead of us, each one hoping to experience a rare moment of euphoria on an empty mountain with only the moon to guide the way.

'It's a lot of effort for a ten-minute ski,' I grumbled through my balaclava, as I concentrated on putting one foot in front of the other.

'What do you mean? This is amazing,' Liv said, her eyes to the starry sky, hot breath puffing smoke into the night air as she looked around in awe. 'The whole experience is once in a lifetime, Holly, starting half an hour ago. It's not just the skiing part.'

'When else in your life will you live on a mountain and have the chance to do something like this?' Xavier added.

Oh. This bit was supposed to be fun as well then.

'True. Sorry, it's because I'm lazy and worried about being cold.'

'And are you cold?' Xavier looked at me quizzically.

I took a moment to connect with my body as I carried on the mountain march and realised that I wasn't actually cold at all. If anything, I was too warm.

'Just my nose, I think,' I said, smiling.

Xavier pulled a red nose out of his pocket and offered it to me.

'Would this help?' he asked.

'That's a weird thing to have in your pocket?' I laughed, taking it from him.

'It gets weirder,' he said, producing two more. 'In case of cold nose emergency, and to go with the antlers for a photo. Illumination is optional.' He squeezed the noses in his hand and they both lit up.

'I've got headtorches for the run down,' Liv said, tapping her rucksack, 'and brandy for when we reach the top.'

This was nature's free playground and it was happening right here, right now. Nothing but effort required to have an unforgettable time. I dug my boots in a little deeper and quickened my pace, taking a big breath of fresh, night air.

'I'm so sorry guys, I haven't contributed anything at all – apart from a bad attitude,' I said, feeling ashamed of all the moaning.

'No worries, mate. You haven't done it before; you'll see what a treat it is when we get up there,' Liv replied.

Xavier and Liv dragged their boards behind them as

I clonked along with my skis on my shoulder and just at the moment I thought I might keel over and die, we turned a corner and saw flashing lights from all the mobile phones congregating in one place.

'Nearly there, mate; just this final push to go and you'll be freewheeling it all the way home,' Liv huffed next to me, while Xavier carried on walking slow and steady next to her. I couldn't speak so I gave an affirmative noise instead and kept my head down. One step at a time, crunch, crunch, crunch. It was a beautiful, clear night and the full moon was shining brightly, but it was hard to appreciate while gasping for air.

We got to the top of the pathway and the three of us took a moment to gather ourselves. Liv did some sort of moon salutation, Xavier was breathing deeply, and I lay on my back and could literally see stars. The only thing less tempting than walking all the way up here was the thought of having to get back down again. In the dark. But I was here to smooth things over with Liv and Xavier, and arguably I'd already done the hard bit. The physically hard bit anyway.

'I made us a little something to see us through,' Xavier said, pulling an enormous flask out of his backpack.

'Mulled wine?' I asked hopefully.

'Close,' he replied, 'Irish coffee, with a lot of Irish in it.'

'Good thinking, Batman,' Liv said. 'Make mine a double.'

Xavier unscrewed the flask and a delicious whisky steam wafted around us as he poured the coffee into three plastic cups. He handed them to us then pulled out a wedge of chocolate cake, cut into three fat pieces. The situation was getting better by the minute. There were several small groups of moonlight skiers crazy enough to make the trek up here, and their gentle chatter and laughter was a strange comfort. We were all in it together. In fact, now that my breathing was back to normal and I had coffee and cake, I was feeling much better about the situation.

'A Leap Year full moon,' Liv said looking up at it wide eyed. 'The Snow Moon, a magical day.'

'The Snow Moon is very apt,' Xavier said.

'I wonder how long it will be before there's another full moon on 29th February,' I said. 'Are you thinking of proposing, Liv?'

'No chance. I don't really believe in marriage, to be honest – no offence.' I wasn't sure if she was talking to me or Xavier. 'I'm more of a free spirit.'

'Totally,' Xavier nodded.

'How can you agree when you're the only married one here?' I said.

'He's got the T-shirt, mate – the only one of us who can speak from experience.'

'I'm a one-woman man, but I have my doubts about the marital framework. Feels more like a governmental control mechanism than anything else.'

'Totally,' Liv agreed, taking a sip of her coffee.

'So how does it work, then? Does everyone ski down together or do we just head down whenever we like?'

'It's very cool,' Liv said, 'there are six fire lighters that ski down first, leaving torches to light our way on either side of the piste. Then two hours later, another six go down and collect them all.'

'So we have two hours from when the flames are lit to get down the piste and it's a twenty-minute run – ten if you're a top skier – so there's plenty of time to enjoy it,' Xavier added. 'We can take it nice and easy.'

'Just a heads up that I'll be in the ten-minute gang,' Liv said. 'I want to hoon it down as fast as I can.'

'Absolutely,' I said. 'I don't want to hold either of you back. Xavier, feel free to hoon down too; I'll be fine on my own.'

'Holly, how many times? What is the first rule of the slopes?'

'Look after your mates,' I said.

'*Exactement*,' Xavier replied.

'Apart from Liv,' I said.

'Apart from Liv the lone wolf,' he smiled.

'A lone wolf boarding in the moonlight, a-wooooooo,' Liv howled and one or two of the other skiers looked over.

'At least we all made it up here together,' I said, 'and this coffee and cake is a treat. Thank you, Xavier.'

'There's more where that came from,' Xavier said. 'I like to be prepared for these things.'

'I'm glad all that weirdness with Luca has been sorted out,' Liv said. 'Mates before dates and all that.'

'Totally. Hopefully, the three of us will stay mates once the season ends?'

'Of course we will – you can come and visit me in Italy anytime,' Xavier said.

'And me in Bali,' Liv added.

'What?! Is that where you'll both be?' My stomach went funny at this news. I'd only just settled into life in Verbier, and the cards were already being reshuffled and thrown back in the air. London didn't feel anywhere near as exciting.

'I hope so. I've applied to run a cookery school in Tuscany and if I get the job, I'll be opening a second Lavedrine X in San Gimignano in the autumn,' Xavier said.

'With Luca as your business partner?' I asked, remembering the argument they'd had on my birthday.

Xavier snorted. 'Certainly not. He signed the paperwork over last week as agreed. Genevieve had a persuasive word with him and gave him an ultimatum – it was either a happy Xavier or a very unhappy Fern. I completed my side of the deal; it was Luca's turn to complete his.'

'Me and Bella are travelling across Indonesia and I've booked onto a yoga teacher training course in Bali,' Liv said. 'I want to get my qualification and start taking it seriously.'

'I'm supposed to go back to the bistro and take all my new recipes with me,' I said. 'Margot said that if I've learnt even a tenth of the skill of the great Xavier Lavedrine, she'll make me head chef.'

'Amazing mate, congrats!' Liv said.

'You are way better than a tenth,' Xavier said. 'Some of your experimentations have been really impressive. And your range is phenomenal. Your mac 'n' cheese is the most delicious I've ever tasted.'

I felt a warm glow at his praise. Maybe I wasn't a complete buffoon in the kitchen after all. The three of us sat side by side, looking down the piste to Verbier below. There was a collective hush as the torches were lit and the fire lighters started to make their way down the piste. The moon was bright, but these golden beacons made a huge difference to the visibility. Just enough light to see my hands in front of me and watch out for huge moguls on the way down.

The short sharp ting of a cowbell sounded and all the ten-minute keenos started shuffling.

'That's my cue,' Liv said, 'hate to leave you both, but have to go. Wooooooo.'

She gave me a high five and put her night goggles on. A quick wave to Xavier and off she went, to enjoy her Leap Year moon hoon.

'Are you sure I'm not ruining your fun?' I asked, concerned.

'Not at all. You are prolonging it, in fact,' Xavier said. 'And actually, there's something I wanted to talk to you about.'

'Is there?' I hoped it wasn't the accidental spooning at Maxim's.

'I don't want you to think I'm a callous bastard, so I have to tell you the truth.'

'About what?' I felt nervous for some reason. What would he need to explain to me?

'About Christina,' he said.

'Christina, your wife?'

'Yes. Christina my wife. Well. That's the thing I wanted to explain. She is technically my wife, but only on paper. We were students together at Cordon Bleu and very good friends. When the new Brexit rules came in, she could no longer live full-time in Paris and was having to give up her life to go back to London. When Chantal called off our engagement, I was a total mess. The restaurant was the only thing I had left and I needed a steady hand to run it. The deal I'd done with Luca meant I'd be working here, so I needed someone in Paris I could trust and Christina needed a way to be able to stay in France. At the time, it felt like the perfect solution. When Chantal ran off, I decided that was it for me – I would never get married. Not for love, anyway.'

'So it made sense to marry Christina for business instead? For your love of food.'

'Exactly. A marriage of convenience.'

'That explains a hell of a lot,' I said, realising this perfect, married man, wasn't married at all, and was in fact just… perfect. 'Why didn't you tell me before?' I asked, lost in thought.

'Very few people know. It's rare for me to let anyone in – especially these days, after everything that happened with Chantal – and then you showed up. The arrangement with Christina is a delicate matter and it isn't just my information to share; it's her life too. I was going to tell you on your birthday, but with Luca there, we didn't get any time on our own and the moment passed.'

I'd tried so hard to ignore my feelings for Xavier, knowing he was married and off limits and now he'd dropped this bombshell, I couldn't bring myself to trust how I felt. Things could have been so different between us if I'd known he was secretly single. But then, *he knew* and he could have told me sooner if he'd wanted something to happen. Why was he bothering to tell me now? When it was too late? He'd been such a wonderful friend, but that was clearly all it was on his side – *friends*.

We waited for everyone else to ski down before setting off, so there was no fear of being hit from behind or colliding into anyone in front.

'I got you these,' Xavier said, handing me some hand

warmers. I shook the two little bags of magic sand to activate the heat and put them in my pockets.

'You're always one step ahead,' I said. 'The best I could think of were glow sticks.' I pulled out a handful from my inside pocket and cracked them all awake. Luminous pink, blue and green glowed bright, as I made a crown for Xavier and three bracelets for myself.

'Very stylish,' he said, when we were both glowed up and ready to go. We stood side by side and peered over the edge down the fire-lit run.

'Ready?' he asked.

'Ready,' I replied.

We set off together, gliding over the fresh snow and for the first time, I didn't feel like I was slowing him down. Me on skis and Xavier on his board, shlooping down the piste together, taking forty minutes to do the twenty-minute run at a smooth and gentle pace. Enjoying the moon and the flames and the freedom.

Thirty-One

14th March

Xavier was poring over his recipe notebook, chewing the end of his pen, brow furrowed deep in thought, with a week to go to the party. It had been two weeks since Luca had gone back to Paris and weirdly, I hadn't missed him at all. I'd missed the free Champagne, though. I'd really missed the free Champagne.

'Once you've decided on the main dish, I'll have a chat with David about the wine,' I said, interrupting his reverie.

'I've already decided,' he announced. 'I'm going with Duck Magret. Indulgent but unexpected and ducky: the prince of meats.'

'The duckiest of meats,' I laughed.

'We'll do stuffed mushrooms, tempura vegetables and potato croquettes with local cheeses. I'll make it finger food, so people don't need to sit down.'

'Nice one, Xavier,' Liv said, 'then we can take it in turns to run the bar and enjoy the party ourselves. Bella's bringing her decks, so that's all sorted.'

'I'll go up and see David now then,' I said. 'Shall I ask Rachael about the cakes on the way?'

'I'll come with you,' Xavier said. 'I've got something specific I want to ask her.'

I popped back to my room and threw my jacket and snood on, tying my hair into a high ponytail and smoothing it down with a headband. My hair had now grown way past my shoulders and was always in a tangle. I gave it a quick brush to glossy it up, catching myself in the mirror and stopping for a second. For the first time in a long time, I looked kind of… right. The London vibes had gone. My skin was smooth and tanned and my eyes were shining. My outfit was sleek. I looked like a skier. Like I belonged here.

I swung by the kitchen to get Xavier.

'Are you coming too?' I called to Liv as she poured herself a coffee.

'Nope, I'm on episode nine of "Be What You See" to align more with nature,' she said, pointing at her headphones, which had been permanently glued to her head for weeks. 'I'm going to stay in and finish it up.'

Xavier and I headed outside. The weather was now bright sunshine every day. March was a joy in Verbier, and I stuffed my snood in my pocket the second we left the chalet. Xavier was much more weather-savvy in a long-sleeved Beatles T-shirt and faded jeans, his green eyes pinging against the violet in his top.

'I had some good news yesterday,' he said, as we walked up the hill, the sun on our cheeks.

'Go on,' I said, 'don't keep me in suspense.'

'I got the job in Tuscany.' He couldn't keep the smile off

his face. 'I'm going to be running the cookery school in San Gimignano, for an old, Italian, Michelin-star master.'

'That's fantastic news, Xavier, congratulations.' My stomach gave a little flutter as I hugged him, wrapping my arms around his back. 'I've been to Tuscany lots of times to nose their wine, but it would be amazing to live there.'

'I know, I can't wait. I head out next Sunday, once the end-of-season party is done.'

'So soon?' I said in surprise. 'So this is our last week together?' It suddenly hit me how close the end of season really was. I thought there'd be a few wind-down days after the party. Some sad packing days, some saying goodbye days and then we'd maybe all travel back to the train station and have a group cry for a day. But no, Xavier was heading off as soon as he possibly could. I wondered when Liv was leaving. And what I was doing. Oh God, I needed some jealousy-inducing plans too. Something to look forward to.

'Yup,' he said, tinkling into Rachael's.

'I've been thinking about going to Chile for the summer to check out their Malbec region. Or maybe Australia?' Two massive lies.

'You could do both?' Xavier said, smiling.

'I could!' I said. My bank balance had been around £127 the last time I'd checked, but the money from the house sale would be coming through soon.

'Do both what?' Rachael asked, beaming at us from behind the counter.

'Holly's planning world wine domination once the season ends next week.'

'Sounds good. David and I are off to Bermuda,' she said

without batting an eyelid. What the actual fuck? Is this how other people lived?

Xavier nodded casually. 'It's supposed to be awesome this time of year,' he said. I nodded along with him. I was so jealous I could cry. I wanted to go to Bermuda or Italy or anywhere but boring old London where no doubt, I'd bump into Gippa every five minutes. Apart from seeing Margot, Abi and my family, there was nothing there for me anymore.

'And Liv and Bella are off to Bali,' I added.

'Yeah, and then they've got tickets for Burning Man,' Rachael said.

'Have they?' I said, incredulous. How had everyone organised all these things? What was I doing with my time?

'She's been going on about it all week. I thought you guys shared a room?' Rachael said.

'We do, but I haven't been the best of room-mates recently; I've been a bit preoccupied,' I said, feeling slightly ashamed. I was suddenly fearful of it all coming to an end. I felt left out, but also really sad. I'd only just got into the swing of things, and it was about to all be over. We were all going to move on with our lives and that would be that. The occasional WhatsApp message, but otherwise living in different countries, maybe even different continents, in completely new jobs.

'Shall we talk about the cakes?' Rachael asked, changing the subject.

'I'm thinking macarons in every colour you can do,' Xavier said, grabbing some from the counter.

'Uh-hmmm,' Rachael said, scribbling on her order pad.

'But I want them stacked in fives, multicoloured and

layered with different flavours of buttercream,' Xavier crammed the macarons together to demonstrate.

'Okaaaayyy,' Rachael said, nodding.

'And maybe some glitter?' Xavier added. 'Unicorn macarons. Can you do them?'

'Ah, a sparkly little Holly touch… but of course! Think of me as your personal Willy Wonka.' I could just imagine the colourful cakes on platters throughout the chalet, adding a magical feeling to the party. I'd have to do something to match it with the drinks, which meant cocktails and Champagne over wine. Or maybe I'd get both. We couldn't have guests eating duck and unicorns and drinking Sex on the Beach. Very uncivilised. We put the order in for 150 macarons and Xavier went back to the chalet as I went on the hunt for David. I found him holding court on his wine stand, surrounded by a crowd of 'temporary friends' all enjoying a free snifter of his latest batch of Chianti.

'The driest of dry, I think you'll agree, but a delicious Chianti nonetheless and I only have two cases. Give it a try and let me know if you want to buy,' David said, winking at me.

I pulled 20 Swiss francs out of my wallet. 'I'll take one please.' David took the note from me, wrapping up a bottle in brown paper and handing it back as the feeding frenzy ensued. Both cases were sold in minutes, with all the happy holidaymakers on their way.

'*Bonjour, bonjour*,' David said, pouring me a small brandy and adding a slug of amaretto. 'This is a cocktail called The French Connection,' he said, which seemed appropriate. We clinked our glasses and took a swig.

'Delicious,' I said, and took another drink. A double hit

of alcohol, but the combination of brandy and amaretto was both warming and hearty. 'I think this is the one,' I said, delighted that I wouldn't end up on a wild goose chase. 'I was going to ask your advice for a cocktail option for next Saturday, but I think this is it.'

'I like to be of service, as you know,' David said, bowing low, handing me my money back and relieving me of the Chianti.

'Five bottles of brandy and one Amaretto should be plenty.'

'Of course. Always a pleasure doing business with you,' David said, scribbling the order down. 'So did you have fun at your birthday dinner? I told Xavier two bottles of Amaretto would be too much for just the two of you, but I guess I was wrong if you've already gone through it!'

My heart nearly stopped. 'What do you mean?' I thought back to my birthday meal and Luca pouring the Amaretto out for the two of us. '...for Luca?'

'Erm, no? For the dinner Xavier organised for you; he spent weeks looking for all your favourite things, I got him another bottle of that Sicilian Fiano you loved and he took a back-up bottle of Amaretto as he knew it was your favourite. Was I not supposed to say?'

'No, not at all,' I said, in shock. How could I have been such an idiot?

'He might be planning to give it to you as a gift, so don't say I said anything,' he said with a wink.

'OK,' I said, blankly.

'I'll drop these bottles into you on Friday. That do you?'

'Perfect,' I said, the cocktail going to my head.

Thirty-Two

21st March

I was almost party-ready and it was only 9 a.m. My hair was washed and wound in heated rollers, legs shaved – entire body shaved, in fact – face plucked, all over moisturisation complete, and wonky mani-pedi done. Just my make-up left to do before I put on my sparkly jumper-dress and doused myself in the glitter puff. And *finally*, an appropriate occasion for the Louboutins. It felt surreal that there were only twenty-four hours left of our winter season. I had to keep reminding myself to enjoy every moment, right up to the end.

Liv was serving breakfast, so I had the bedroom to myself. I looked around our cosy little space, the ten square-metres we'd called home for the past six months, and couldn't believe we'd lived so happily in this tiny patch of chaos. Liv had already pulled her suitcase out from under the bed and started dismantling her half of the room, while everything of mine stayed staunchly in position. I pulled out the *Culinary Guide to Bali* I'd bought as a little surprise and popped it on top of her suitcase. I had to accept we were all moving on. I threw my soft tracksuit on and skidded down to the kitchen in my socks. I wasn't officially working until lunchtime, but Xavier was already hard at it, stirring pots and sprinkling herbs and spices, surrounded by swirls of steam.

'Morning,' I said, startling him from his alchemy, 'I'm here to help.'

'Excellent,' he said, passing me a sack of potatoes and a peeler. 'You can start with these. I need the whole bag for the croquettes.'

There was something so satisfying about washing the soil off a potato and stripping its skin to reveal a bright-white underbelly. I worked through the enormous sack, the repetition almost meditative as I peeled and plopped each naked potato into a pan of salted water. My stomach made a low growl as I imagined this sea of tiny bald heads as a pile of buttery mash. I was starving.

'*Merci*,' Xavier said, taking the pan from me, 'a sous-chef *par excellence*.'

I had to admit, I peeled a bloody good potato.

'The duck is already in and slow-roasting and I'm preparing the vegetables to have everything ready for 4 p.m.,' he said, 'then it's just a few pieces to serve hot when the party starts.'

I followed my nose to the oven, where four fat ducks were roasting on a timer, the skin already starting to bubble and crisp. Xavier was all over it and well ahead of schedule.

'I've very much focused on getting *myself* ready so far this morning,' I said, 'but don't worry, the glasses will be frosted and the Champagne will be chilled in time for the guests to arrive.'

'I don't doubt it,' Xavier said. 'I think there will be around twenty in total. Everyone has accepted: Mimi and Frank, Rachael and David, Bella of course and I've invited Maxim. Genevieve has several groups of friends coming from Paris.'

'Weird to think Luca won't be at his own end-of-season party,' I said gingerly.

'Apparently he's in Cannes checking out a new restaurant,' Liv said, wafting into the kitchen, her jasmine perfume light and breezy in contrast to the meaty feast in the oven.

'Of course he is,' Xavier said.

'Have the macarons arrived?' I asked, desperate to see them.

'Here they areeeee!' Rachael appeared in the doorway with two bags full of boxes, followed by David and the booze.

'*Bonjour*, happy end-of-season party day, Chalet Blanchet!' Rachael said, smiling. 'Something smells delicious.'

'*C'est moi*,' Xavier said, with a confident nod, 'it's called "French Man".'

'Of course it is,' she laughed, double kissing him, then giving me a hug.

'I'm wearing it too,' David said, offering Rachael his arm pit.

'I get plenty of that, thank you very much,' she said, batting him away.

The party was in full swing as I went outside to get some fresh air. I couldn't stop thinking about my birthday dinner. The little voice in my head had known it hadn't made sense that Luca had organised it, but I'd let myself get swept away in the Blanchet high life. It was Xavier behind it all. Of course it was. Xavier had been the thoughtful one, the kind one, putting me before everyone else. Listening to me, helping me, waiting for me. And he wasn't even properly married and now it was too late. The evening air was almost warm as I looked up at the mountain, breathing it all in and enjoying my third glass of Champagne.

George: *I've accepted the highest offer and the house is officially off the market. The good news is we've made £40k profit, so you'll be getting £32k instead of £12k xx*

Thirty-two thousand pounds! I couldn't believe it. My money worries were over. I could do whatever I wanted with that amount of cash. Go anywhere. But there was nowhere I wanted to be other than right here, living this new life I'd discovered and only just started to enjoy.

'Holly?' I turned and Xavier was stood in the doorway, holding two of my excellently mixed French Connections. He'd changed into a tuxedo and looked ab-so-lute fire. His auburn hair fresh and glossy, eyes gleaming. The face of a man whose work was done. He'd paid his dues and his season was over. In fact, all three of his seasons were now over. I was going to miss that face.

'Hi,' I said shyly, taking in this new version of him. 'Love the suit. Amazing food as always. Twenty empty platters plus twenty empty bowls equals one fantastic chef.'

'*Merci, merci*,' Xavier said, bowing in mock modesty and handing me a French Connection. 'Two fantastic chefs, I think. Thank you for all your work this week to get us here – and great job on the cocktails! We are a formidable team.'

'Were. We *were* a formidable team. And now it's over,' I said. 'Your final canapé served, your final moule marinière-d.'

'There's always a moule to marinière somewhere,' he laughed, 'but yep, that's Switzerland ticked off the list. Next stop, Italy. The land of prosciutto, pasta and Prosecco. And non-stop sunshine. It'll be nice to get my year-round tan back.'

We clinked glasses and leant against the balcony, looking up at the moon, which was close to full and cheesy, stars glinting through the clouds.

'I wanted to say thank you for my lovely birthday meal,' I said. 'David let it slip last week that you organised it for me and it had nothing to do with Luca.'

'Did he?' Xavier took a sip of his cocktail and avoided my eyes.

'Why didn't you tell me?'

Xavier shrugged, 'Luca claimed it as his own and I couldn't show him up in his own chalet. It would have ruined your birthday if I'd argued with him and you looked so happy when you saw it all.'

'I thought it seemed strange that he'd got everything so spot on, but you were both so convincing that he'd organised it.' I shook my head.

'Luca shouldn't have even been there; he was meant to be in Paris. He forgot his passport and came back for it as I was finishing everything off. Then we got into an argument about Lavedrine X and you walked in.'

'It's the nicest thing anyone's ever done for me, and I gave the credit to the wrong man. I feel like such an idiot.'

'I'm sorry, Holly. It wasn't anything to do with your

birthday for him. He just wanted to show me who's boss. I had to suck it up and let it go.'

'And let me go too?' I whispered.

Xavier nodded wistfully. 'What's done is done. It's too late now,' he said, taking a swig of his drink.

'Is it?' I took Xavier's hand, which was warm and soft. 'Maybe it's not too late. Maybe there's still a chance for something?'

Xavier looked me straight in the eyes as the balcony doors rattled open and Liv came out bum first carrying a box of fireworks. She was followed by two sturdy men in yellow overalls and black rubber boots – fire marshals at the ready for the finale display.

'Alright you two – not missing anything important, am I?' she shouted with a wink, as she led them into the garden. We watched as the three of them set about wedging differently shaped fireworks into the soil, working away with a tape measure to ensure they were far enough from the pine trees to trace a clear path into the sky. Xavier was still holding my hand as we sipped our drinks. Eventually, he turned to me, and I held my breath.

'I know I've missed my chance, but…' Xavier started.

'You haven't missed your chance,' I interrupted, squeezing his hand.

'Haven't I?' His eyes searched mine, not understanding. I leant in and kissed him softly on the lips to make it crystal clear.

'I didn't even know there was a chance until two weeks ago,' I said, looking away shyly. 'I thought you were married?' I traced my finger along the stitching of his lapel;

his chest was bursting out of his suit and my heart gave a little flutter.

'I'm so sorry I didn't tell you sooner. I had to be sure I could trust you, as Christina and I need to be married for another year at least before she can stay permanently in France.'

Xavier pulled me towards him and kissed me hard, his hand on my cheek. It felt so perfect, so right to be here in his arms, but I couldn't help feeling a tiny bit heartbroken that this was our first genuine kiss and might also be our last. Time had run out for us and now it was all happening too late.

'This can't be the end,' I said, as the first firework shot into the air, signalling the start of the display. Genevieve led everyone out onto the balcony in a posh conga to watch as the sky exploded in a shower of colour, fireworks banging and screeching. She looked down and caught my eye, giving me a knowing smile.

'I don't want to let you go,' he said, kissing me again.

'I'm not going anywhere,' I said, kissing him back.

'Really?' Xavier said, a twinkle in his eye. 'What about if you came with me to… Tuscany?'

I stared at him, shocked, as a feeling I couldn't quite place hit me in the stomach. I couldn't go to Tuscany, could I? I felt so happy at the thought of it. Being with Xavier in Italy, with all the food and wine and sunshine. Why couldn't I go? Why wouldn't I go?

'Really?' I replied, eyes shining. 'Do you really mean it?'

Xavier nodded. 'I can't imagine my kitchen without you in it anymore. And I can always use a reliable sous-chef.'

Oh. He meant to work with him. Of course he did.

My face dropped as Xavier reached out and lifted my chin to him, his big, green eyes staring down at me. I didn't know where to look.

Oh. My. God.

'And I can't do this if you're in London, can I?' Xavier said, kissing me again and then on both cheeks as the fireworks went off above us.

Acknowledgements

Thank you to the entire team at Aria for all the work that has gone into bringing *Escape to the Swiss Chalet* into being, particularly to Martina Arzu, my brilliant editor, who has given so much of herself to this book. Her time, energy and ideas have made the creative process a total joy. Thank you also to my copy editor Paul Sellars for his eagle eyes when I couldn't see the wood for the trees, and to Meg Shepherd for the gorgeous cover design.

A special thank you to Rachel Faulkner-Willcocks for believing in me and my writing. I will never forget the moment I opened your email with the offer of the book deal.

Thank you to Helen Lederer and the team at the Comedy Women In Print awards – specifically Maureen, who chased me down when I missed the email saying I'd made the longlist. CWIP is an amazing endeavour, encouraging witty women to write and bringing them together to champion one another. Sue Townsend, Helen Fielding and Marian Keyes gave me a love of reading way before I started writing and made me think differently about what being a writer could be.

Thank you to The Faber Academy and Joanna Briscoe for the excellent 'Writing a Novel' course which was a significant milestone on my writing journey. A moment of self-investment and a decision to change my career and start taking my writing seriously. My Faber friends remain my regular writing gang. Thank you, Liz Webb, for your ideas and encouragement, Katherine Tansley for your incisive questions, Sarah Lawton for being such a thoughtful problem-solver and Marija Maher-Diffenthal for always layering on the laughs.

And finally, to my champions: Marianne for telling me to not be SO RIDICULOUS when I had doubtful moments along the way, my sister Claire for reading early drafts and laughing in all the right places. My Dad for my silly sense of humour and ability to find the funny. My Mom for always pushing me to go for it (whatever it happens to be that week) and my brother Justin for keeping my feet on the ground (Pre-order? Can't you just email me the PDF?).

Thank you to Rachel Lyon, who has always believed in my writing beyond all sense and reason. Relentless in her dismissal of my other career choices, she's never accepted that writing wouldn't be part of my path. Thank you for reminding me of my dreams when I'd buried them away somewhere in the pursuit of a *real job*.

And the biggest thank you to my husband Rob who has lovingly supported me as I've written, re-written, edited and re-edited this book. Thank you for trusting me to take the leap. For keeping me safe when I've been beyond wild. For letting me be me. I love you.

About the Author

CARRIE WALKER is a Brummie-born rom-com lover with a lifelong passion for travel. She has lived in a ski resort, by a beach, in the country and in the city, and travelled solo through Asia, South America and Europe. Her own love life was more com than rom until she met her husband, Rob, a few years ago and settled down with him, and her dog Ziggy, in a pub-filled village in Essex.

Longlisted for Helen Lederer's Comedy Women in Print prize in 2021, writing has long been Carrie's side hustle, penning columns and features for newspapers and magazines, while working in many other jobs. She has been the CEO of a global disability movement, a board director of a brand agency, the editor of a newspaper, a radio presenter, a football mascot, dressed up as a carrot for the BBC and now she is writing books.

Escape to the Swiss Chalet is her debut novel.